4

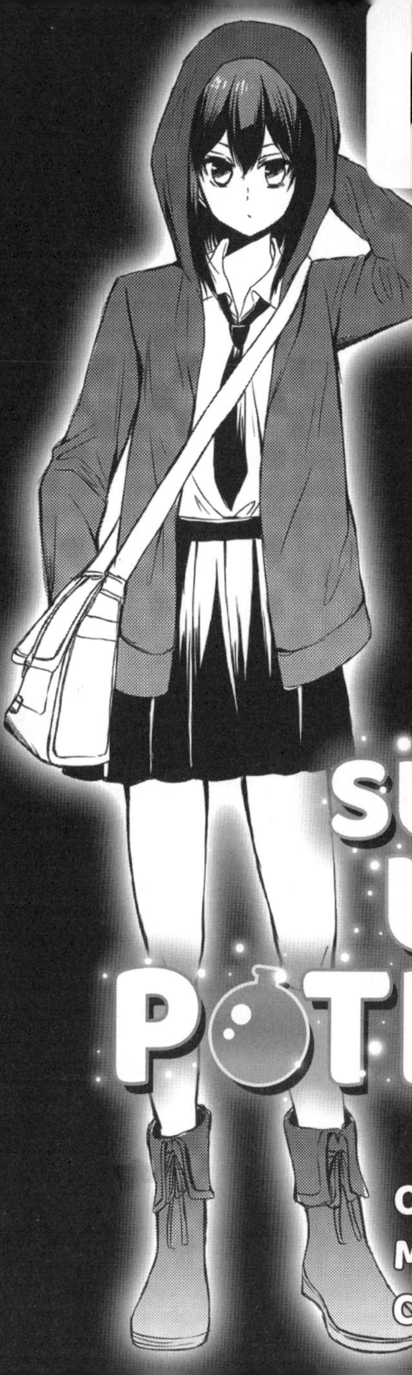

I SHALL SURVIVE USING POTIONS!

Original Work: FUNA
Manga: Hibiki Kokonoe
Character Design: Sukima

TABLE OF CONTENTS

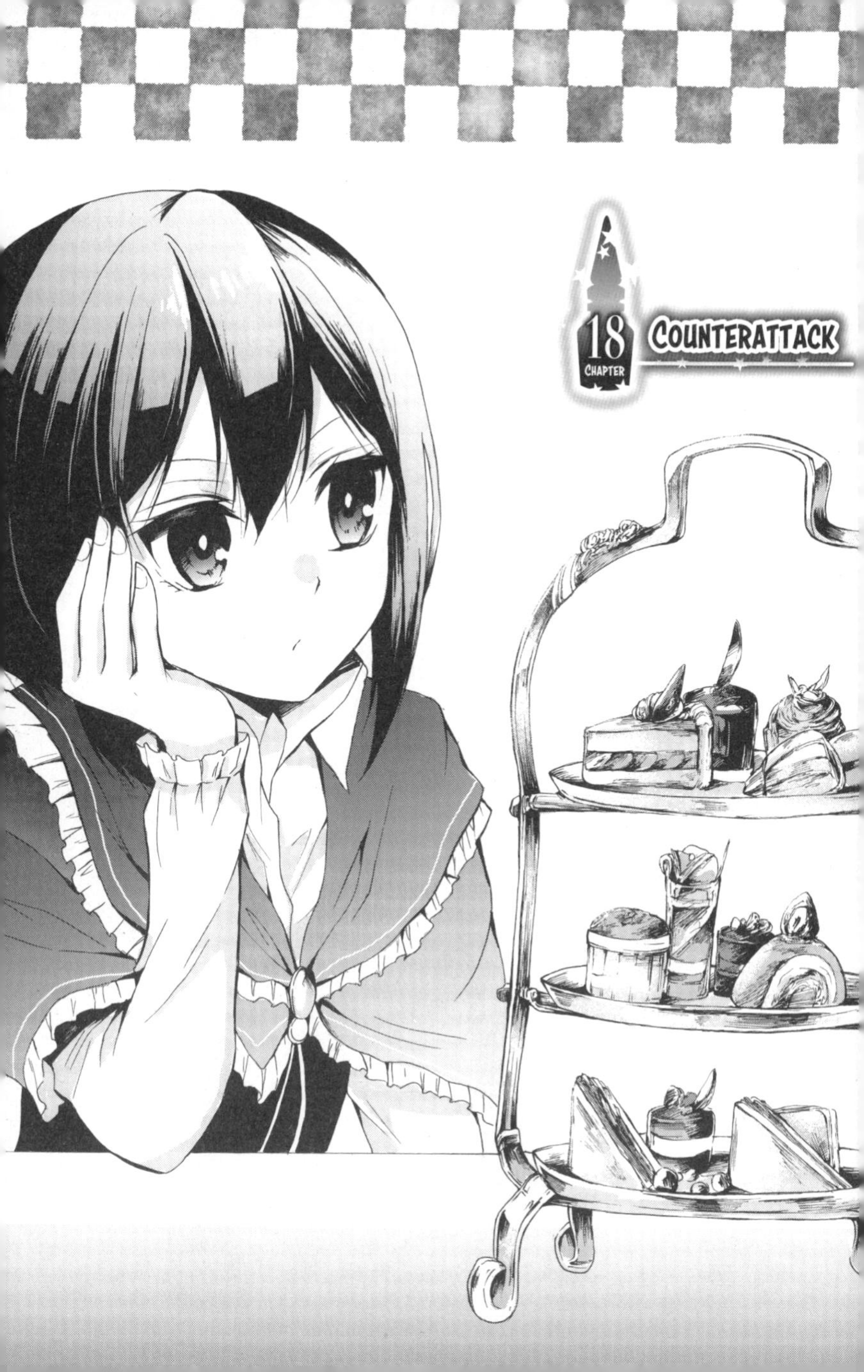
18
CHAPTER
COUNTERATTACK

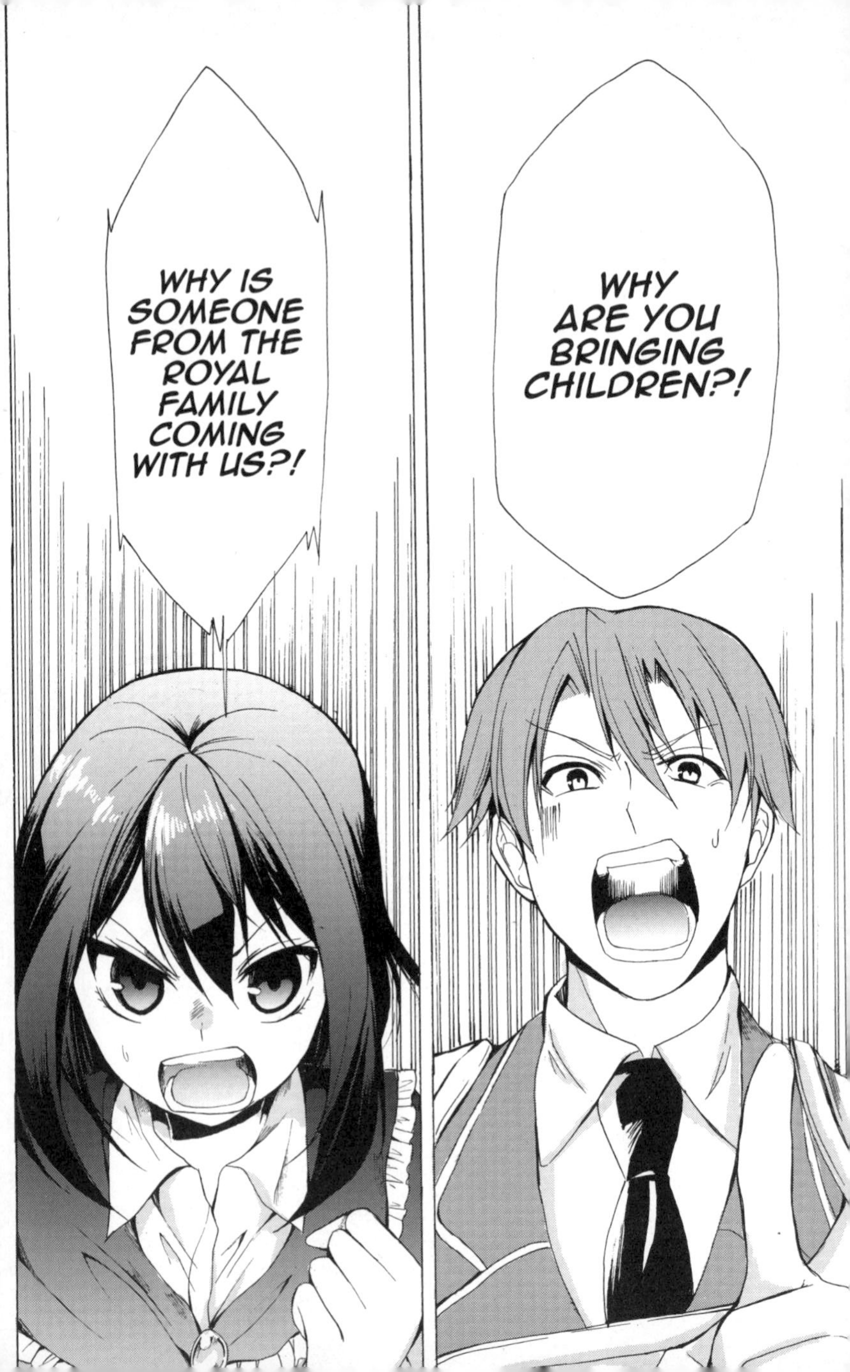
WHY ARE YOU BRINGING CHILDREN?!
WHY IS SOMEONE FROM THE ROYAL FAMILY COMING WITH US?!

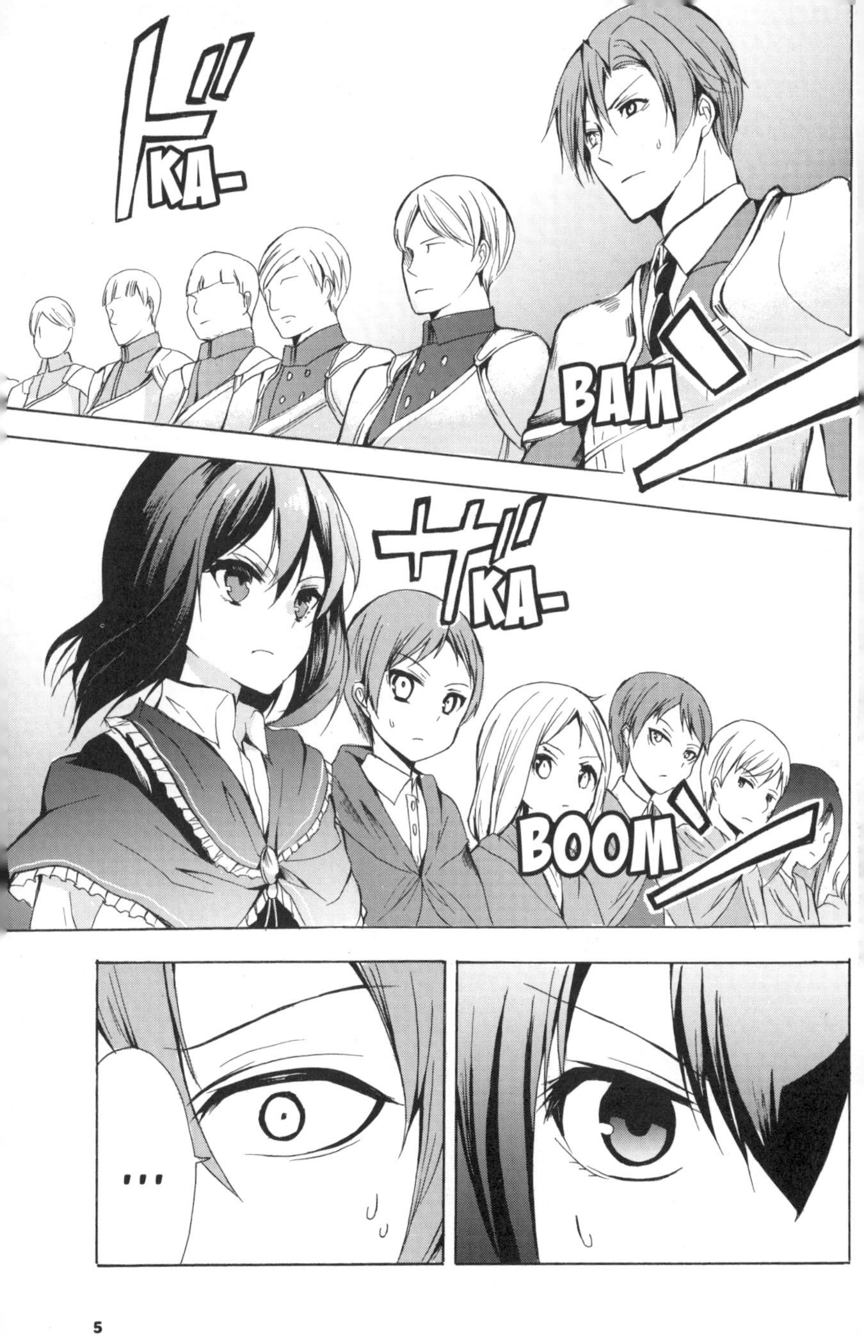
ドKA-
BAM
ザKA-
BOOM
...

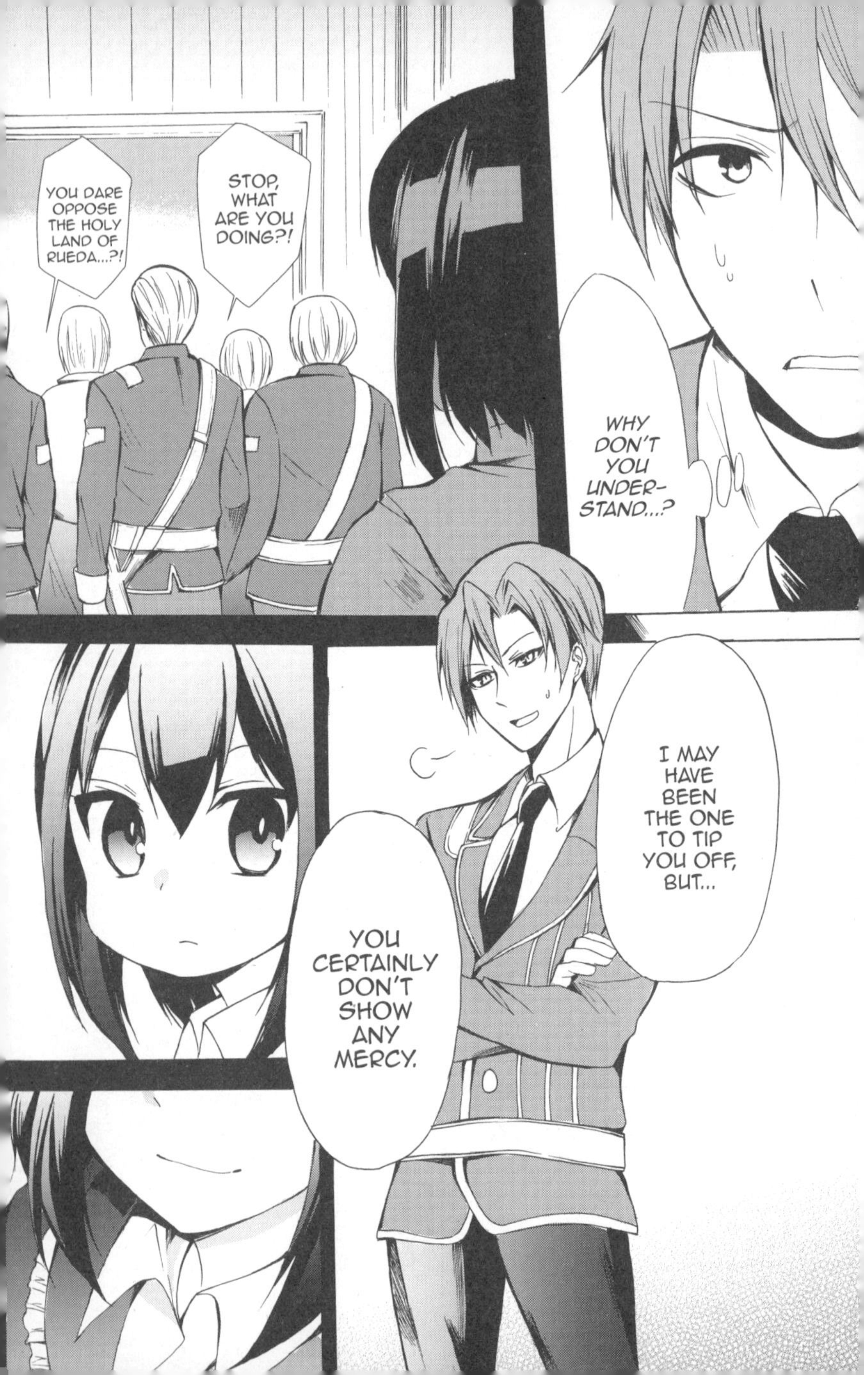
WHY DON'T YOU UNDER-STAND...?
STOP, WHAT ARE YOU DOING?!
YOU DARE OPPOSE THE HOLY LAND OF RUEDA...?!
I MAY HAVE BEEN THE ONE TO TIP YOU OFF, BUT...
YOU CERTAINLY DON'T SHOW ANY MERCY.

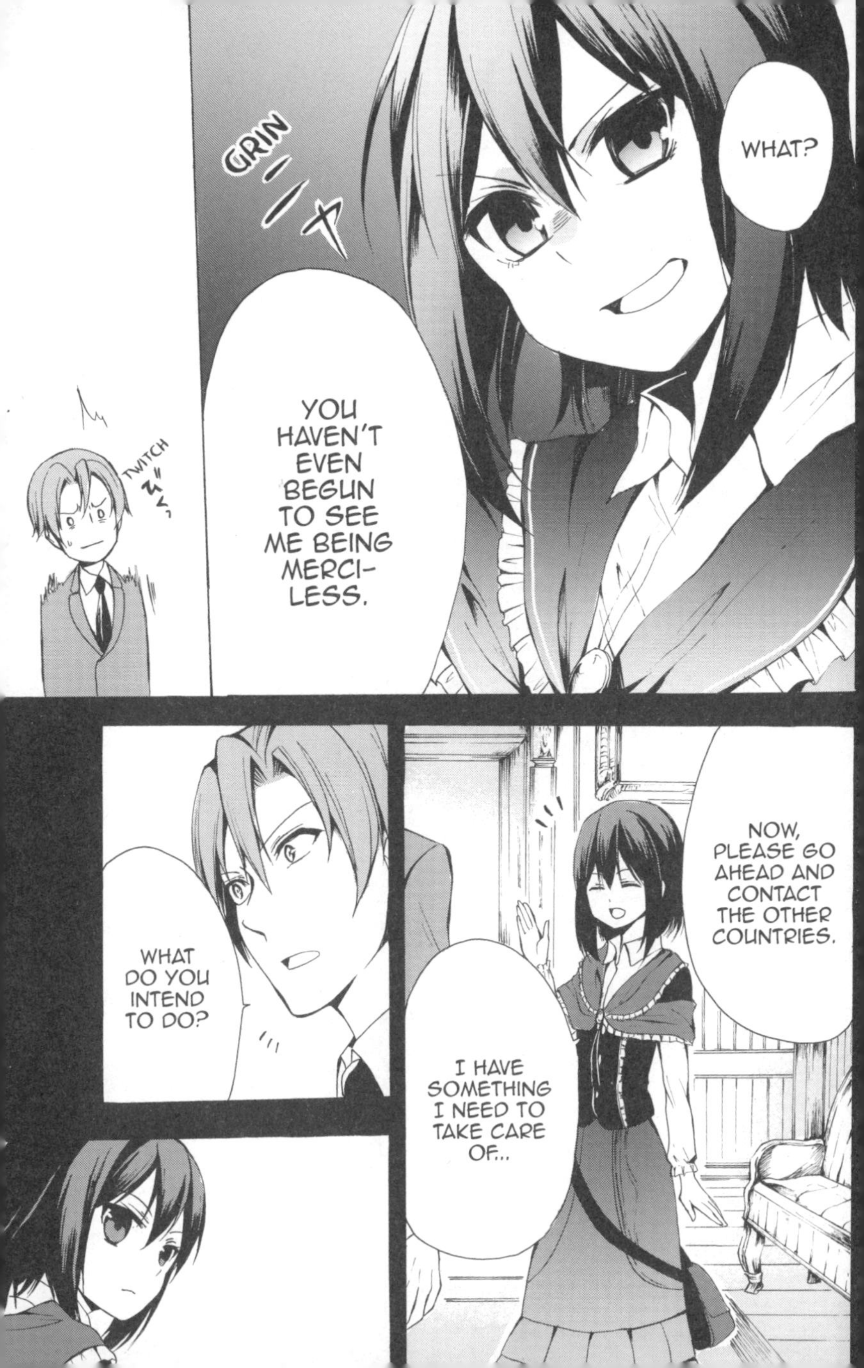
WHAT?
GRIN
YOU HAVEN'T EVEN BEGUN TO SEE ME BEING MERCI-LESS.
TWITCH
NOW, PLEASE GO AHEAD AND CONTACT THE OTHER COUNTRIES.
I HAVE SOMETHING I NEED TO TAKE CARE OF...
WHAT DO YOU INTEND TO DO?

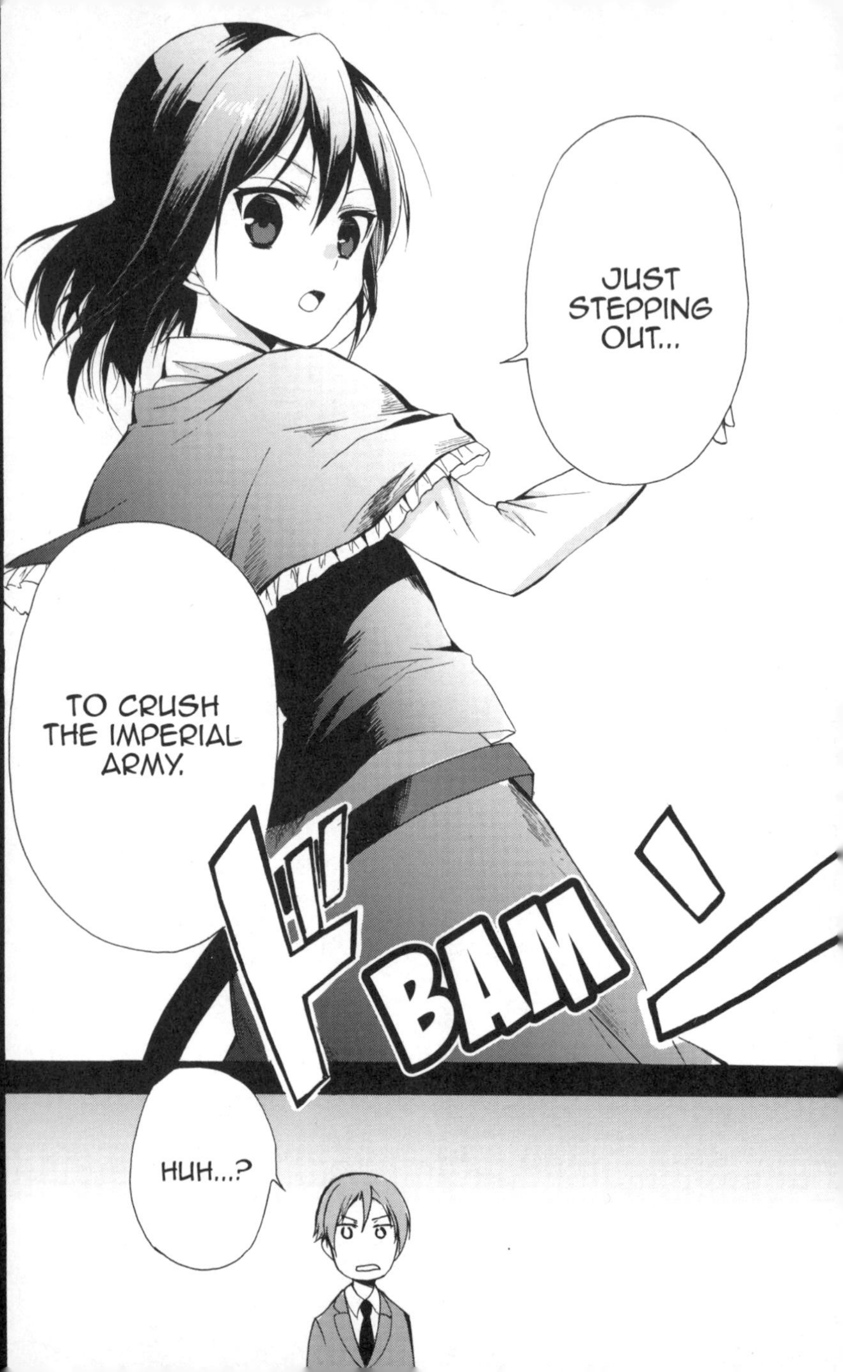
JUST STEPPING OUT...
TO CRUSH THE IMPERIAL ARMY.
BAM
HUH...?

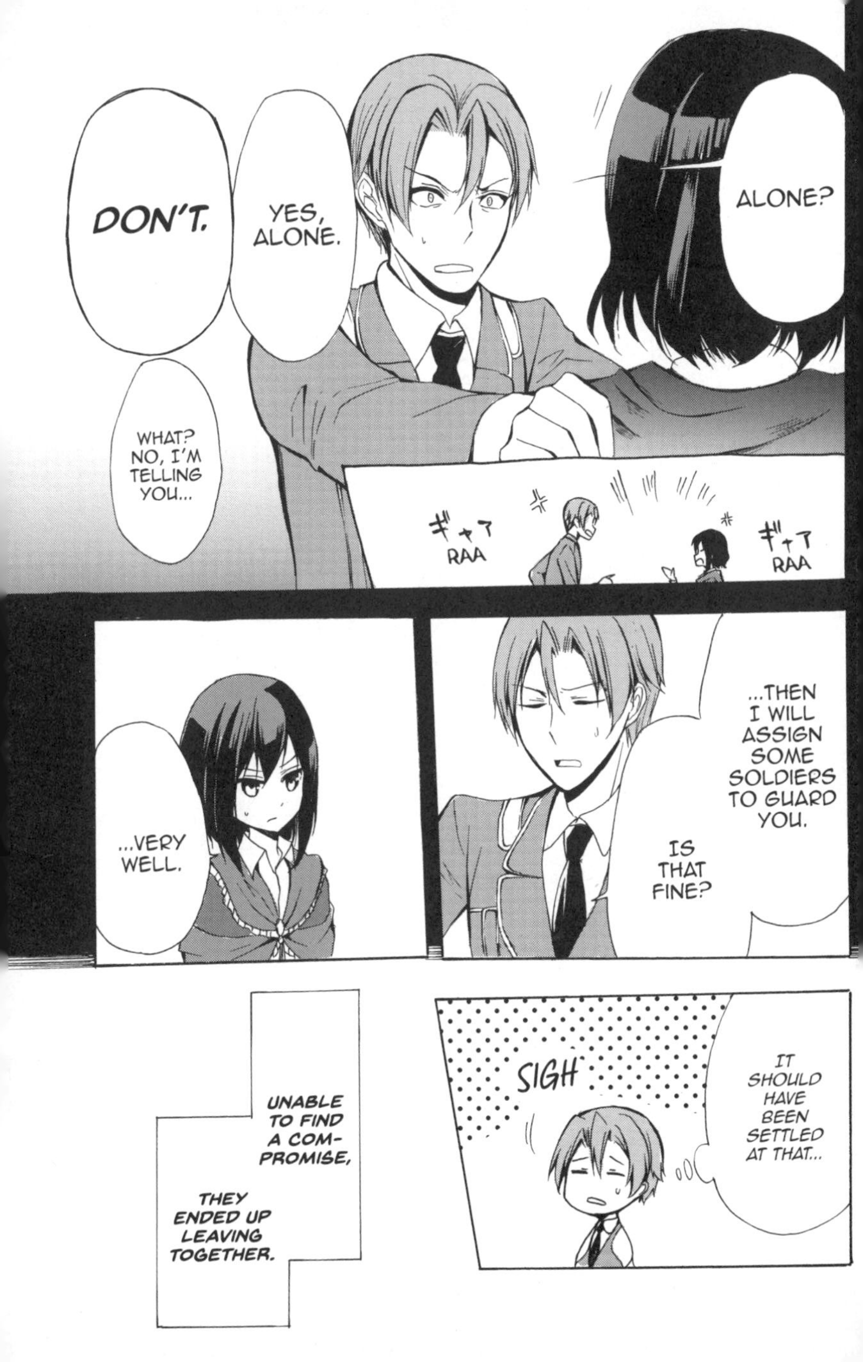
ALONE?
YES, ALONE.
DON'T.
WHAT? NO, I'M TELLING YOU...
ギャア RAA
ギャア RAA
...THEN I WILL ASSIGN SOME SOLDIERS TO GUARD YOU.
IS THAT FINE?
...VERY WELL.
IT SHOULD HAVE BEEN SETTLED AT THAT...
SIGH
UNABLE TO FIND A COM-PROMISE,
THEY ENDED UP LEAVING TOGETHER.

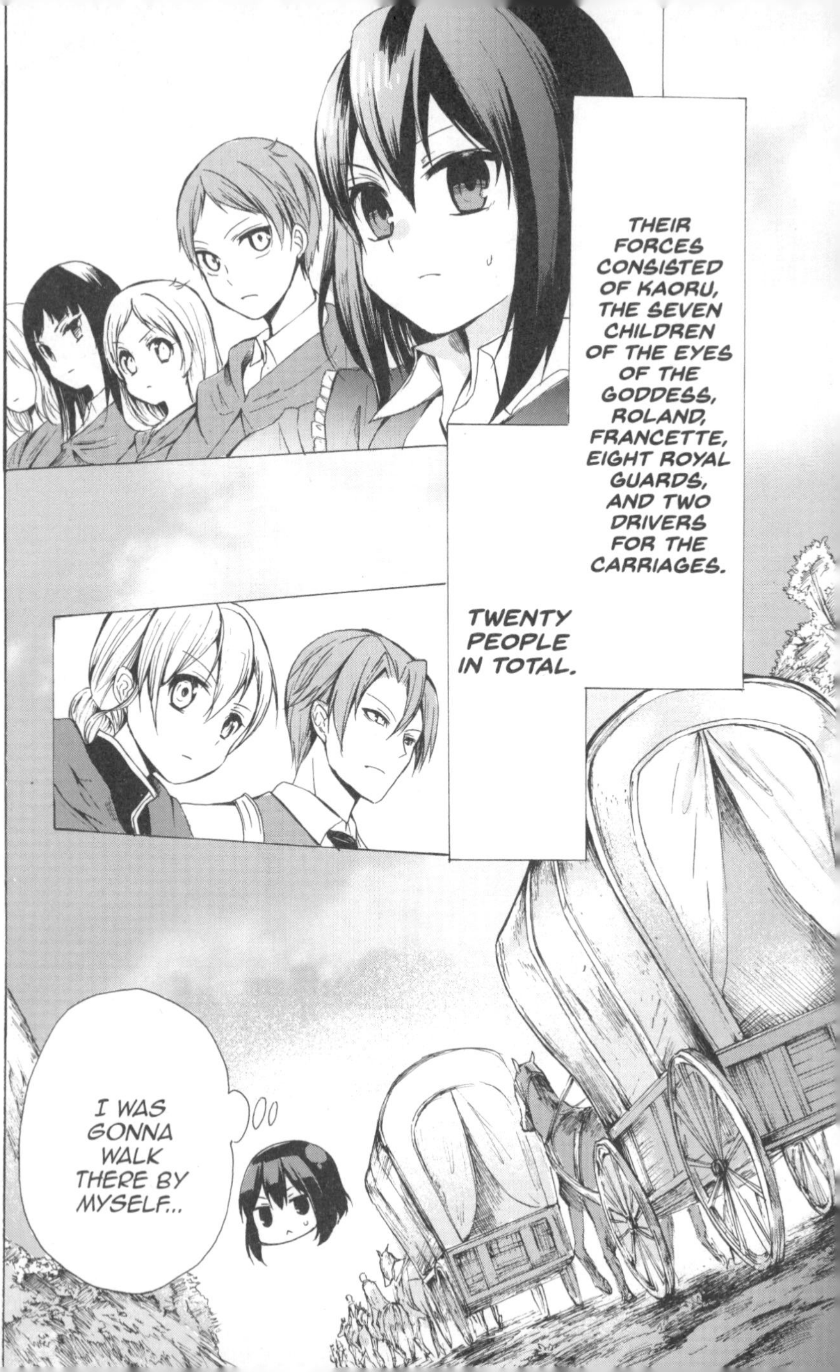
THEIR FORCES CONSISTED OF KAORU, THE SEVEN CHILDREN OF THE EYES OF THE GODDESS, ROLAND, FRANCETTE, EIGHT ROYAL GUARDS, AND TWO DRIVERS FOR THE CARRIAGES.
TWENTY PEOPLE IN TOTAL.
I WAS GONNA WALK THERE BY MYSELF...

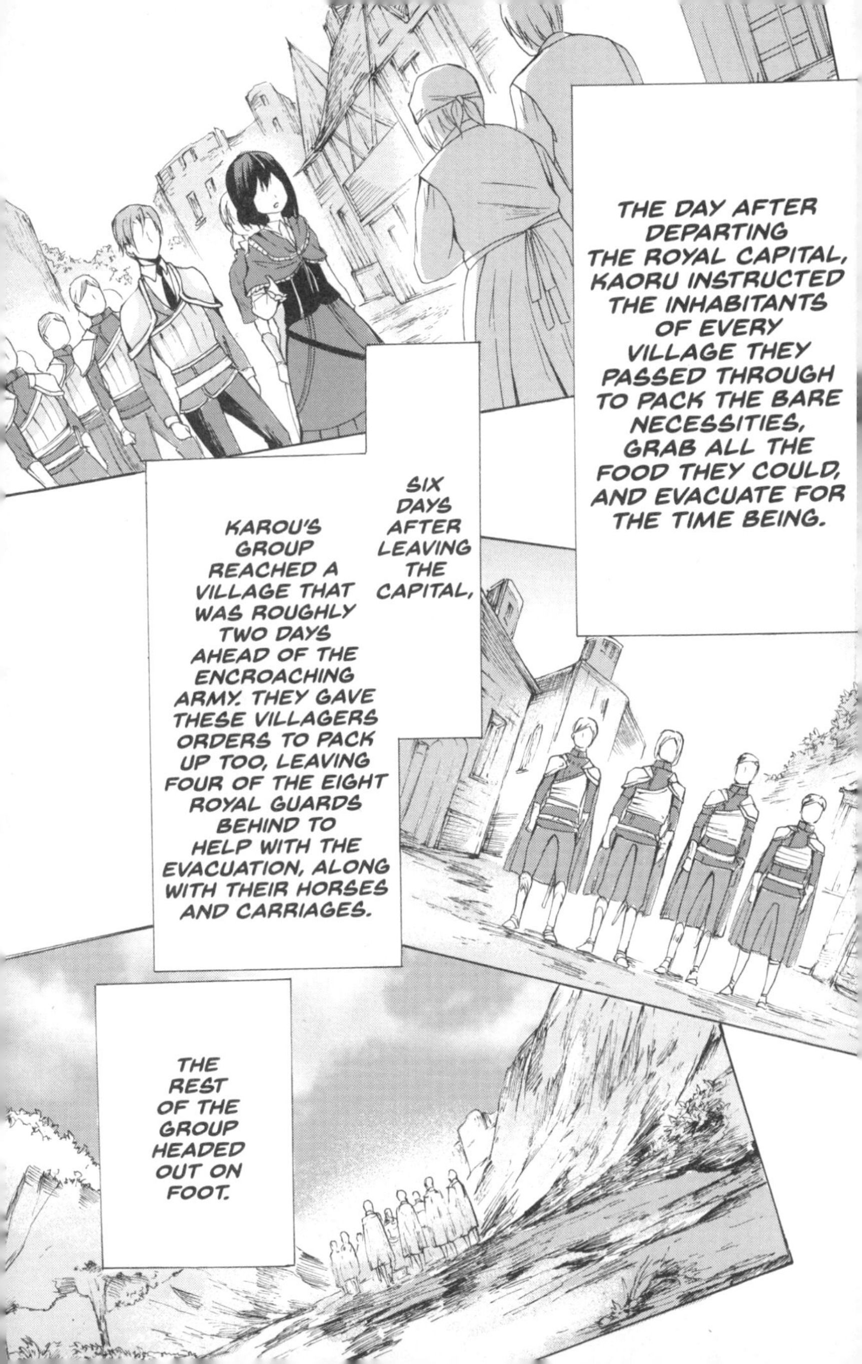
THE DAY AFTER DEPARTING THE ROYAL CAPITAL, KAORU INSTRUCTED THE INHABITANTS OF EVERY VILLAGE THEY PASSED THROUGH TO PACK THE BARE NECESSITIES, GRAB ALL THE FOOD THEY COULD, AND EVACUATE FOR THE TIME BEING.
SIX DAYS AFTER LEAVING THE CAPITAL,
KAROU'S GROUP REACHED A VILLAGE THAT WAS ROUGHLY TWO DAYS AHEAD OF THE ENCROACHING ARMY. THEY GAVE THESE VILLAGERS ORDERS TO PACK UP TOO, LEAVING FOUR OF THE EIGHT ROYAL GUARDS BEHIND TO HELP WITH THE EVACUATION, ALONG WITH THEIR HORSES AND CARRIAGES.
THE REST OF THE GROUP HEADED OUT ON FOOT.

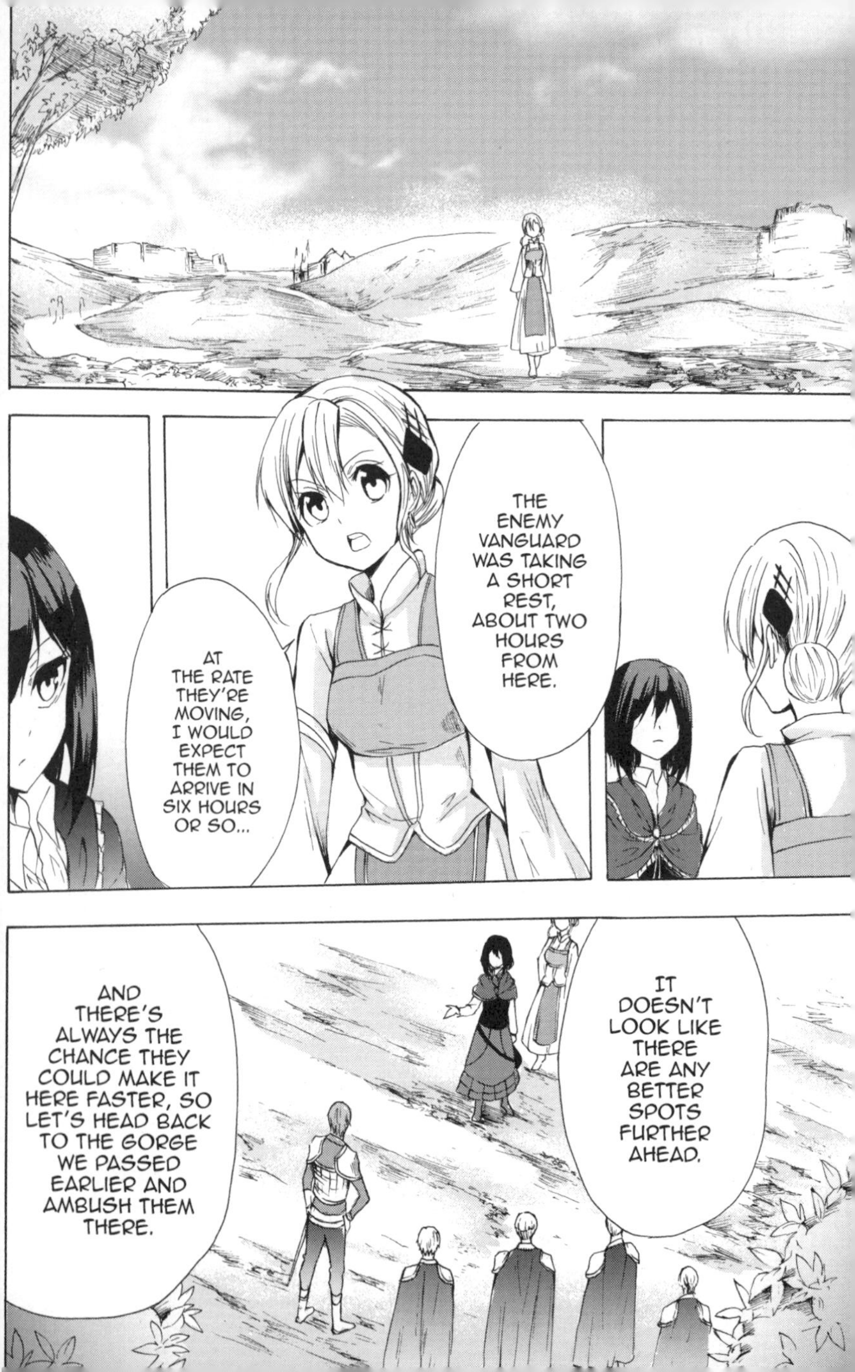
THE ENEMY VANGUARD WAS TAKING A SHORT REST, ABOUT TWO HOURS FROM HERE.
AT THE RATE THEY'RE MOVING, I WOULD EXPECT THEM TO ARRIVE IN SIX HOURS OR SO...
IT DOESN'T LOOK LIKE THERE ARE ANY BETTER SPOTS FURTHER AHEAD.
AND THERE'S ALWAYS THE CHANCE THEY COULD MAKE IT HERE FASTER, SO LET'S HEAD BACK TO THE GORGE WE PASSED EARLIER AND AMBUSH THEM THERE.

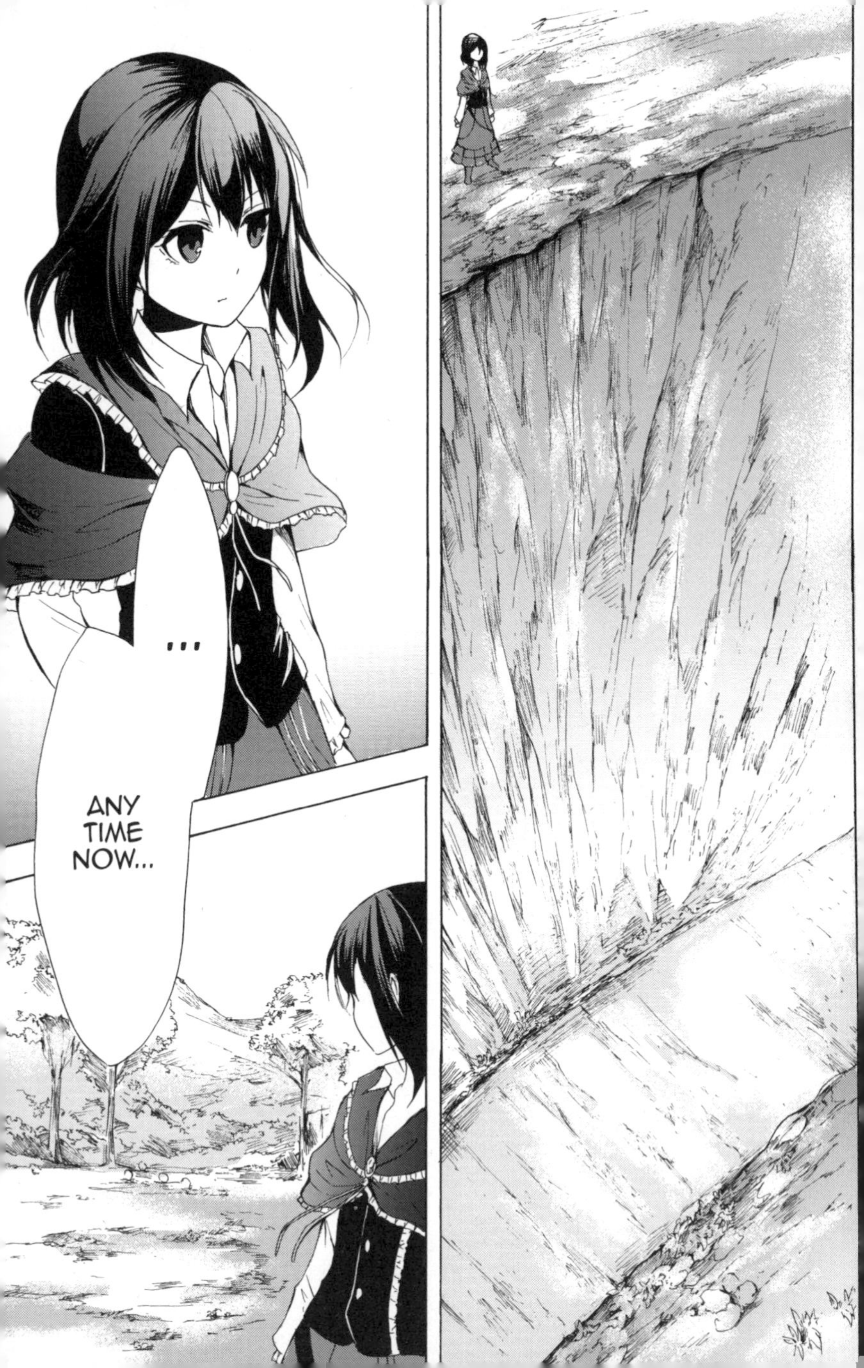
...
ANY TIME NOW...

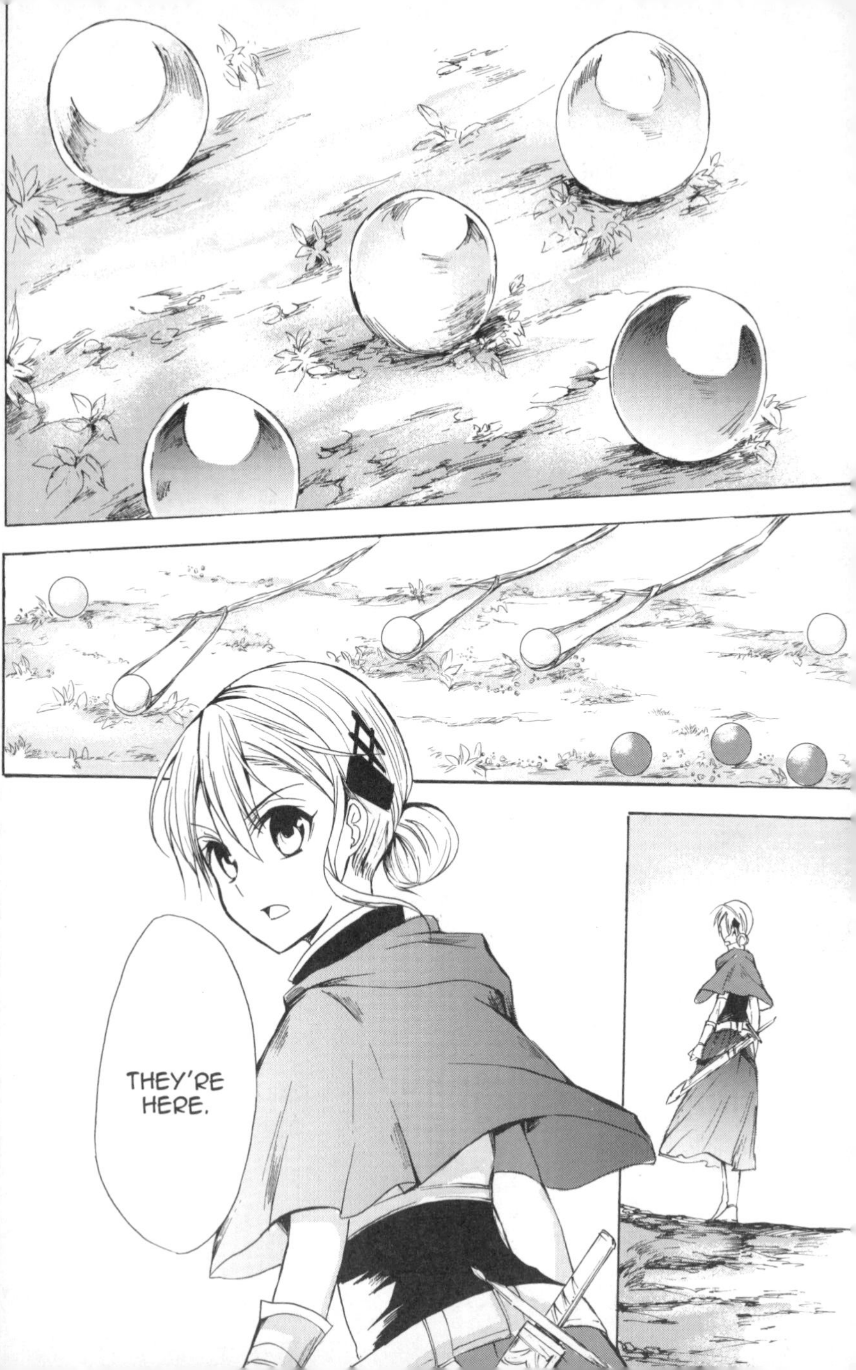
THEY'RE HERE.

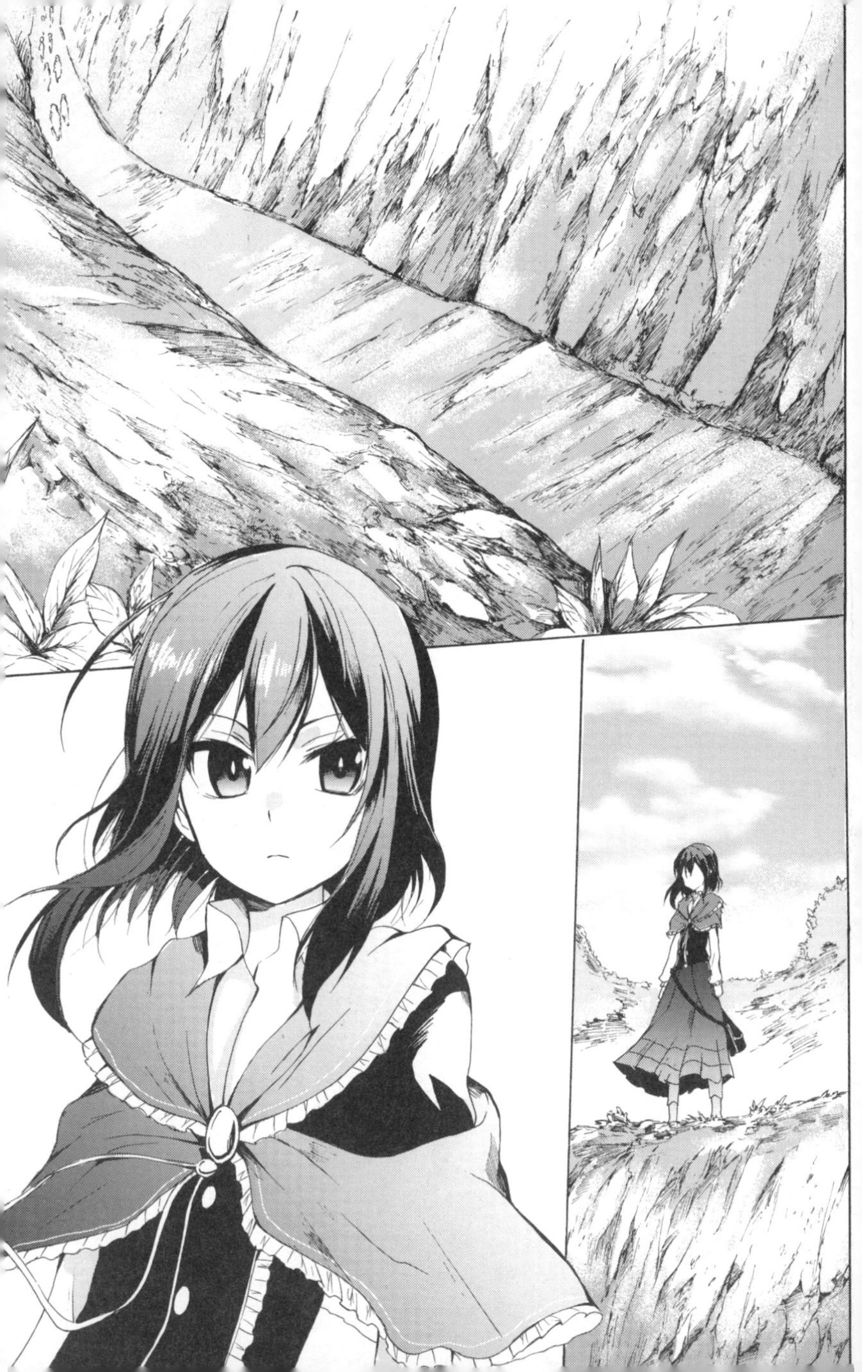

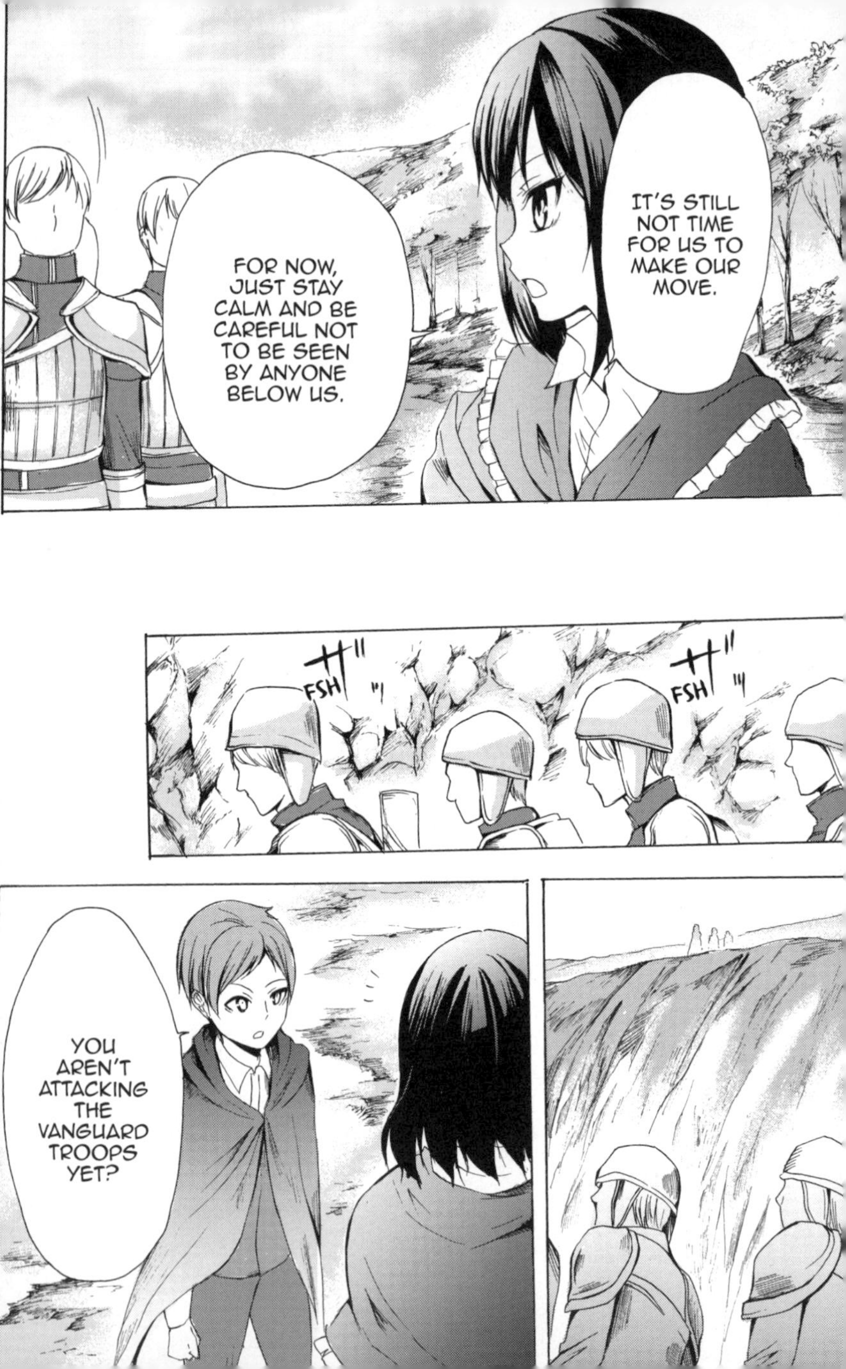
IT'S STILL NOT TIME FOR US TO MAKE OUR MOVE.
FOR NOW, JUST STAY CALM AND BE CAREFUL NOT TO BE SEEN BY ANYONE BELOW US.
FSH
FSH
YOU AREN'T ATTACKING THE VANGUARD TROOPS YET?

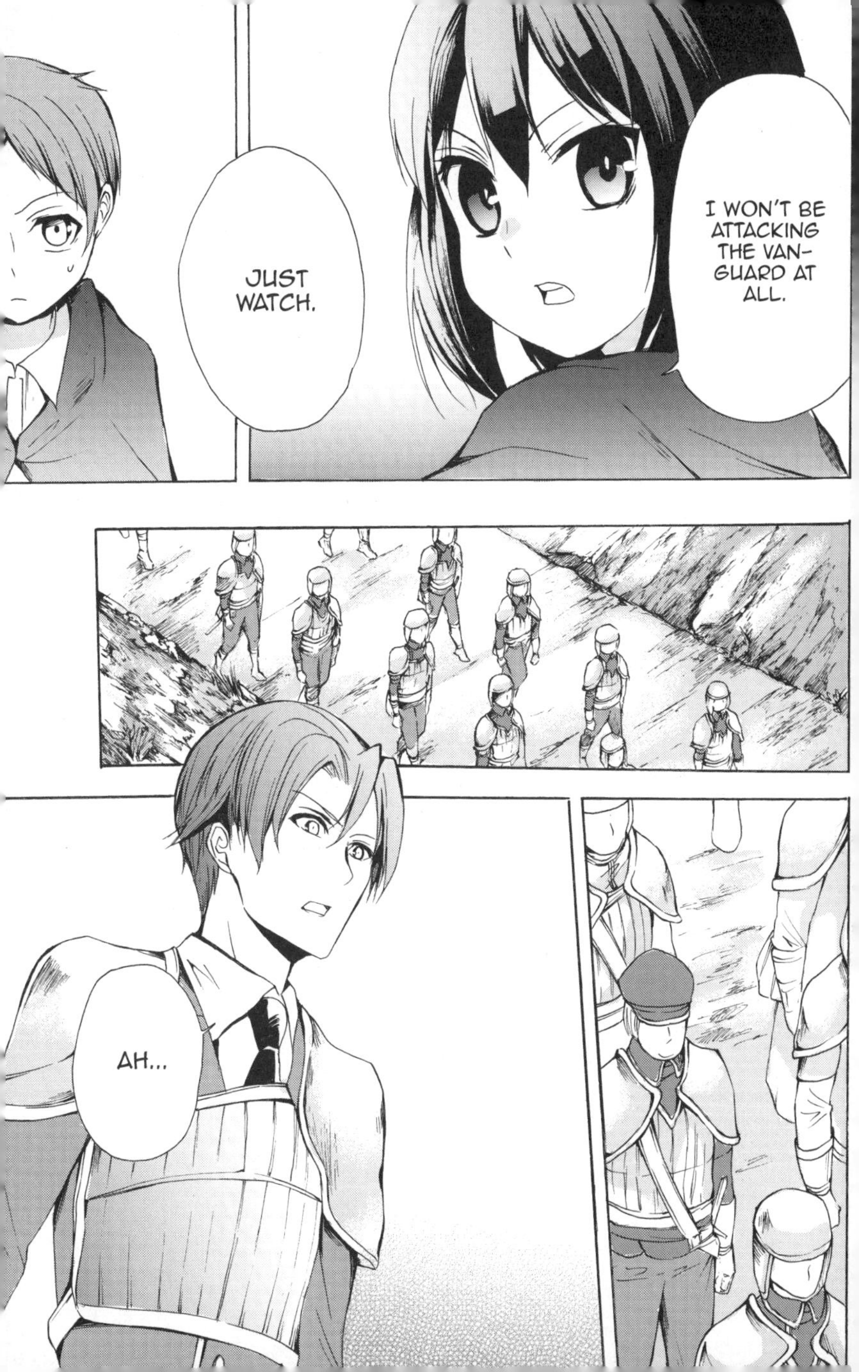
I WON'T BE ATTACKING THE VAN-GUARD AT ALL.
JUST WATCH.
AH...

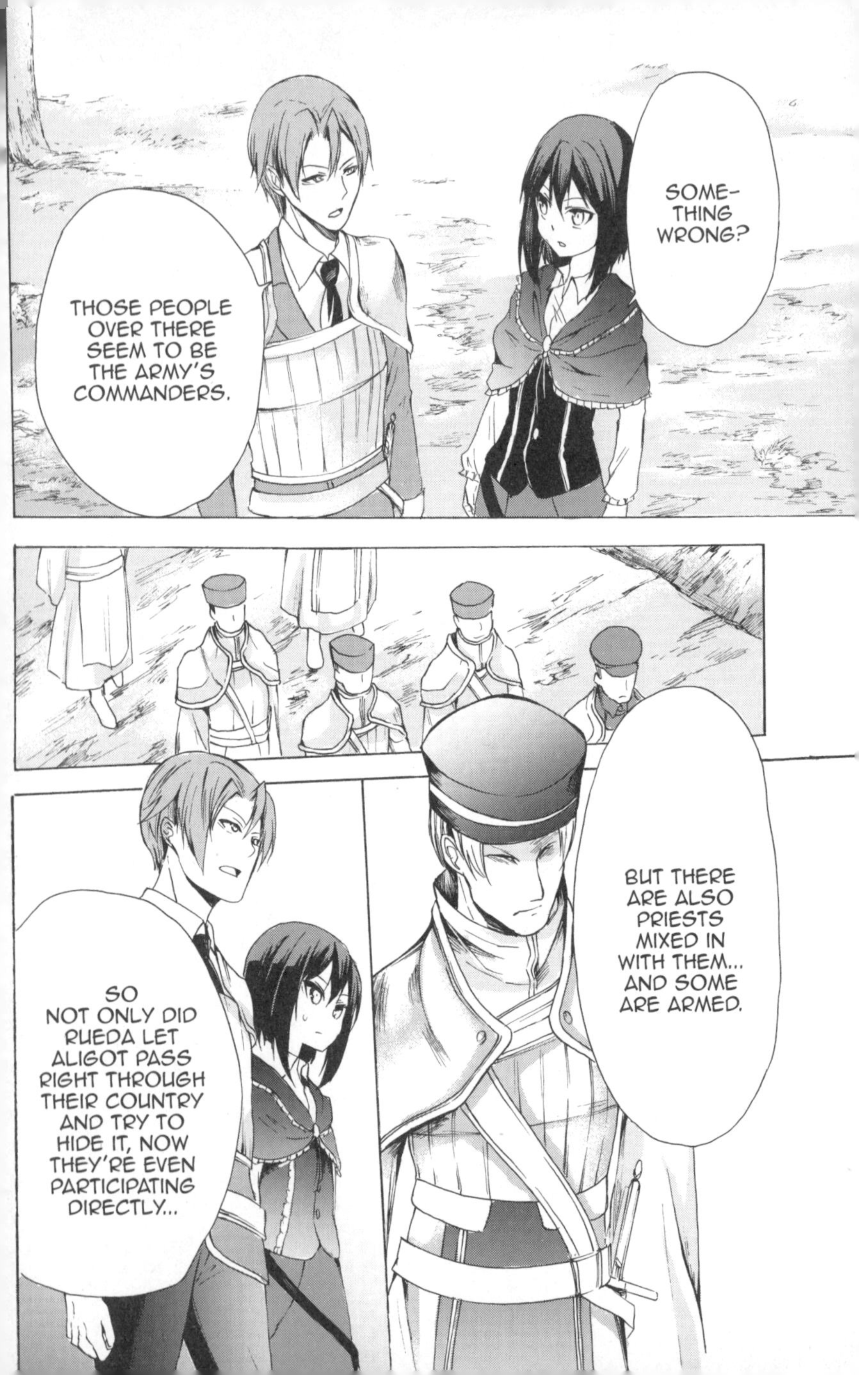
SOME-THING WRONG?
THOSE PEOPLE OVER THERE SEEM TO BE THE ARMY'S COMMANDERS.
BUT THERE ARE ALSO PRIESTS MIXED IN WITH THEM... AND SOME ARE ARMED.
SO NOT ONLY DID RUEDA LET ALIGOT PASS RIGHT THROUGH THEIR COUNTRY AND TRY TO HIDE IT, NOW THEY'RE EVEN PARTICIPATING DIRECTLY...

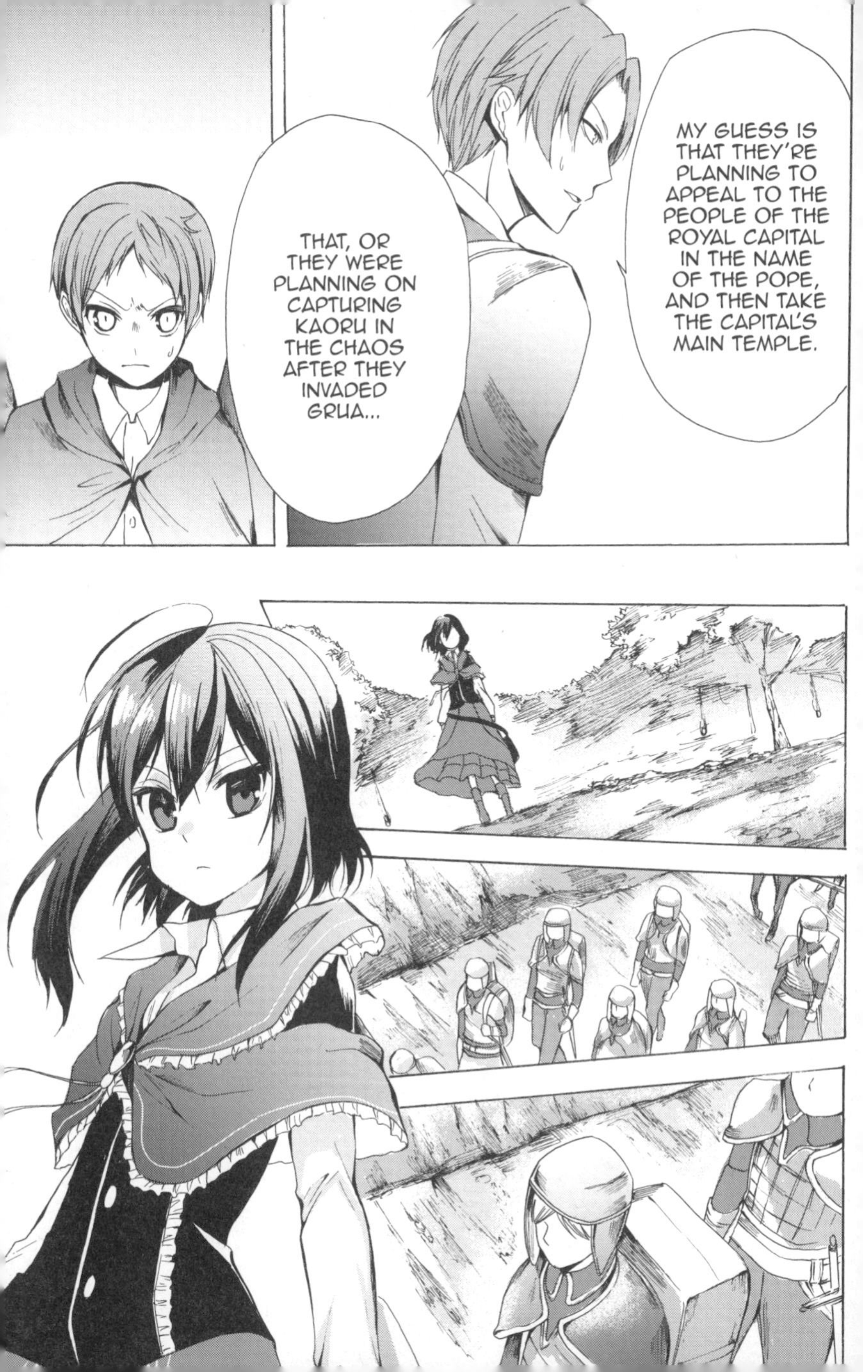
MY GUESS IS THAT THEY'RE PLANNING TO APPEAL TO THE PEOPLE OF THE ROYAL CAPITAL IN THE NAME OF THE POPE, AND THEN TAKE THE CAPITAL'S MAIN TEMPLE.
THAT, OR THEY WERE PLANNING ON CAPTURING KAORU IN THE CHAOS AFTER THEY INVADED GRUA...

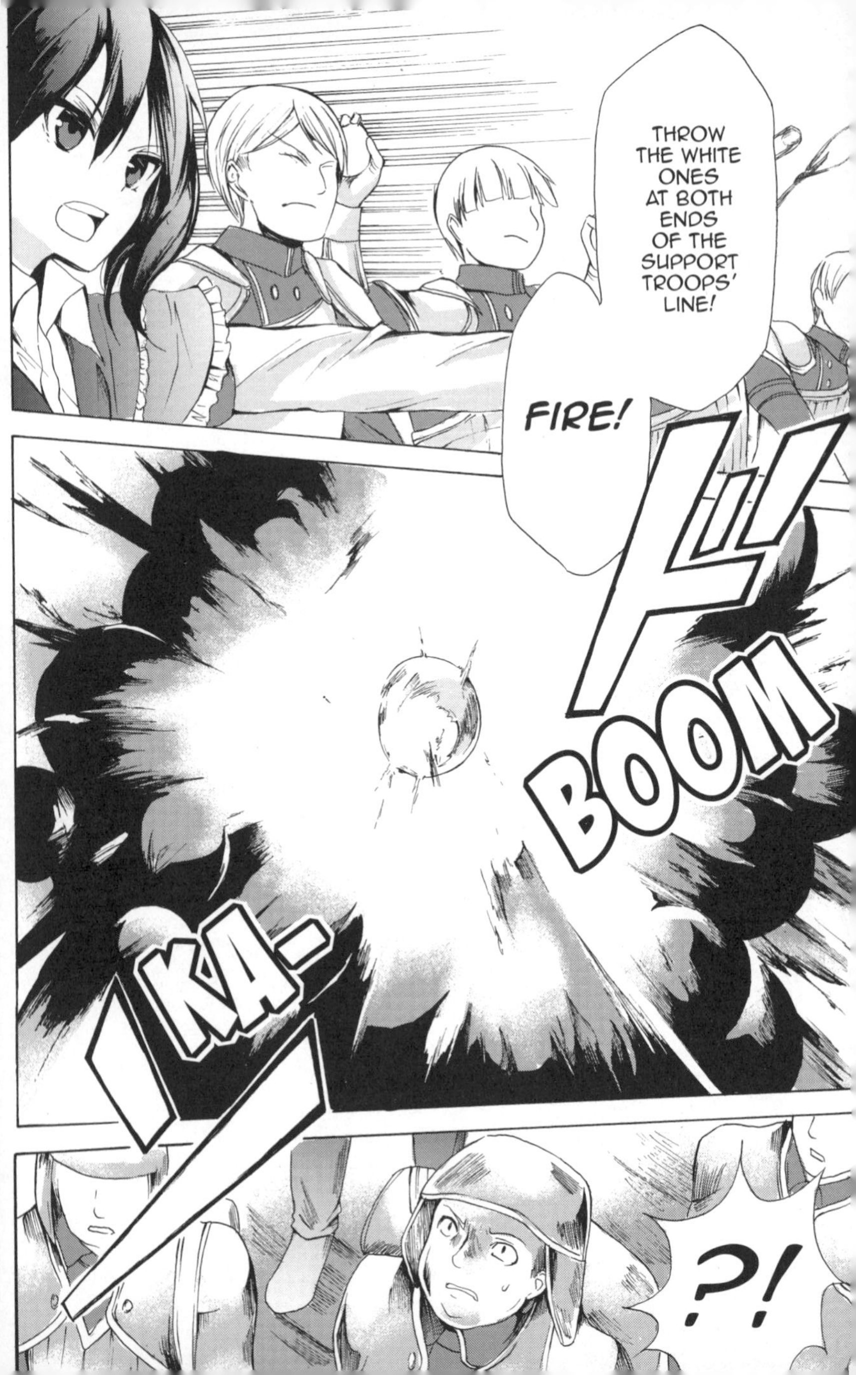
THROW THE WHITE ONES AT BOTH ENDS OF THE SUPPORT TROOPS' LINE!
FIRE!
KA-BOOM
?!

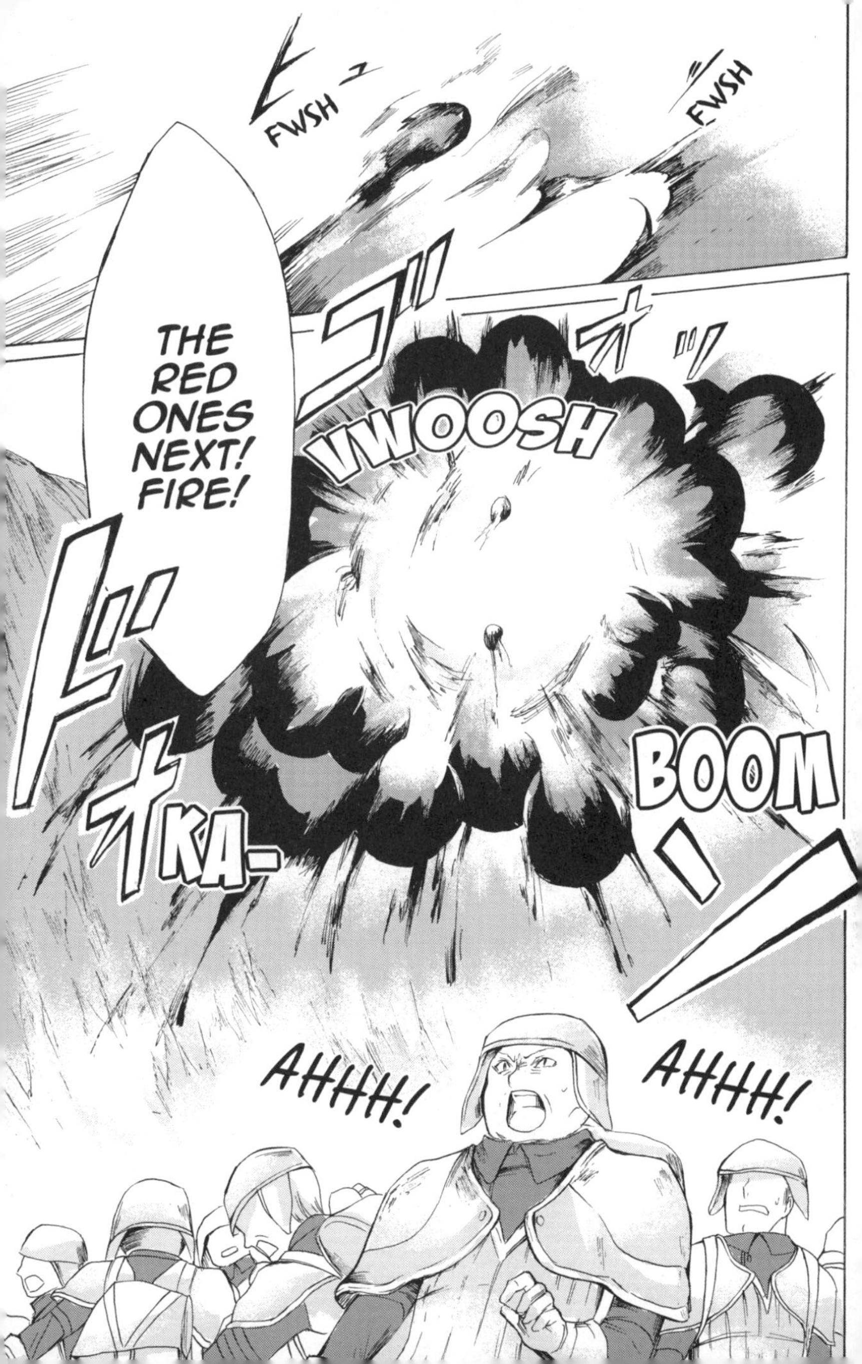
FWSH
FWSH
THE RED ONES NEXT! FIRE!
VWOOSH
BOOM
KA-
AHHH!
AHHH!

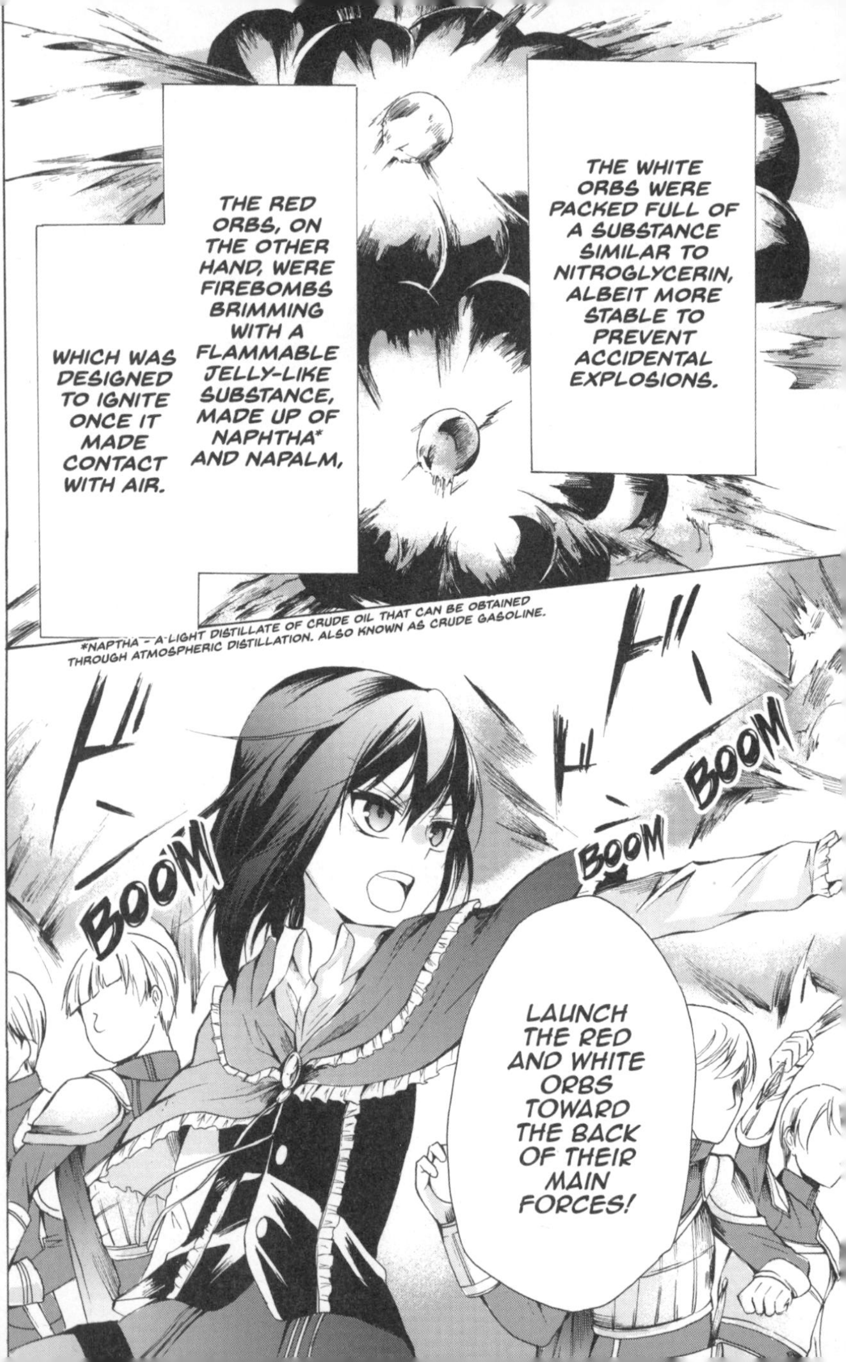
THE WHITE ORBS WERE PACKED FULL OF A SUBSTANCE SIMILAR TO NITROGLYCERIN, ALBEIT MORE STABLE TO PREVENT ACCIDENTAL EXPLOSIONS.
THE RED ORBS, ON THE OTHER HAND, WERE FIREBOMBS BRIMMING WITH A FLAMMABLE JELLY-LIKE SUBSTANCE, MADE UP OF NAPHTHA* AND NAPALM,
WHICH WAS DESIGNED TO IGNITE ONCE IT MADE CONTACT WITH AIR.
*NAPTHA - A LIGHT DISTILLATE OF CRUDE OIL THAT CAN BE OBTAINED THROUGH ATMOSPHERIC DISTILLATION. ALSO KNOWN AS CRUDE GASOLINE.
BOOM
BOOM
BOOM
BOOM
LAUNCH THE RED AND WHITE ORBS TOWARD THE BACK OF THEIR MAIN FORCES!

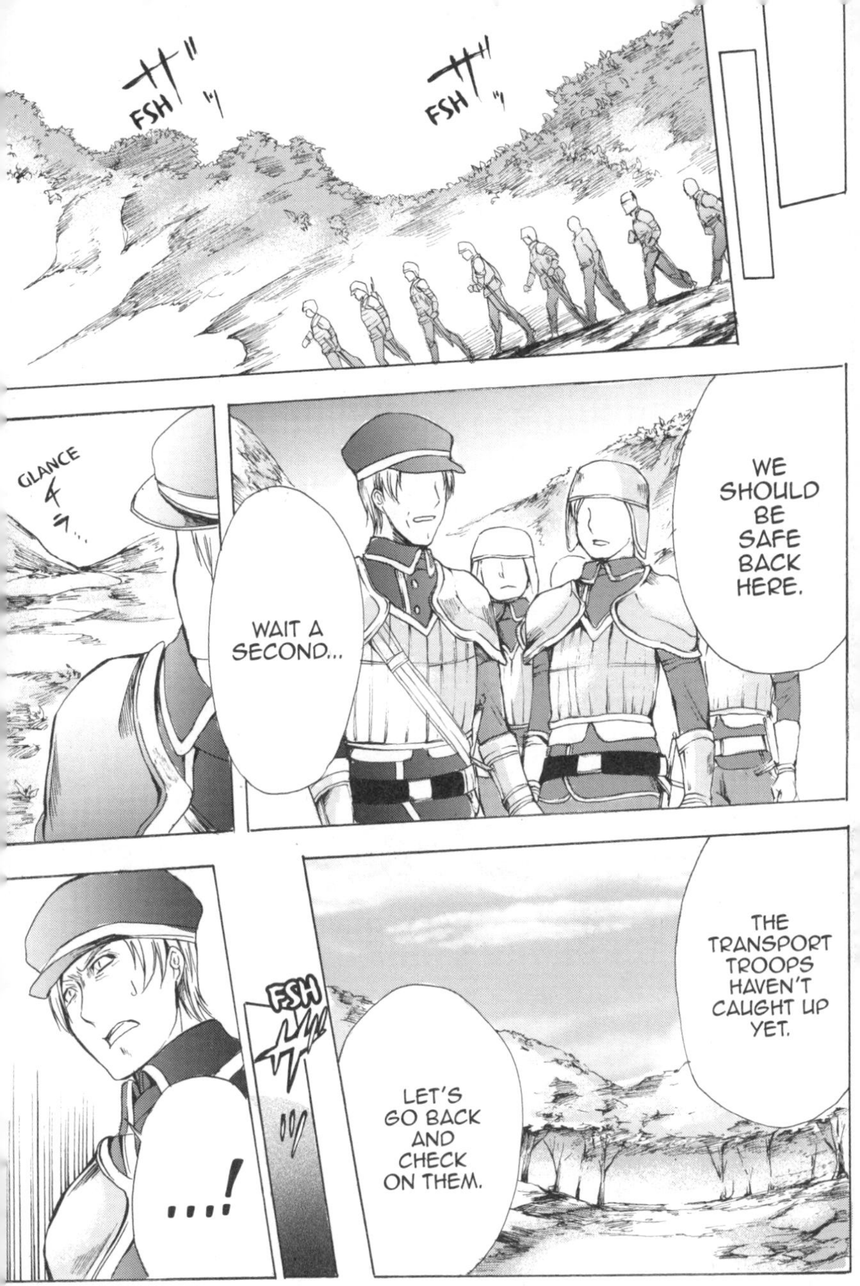
FSH
FSH
WE SHOULD BE SAFE BACK HERE.
WAIT A SECOND...
GLANCE
THE TRANSPORT TROOPS HAVEN'T CAUGHT UP YET.
LET'S GO BACK AND CHECK ON THEM.
FSH
...!

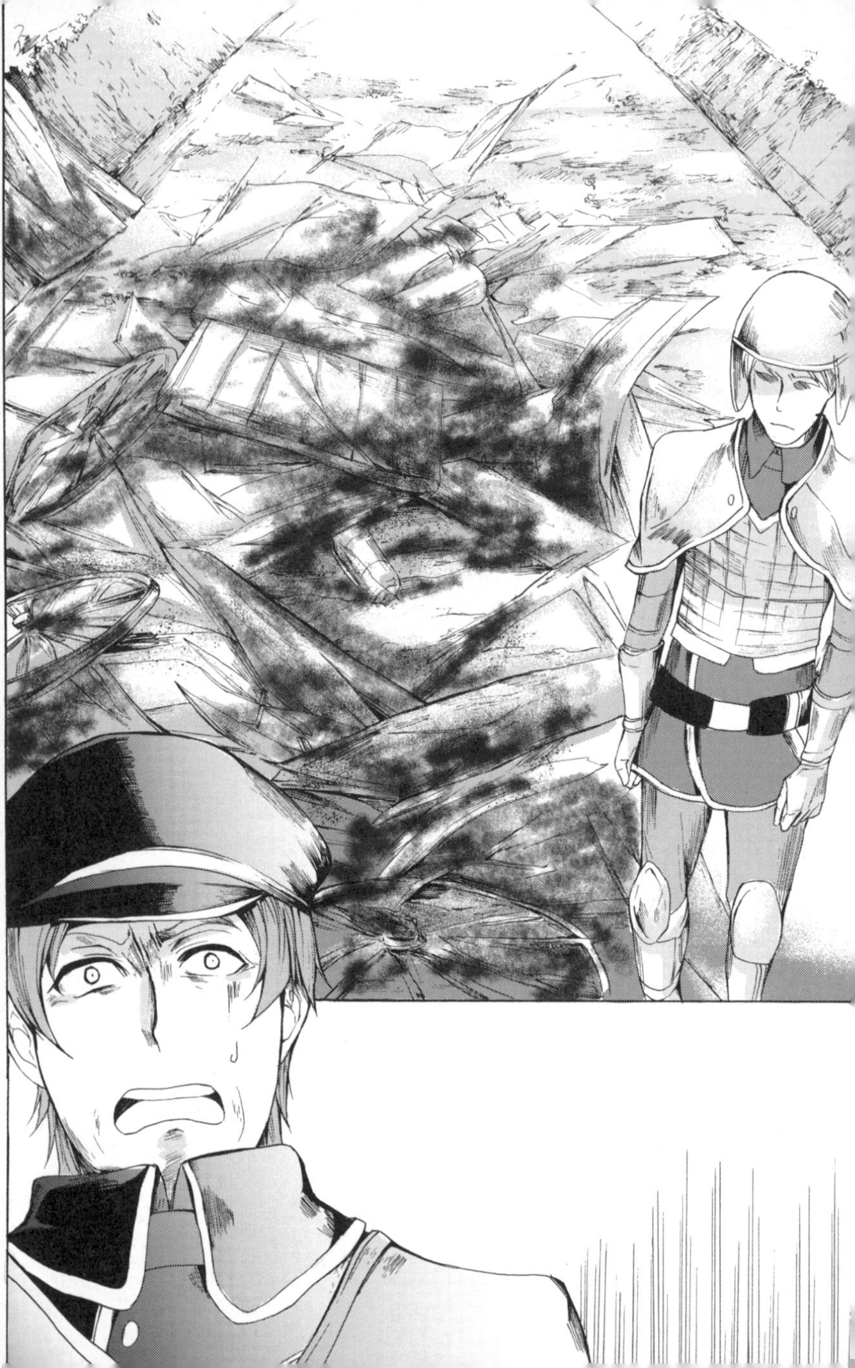

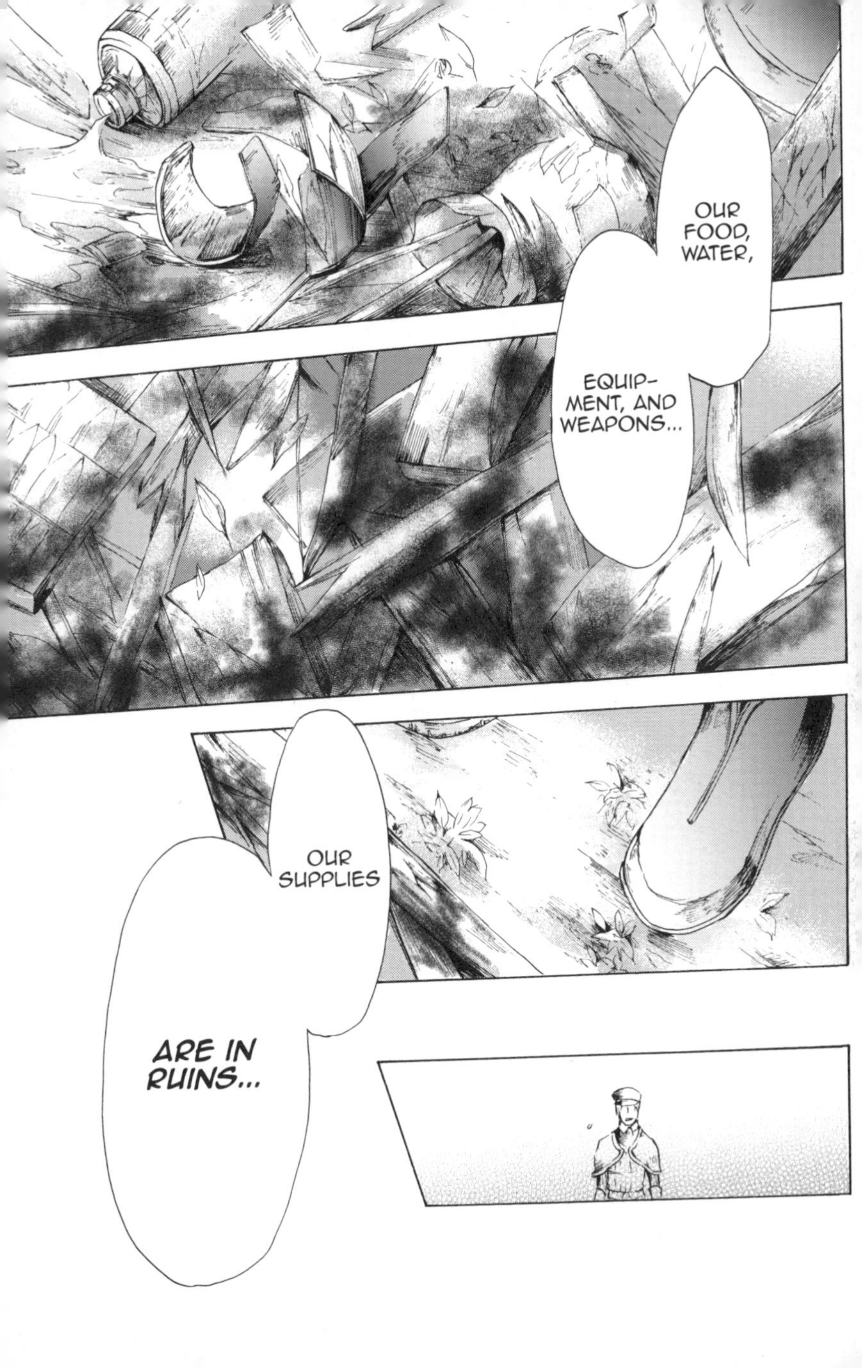
OUR FOOD, WATER,
EQUIPMENT, AND WEAPONS...
OUR SUPPLIES
ARE IN RUINS...

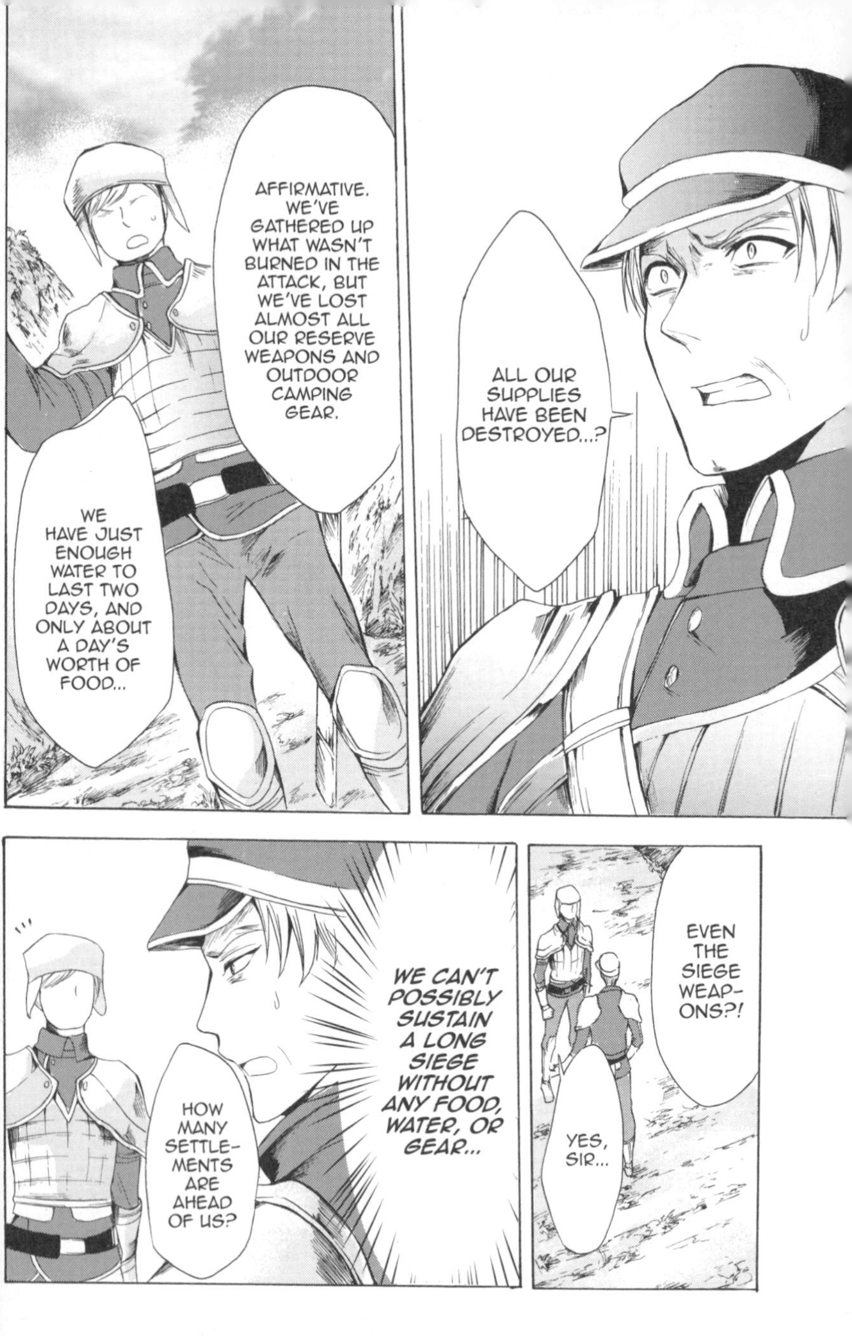
ALL OUR SUPPLIES HAVE BEEN DESTROYED...?
AFFIRMATIVE. WE'VE GATHERED UP WHAT WASN'T BURNED IN THE ATTACK, BUT WE'VE LOST ALMOST ALL OUR RESERVE WEAPONS AND OUTDOOR CAMPING GEAR.
WE HAVE JUST ENOUGH WATER TO LAST TWO DAYS, AND ONLY ABOUT A DAY'S WORTH OF FOOD...
EVEN THE SIEGE WEAPONS?!
YES, SIR...
WE CAN'T POSSIBLY SUSTAIN A LONG SIEGE WITHOUT ANY FOOD, WATER, OR GEAR...
HOW MANY SETTLEMENTS ARE AHEAD OF US?

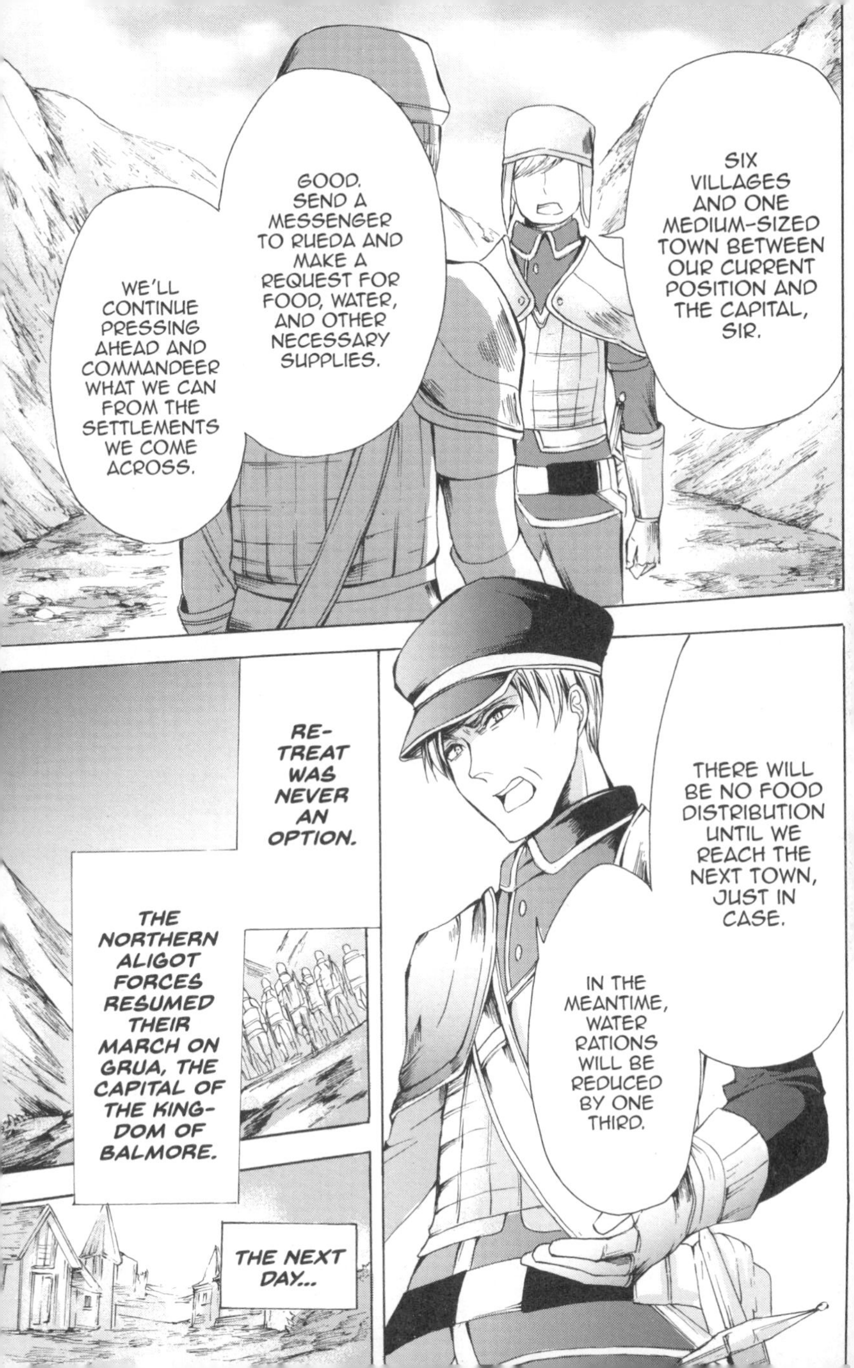
SIX VILLAGES AND ONE MEDIUM-SIZED TOWN BETWEEN OUR CURRENT POSITION AND THE CAPITAL, SIR.
GOOD. SEND A MESSENGER TO RUEDA AND MAKE A REQUEST FOR FOOD, WATER, AND OTHER NECESSARY SUPPLIES.
WE'LL CONTINUE PRESSING AHEAD AND COMMANDEER WHAT WE CAN FROM THE SETTLEMENTS WE COME ACROSS.
THERE WILL BE NO FOOD DISTRIBUTION UNTIL WE REACH THE NEXT TOWN, JUST IN CASE.
IN THE MEANTIME, WATER RATIONS WILL BE REDUCED BY ONE THIRD.
RE-TREAT WAS NEVER AN OPTION.
THE NORTHERN ALIGOT FORCES RESUMED THEIR MARCH ON GRUA, THE CAPITAL OF THE KING-DOM OF BALMORE.
THE NEXT DAY...

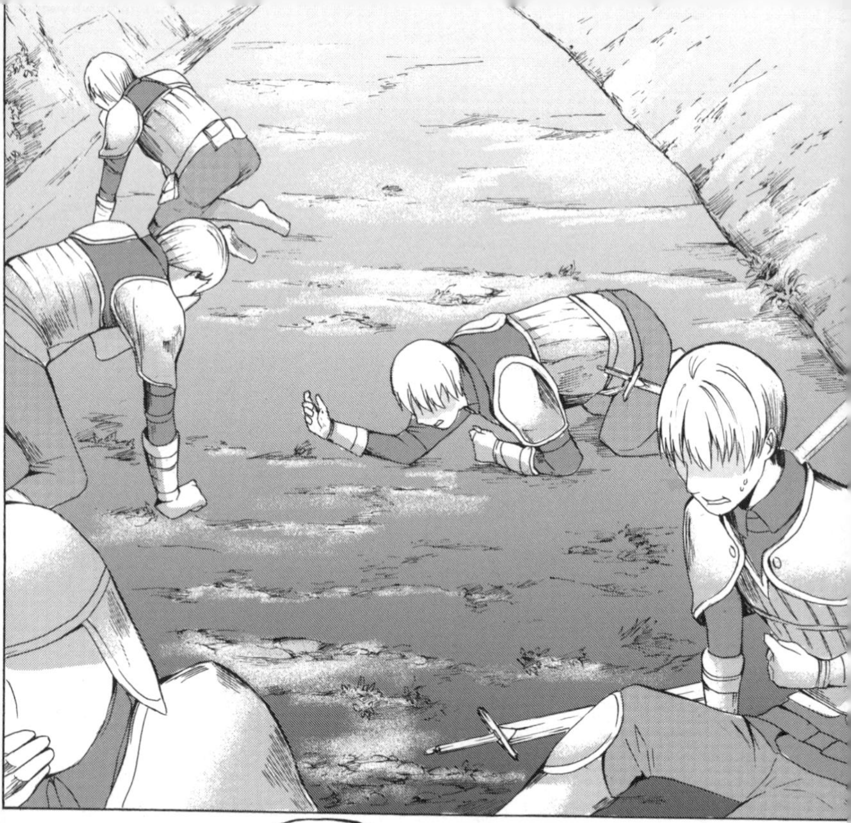

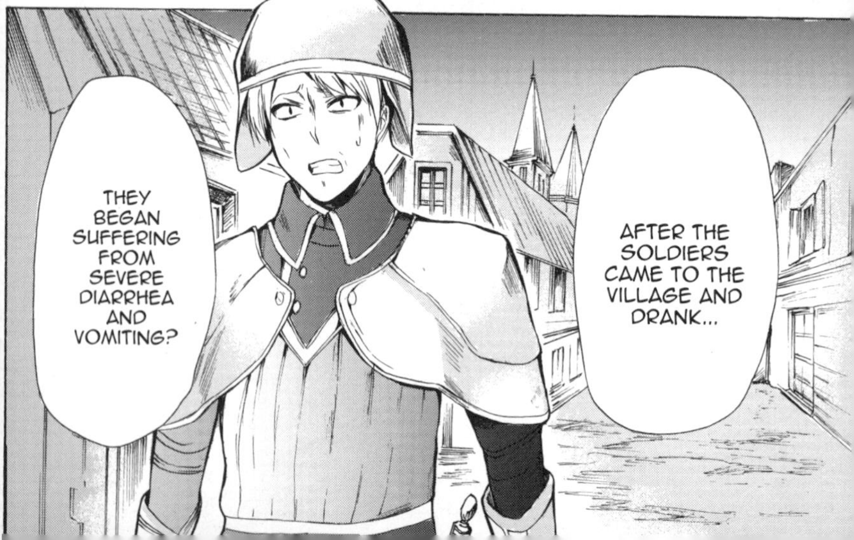
AFTER THE SOLDIERS CAME TO THE VILLAGE AND DRANK...
THEY BEGAN SUFFERING FROM SEVERE DIARRHEA AND VOMITING?

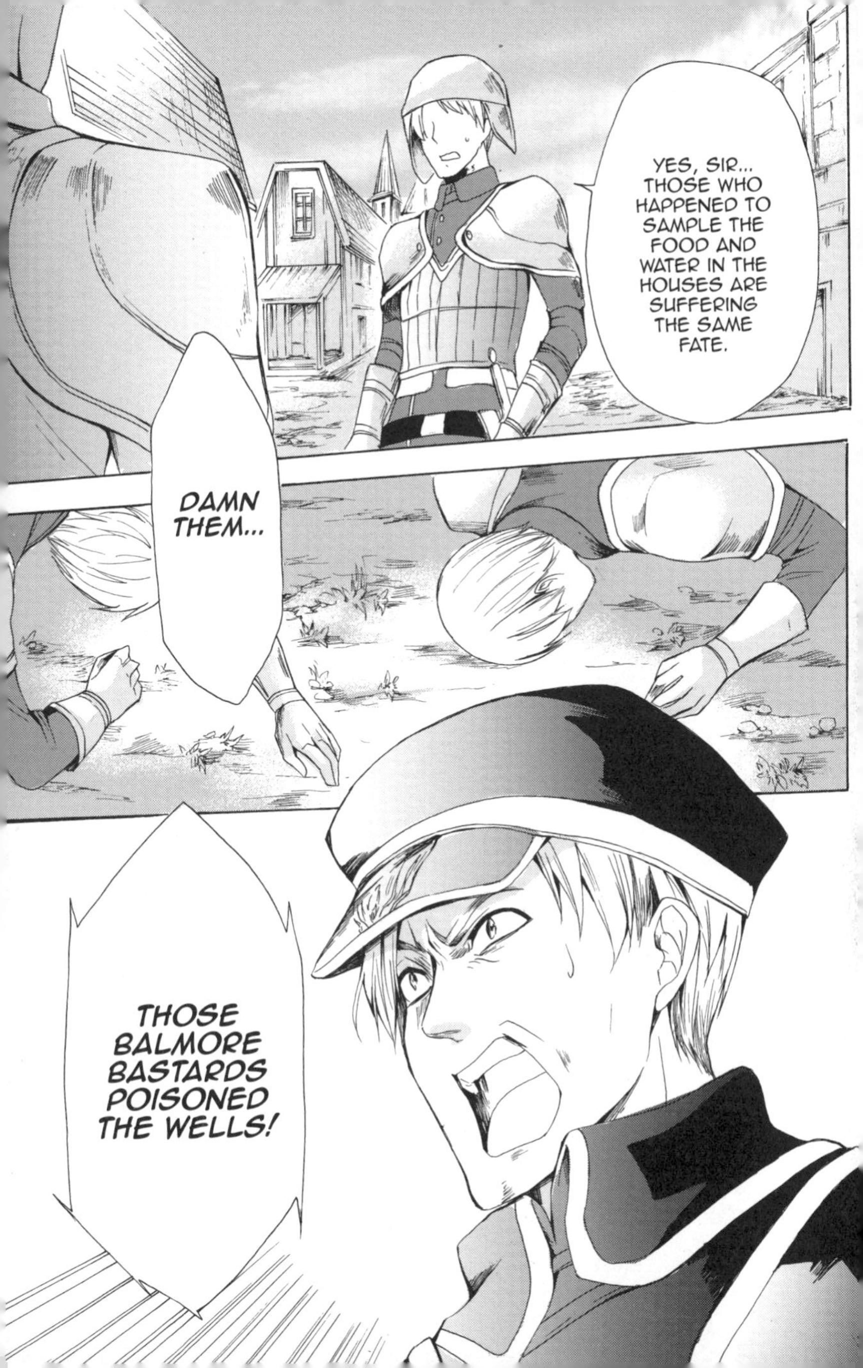
YES, SIR... THOSE WHO HAPPENED TO SAMPLE THE FOOD AND WATER IN THE HOUSES ARE SUFFERING THE SAME FATE.
DAMN THEM...
THOSE BALMORE BASTARDS POISONED THE WELLS!

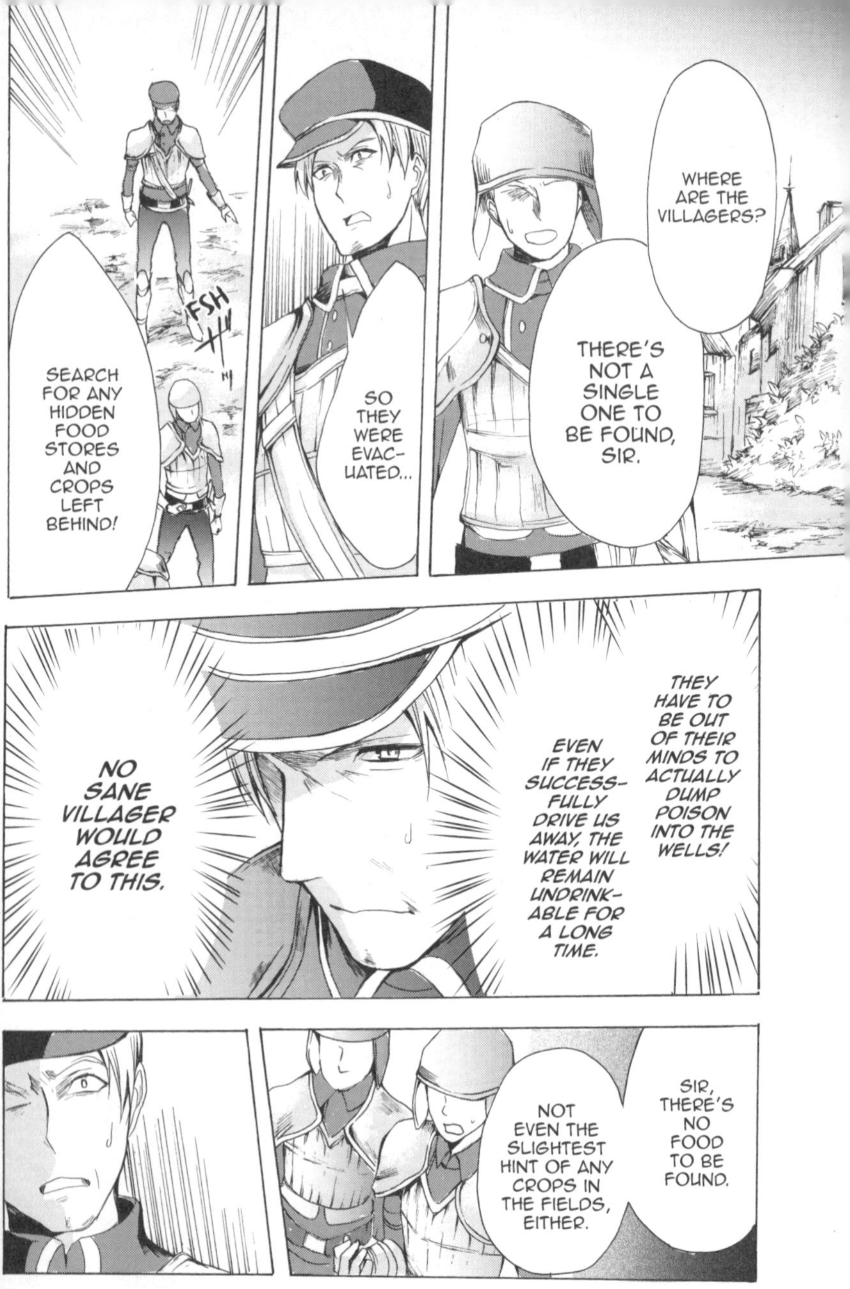
WHERE ARE THE VILLAGERS?
THERE'S NOT A SINGLE ONE TO BE FOUND, SIR.
SO THEY WERE EVAC-UATED...
FSH
SEARCH FOR ANY HIDDEN FOOD STORES AND CROPS LEFT BEHIND!
THEY HAVE TO BE OUT OF THEIR MINDS TO ACTUALLY DUMP POISON INTO THE WELLS!
EVEN IF THEY SUCCESS-FULLY DRIVE US AWAY, THE WATER WILL REMAIN UNDRINK-ABLE FOR A LONG TIME.
NO SANE VILLAGER WOULD AGREE TO THIS.
SIR, THERE'S NO FOOD TO BE FOUND.
NOT EVEN THE SLIGHTEST HINT OF ANY CROPS IN THE FIELDS, EITHER.

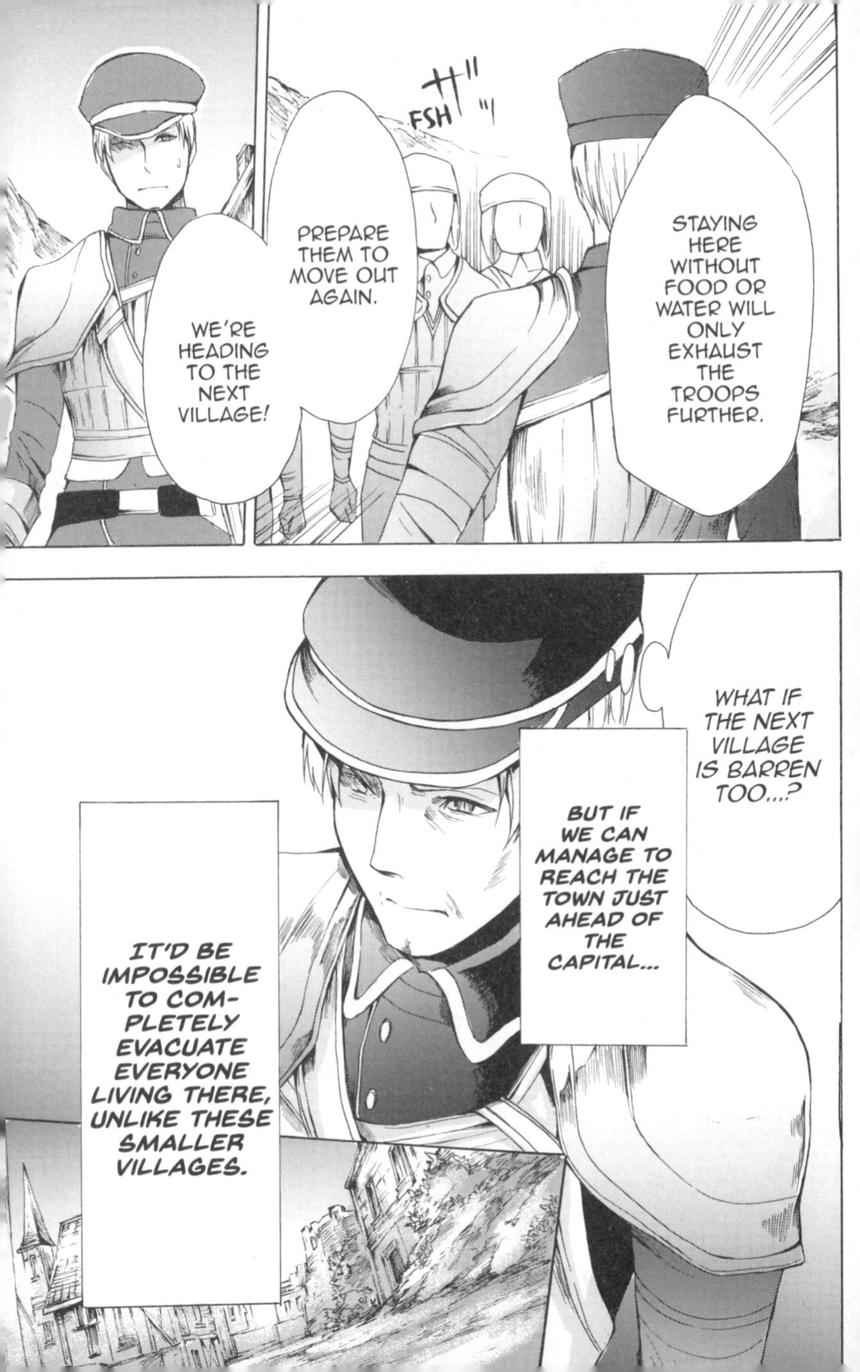
STAYING HERE WITHOUT FOOD OR WATER WILL ONLY EXHAUST THE TROOPS FURTHER.
FSH
PREPARE THEM TO MOVE OUT AGAIN.
WE'RE HEADING TO THE NEXT VILLAGE!
WHAT IF THE NEXT VILLAGE IS BARREN TOO...?
BUT IF WE CAN MANAGE TO REACH THE TOWN JUST AHEAD OF THE CAPITAL...
IT'D BE IMPOSSIBLE TO COM-PLETELY EVACUATE EVERYONE LIVING THERE, UNLIKE THESE SMALLER VILLAGES.

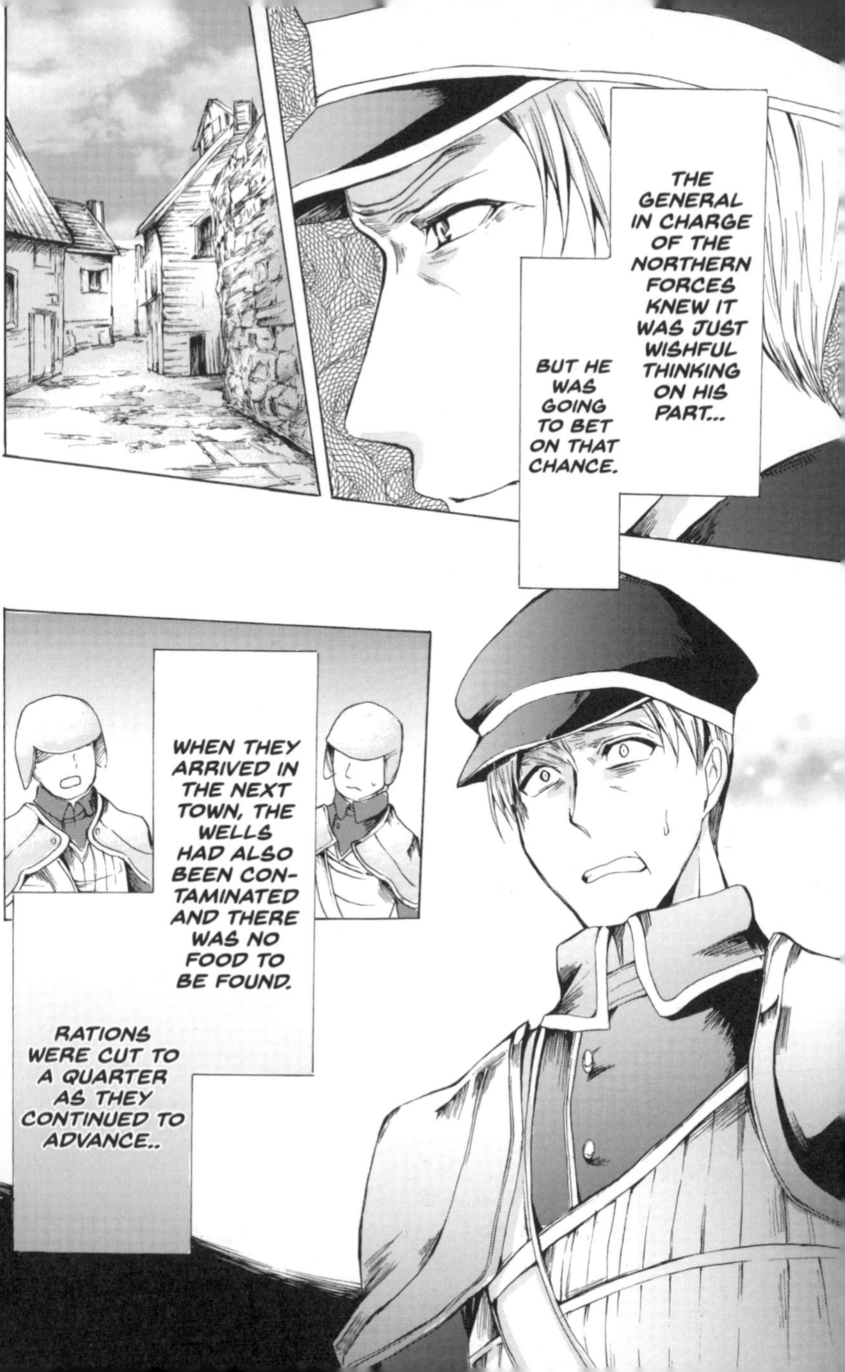
THE GENERAL IN CHARGE OF THE NORTHERN FORCES KNEW IT WAS JUST WISHFUL THINKING ON HIS PART...
BUT HE WAS GOING TO BET ON THAT CHANCE.
WHEN THEY ARRIVED IN THE NEXT TOWN, THE WELLS HAD ALSO BEEN CON-TAMINATED AND THERE WAS NO FOOD TO BE FOUND.
RATIONS WERE CUT TO A QUARTER AS THEY CONTINUED TO ADVANCE..

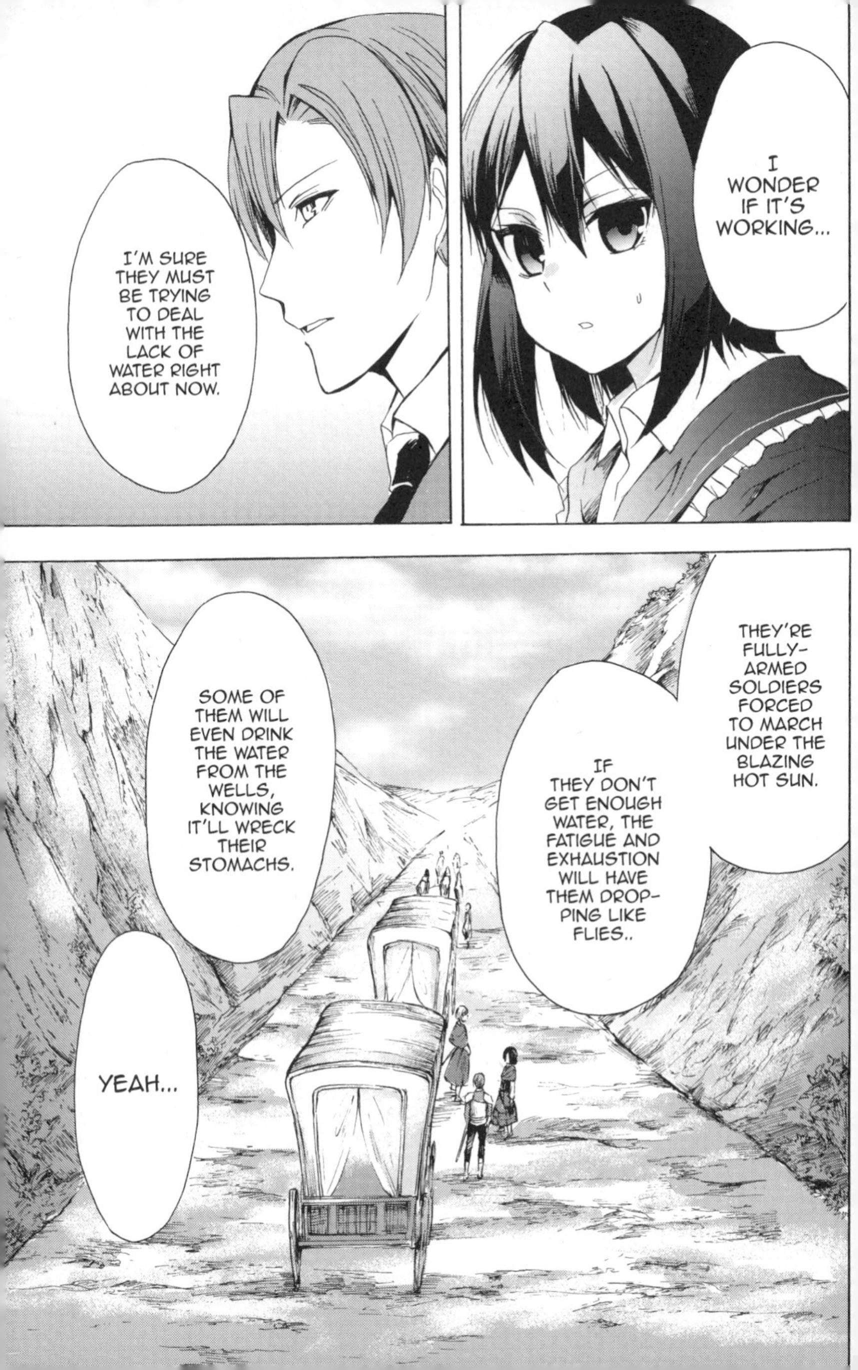
I WONDER IF IT'S WORKING...
I'M SURE THEY MUST BE TRYING TO DEAL WITH THE LACK OF WATER RIGHT ABOUT NOW.
THEY'RE FULLY-ARMED SOLDIERS FORCED TO MARCH UNDER THE BLAZING HOT SUN.
IF THEY DON'T GET ENOUGH WATER, THE FATIGUE AND EXHAUSTION WILL HAVE THEM DROPPING LIKE FLIES..
SOME OF THEM WILL EVEN DRINK THE WATER FROM THE WELLS, KNOWING IT'LL WRECK THEIR STOMACHS.
YEAH...

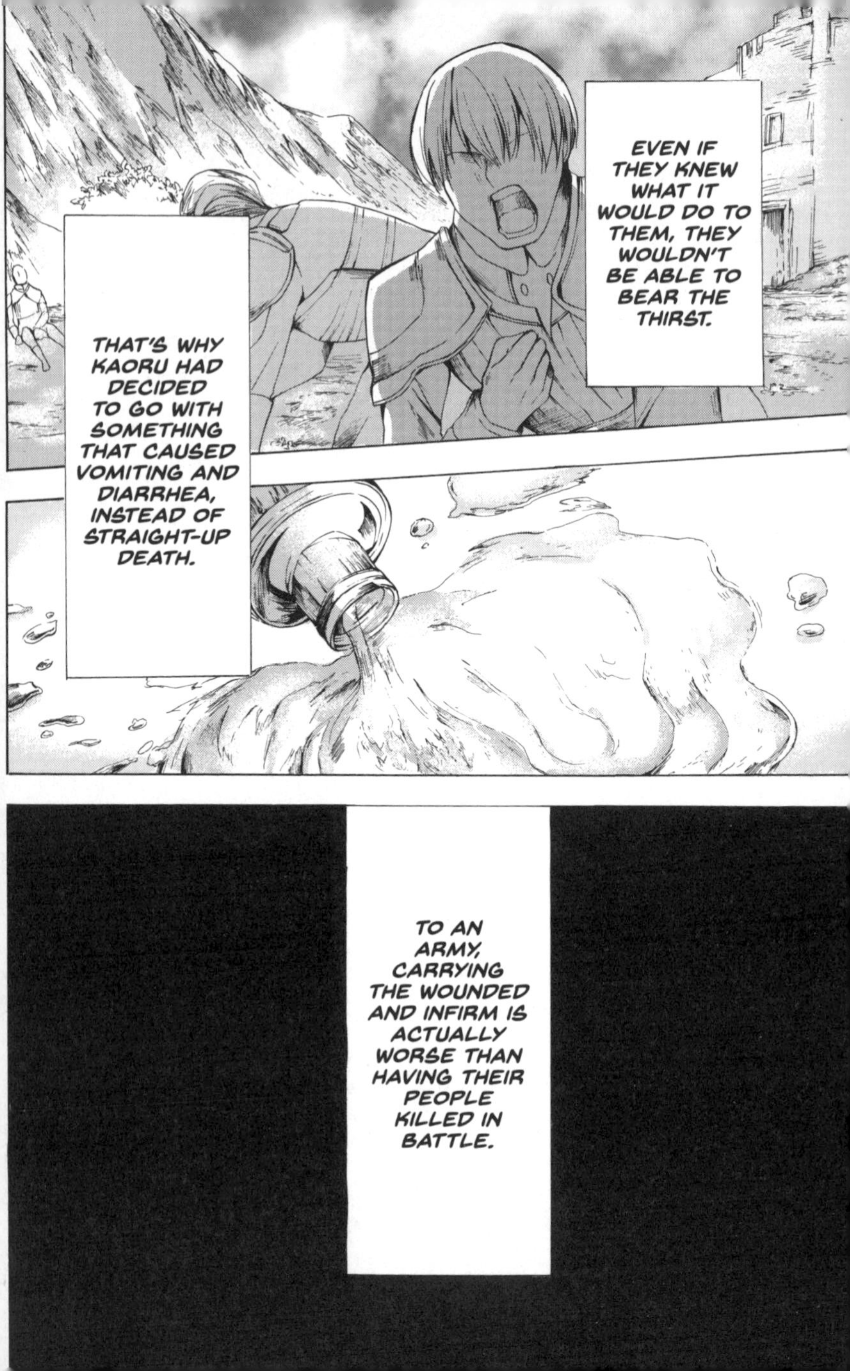
EVEN IF THEY KNEW WHAT IT WOULD DO TO THEM, THEY WOULDN'T BE ABLE TO BEAR THE THIRST.
THAT'S WHY KAORU HAD DECIDED TO GO WITH SOMETHING THAT CAUSED VOMITING AND DIARRHEA, INSTEAD OF STRAIGHT-UP DEATH.
TO AN ARMY, CARRYING THE WOUNDED AND INFIRM IS ACTUALLY WORSE THAN HAVING THEIR PEOPLE KILLED IN BATTLE.

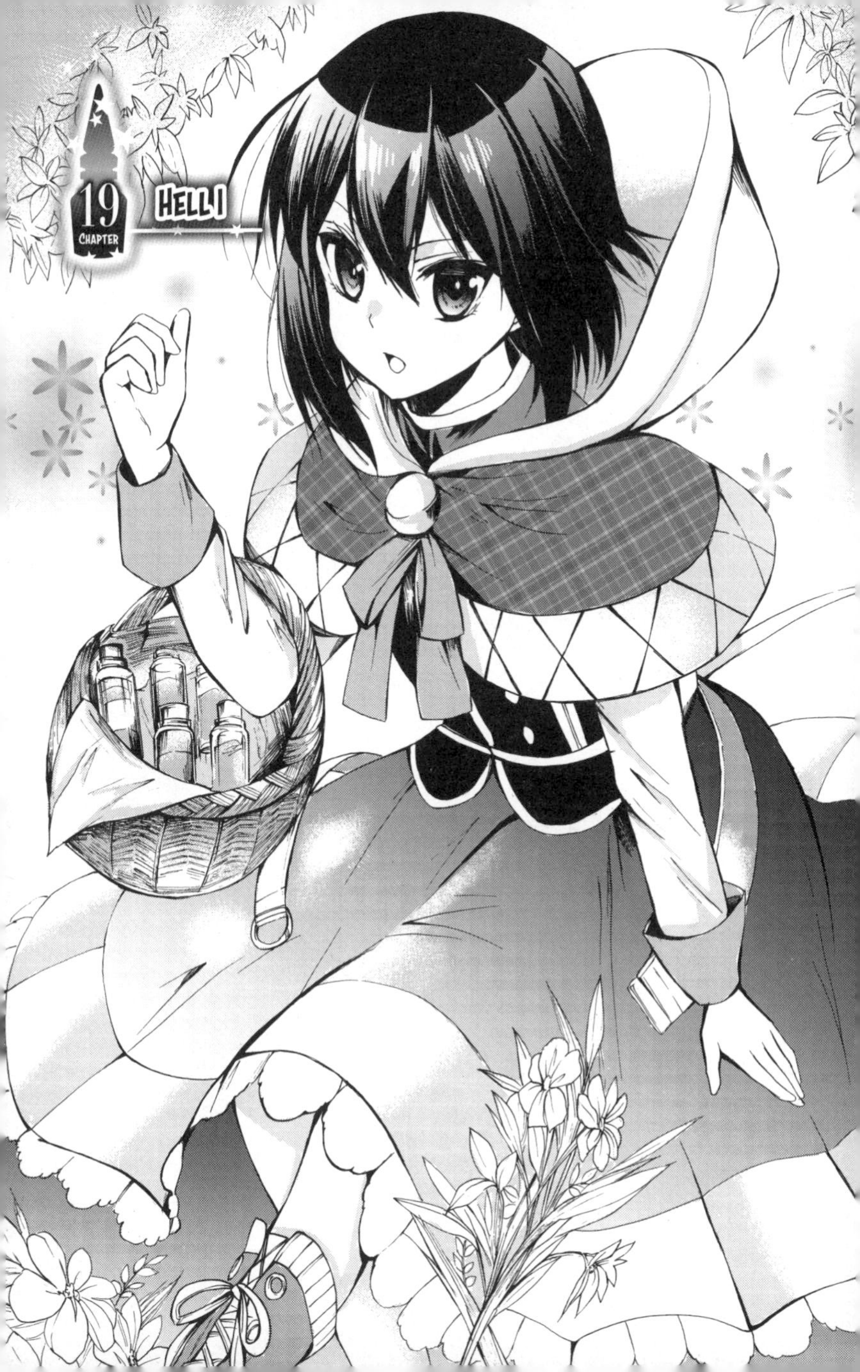
19
CHAPTER
HELL I

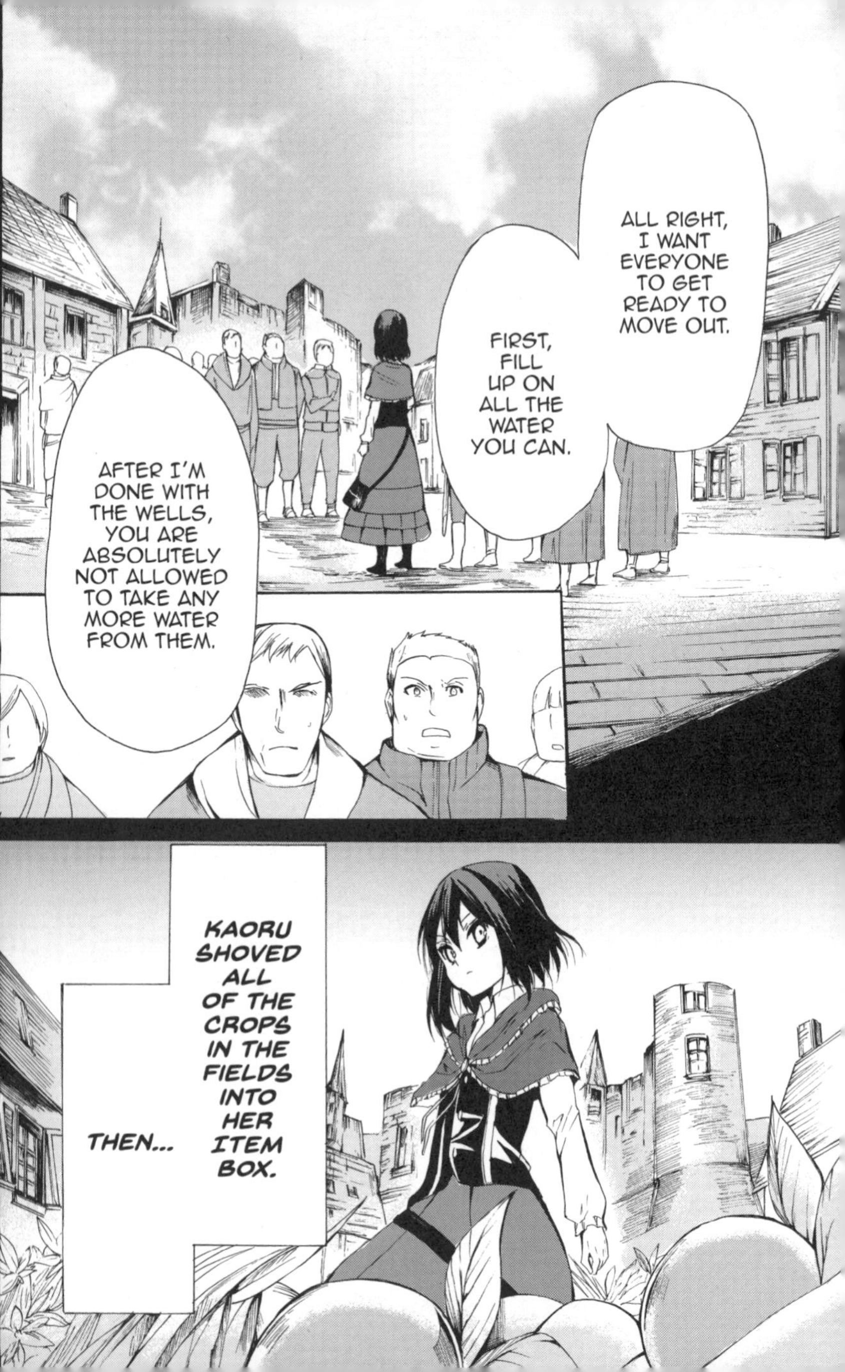
ALL RIGHT, I WANT EVERYONE TO GET READY TO MOVE OUT.
FIRST, FILL UP ON ALL THE WATER YOU CAN.
AFTER I'M DONE WITH THE WELLS, YOU ARE ABSOLUTELY NOT ALLOWED TO TAKE ANY MORE WATER FROM THEM.
THEN...
KAORU SHOVED ALL OF THE CROPS IN THE FIELDS INTO HER ITEM BOX.

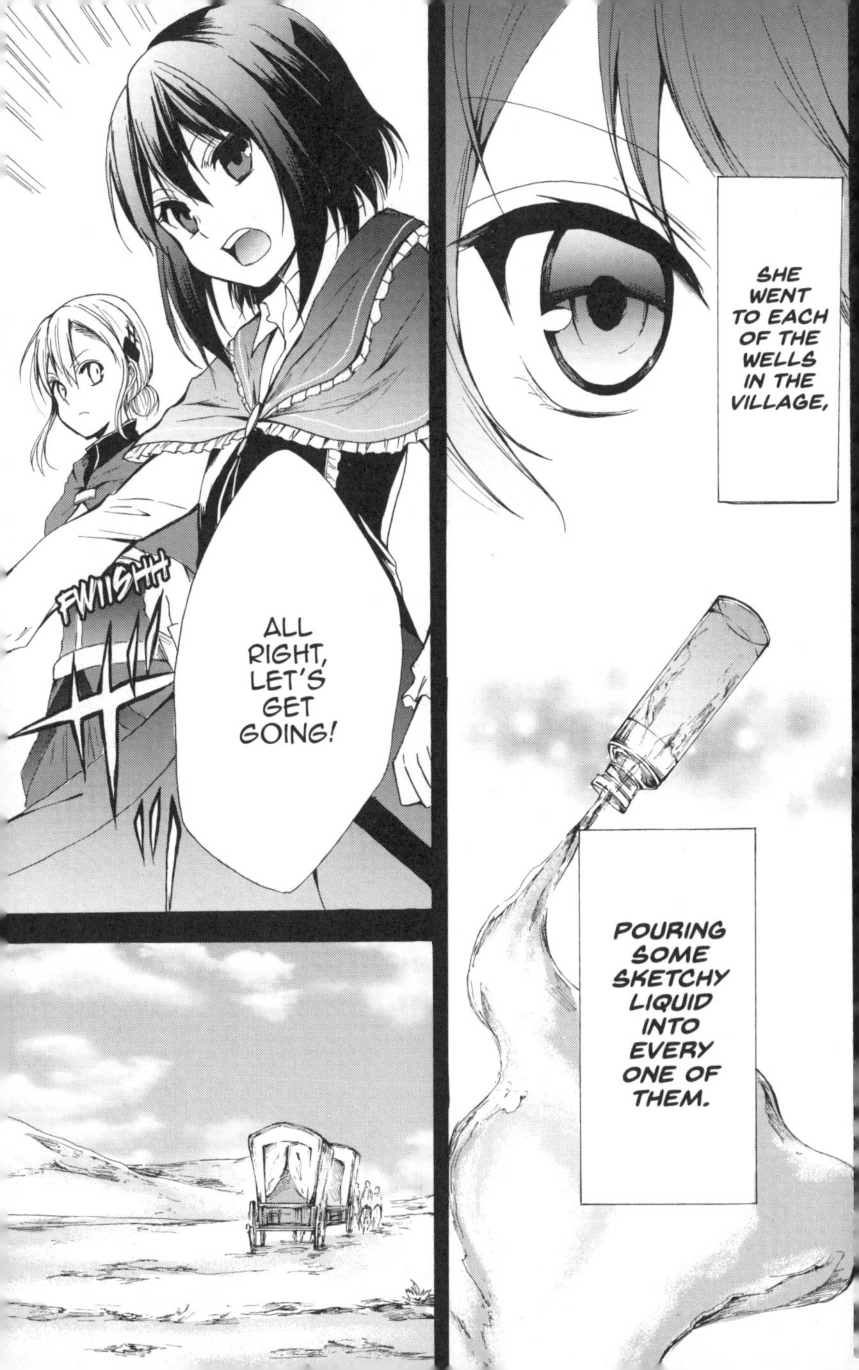
SHE WENT TO EACH OF THE WELLS IN THE VILLAGE,
POURING SOME SKETCHY LIQUID INTO EVERY ONE OF THEM.
ALL RIGHT, LET'S GET GOING!
FWIISHH

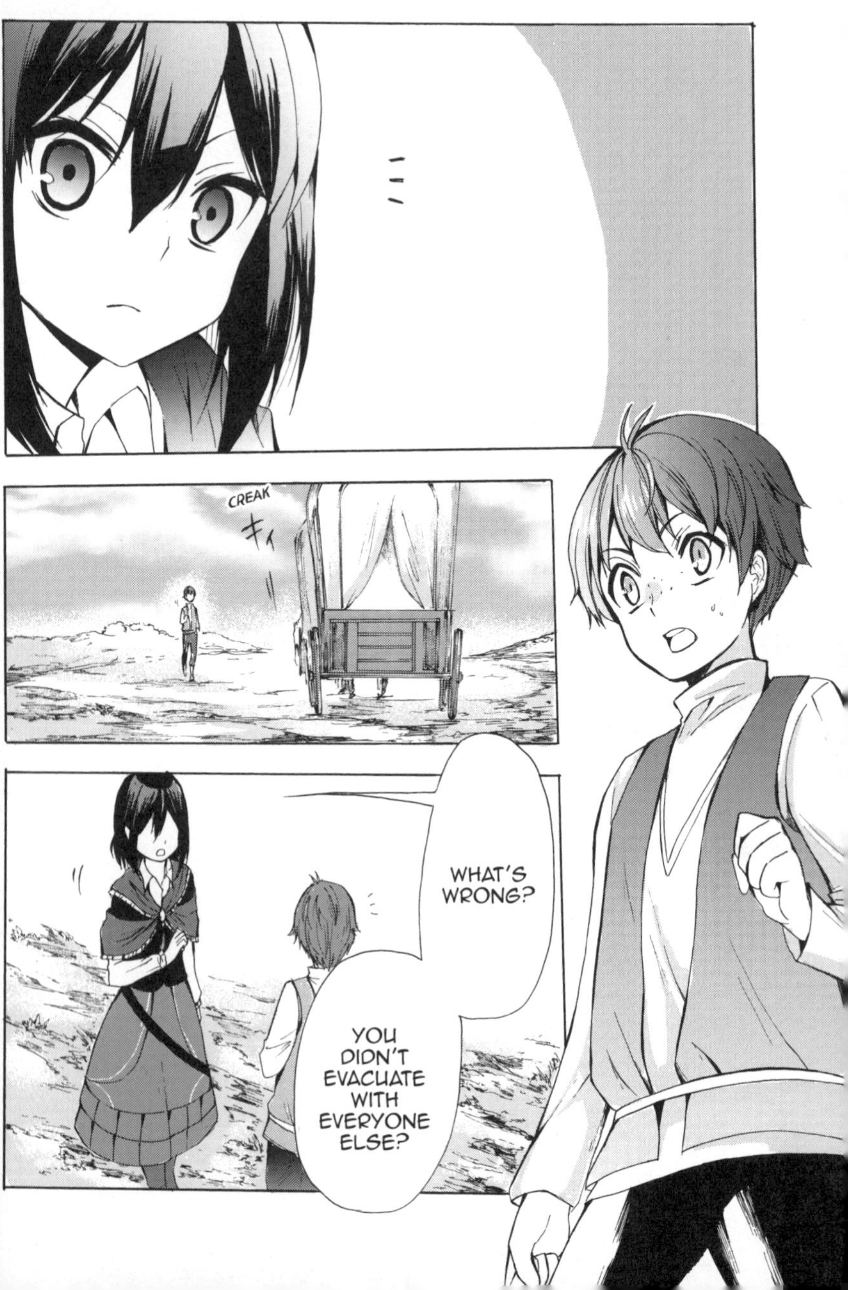
CREAK
キィ
WHAT'S WRONG?
YOU DIDN'T EVACUATE WITH EVERYONE ELSE?

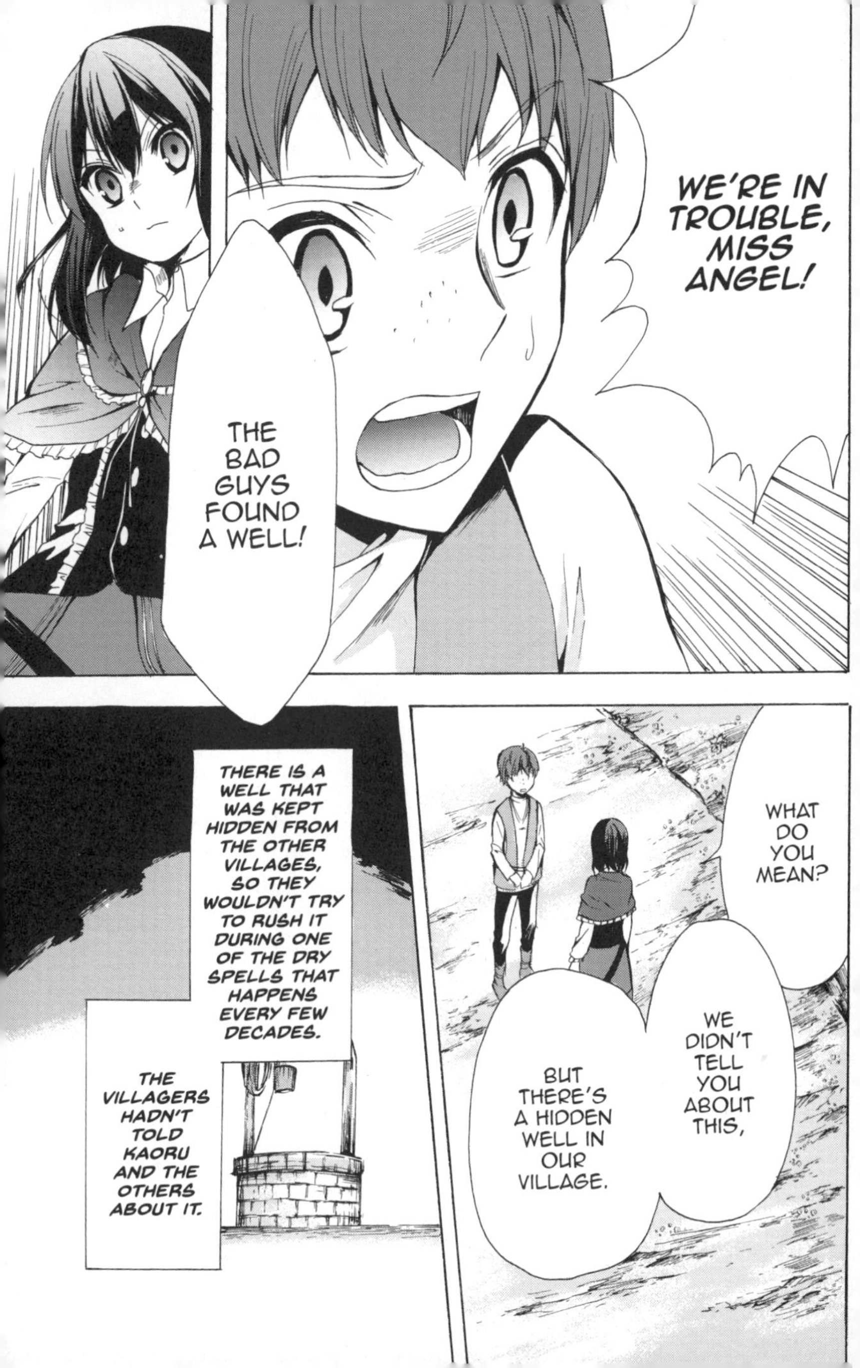
WE'RE IN TROUBLE, MISS ANGEL!
THE BAD GUYS FOUND A WELL!
WHAT DO YOU MEAN?
WE DIDN'T TELL YOU ABOUT THIS,
BUT THERE'S A HIDDEN WELL IN OUR VILLAGE.
THERE IS A WELL THAT WAS KEPT HIDDEN FROM THE OTHER VILLAGES, SO THEY WOULDN'T TRY TO RUSH IT DURING ONE OF THE DRY SPELLS THAT HAPPENS EVERY FEW DECADES.
THE VILLAGERS HADN'T TOLD KAORU AND THE OTHERS ABOUT IT.

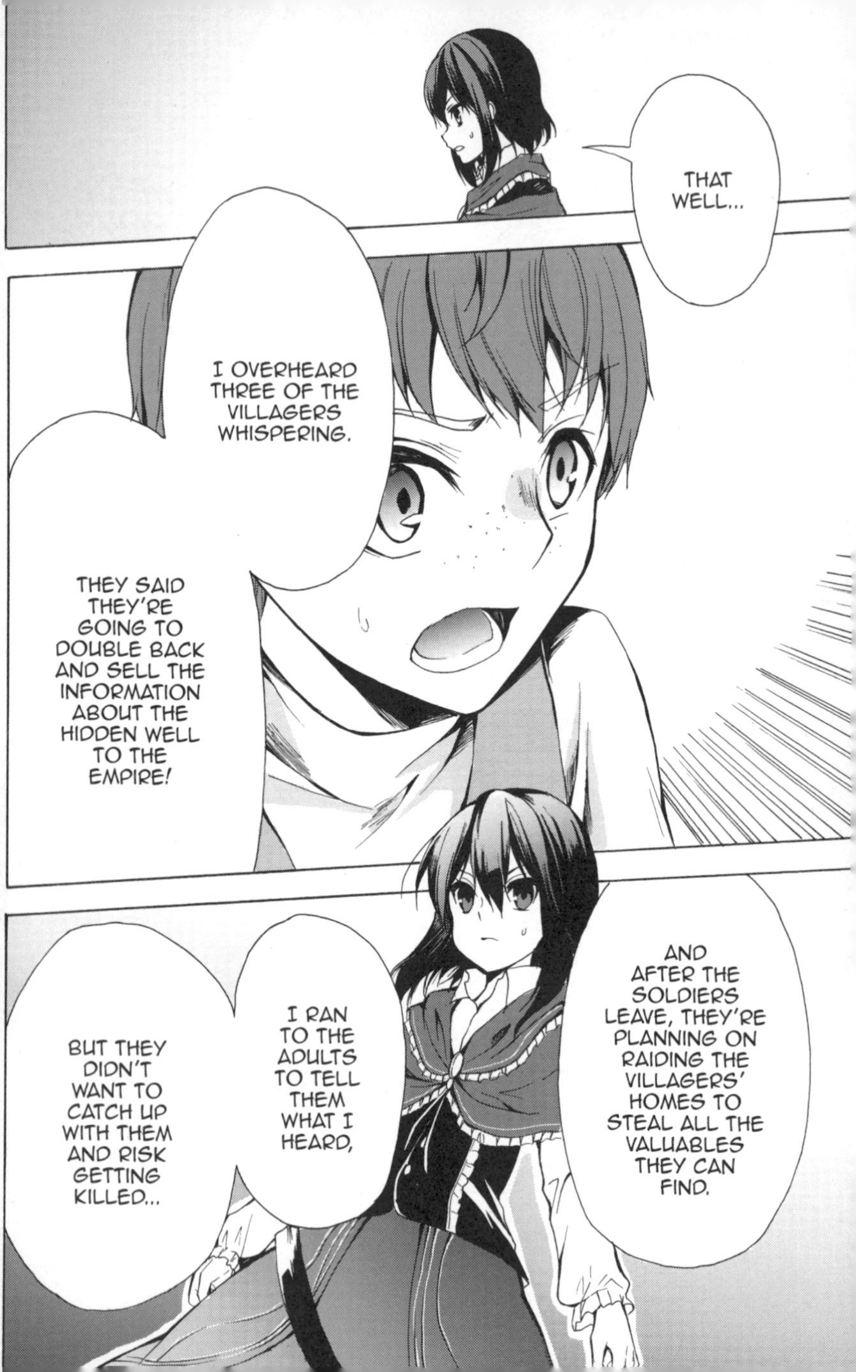
THAT WELL...
I OVERHEARD THREE OF THE VILLAGERS WHISPERING.
THEY SAID THEY'RE GOING TO DOUBLE BACK AND SELL THE INFORMATION ABOUT THE HIDDEN WELL TO THE EMPIRE!
AND AFTER THE SOLDIERS LEAVE, THEY'RE PLANNING ON RAIDING THE VILLAGERS' HOMES TO STEAL ALL THE VALUABLES THEY CAN FIND.
I RAN TO THE ADULTS TO TELL THEM WHAT I HEARD,
BUT THEY DIDN'T WANT TO CATCH UP WITH THEM AND RISK GETTING KILLED...

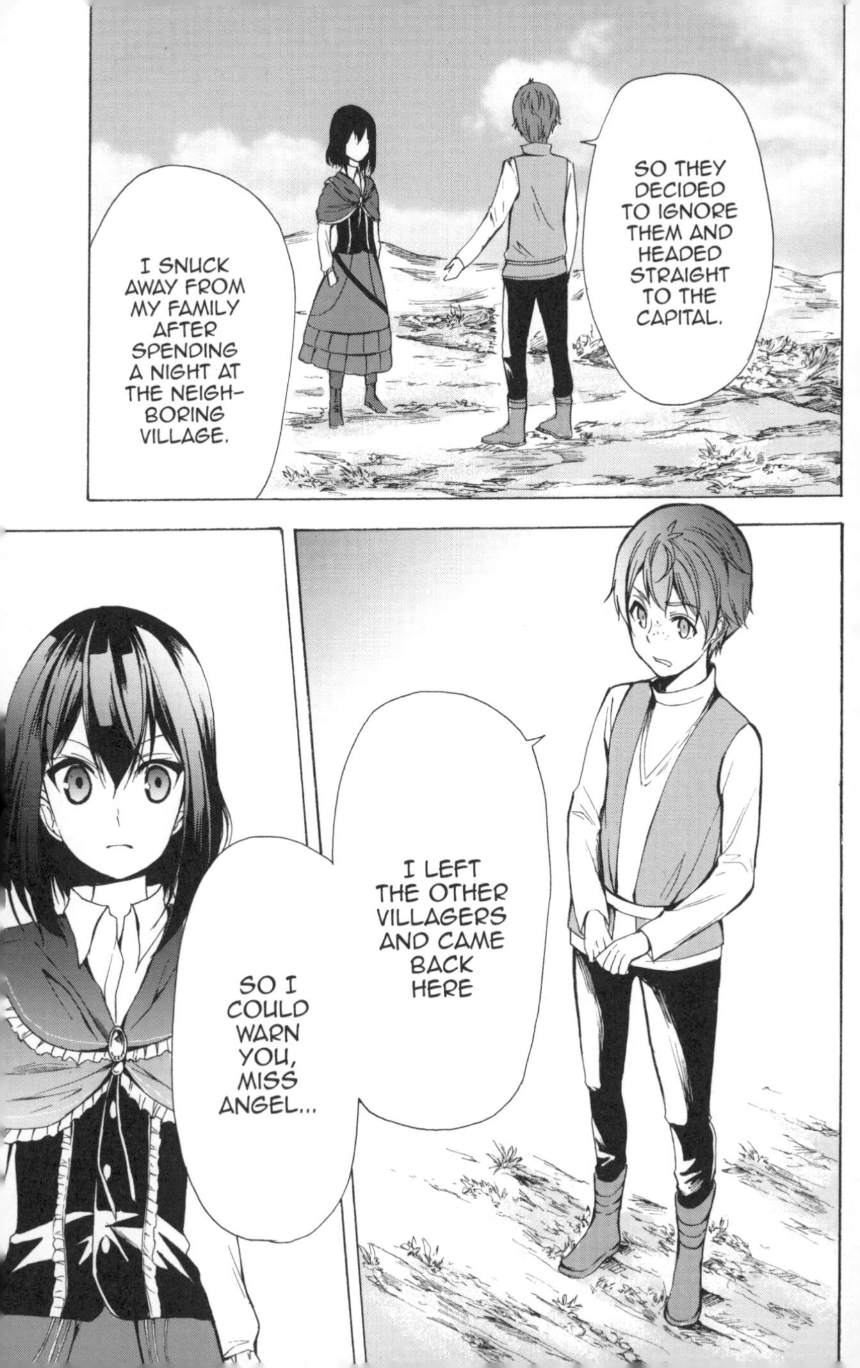
SO THEY DECIDED TO IGNORE THEM AND HEADED STRAIGHT TO THE CAPITAL.
I SNUCK AWAY FROM MY FAMILY AFTER SPENDING A NIGHT AT THE NEIGH-BORING VILLAGE.
I LEFT THE OTHER VILLAGERS AND CAME BACK HERE
SO I COULD WARN YOU, MISS ANGEL...

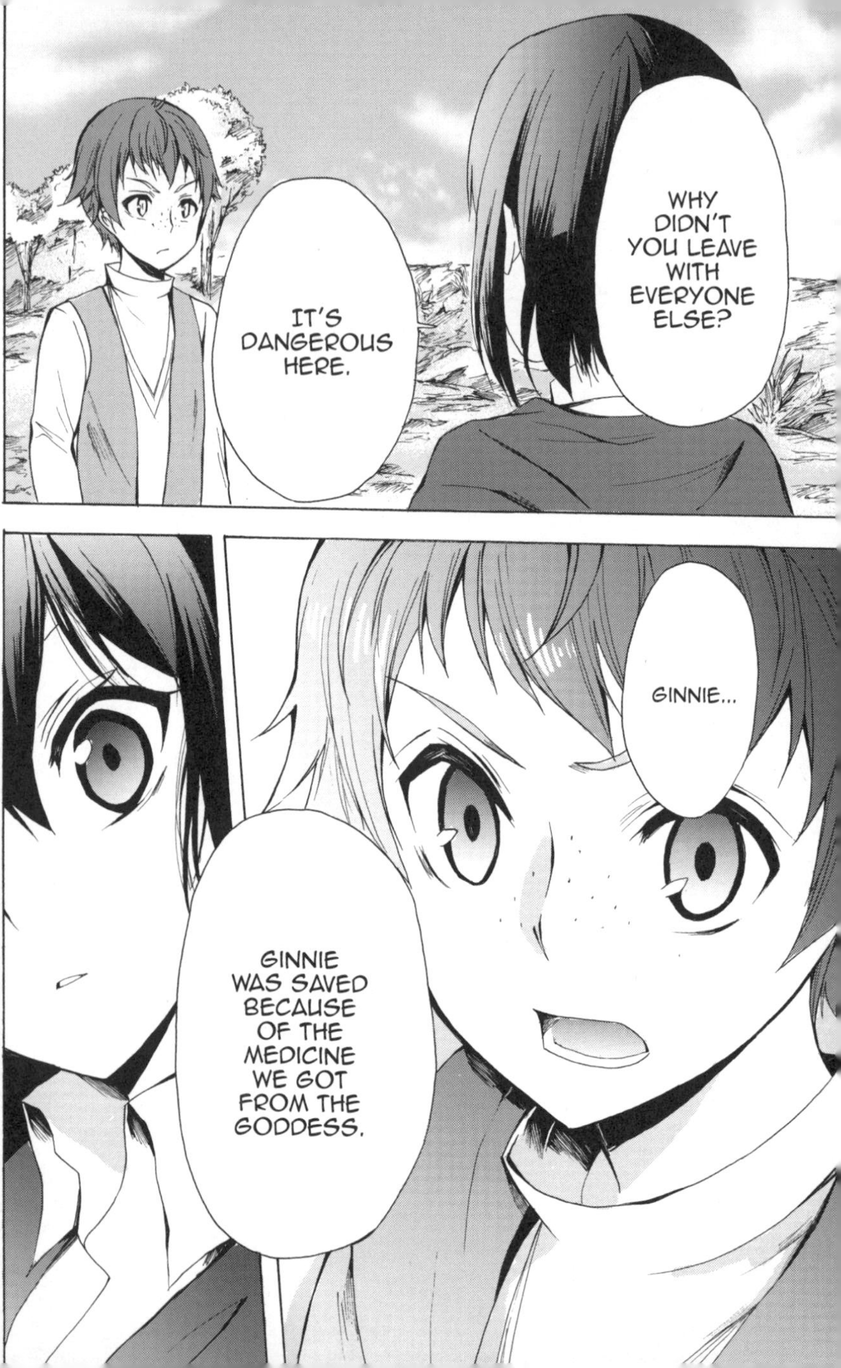
WHY DIDN'T YOU LEAVE WITH EVERYONE ELSE?
IT'S DANGEROUS HERE.
GINNIE...
GINNIE WAS SAVED BECAUSE OF THE MEDICINE WE GOT FROM THE GODDESS.

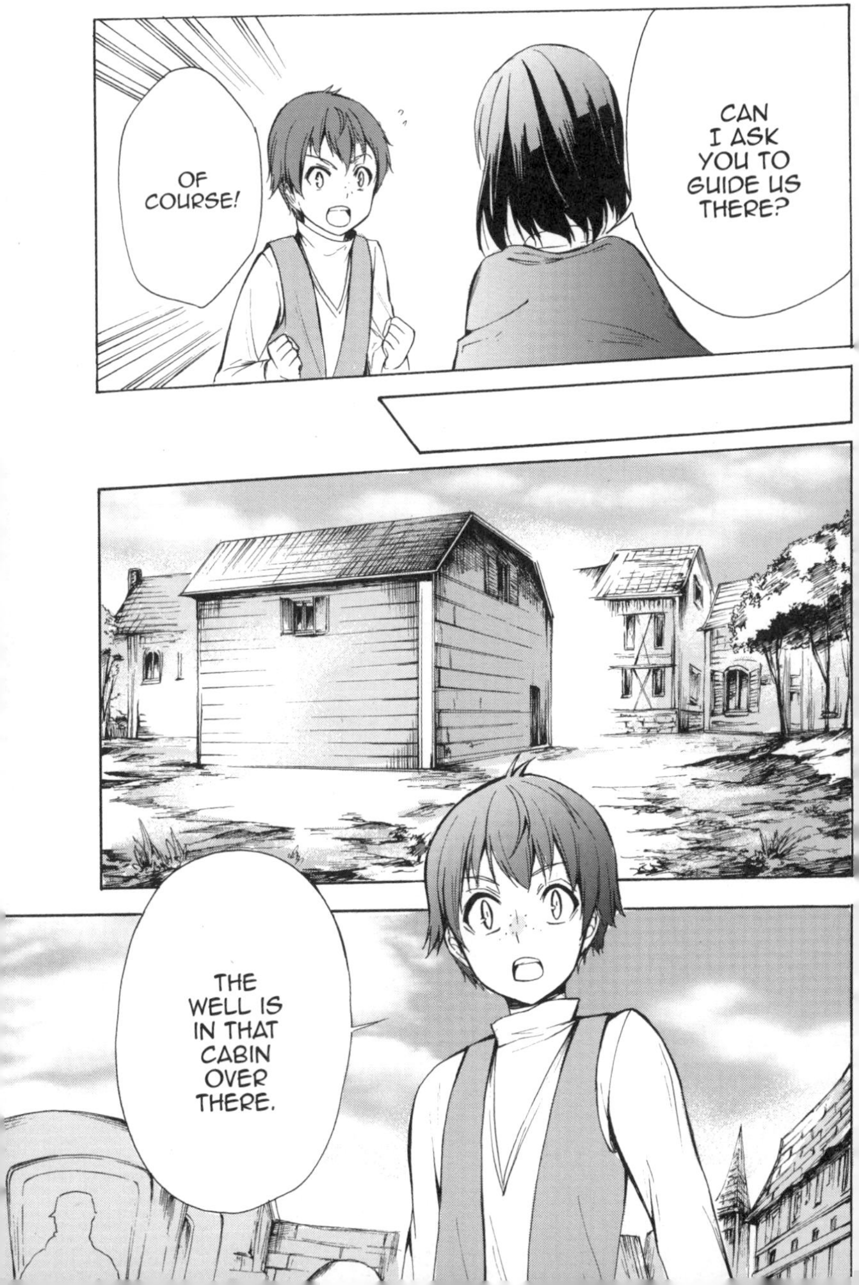
CAN I ASK YOU TO GUIDE US THERE?
OF COURSE!
THE WELL IS IN THAT CABIN OVER THERE.

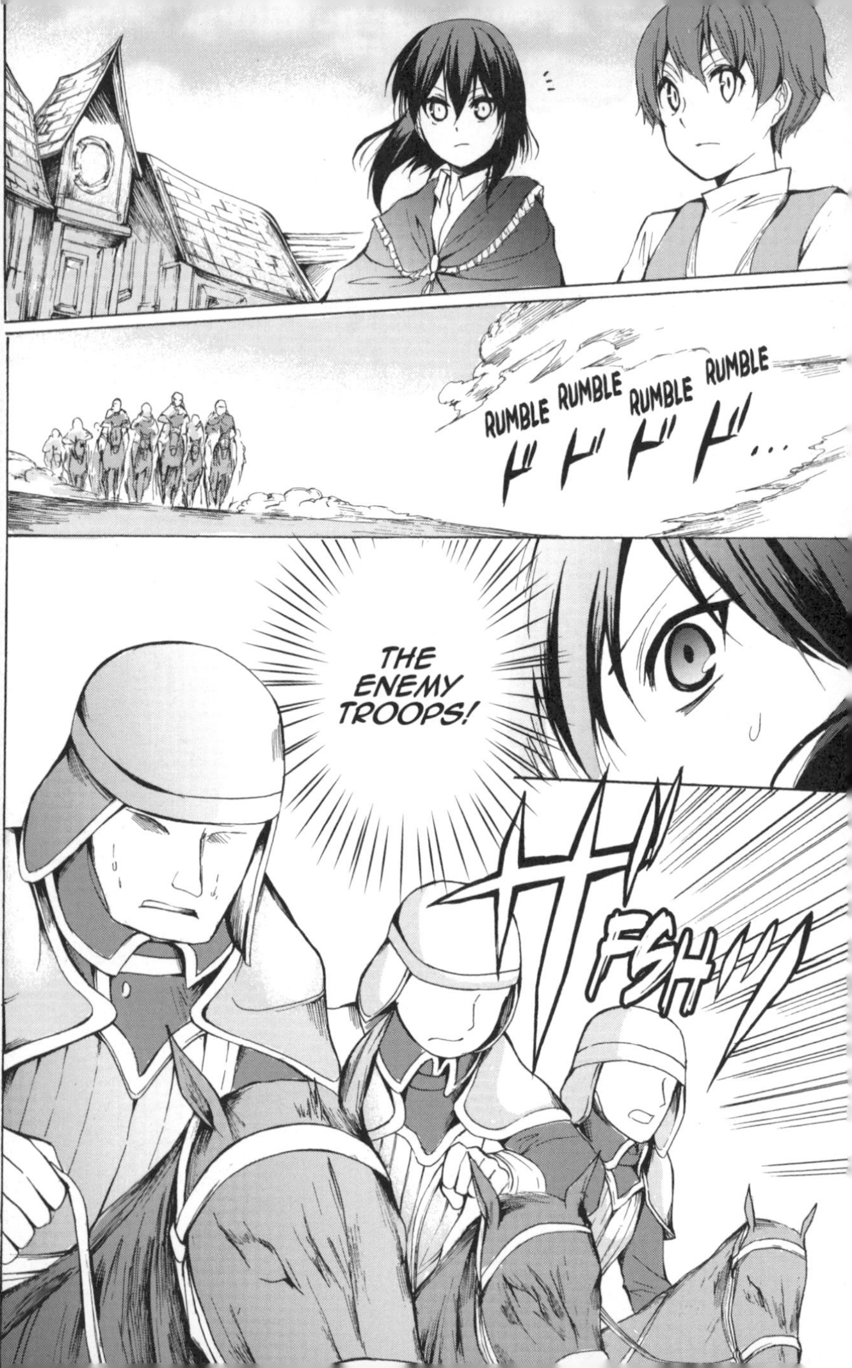
RUMBLE RUMBLE RUMBLE RUMBLE
ドドドド…
THE ENEMY TROOPS!
FSH

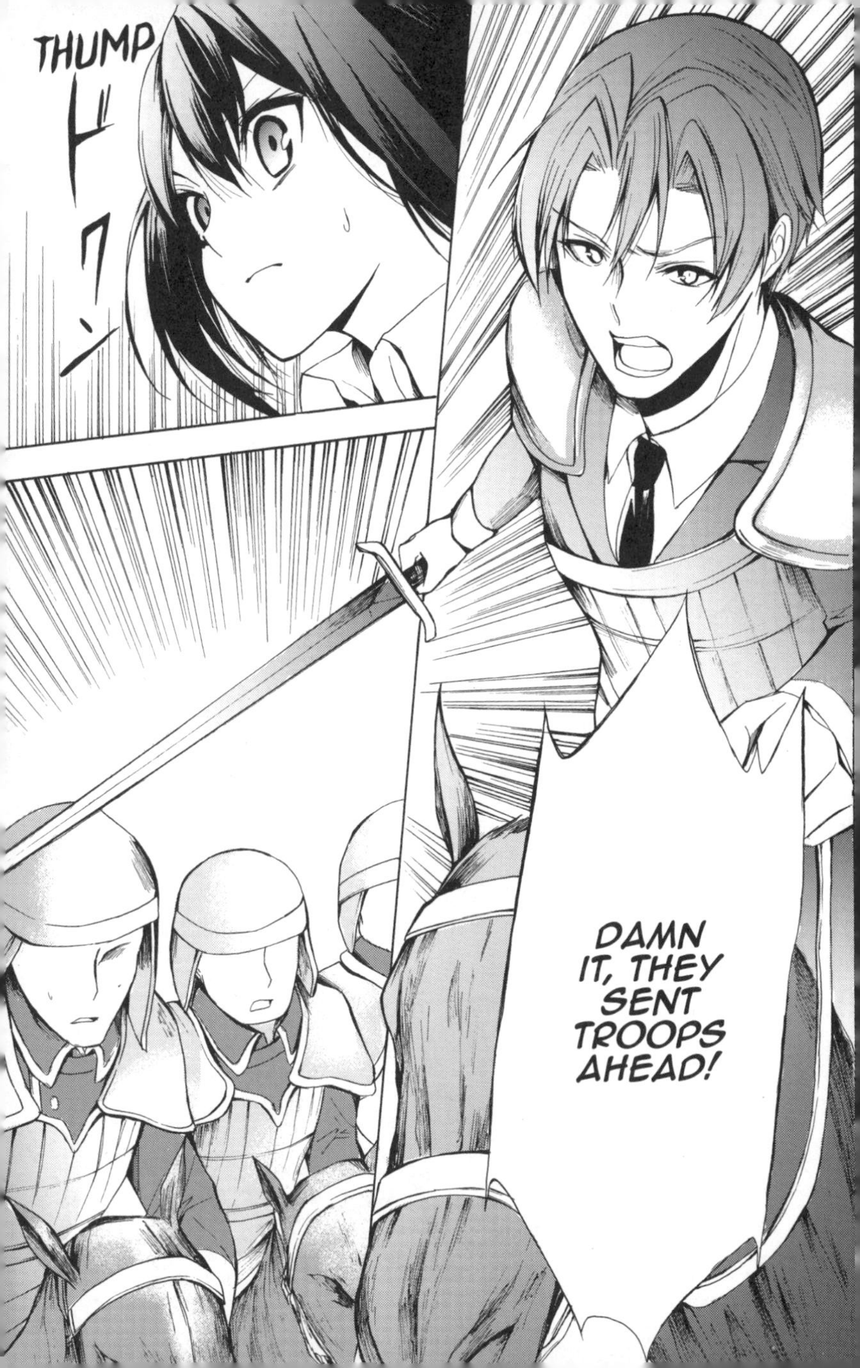
DAMN IT, THEY SENT TROOPS AHEAD!
THUMP
ドクン

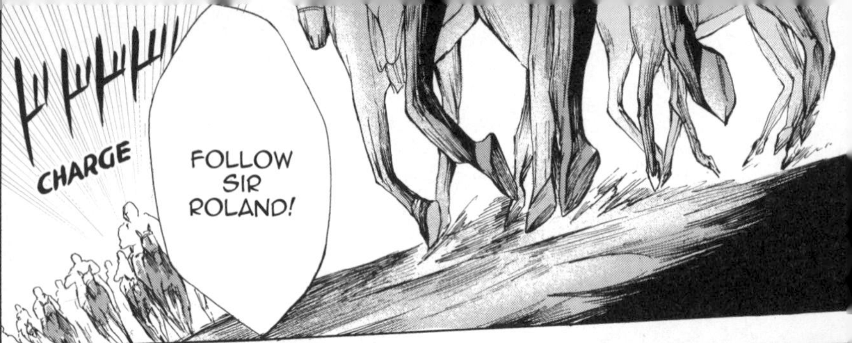
FOLLOW SIR ROLAND!
CHARGE
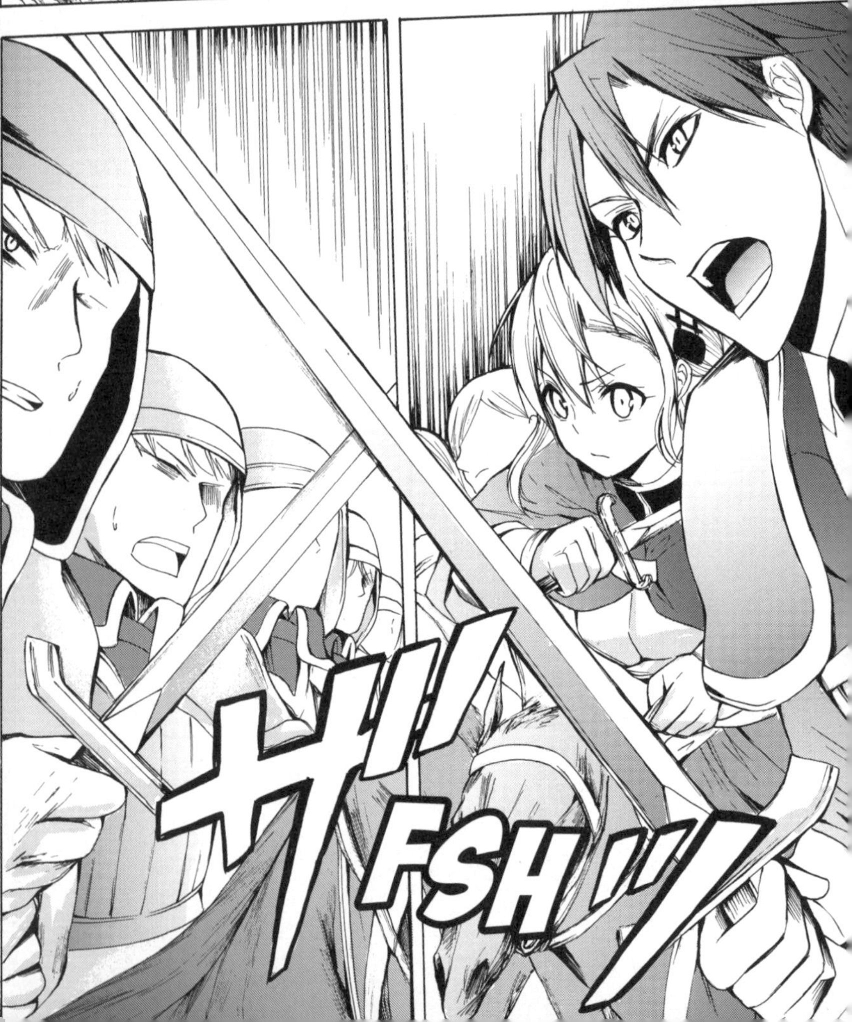
FSH

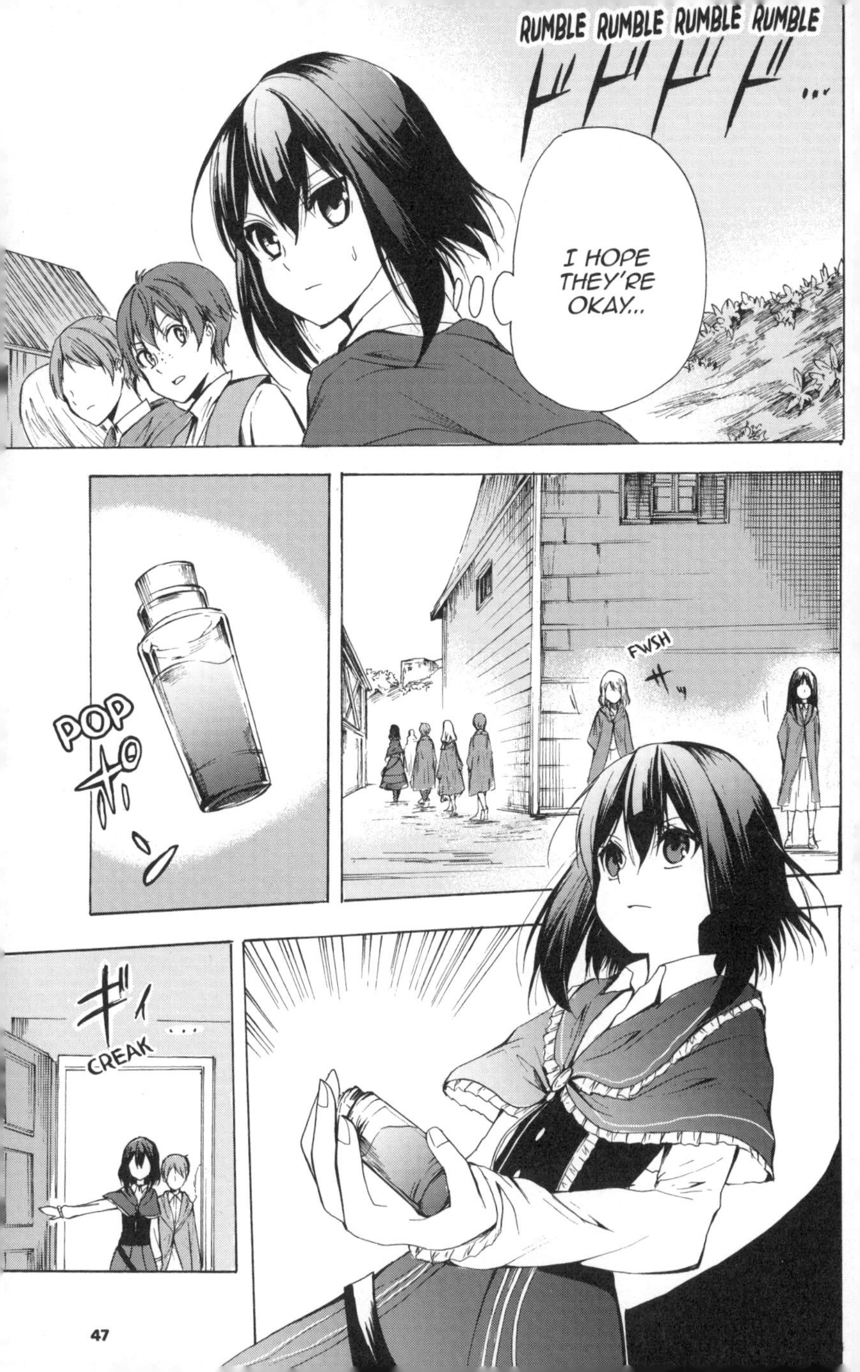
RUMBLE RUMBLE RUMBLE RUMBLE
I HOPE THEY'RE OKAY...
FWSH
POP
CREAK

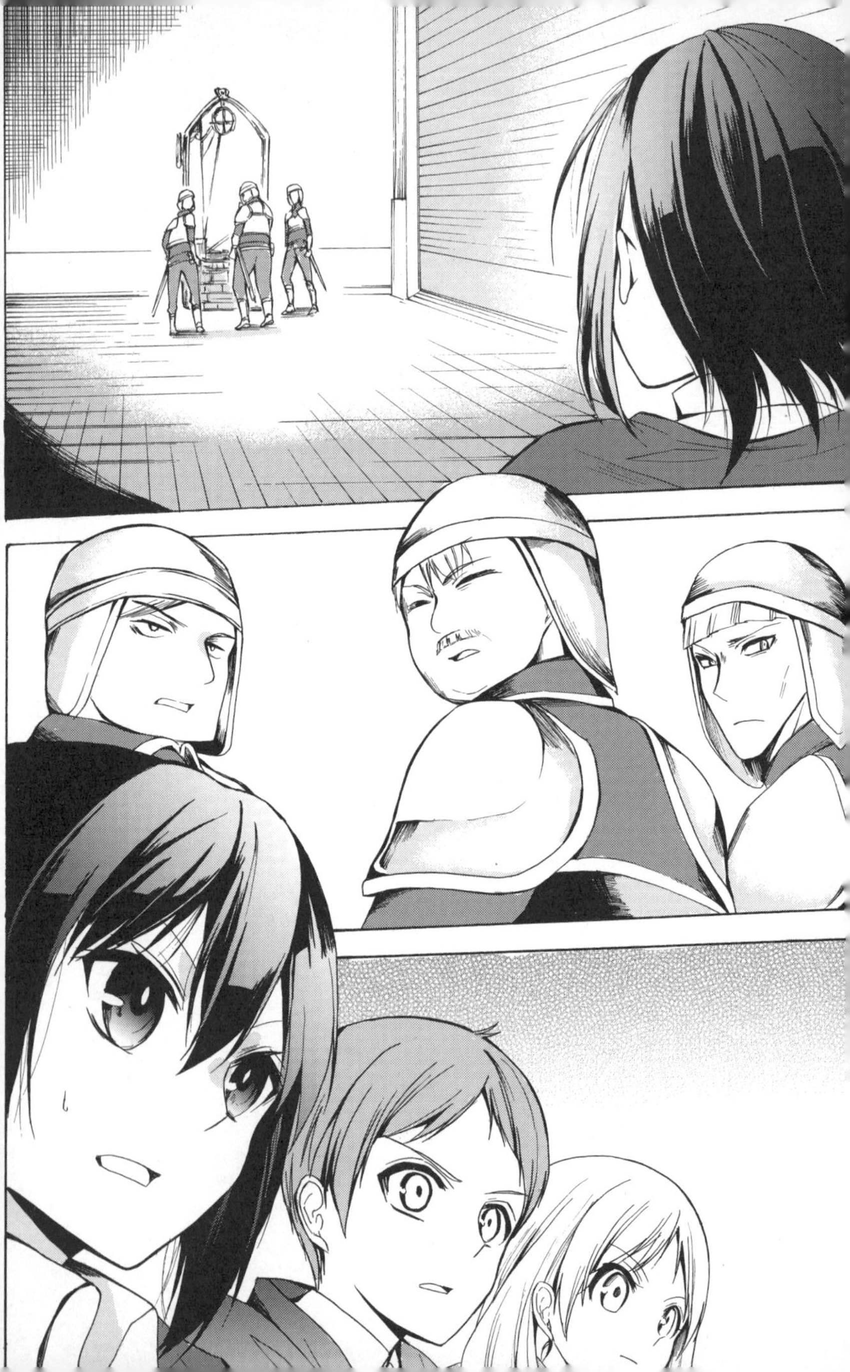

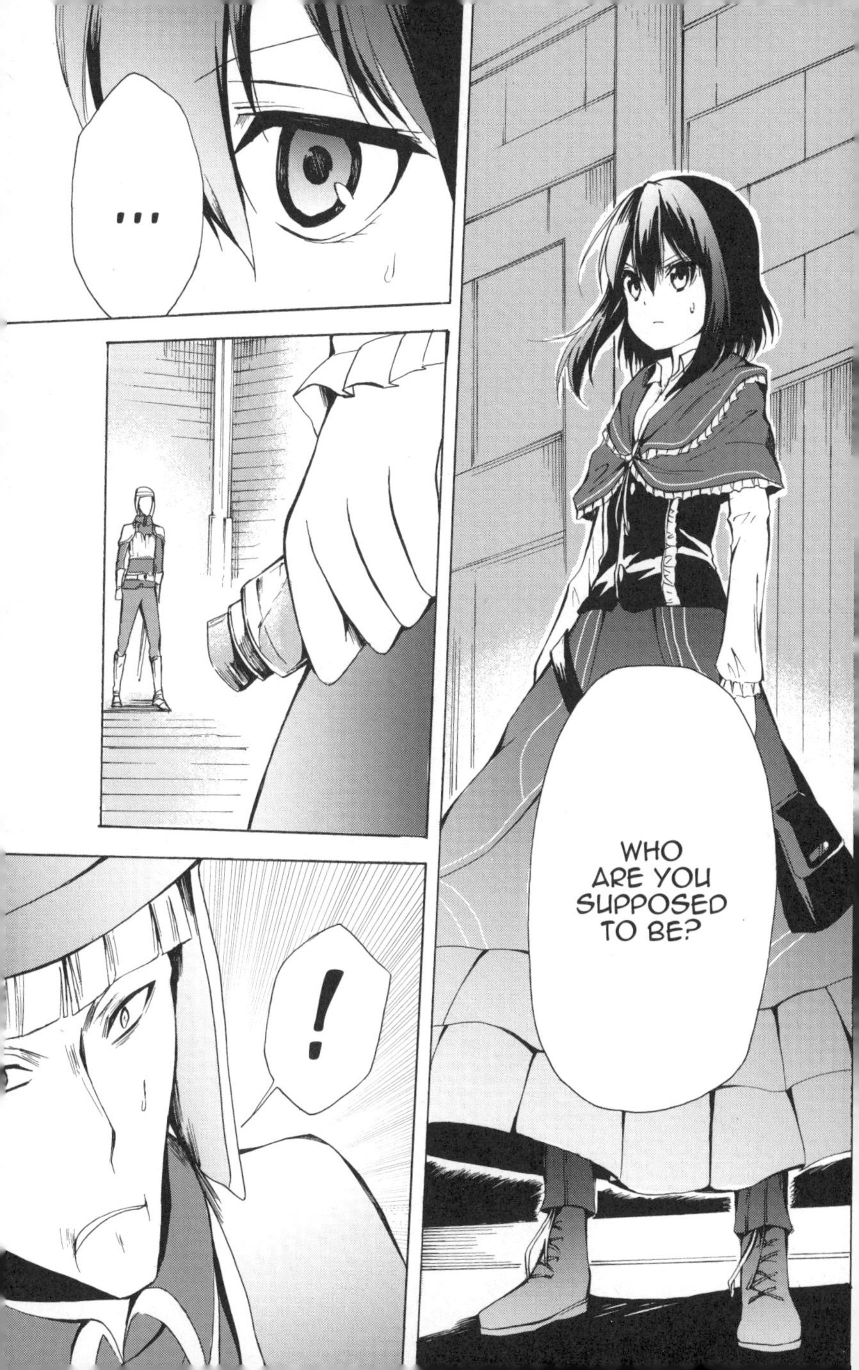
WHO ARE YOU SUPPOSED TO BE?
...
!

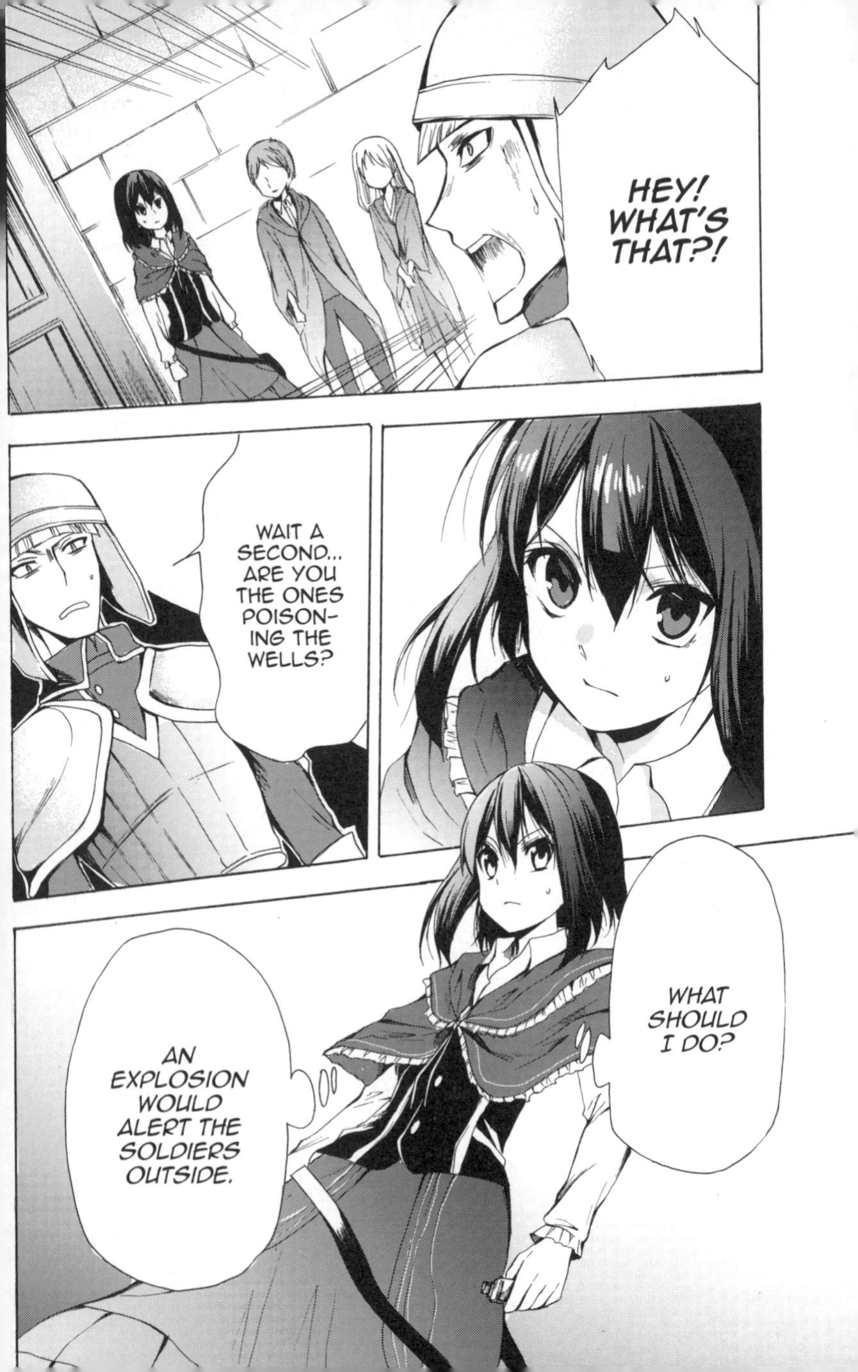
HEY! WHAT'S THAT?!
WAIT A SECOND... ARE YOU THE ONES POISON-ING THE WELLS?
WHAT SHOULD I DO?
AN EXPLOSION WOULD ALERT THE SOLDIERS OUTSIDE.

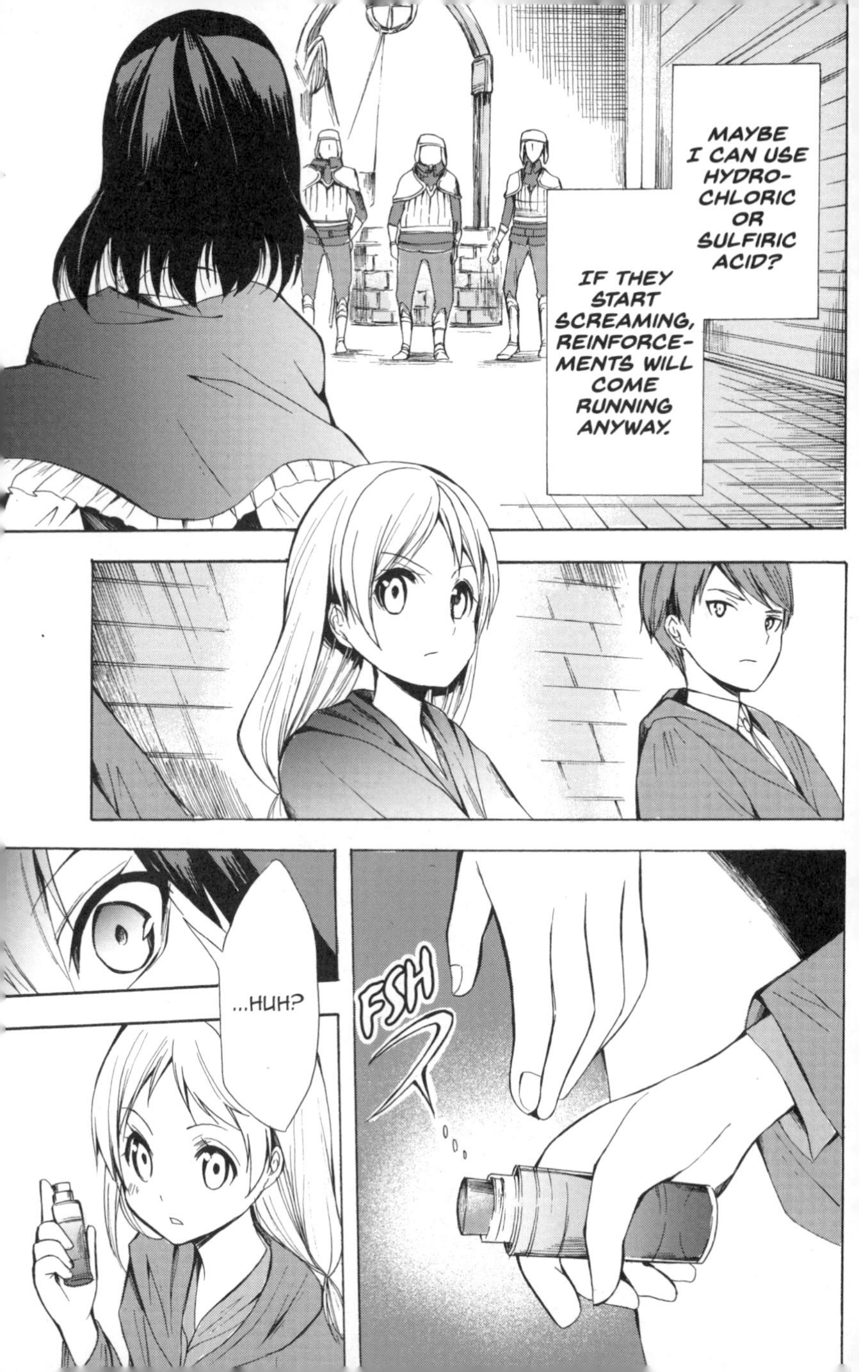
MAYBE I CAN USE HYDRO-CHLORIC OR SULFIRIC ACID?
IF THEY START SCREAMING, REINFORCE-MENTS WILL COME RUNNING ANYWAY.
FSH
...HUH?

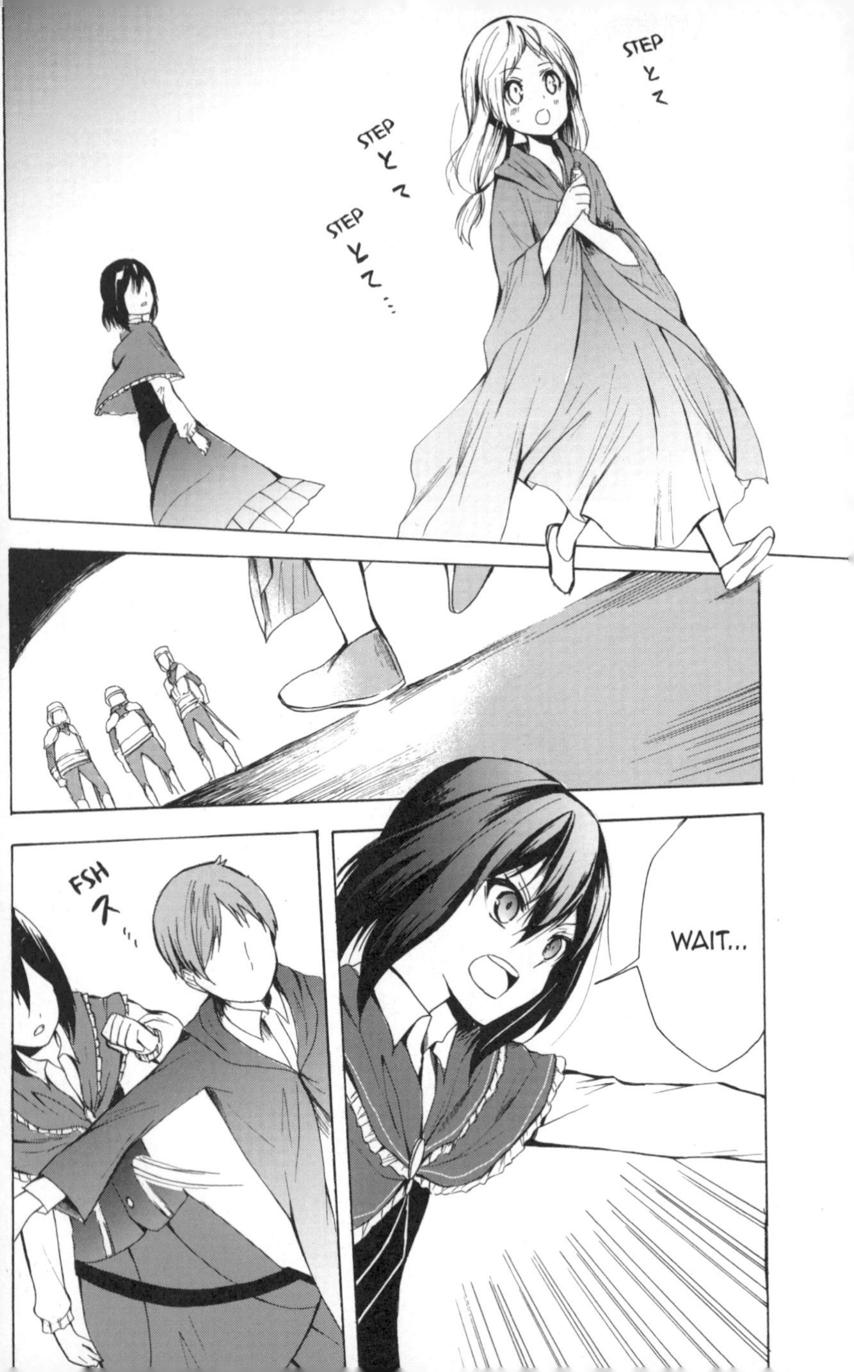

STEP とこ
STEP とこ
STEP とこ...
WAIT...
FSH ス...

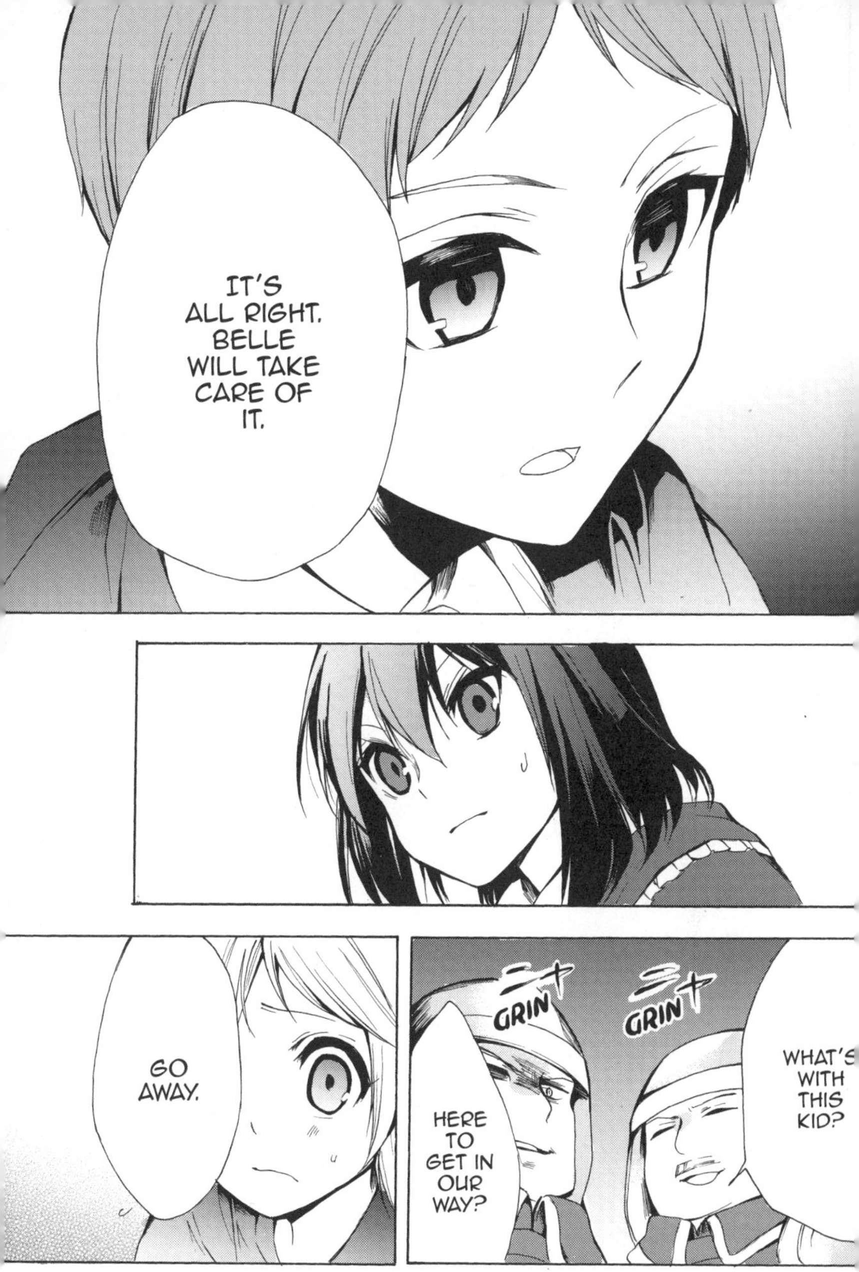
IT'S ALL RIGHT. BELLE WILL TAKE CARE OF IT.
GRIN
WHAT'S WITH THIS KID?
GRIN
HERE TO GET IN OUR WAY?
GO AWAY.

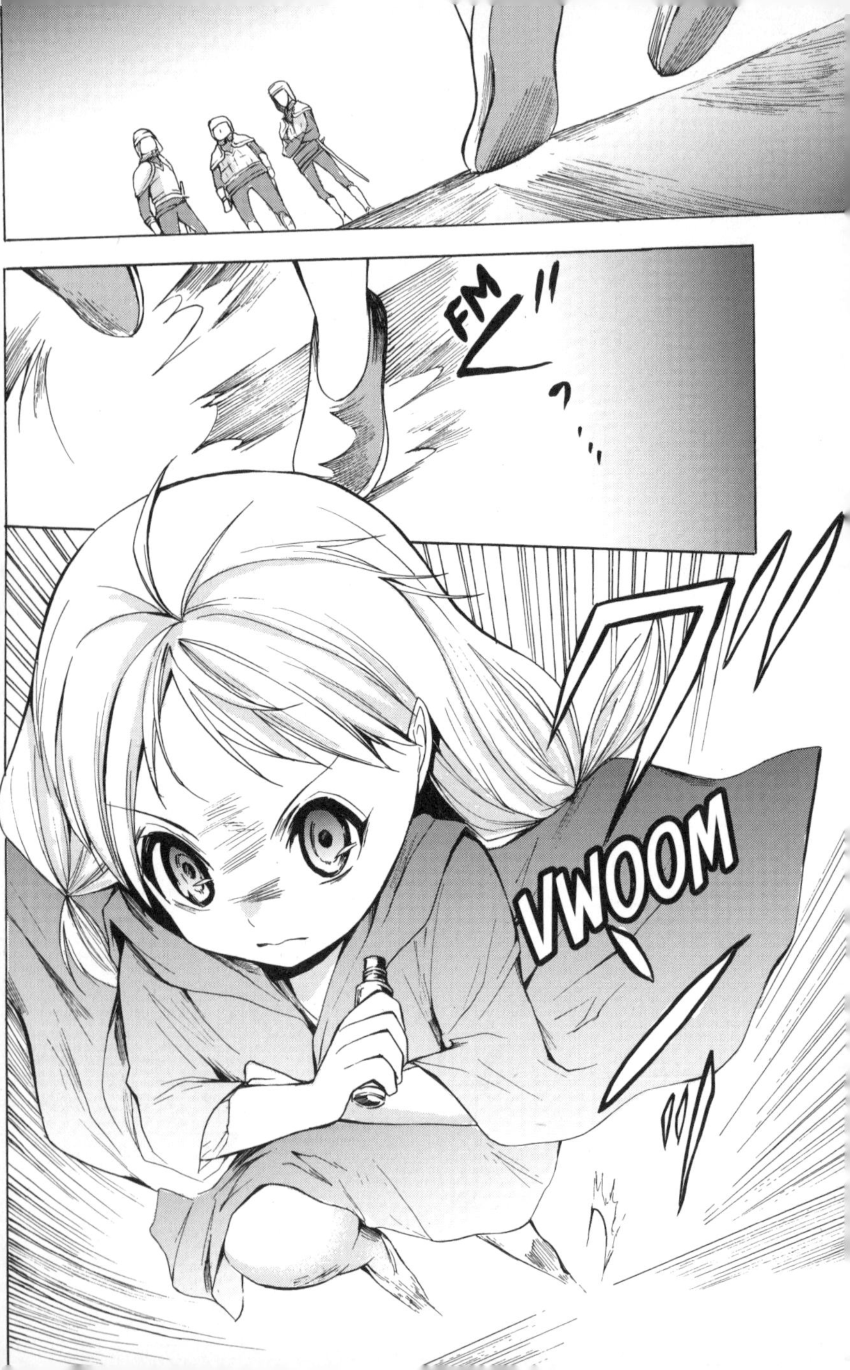
FM
VWOOM

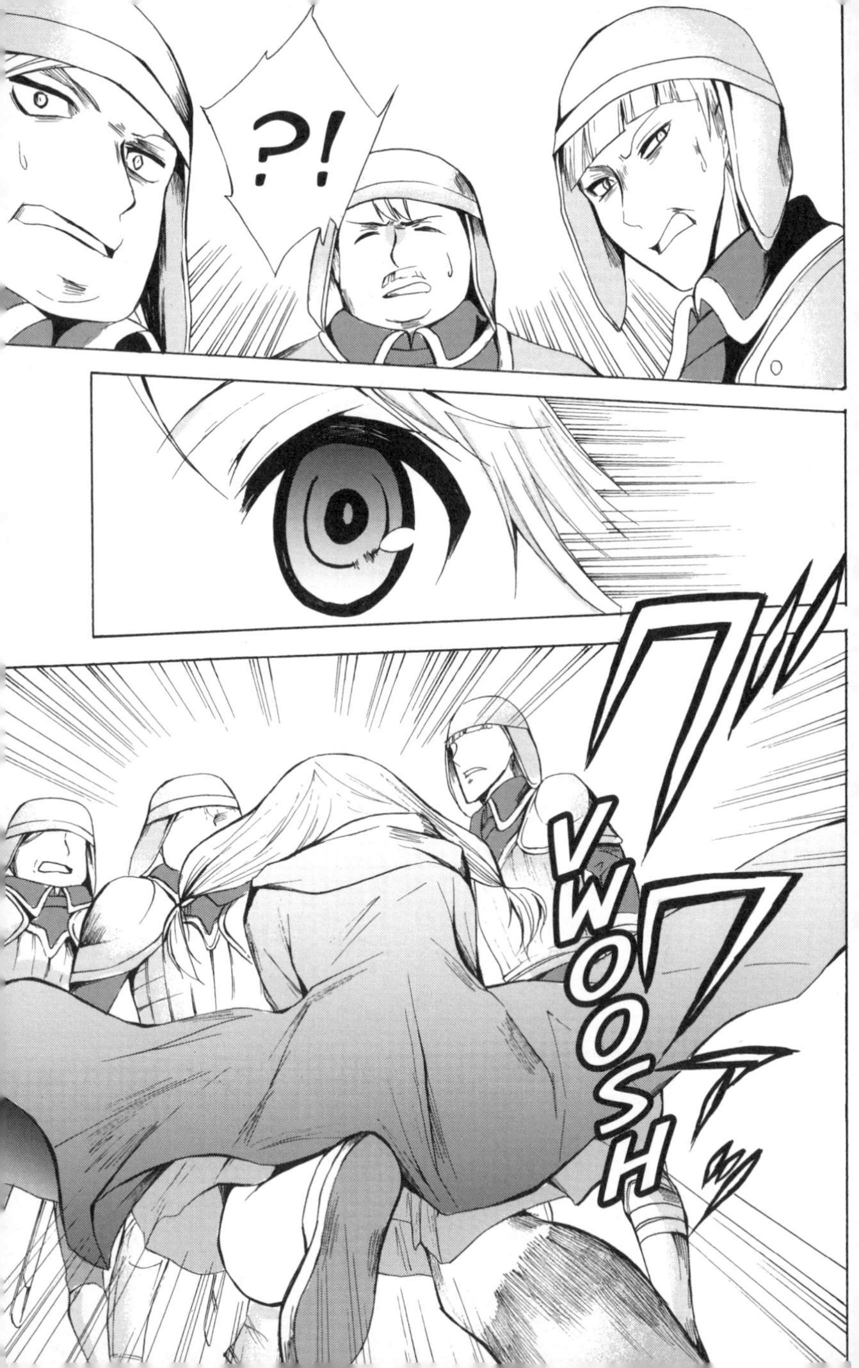
?!
VWOOSH

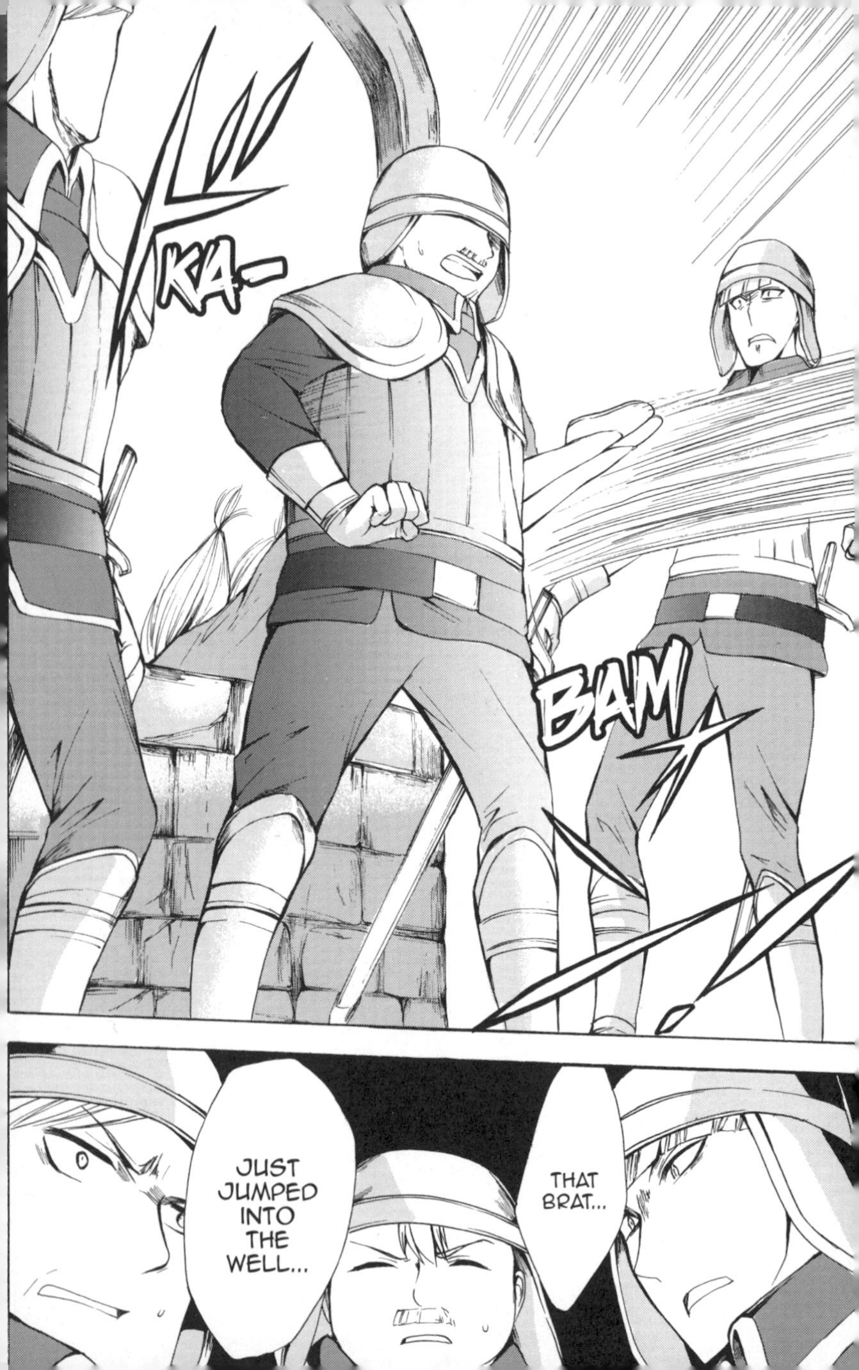
KA-
BAM
THAT BRAT...
JUST JUMPED INTO THE WELL...

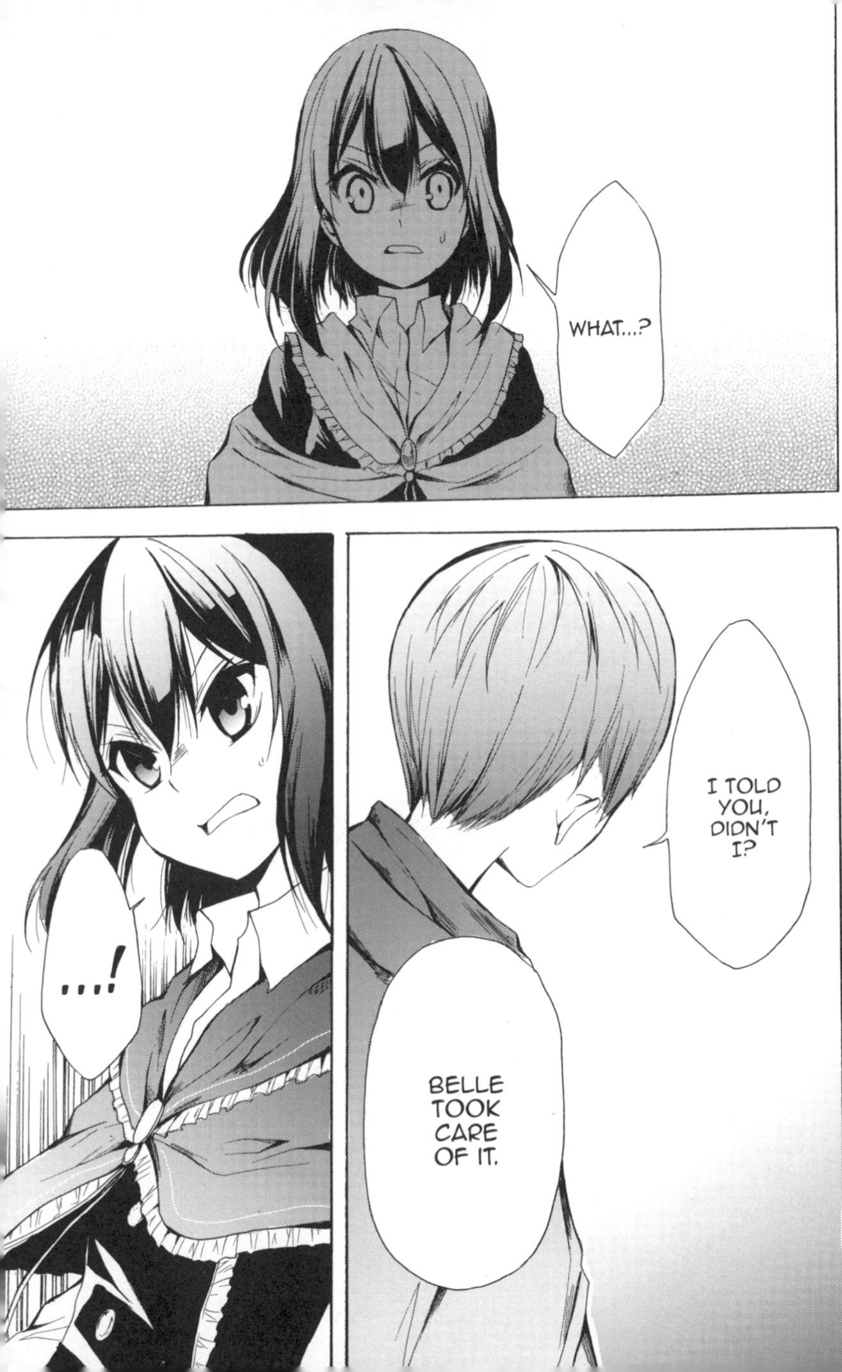
WHAT...?
I TOLD YOU, DIDN'T I?
BELLE TOOK CARE OF IT.
...!

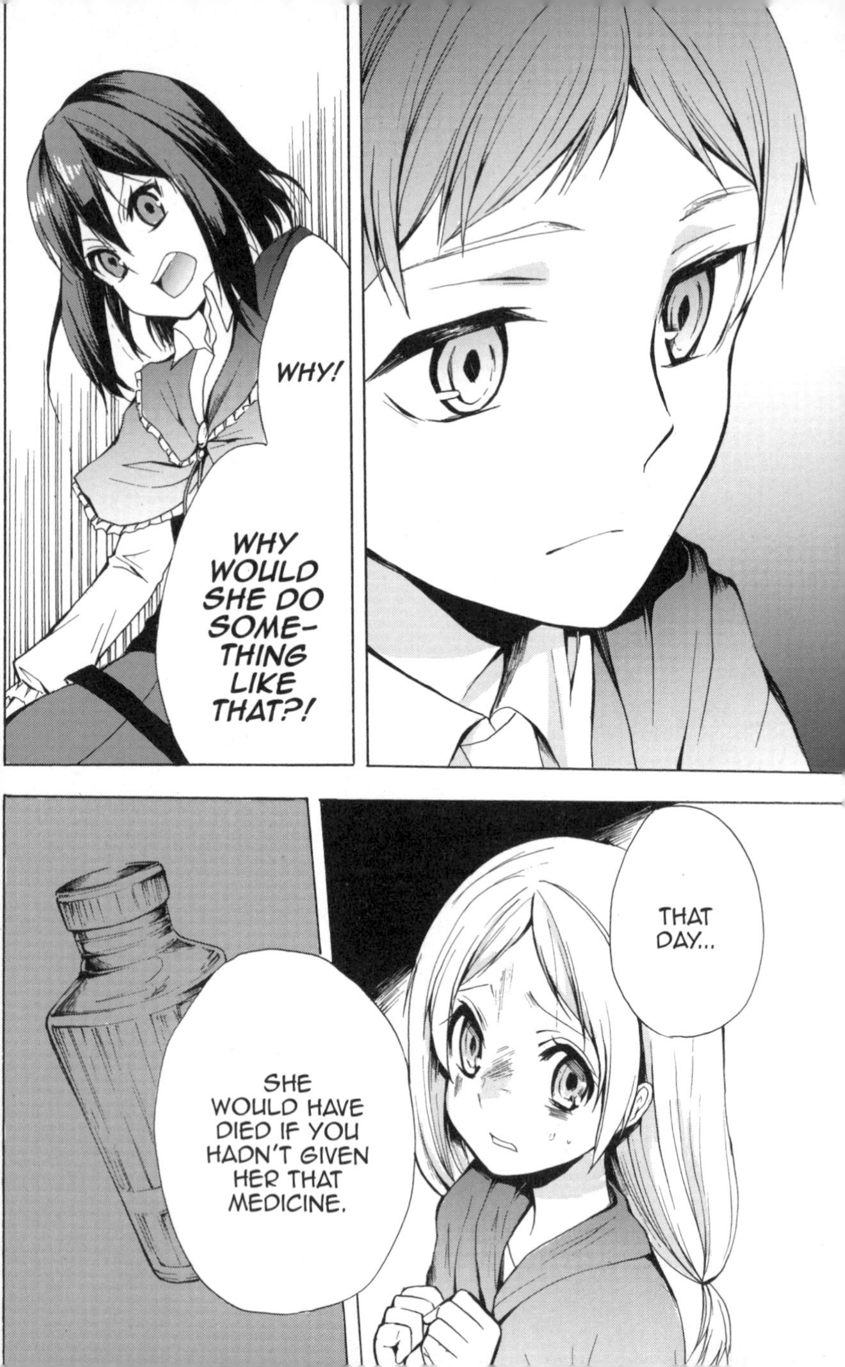
WHY!
WHY WOULD SHE DO SOME-THING LIKE THAT?!
THAT DAY...
SHE WOULD HAVE DIED IF YOU HADN'T GIVEN HER THAT MEDICINE.

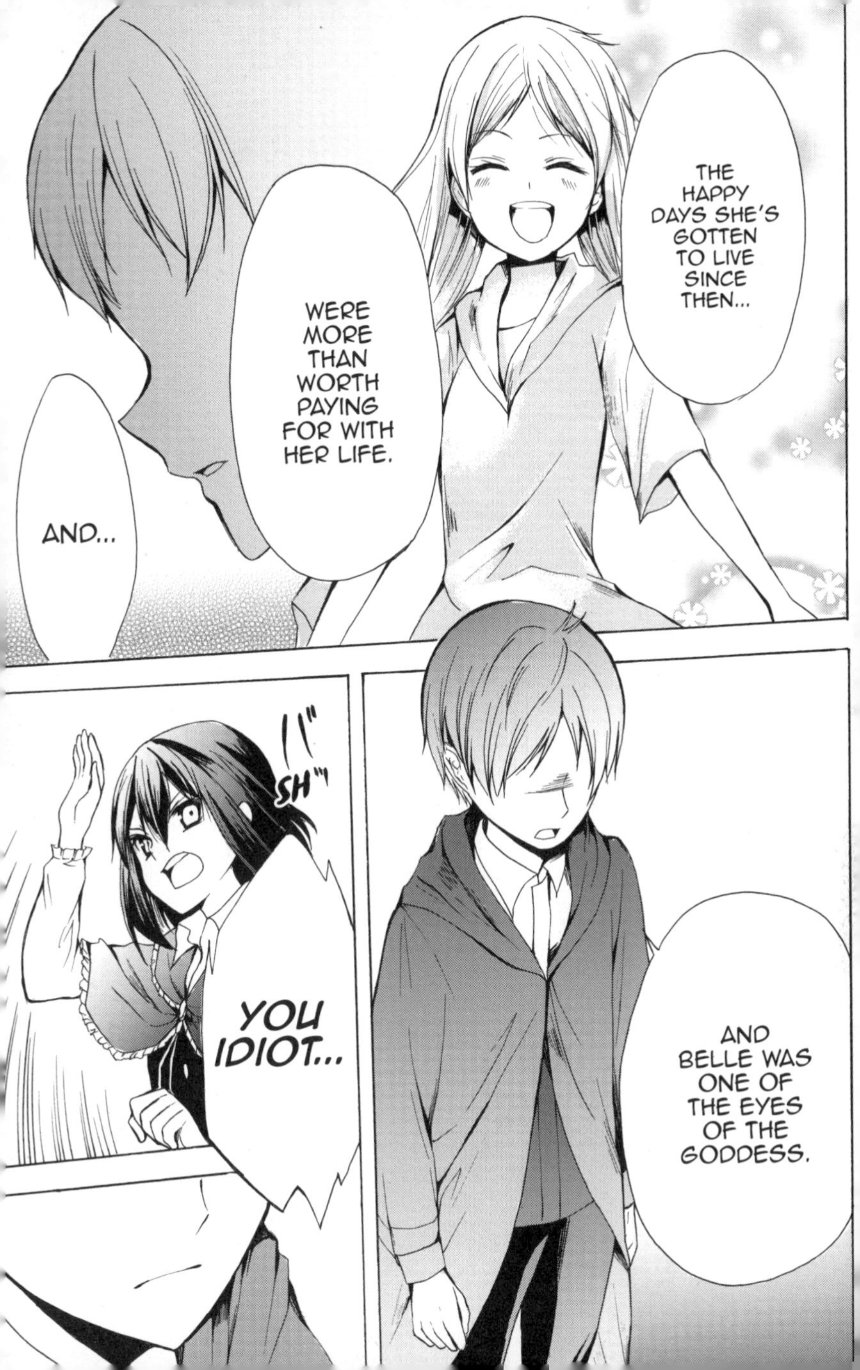
THE HAPPY DAYS SHE'S GOTTEN TO LIVE SINCE THEN...
WERE MORE THAN WORTH PAYING FOR WITH HER LIFE.
AND...
AND BELLE WAS ONE OF THE EYES OF THE GODDESS.
SH
YOU IDIOT...

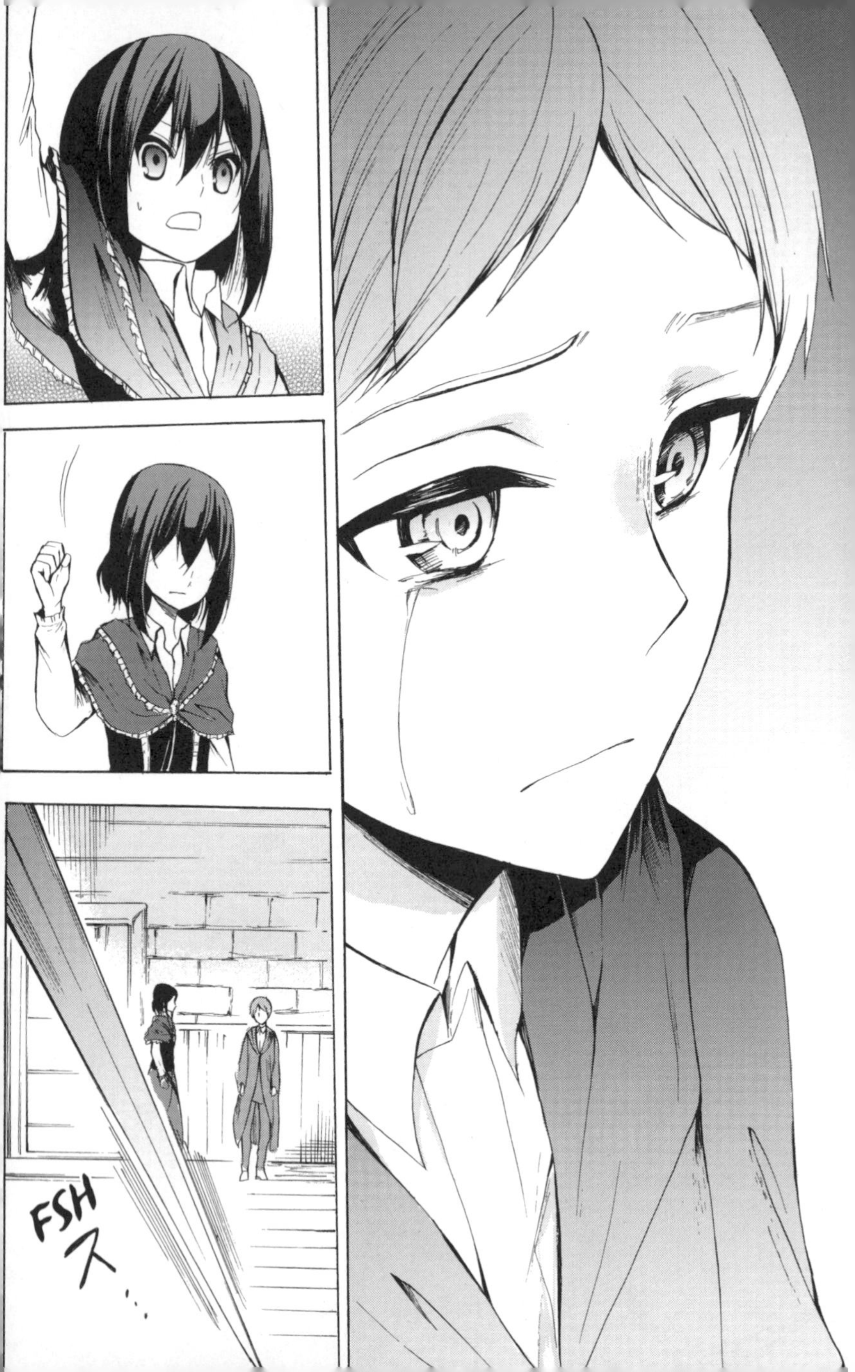
FSH
ス…

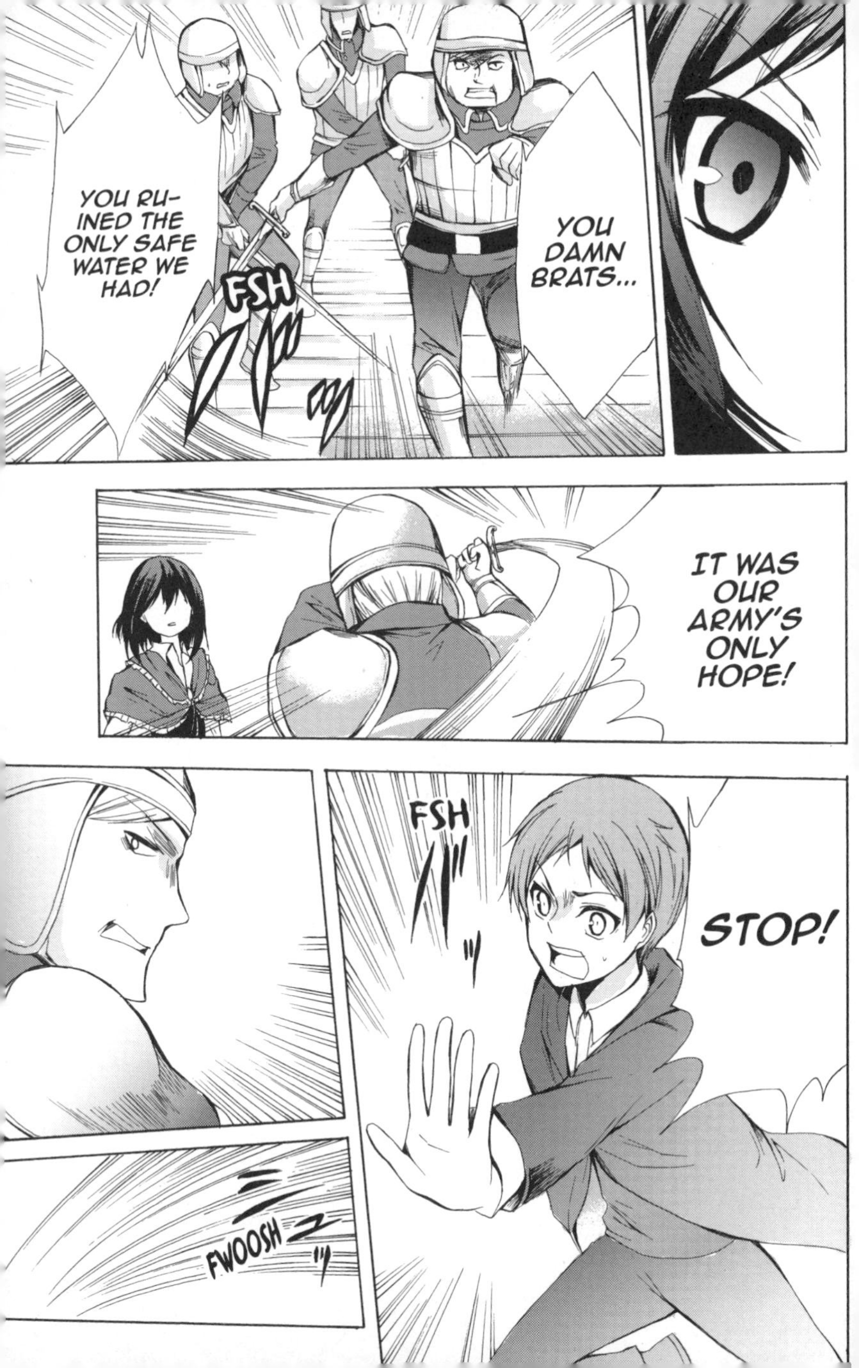
YOU DAMN BRATS...
YOU RU-INED THE ONLY SAFE WATER WE HAD!
FSH
IT WAS OUR ARMY'S ONLY HOPE!
FSH
STOP!
FWOOSH

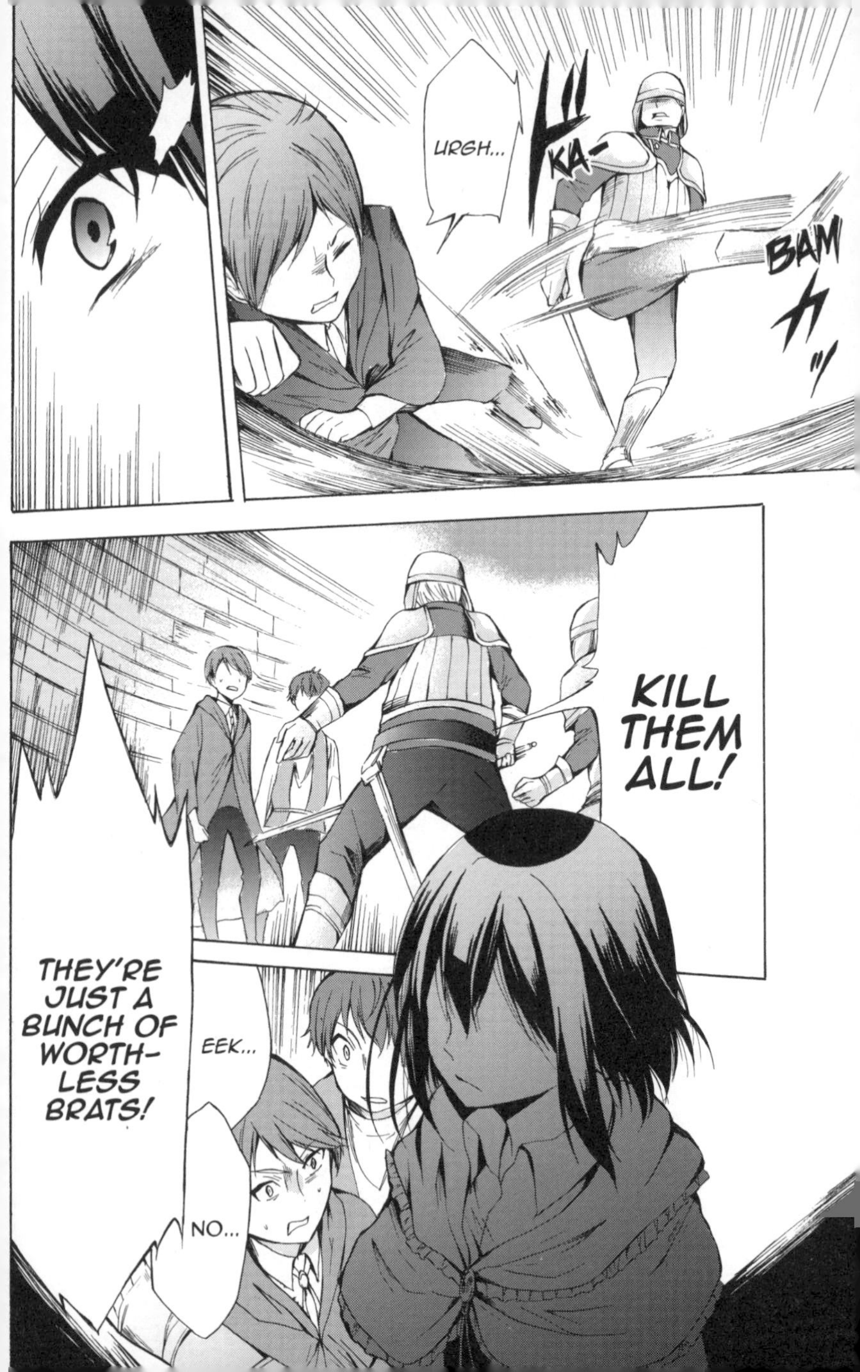
BAM
KA-
URGH...
KILL THEM ALL!
THEY'RE JUST A BUNCH OF WORTH-LESS BRATS!
EEK...
NO...

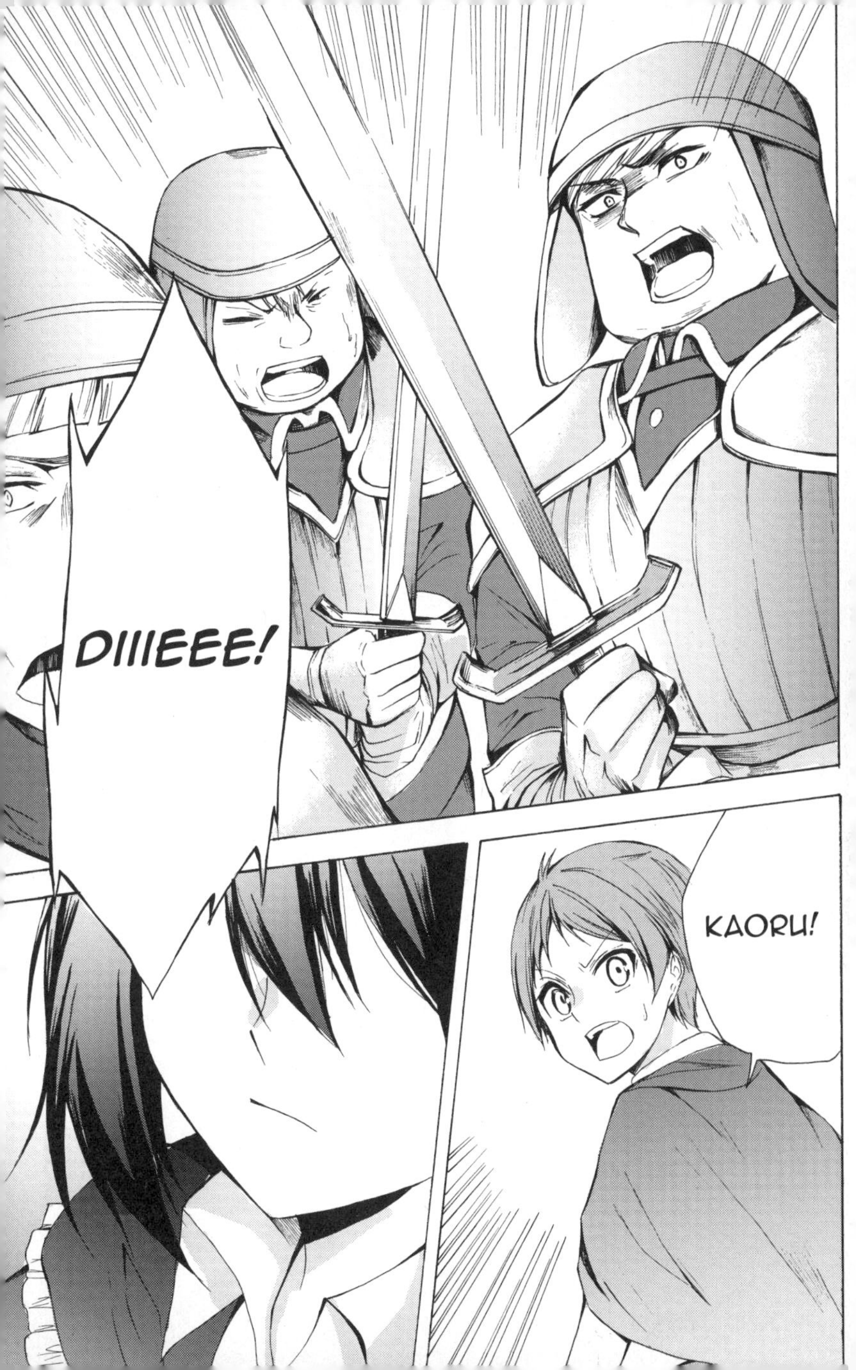
DIIIEEE!
KAORU!

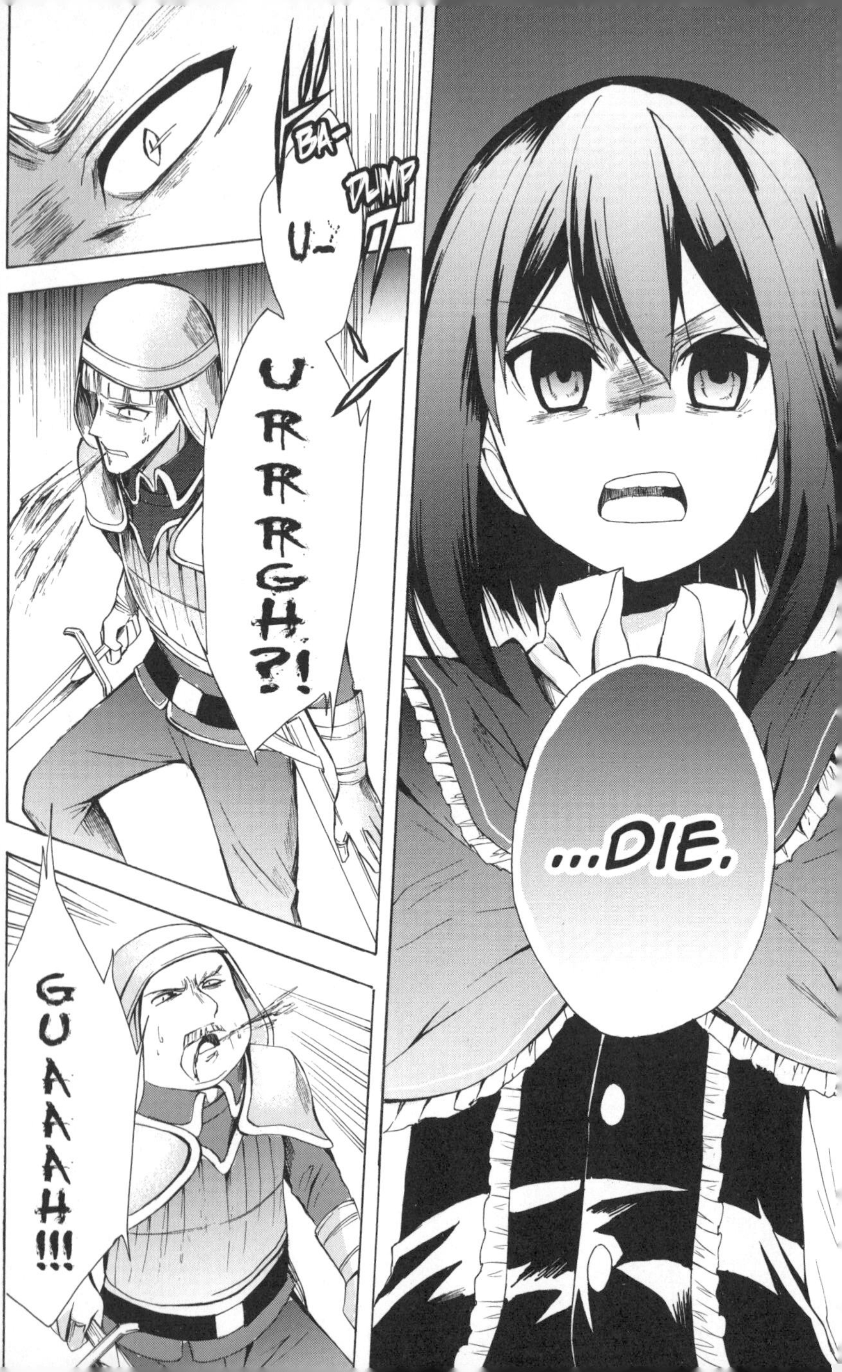
...DIE.
BA-DUMP
U-
URRRRGH?!
GUAAAH!!!

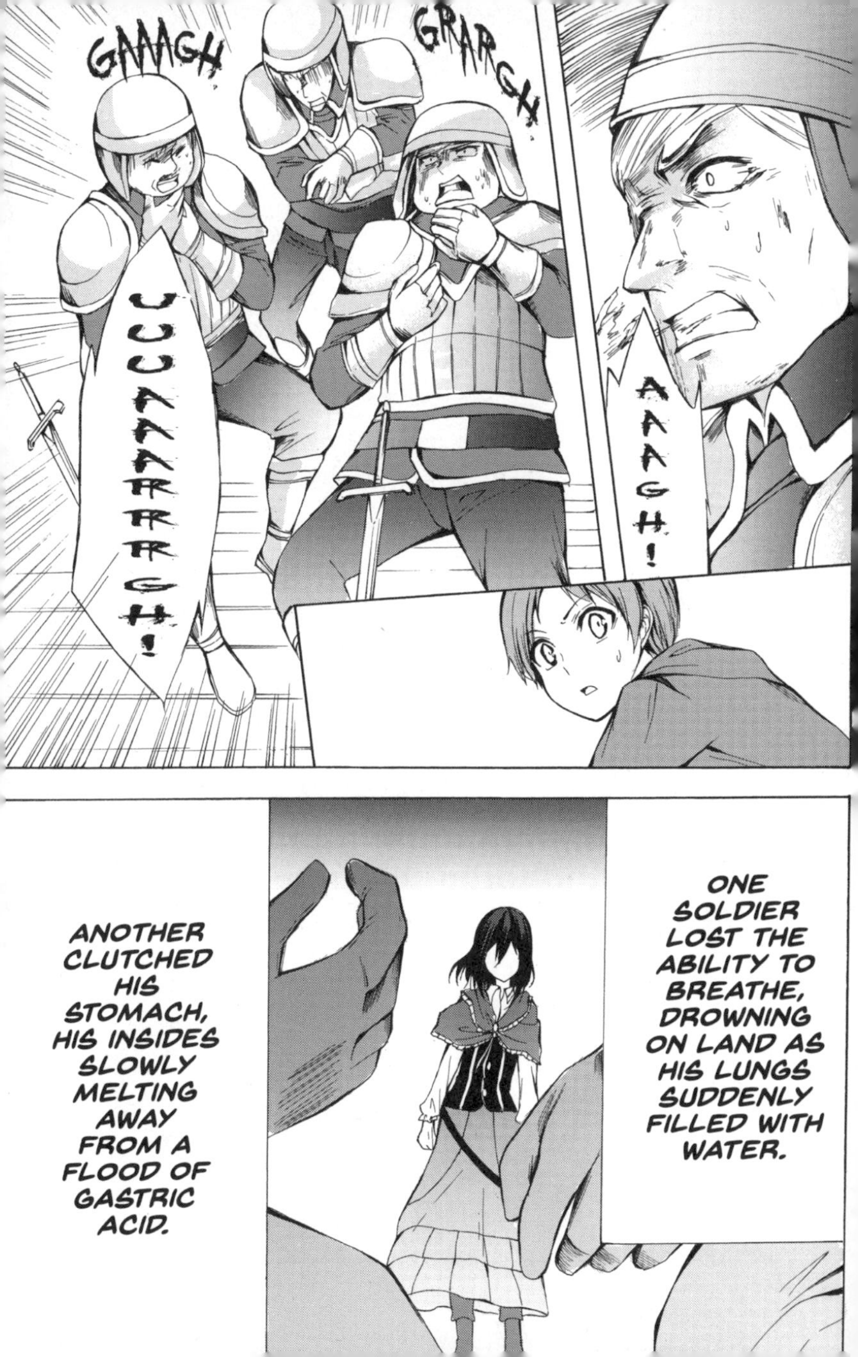
AAAGH!
GRARGH
GAAAGH
UUUAAARRRGH!
ONE SOLDIER LOST THE ABILITY TO BREATHE, DROWNING ON LAND AS HIS LUNGS SUDDENLY FILLED WITH WATER.
ANOTHER CLUTCHED HIS STOMACH, HIS INSIDES SLOWLY MELTING AWAY FROM A FLOOD OF GASTRIC ACID.

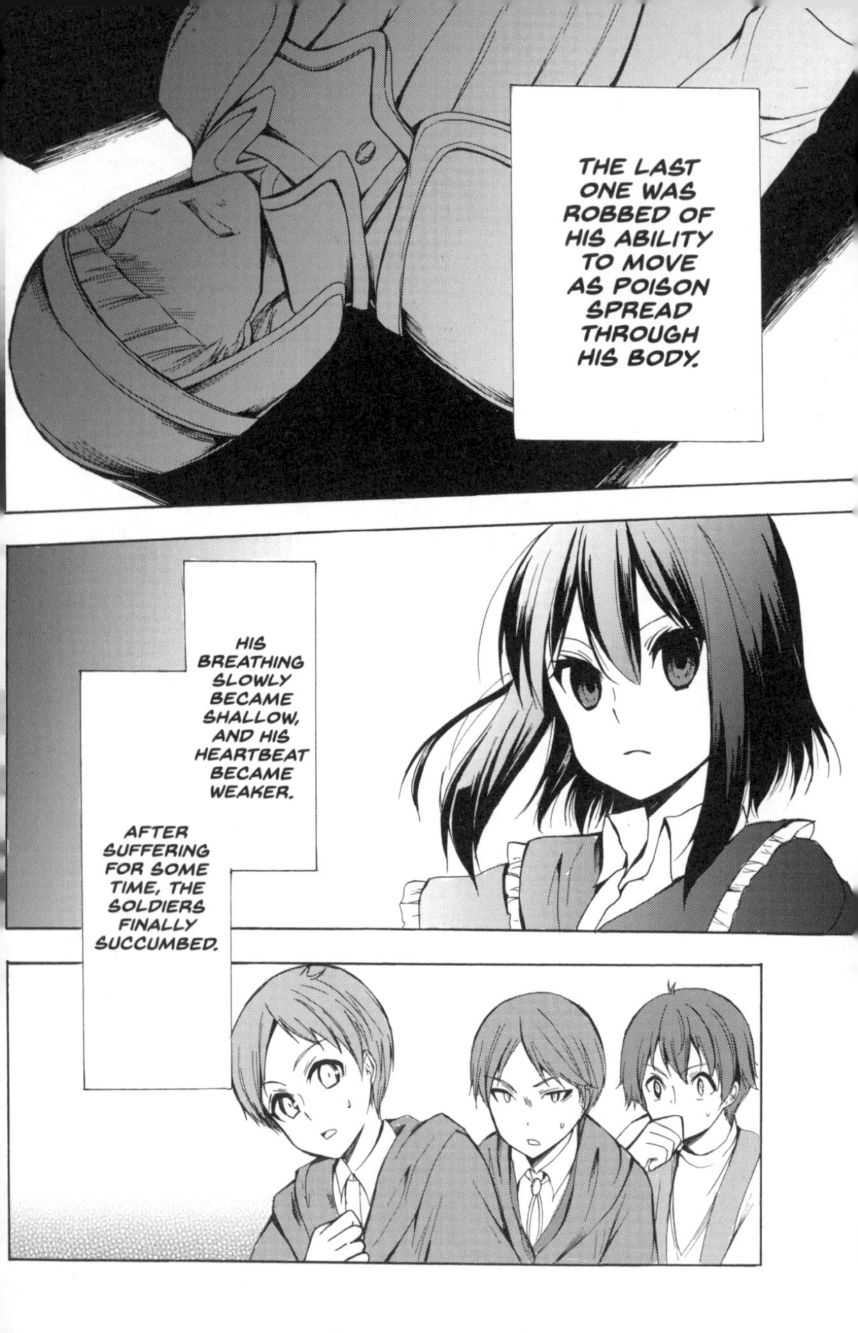
THE LAST ONE WAS ROBBED OF HIS ABILITY TO MOVE AS POISON SPREAD THROUGH HIS BODY.
HIS BREATHING SLOWLY BECAME SHALLOW, AND HIS HEARTBEAT BECAME WEAKER.
AFTER SUFFERING FOR SOME TIME, THE SOLDIERS FINALLY SUCCUMBED.

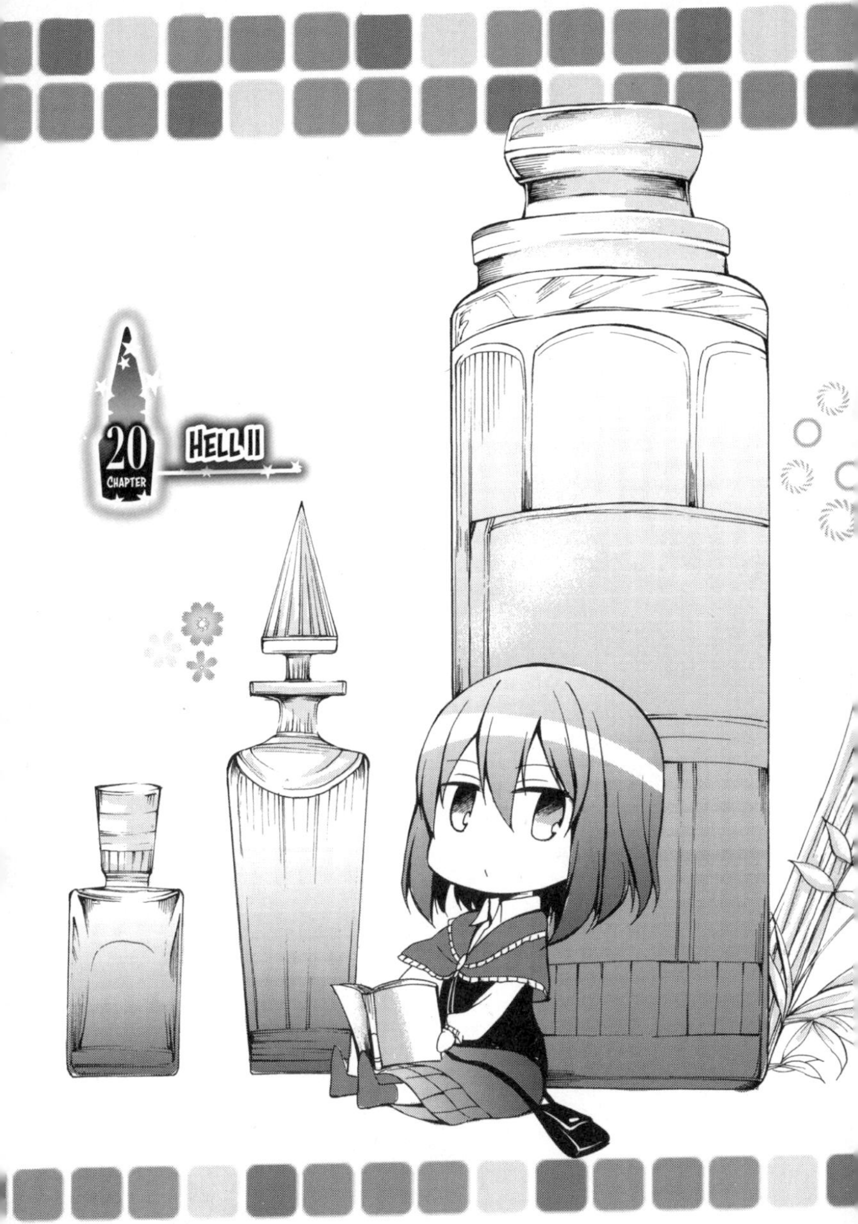
20
CHAPTER
HELL II

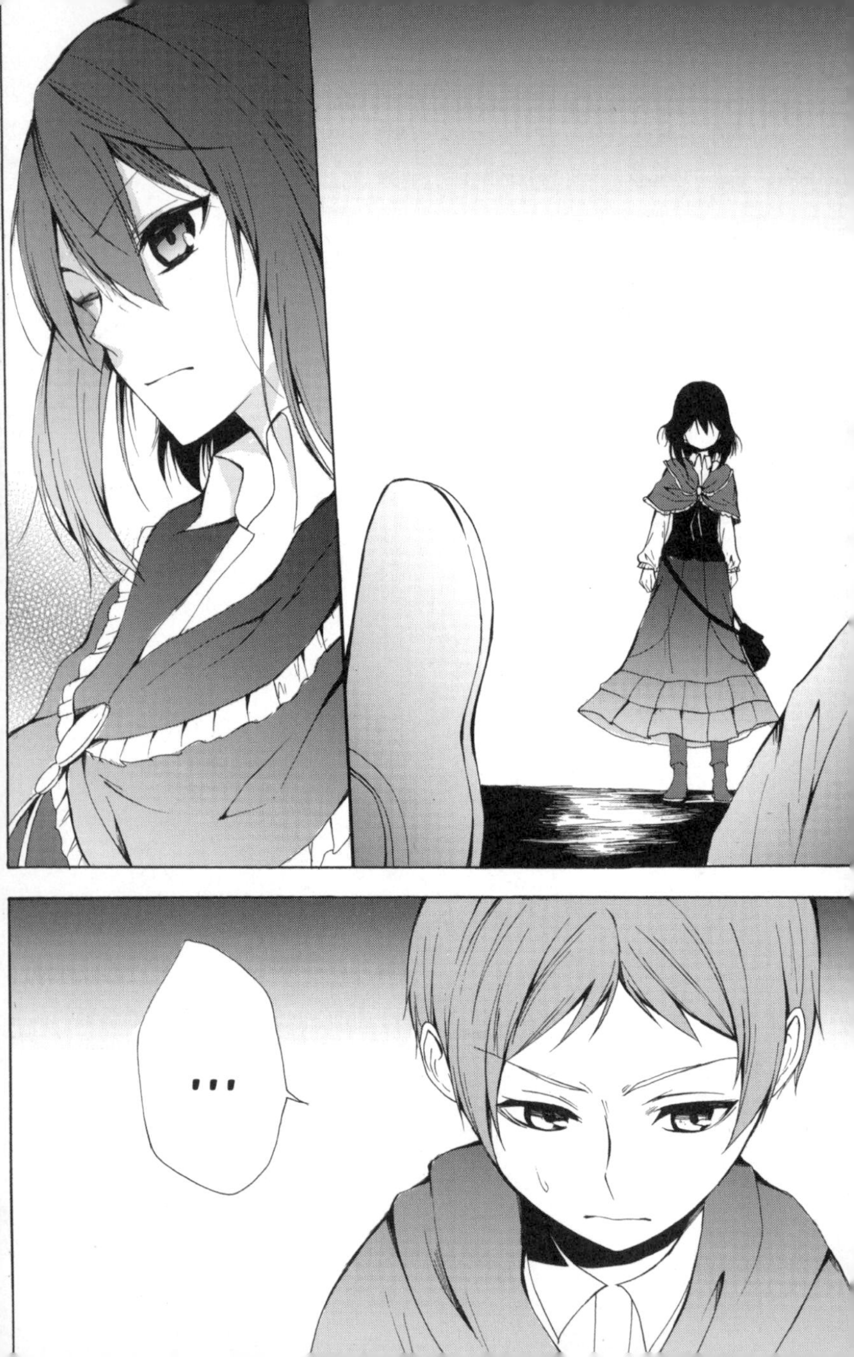
...

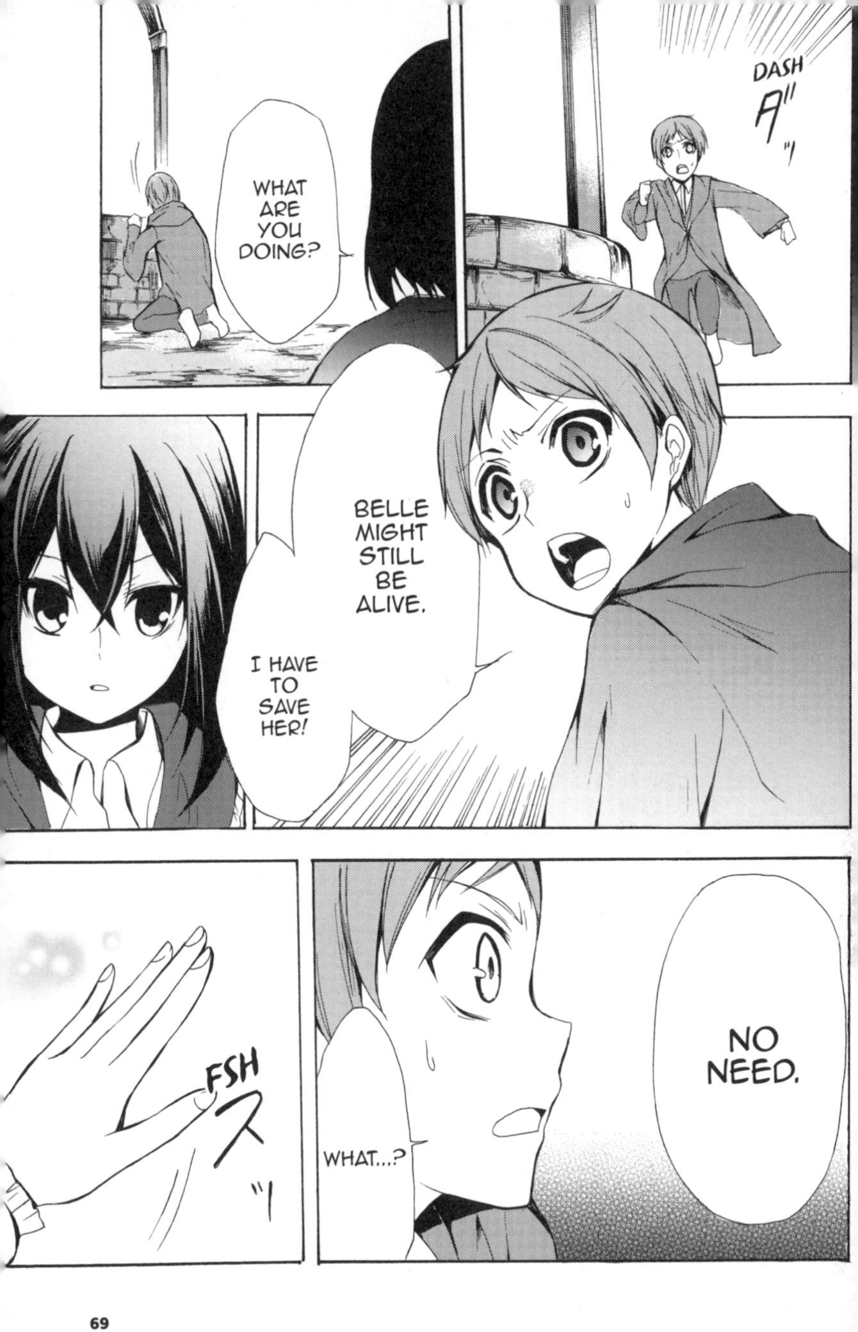
DASH
ダッ
WHAT ARE YOU DOING?
BELLE MIGHT STILL BE ALIVE.
I HAVE TO SAVE HER!
NO NEED.
WHAT...?
FSH
スッ

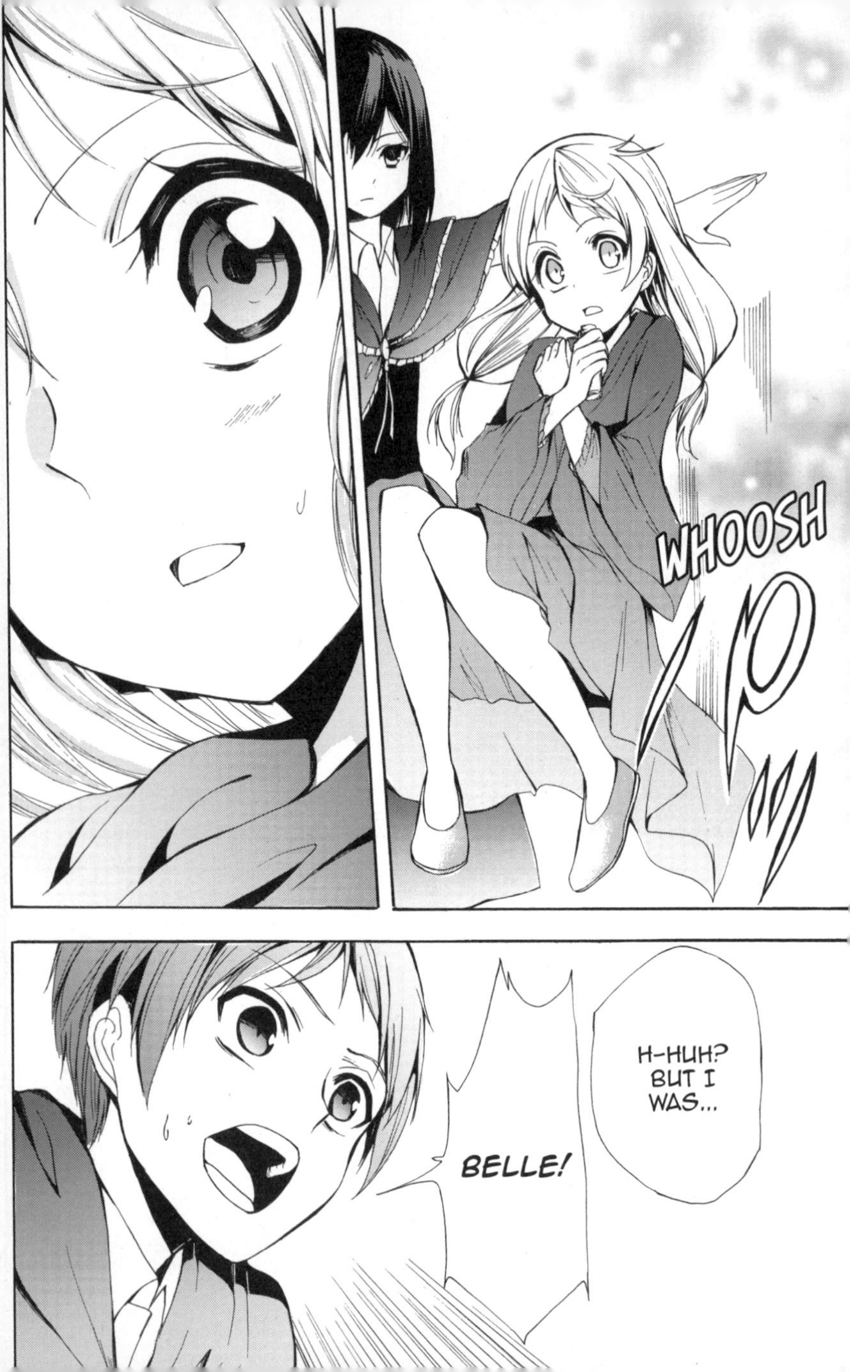
WHOOSH
H-HUH? BUT I WAS...
BELLE!

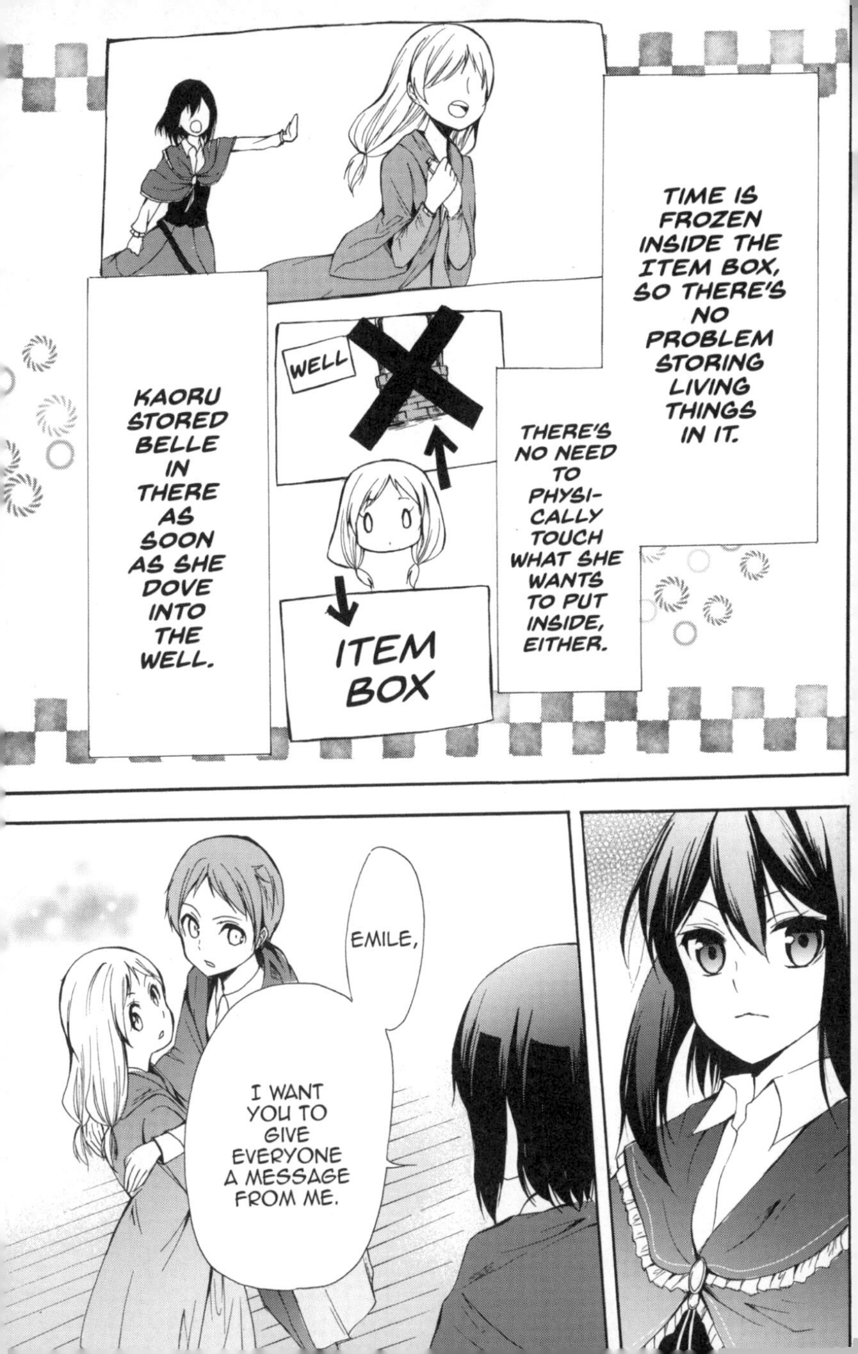
TIME IS FROZEN INSIDE THE ITEM BOX, SO THERE'S NO PROBLEM STORING LIVING THINGS IN IT.
THERE'S NO NEED TO PHYSI-CALLY TOUCH WHAT SHE WANTS TO PUT INSIDE, EITHER.
WELL
ITEM BOX
KAORU STORED BELLE IN THERE AS SOON AS SHE DOVE INTO THE WELL.
EMILE,
I WANT YOU TO GIVE EVERYONE A MESSAGE FROM ME.

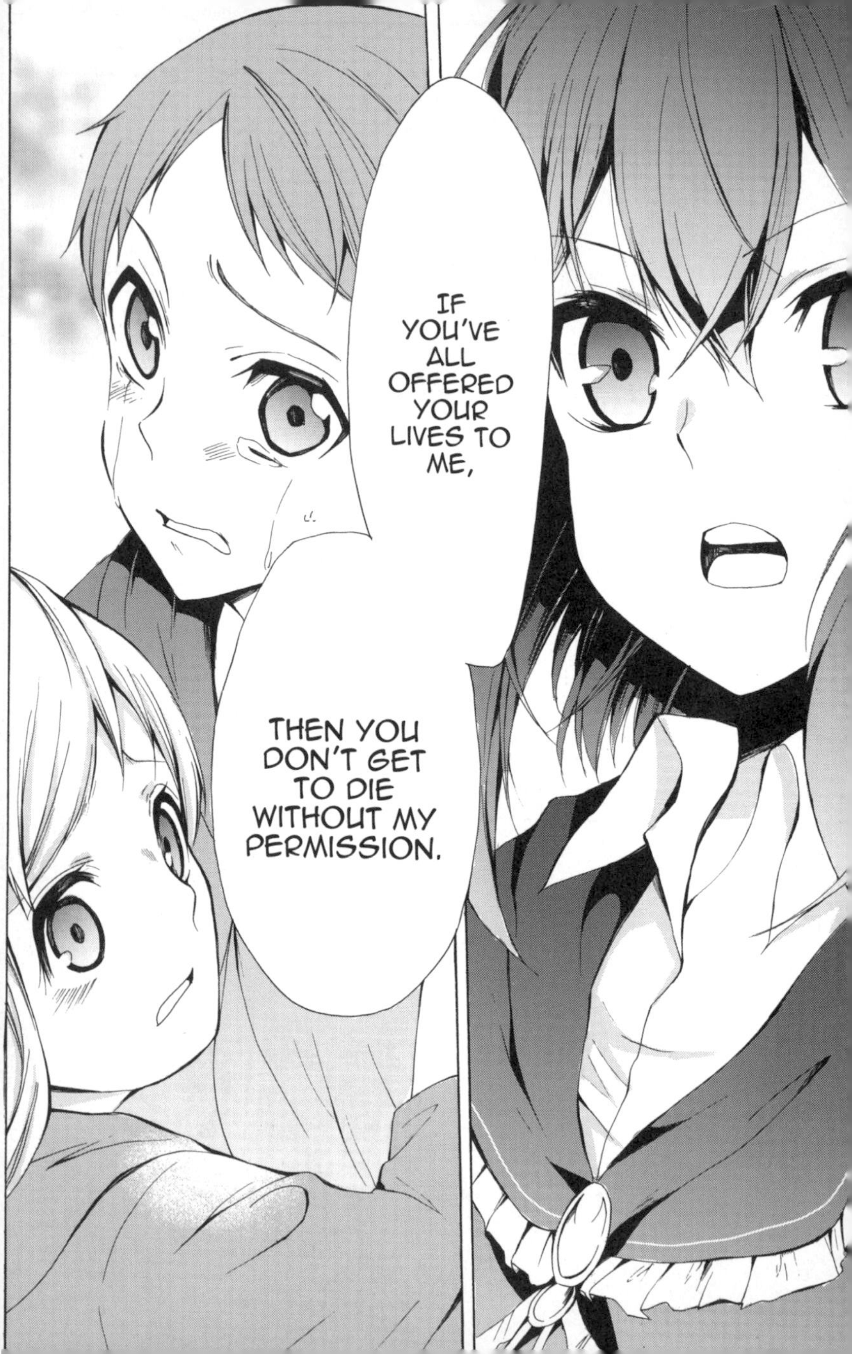
IF YOU'VE ALL OFFERED YOUR LIVES TO ME,
THEN YOU DON'T GET TO DIE WITHOUT MY PERMISSION.

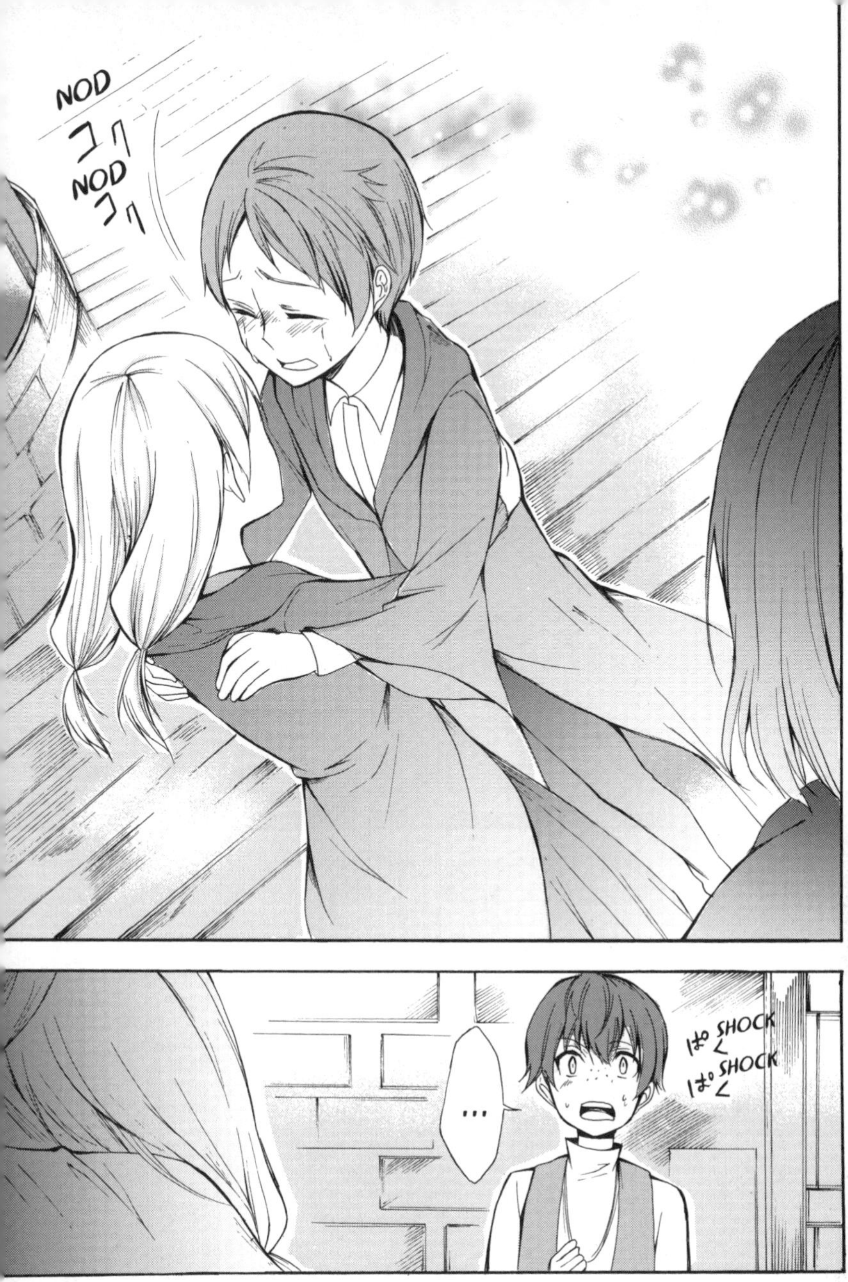
NOD
コク
NOD
コク
ぱく SHOCK
ぱく SHOCK
...

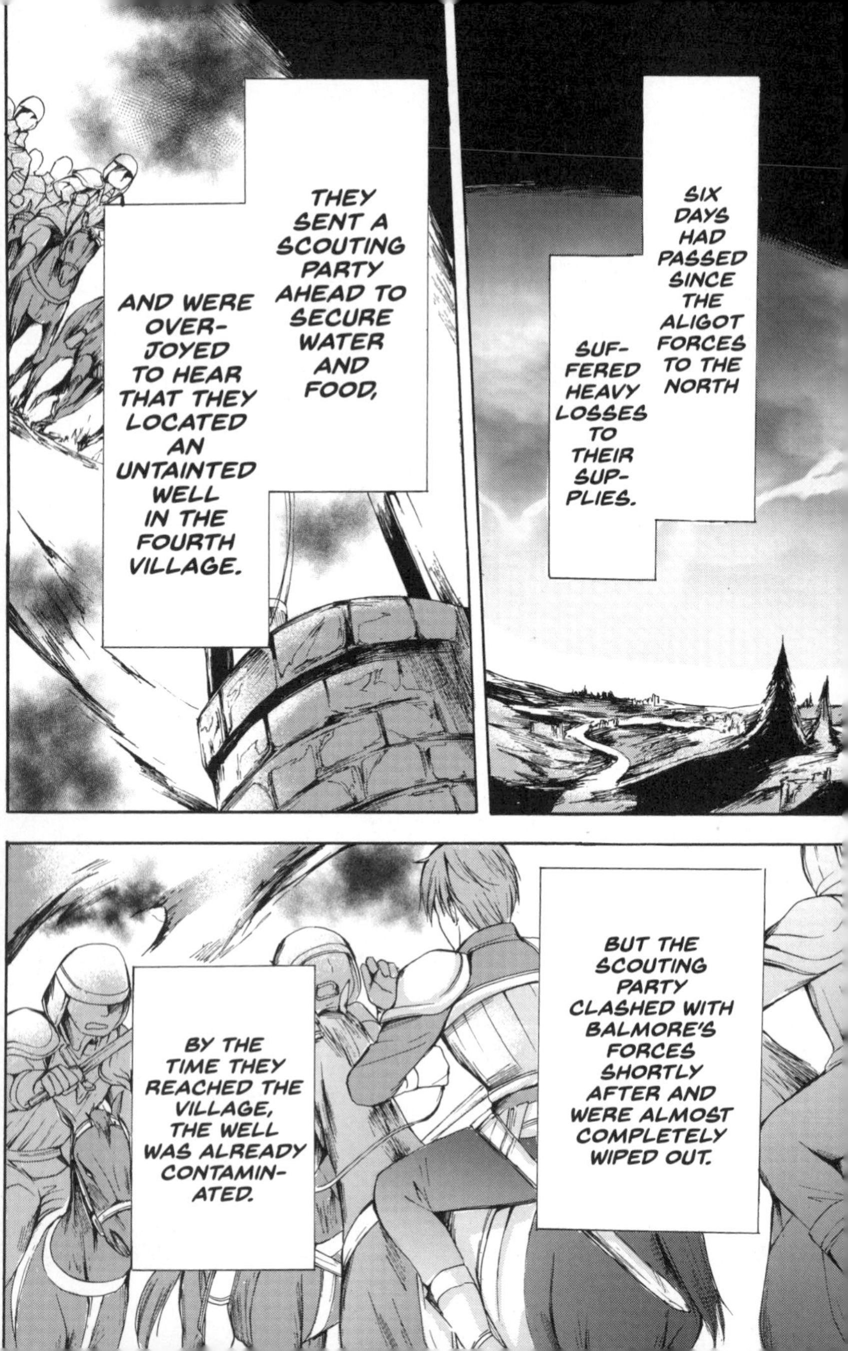
SIX DAYS HAD PASSED SINCE THE ALIGOT FORCES TO THE NORTH
SUF-FERED HEAVY LOSSES TO THEIR SUP-PLIES.
THEY SENT A SCOUTING PARTY AHEAD TO SECURE WATER AND FOOD,
AND WERE OVER-JOYED TO HEAR THAT THEY LOCATED AN UNTAINTED WELL IN THE FOURTH VILLAGE.
BUT THE SCOUTING PARTY CLASHED WITH BALMORE'S FORCES SHORTLY AFTER AND WERE ALMOST COMPLETELY WIPED OUT.
BY THE TIME THEY REACHED THE VILLAGE, THE WELL WAS ALREADY CONTAMIN-ATED.

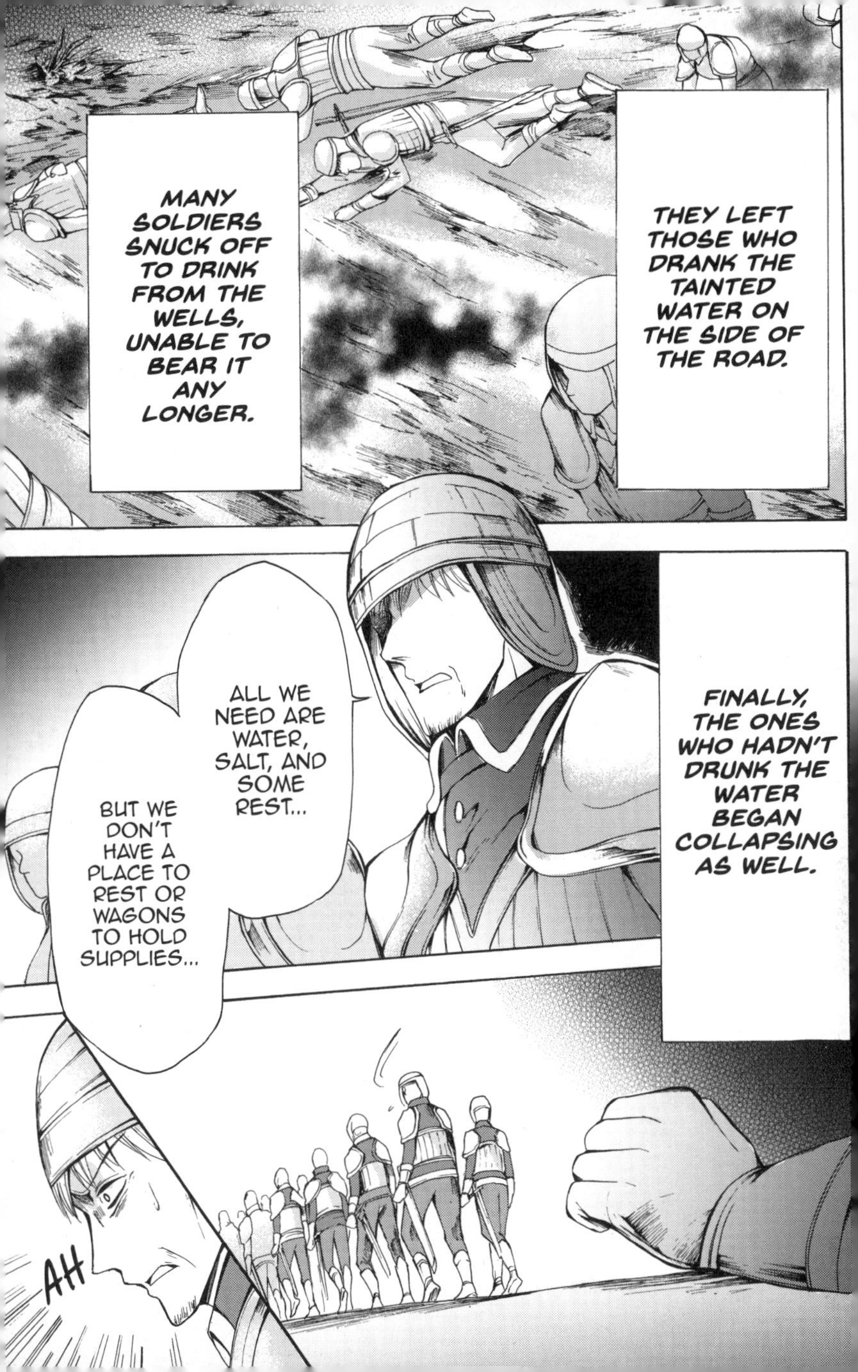
THEY LEFT THOSE WHO DRANK THE TAINTED WATER ON THE SIDE OF THE ROAD.
MANY SOLDIERS SNUCK OFF TO DRINK FROM THE WELLS, UNABLE TO BEAR IT ANY LONGER.
FINALLY, THE ONES WHO HADN'T DRUNK THE WATER BEGAN COLLAPSING AS WELL.
ALL WE NEED ARE WATER, SALT, AND SOME REST...
BUT WE DON'T HAVE A PLACE TO REST OR WAGONS TO HOLD SUPPLIES...
AH

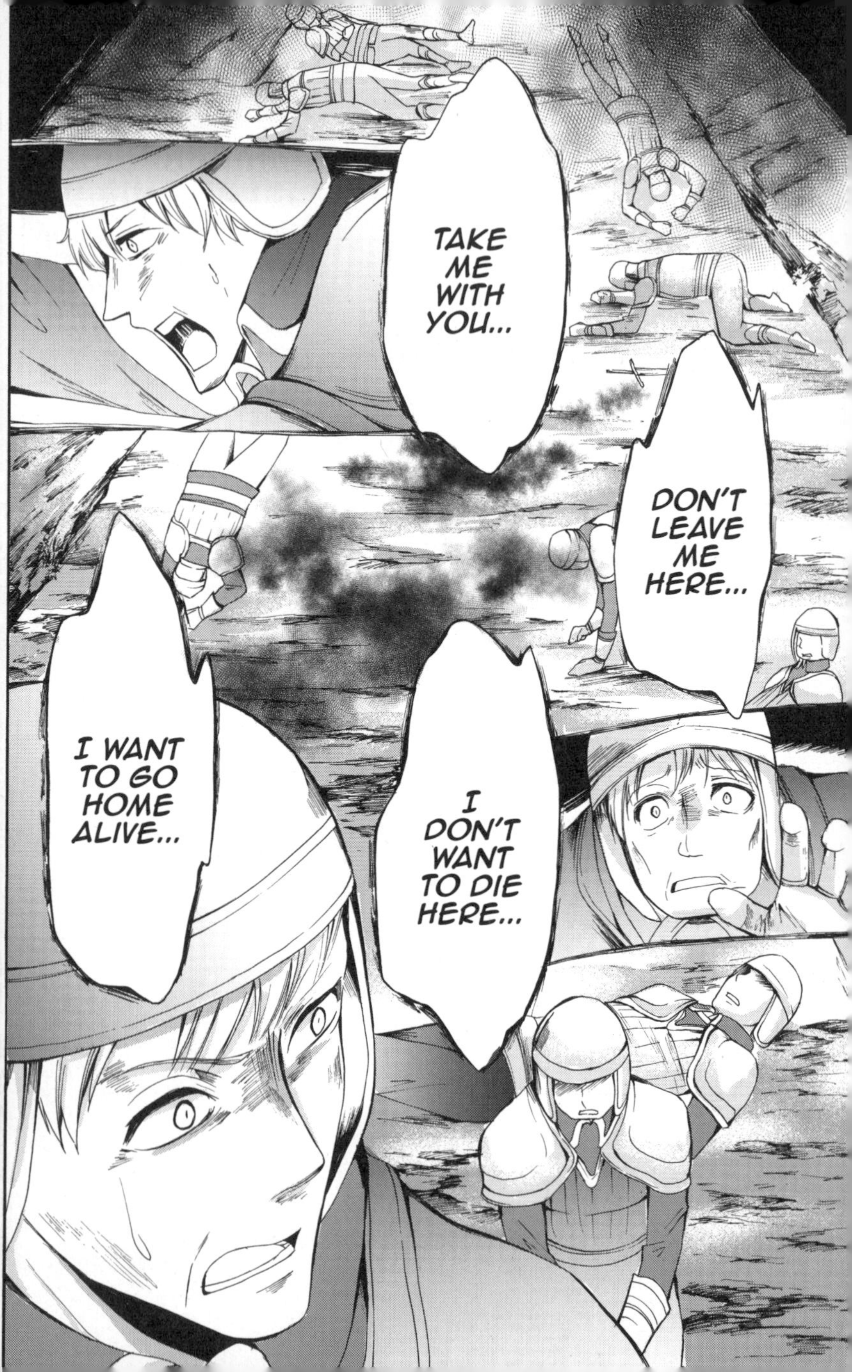
TAKE ME WITH YOU...
DON'T LEAVE ME HERE...
I DON'T WANT TO DIE HERE...
I WANT TO GO HOME ALIVE...

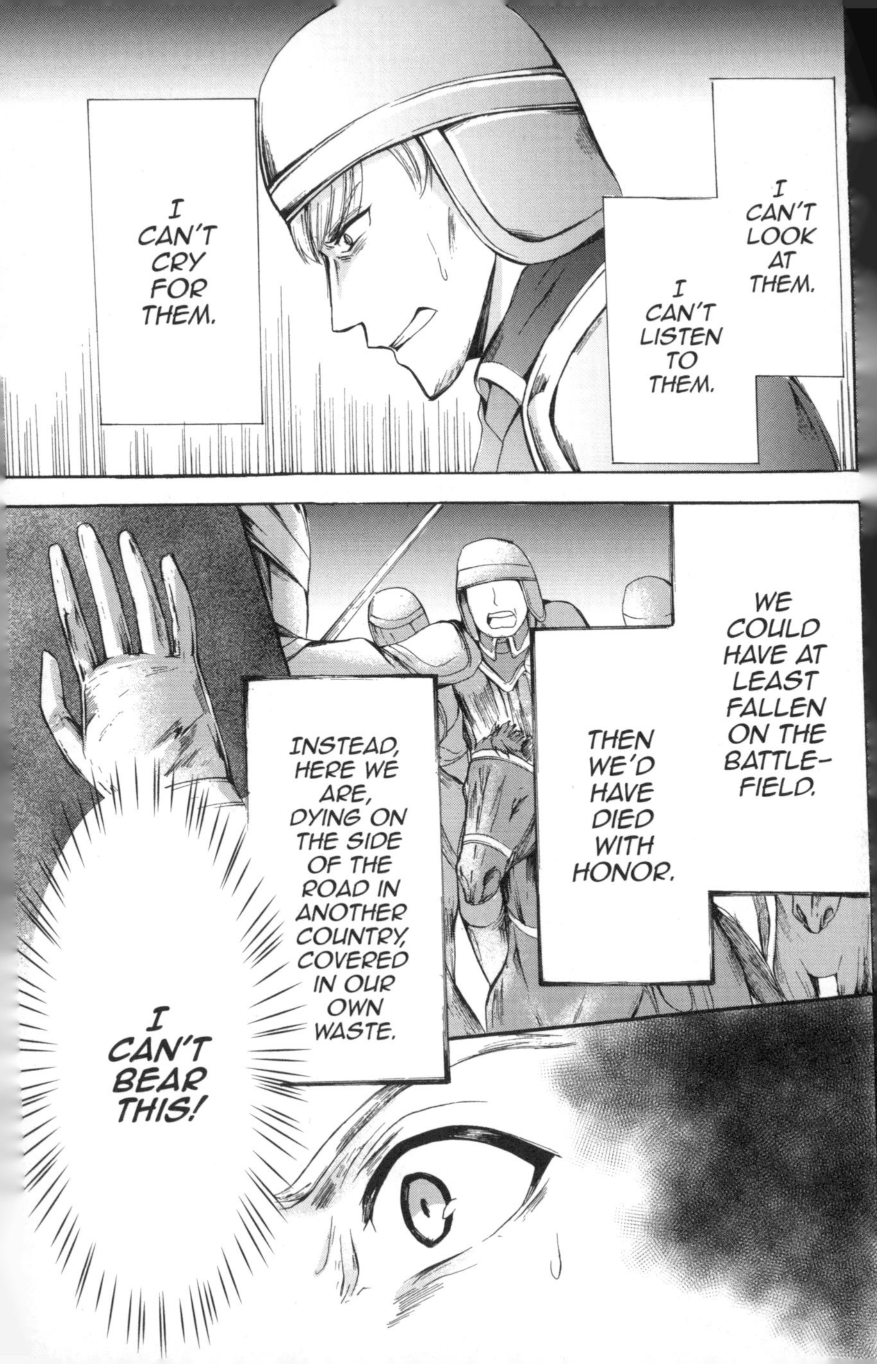
I CAN'T LOOK AT THEM.
I CAN'T LISTEN TO THEM.
I CAN'T CRY FOR THEM.
WE COULD HAVE AT LEAST FALLEN ON THE BATTLE-FIELD.
THEN WE'D HAVE DIED WITH HONOR.
INSTEAD, HERE WE ARE, DYING ON THE SIDE OF THE ROAD IN ANOTHER COUNTRY, COVERED IN OUR OWN WASTE.
I CAN'T BEAR THIS!

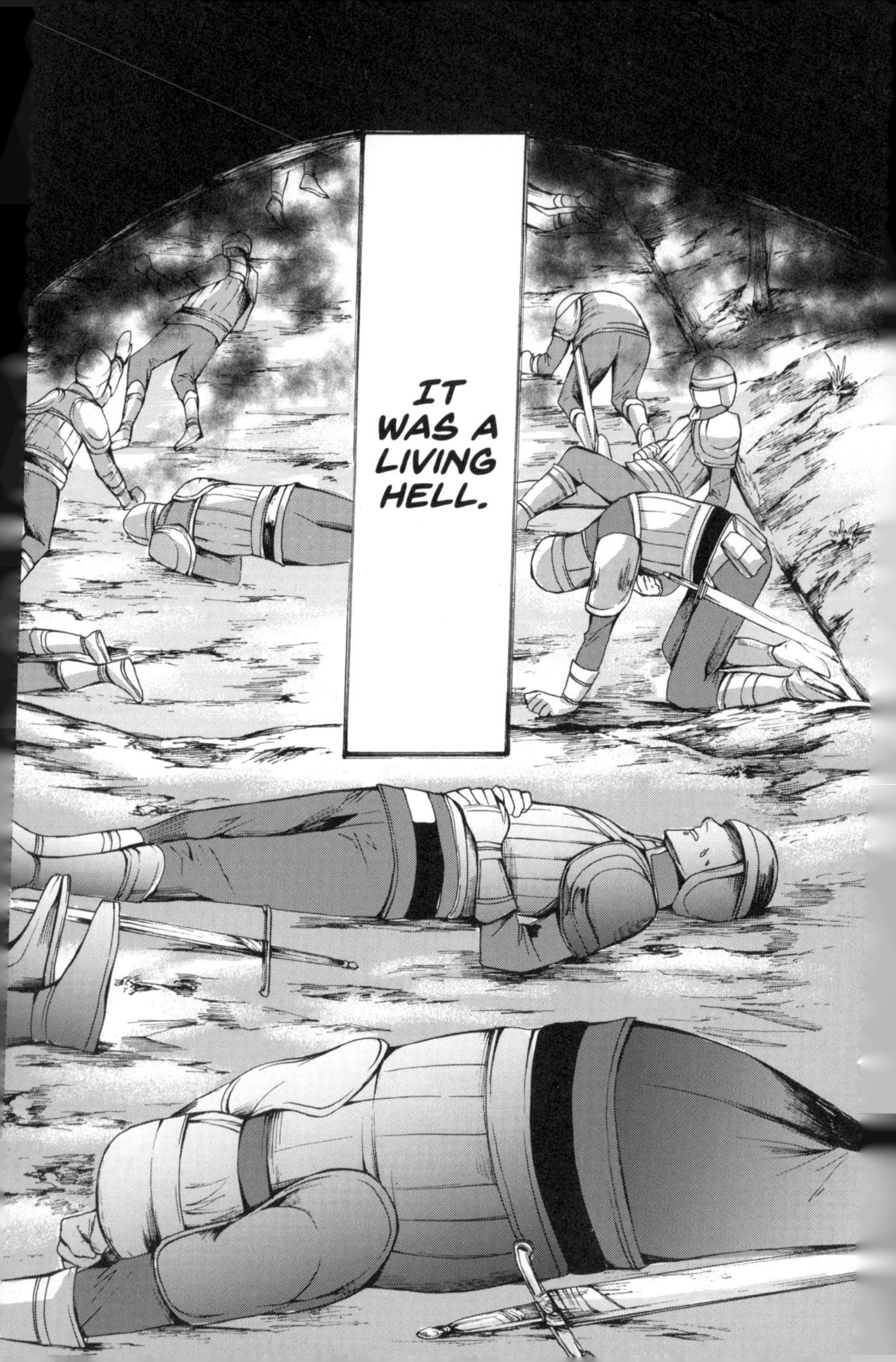
IT WAS A LIVING HELL.

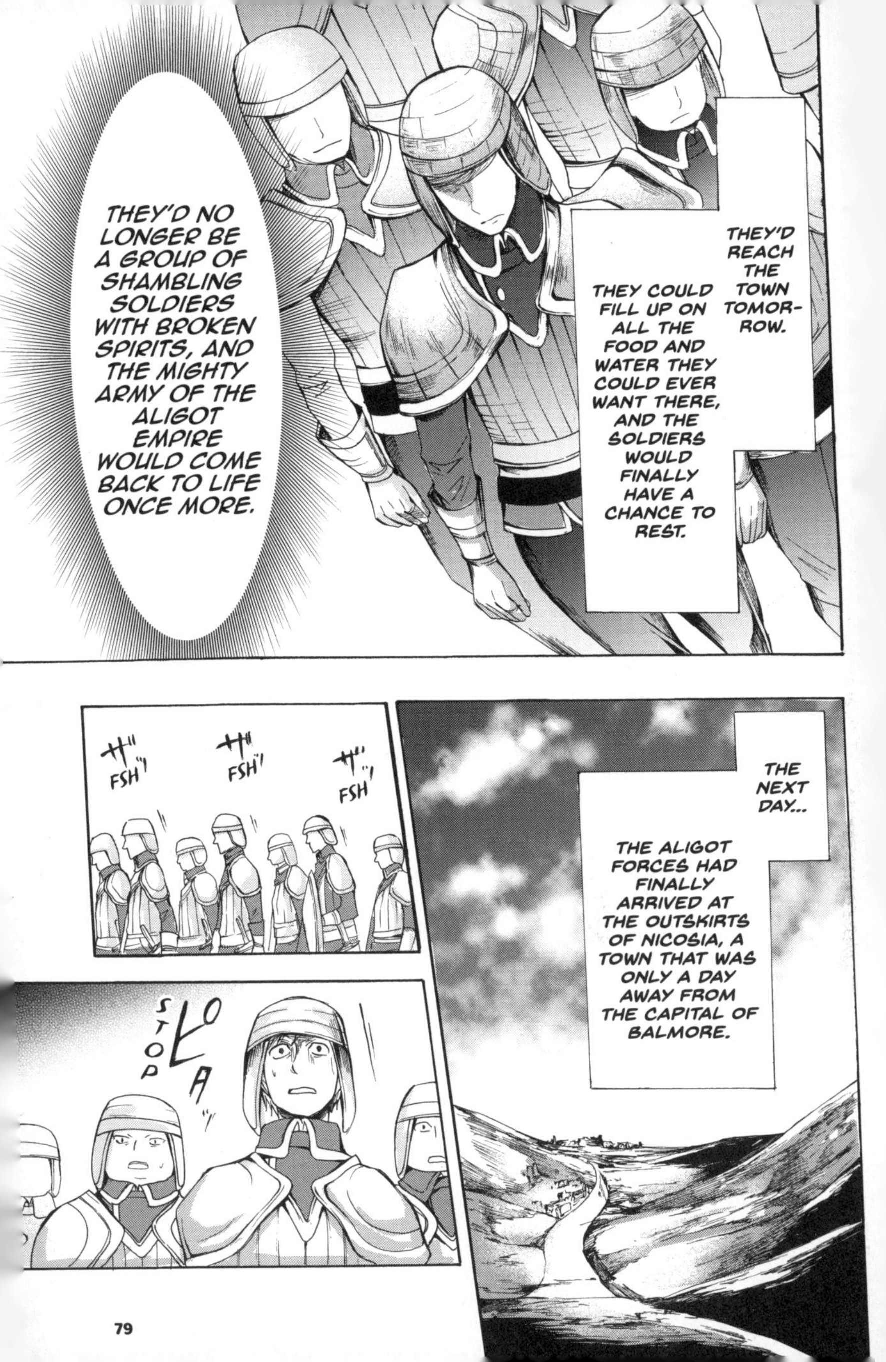
THEY'D REACH THE TOWN TOMORROW.
THEY COULD FILL UP ON ALL THE FOOD AND WATER THEY COULD EVER WANT THERE, AND THE SOLDIERS WOULD FINALLY HAVE A CHANCE TO REST.
THEY'D NO LONGER BE A GROUP OF SHAMBLING SOLDIERS WITH BROKEN SPIRITS, AND THE MIGHTY ARMY OF THE ALIGOT EMPIRE WOULD COME BACK TO LIFE ONCE MORE.
THE NEXT DAY...
THE ALIGOT FORCES HAD FINALLY ARRIVED AT THE OUTSKIRTS OF NICOSIA, A TOWN THAT WAS ONLY A DAY AWAY FROM THE CAPITAL OF BALMORE.
FSH
FSH
FSH
STOP

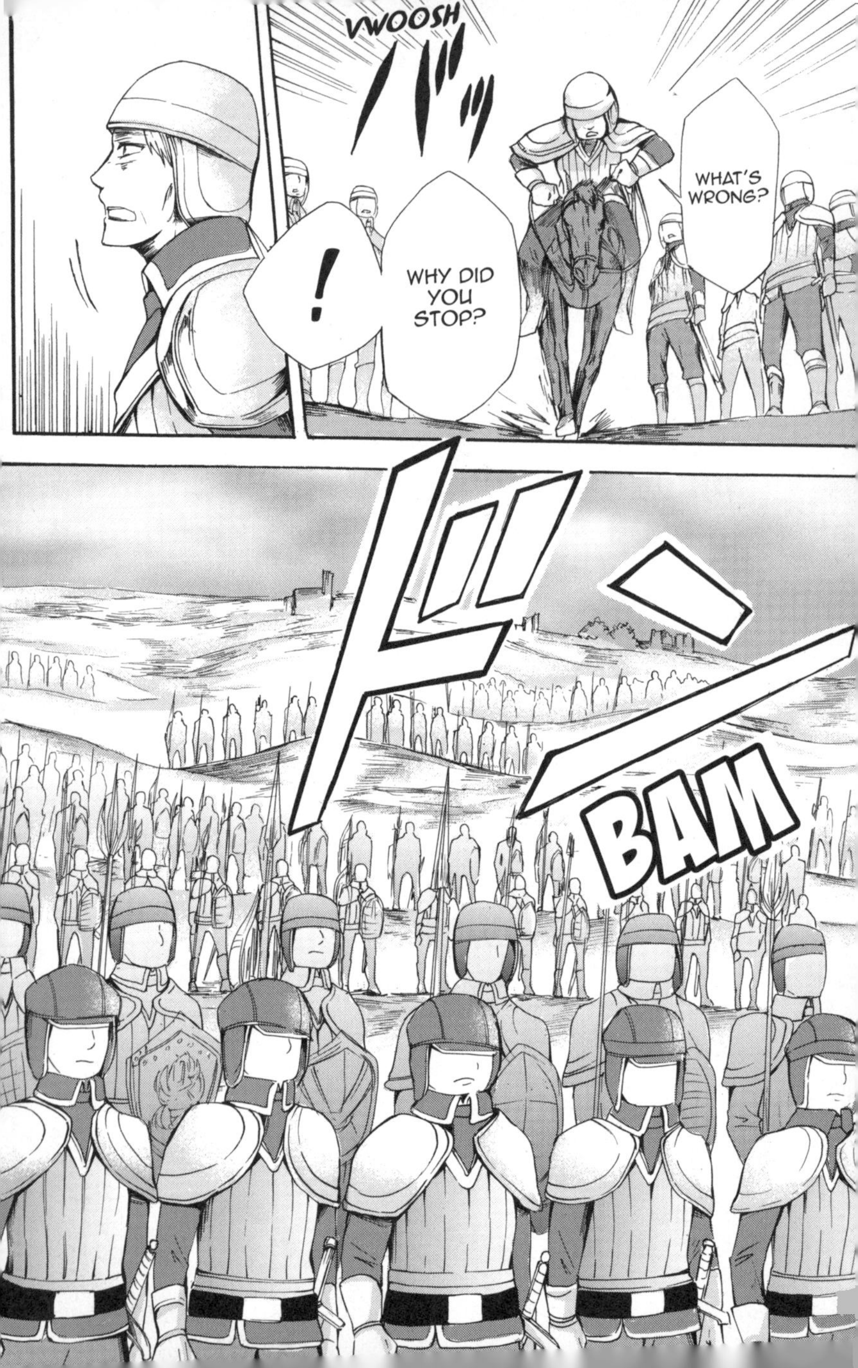
VWOOSH
WHAT'S WRONG?
WHY DID YOU STOP?
!
BAM

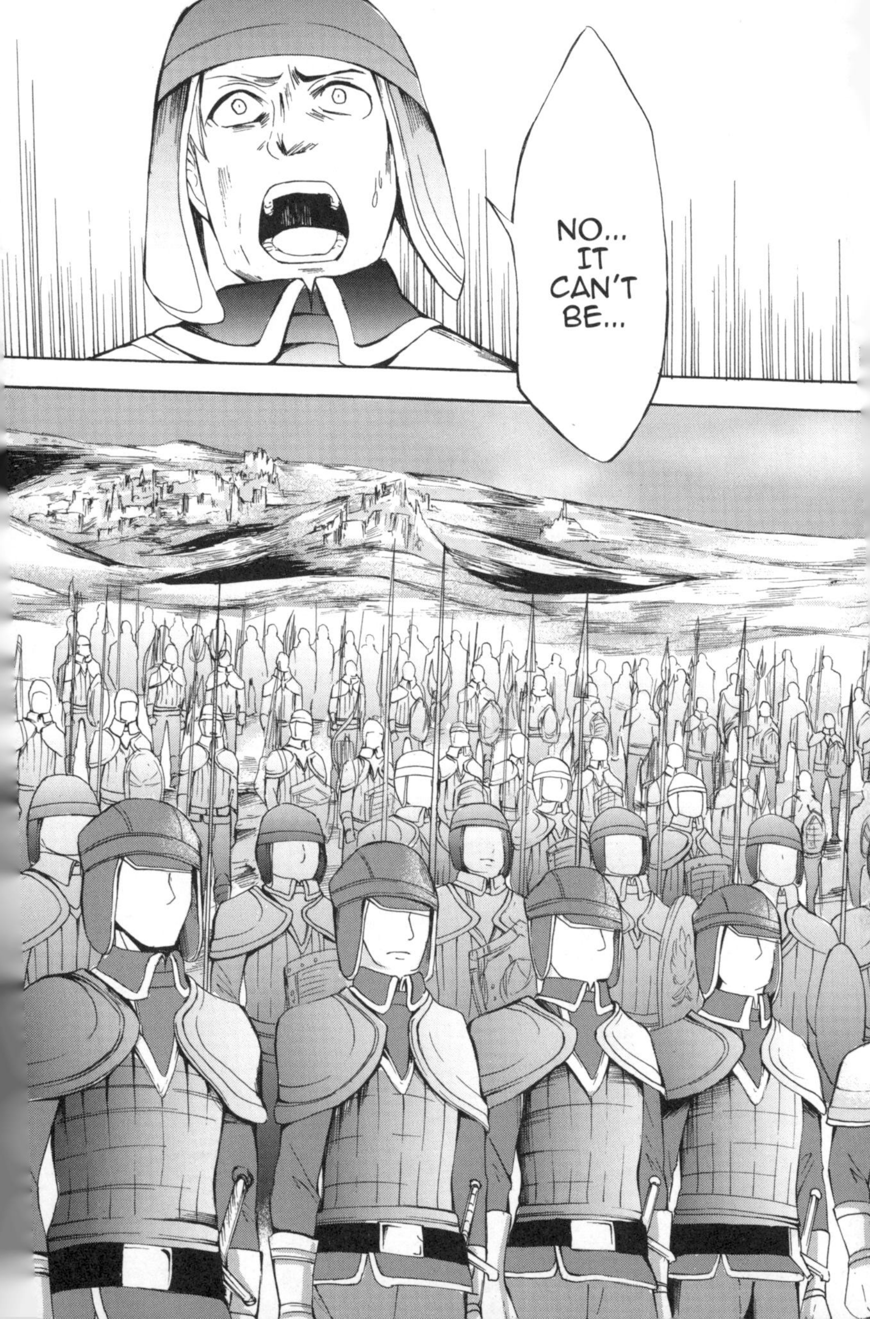
NO... IT CAN'T BE...

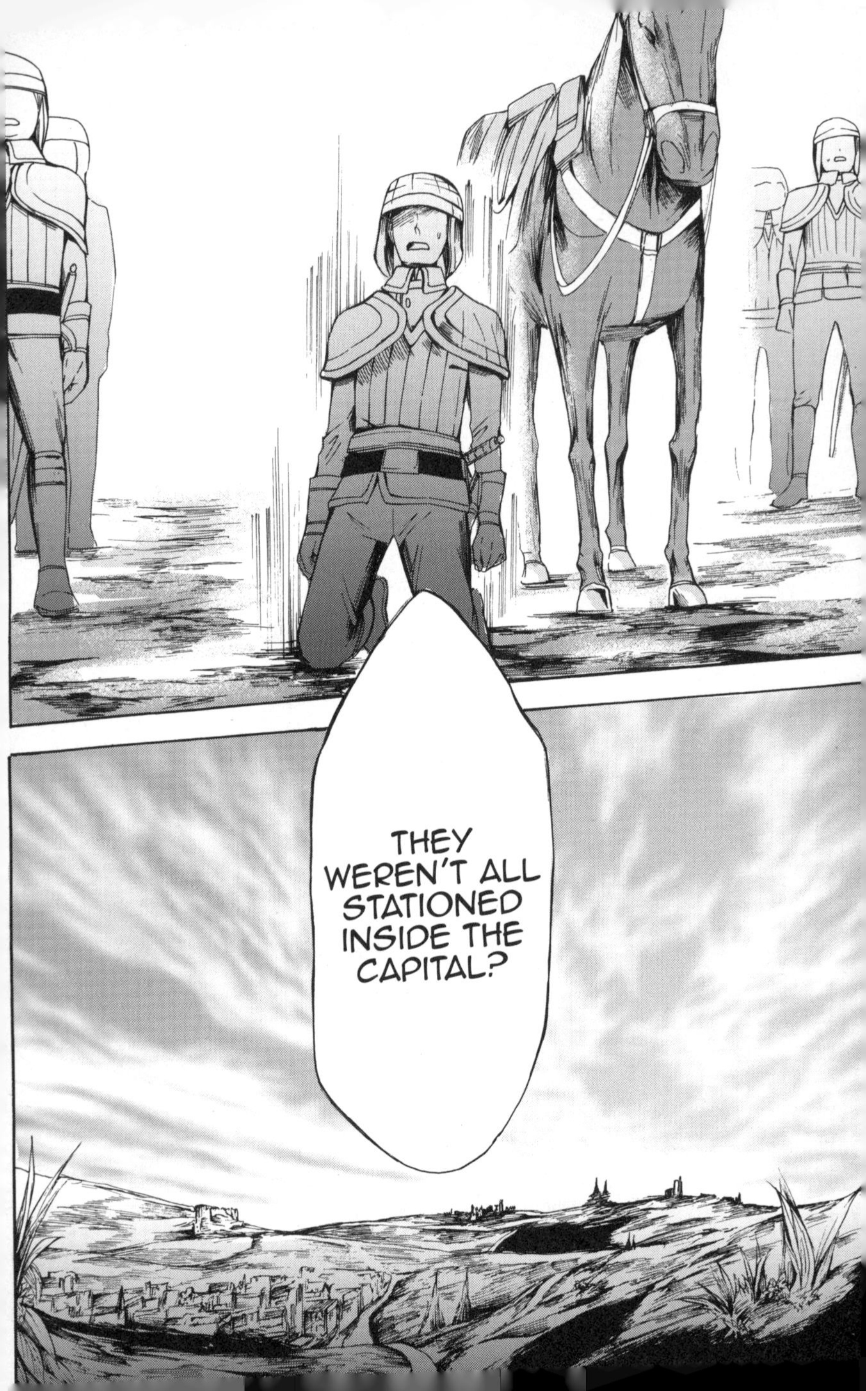
THEY WEREN'T ALL STATIONED INSIDE THE CAPITAL?

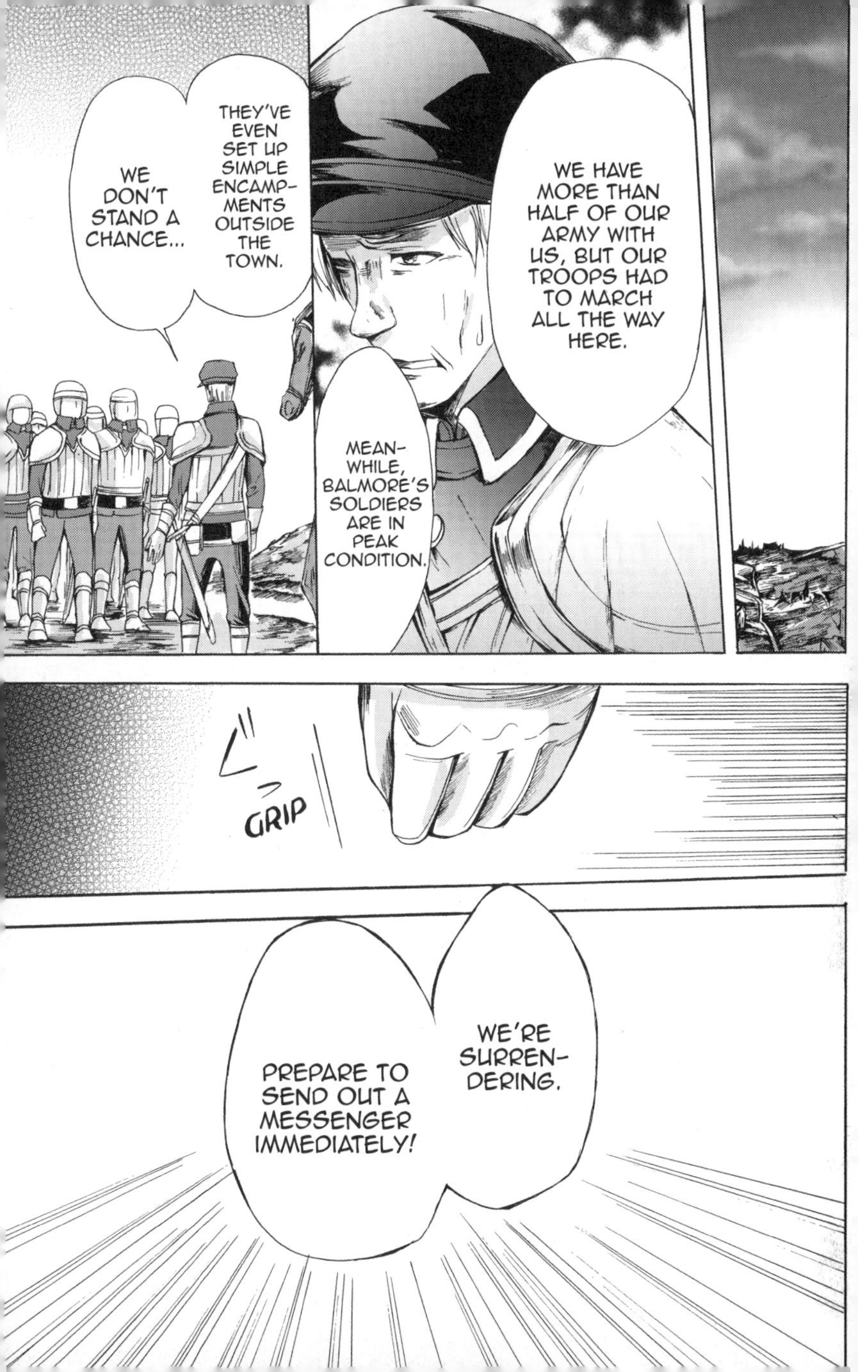
WE HAVE MORE THAN HALF OF OUR ARMY WITH US, BUT OUR TROOPS HAD TO MARCH ALL THE WAY HERE.
MEAN-WHILE, BALMORE'S SOLDIERS ARE IN PEAK CONDITION.
THEY'VE EVEN SET UP SIMPLE ENCAMP-MENTS OUTSIDE THE TOWN.
WE DON'T STAND A CHANCE...
GRIP
WE'RE SURREN-DERING.
PREPARE TO SEND OUT A MESSENGER IMMEDIATELY!

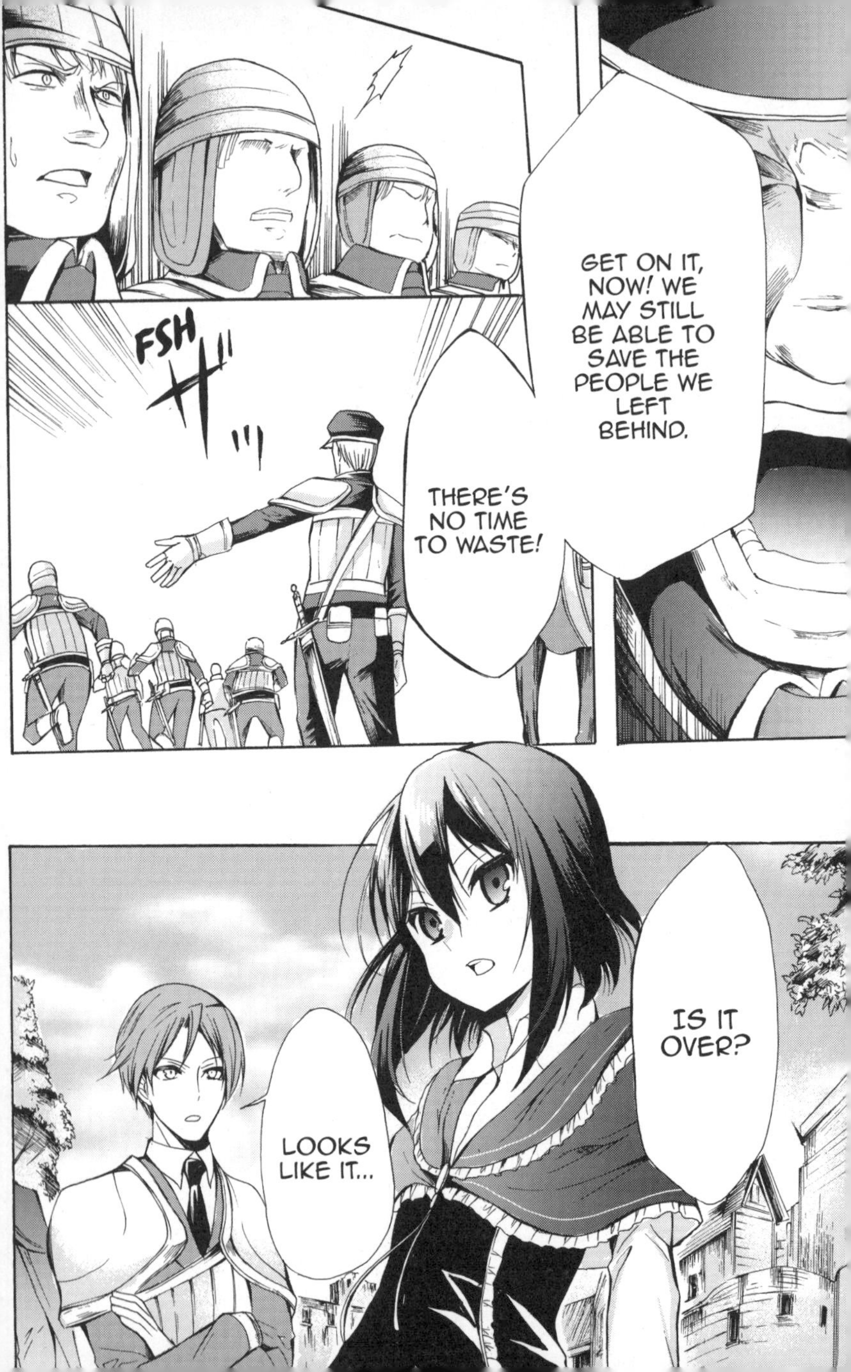
GET ON IT, NOW! WE MAY STILL BE ABLE TO SAVE THE PEOPLE WE LEFT BEHIND.
THERE'S NO TIME TO WASTE!
FSH
IS IT OVER?
LOOKS LIKE IT...

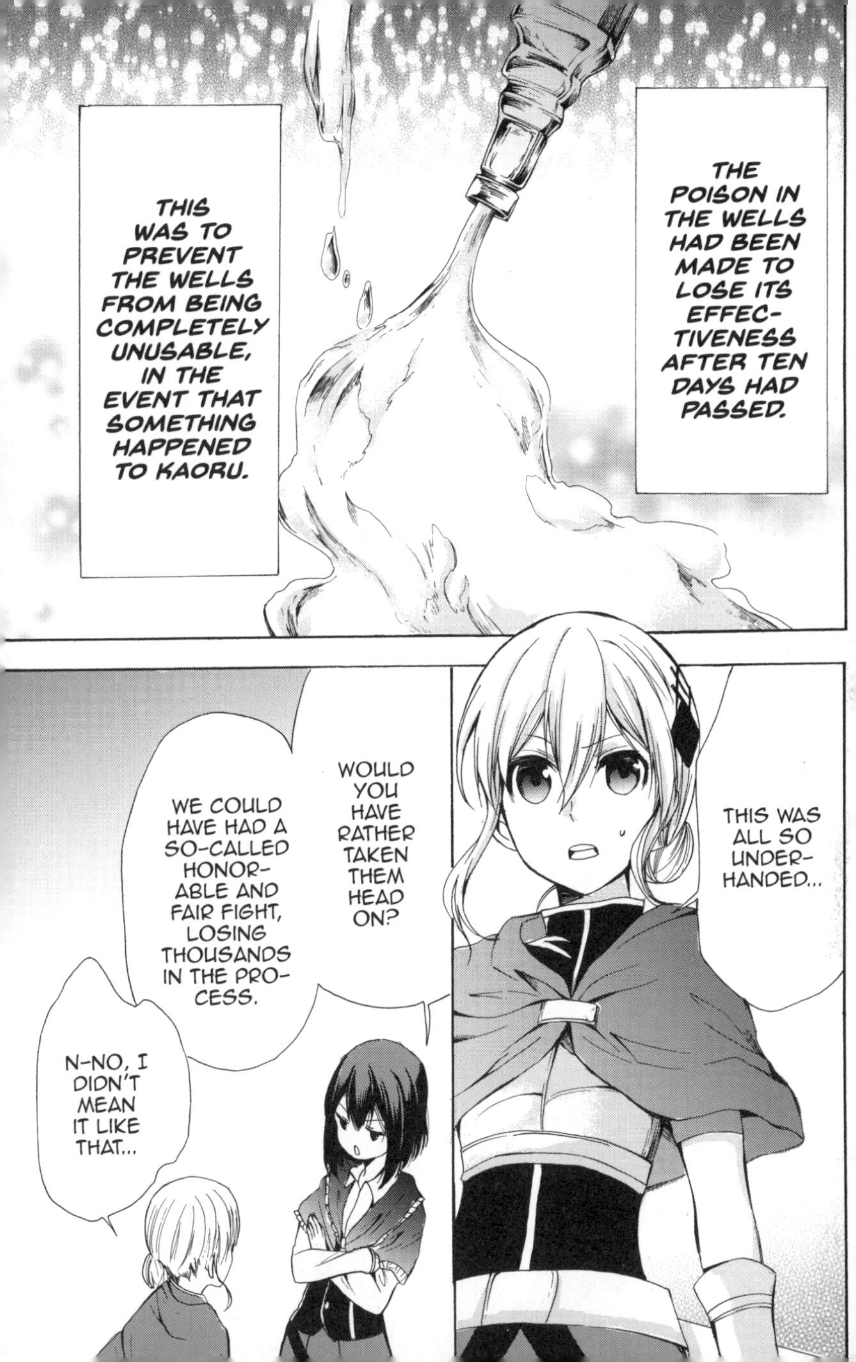
THE POISON IN THE WELLS HAD BEEN MADE TO LOSE ITS EFFEC-TIVENESS AFTER TEN DAYS HAD PASSED.
THIS WAS TO PREVENT THE WELLS FROM BEING COMPLETELY UNUSABLE, IN THE EVENT THAT SOMETHING HAPPENED TO KAORU.
THIS WAS ALL SO UNDER-HANDED...
WOULD YOU HAVE RATHER TAKEN THEM HEAD ON?
WE COULD HAVE HAD A SO-CALLED HONOR-ABLE AND FAIR FIGHT, LOSING THOUSANDS IN THE PRO-CESS.
N-NO, I DIDN'T MEAN IT LIKE THAT...

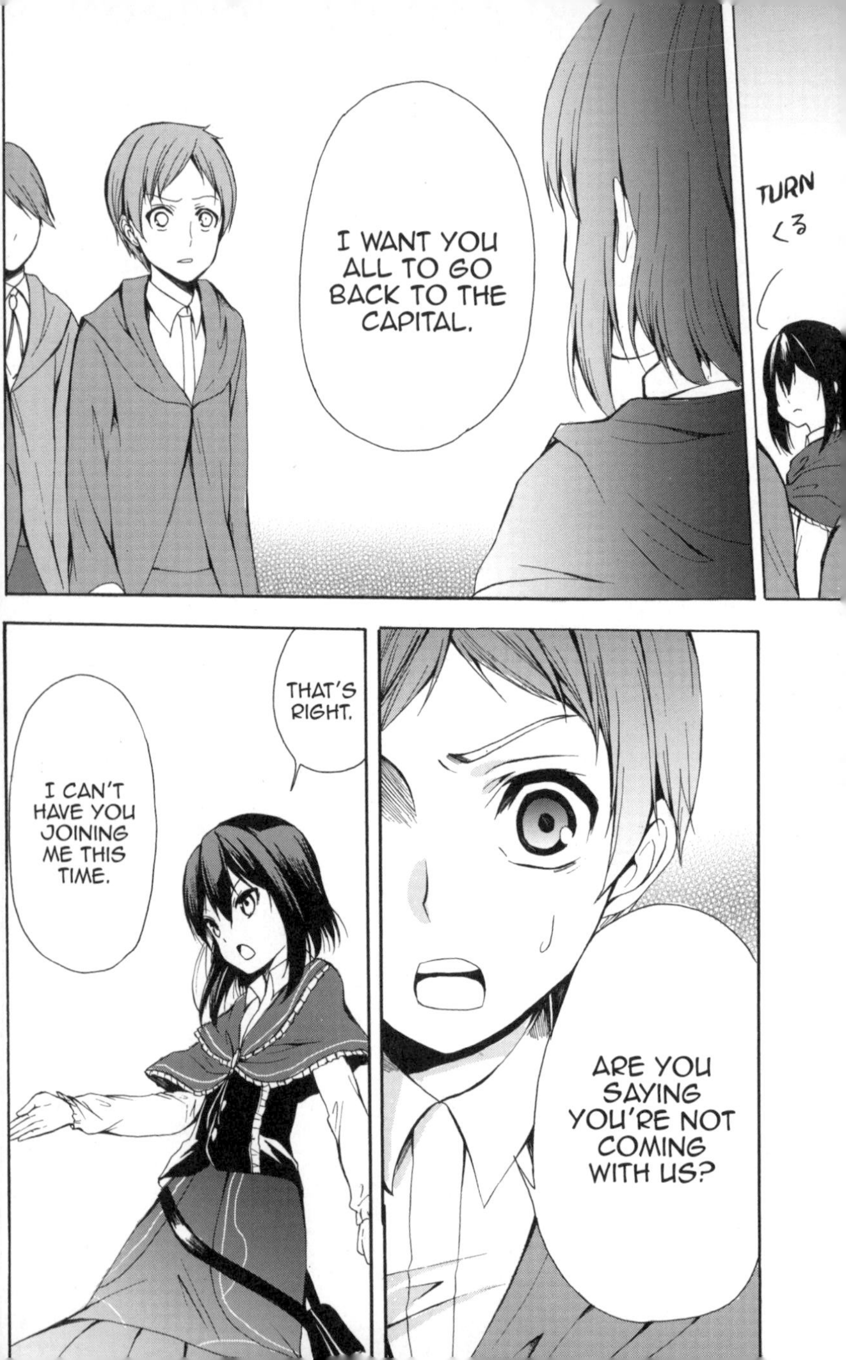
TURN
くる
I WANT YOU ALL TO GO BACK TO THE CAPITAL.
ARE YOU SAYING YOU'RE NOT COMING WITH US?
THAT'S RIGHT.
I CAN'T HAVE YOU JOINING ME THIS TIME.

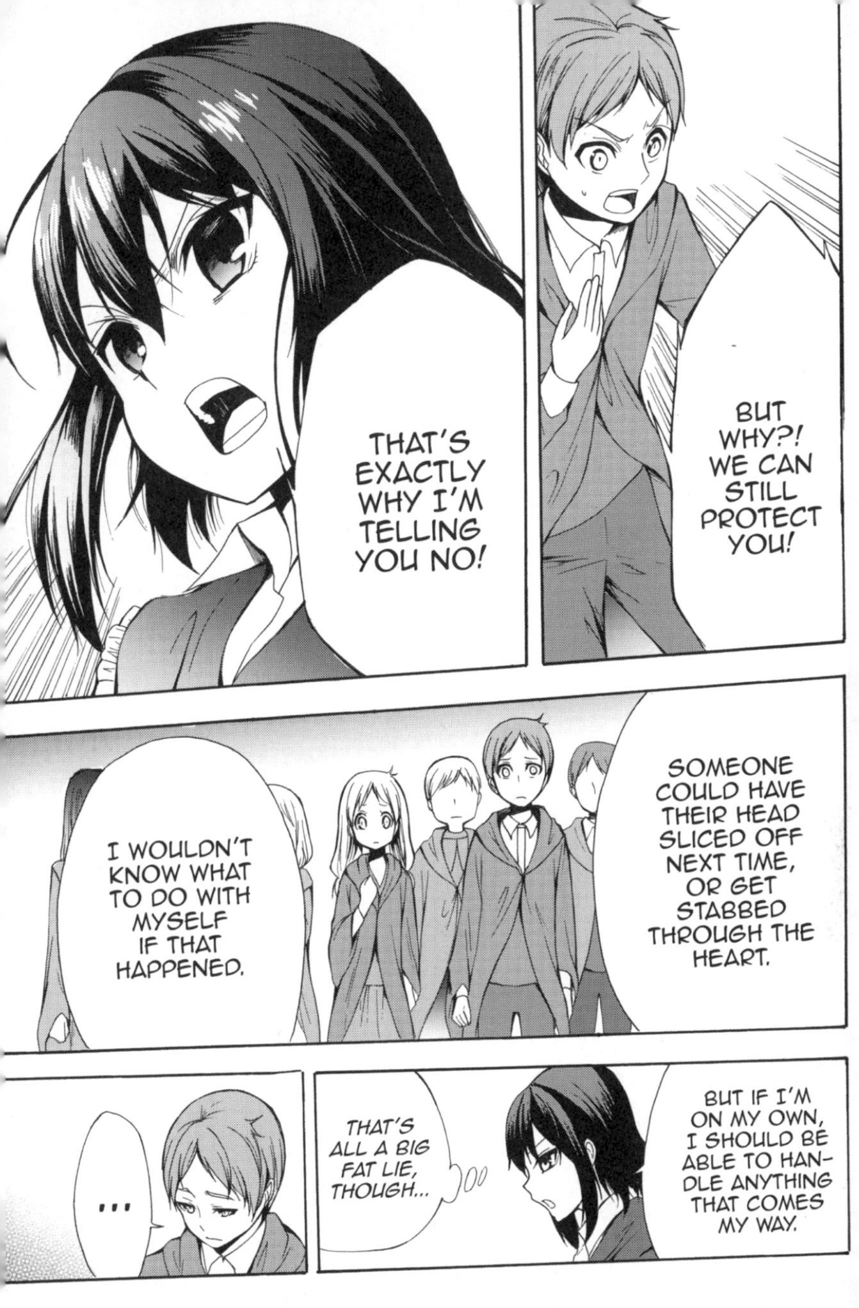
BUT WHY?! WE CAN STILL PROTECT YOU!
THAT'S EXACTLY WHY I'M TELLING YOU NO!
SOMEONE COULD HAVE THEIR HEAD SLICED OFF NEXT TIME, OR GET STABBED THROUGH THE HEART.
I WOULDN'T KNOW WHAT TO DO WITH MYSELF IF THAT HAPPENED.
BUT IF I'M ON MY OWN, I SHOULD BE ABLE TO HAN-DLE ANYTHING THAT COMES MY WAY.
THAT'S ALL A BIG FAT LIE, THOUGH...
...

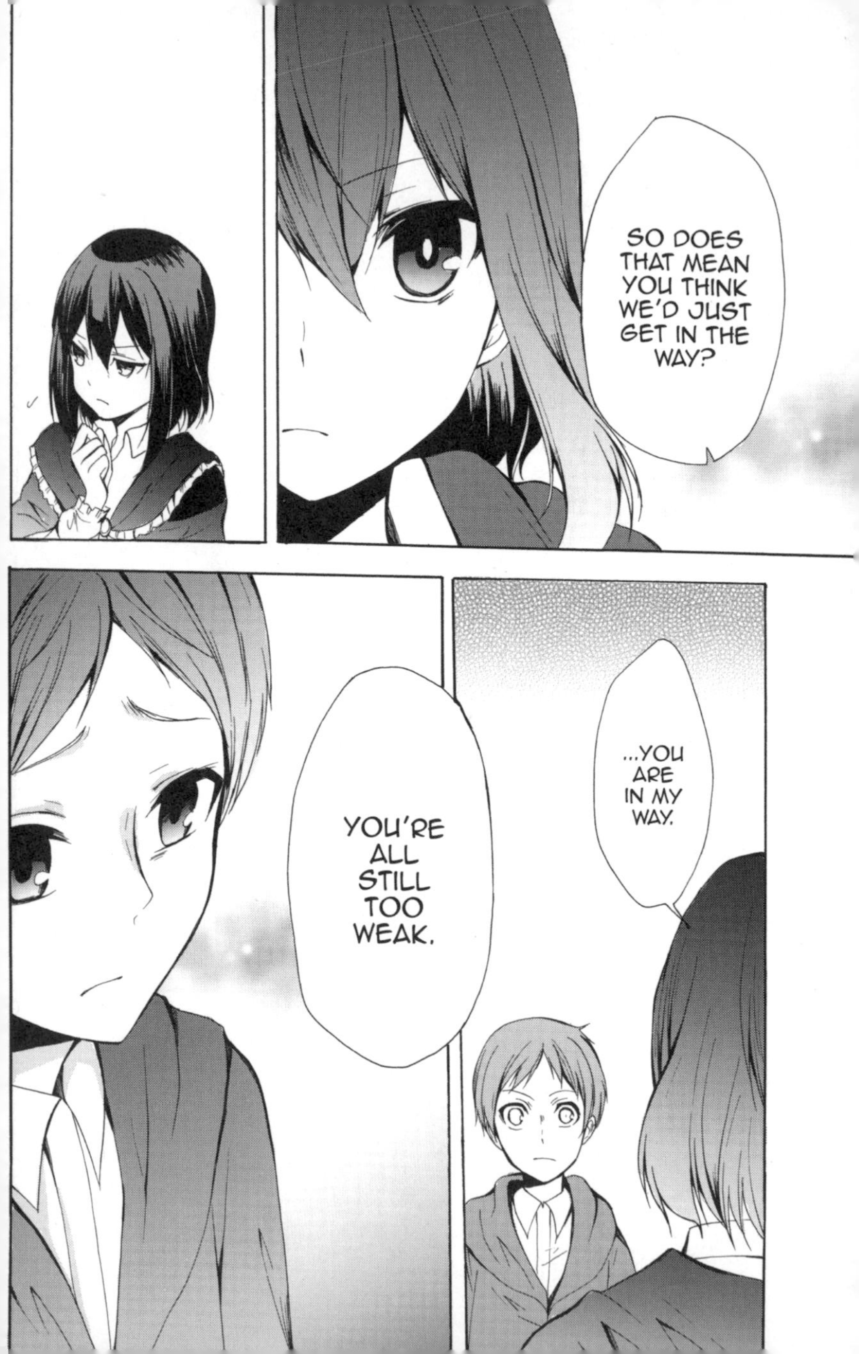
SO DOES THAT MEAN YOU THINK WE'D JUST GET IN THE WAY?
...YOU ARE IN MY WAY.
YOU'RE ALL STILL TOO WEAK.

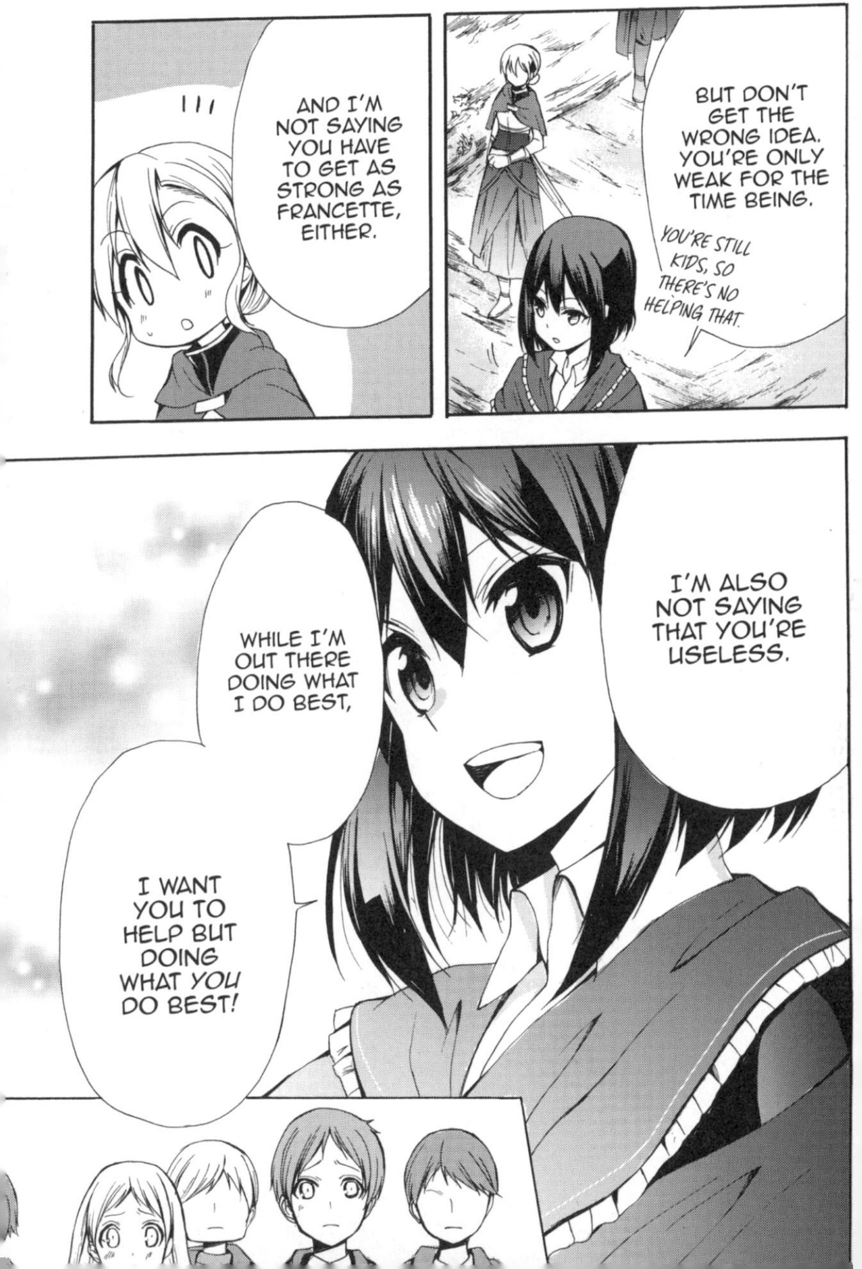
BUT DON'T GET THE WRONG IDEA. YOU'RE ONLY WEAK FOR THE TIME BEING.
YOU'RE STILL KIDS, SO THERE'S NO HELPING THAT.
AND I'M NOT SAYING YOU HAVE TO GET AS STRONG AS FRANCETTE, EITHER.
I'M ALSO NOT SAYING THAT YOU'RE USELESS.
WHILE I'M OUT THERE DOING WHAT I DO BEST,
I WANT YOU TO HELP BUT DOING WHAT *YOU* DO BEST!

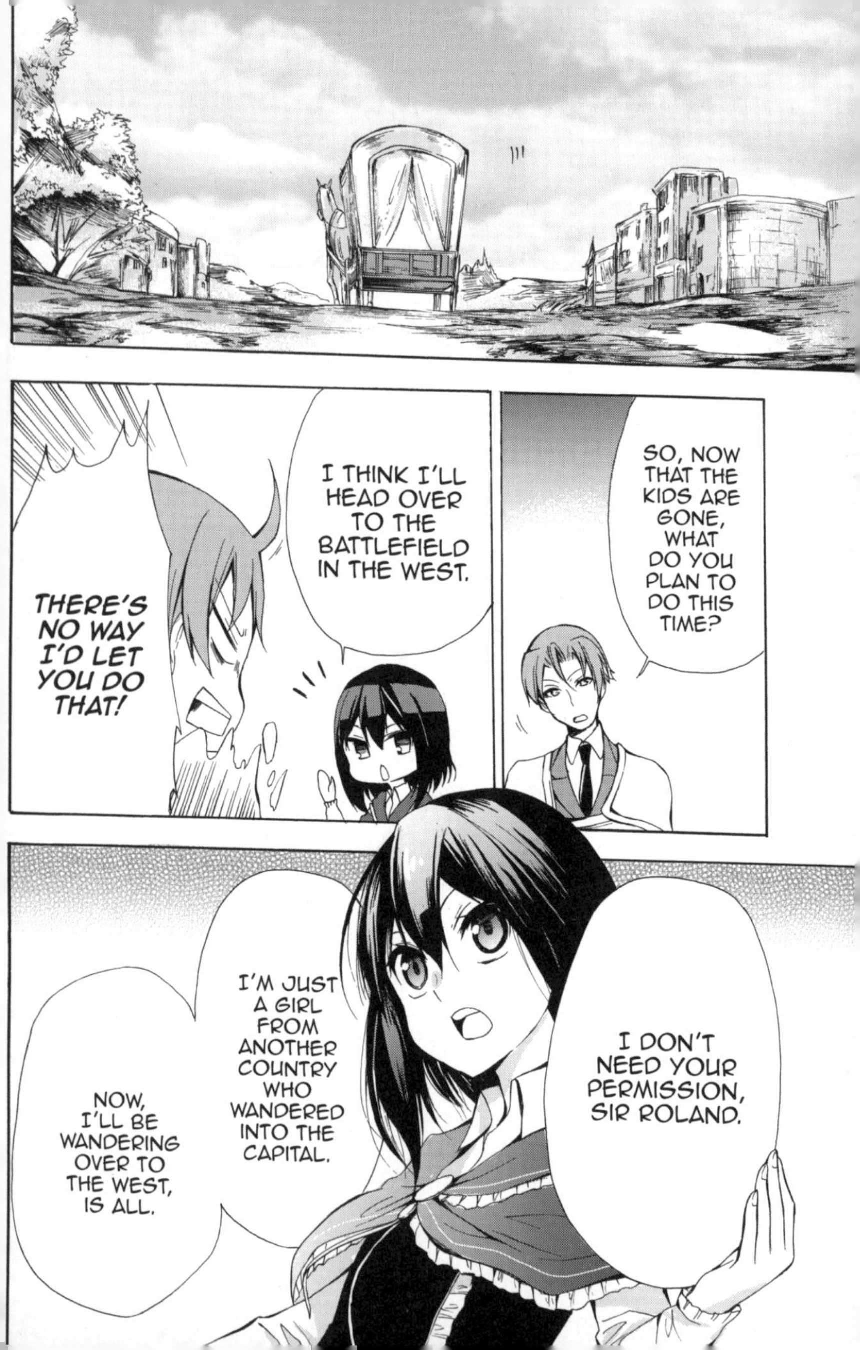
SO, NOW THAT THE KIDS ARE GONE, WHAT DO YOU PLAN TO DO THIS TIME?
I THINK I'LL HEAD OVER TO THE BATTLEFIELD IN THE WEST.
THERE'S NO WAY I'D LET YOU DO THAT!
I DON'T NEED YOUR PERMISSION, SIR ROLAND.
I'M JUST A GIRL FROM ANOTHER COUNTRY WHO WANDERED INTO THE CAPITAL.
NOW, I'LL BE WANDERING OVER TO THE WEST, IS ALL.

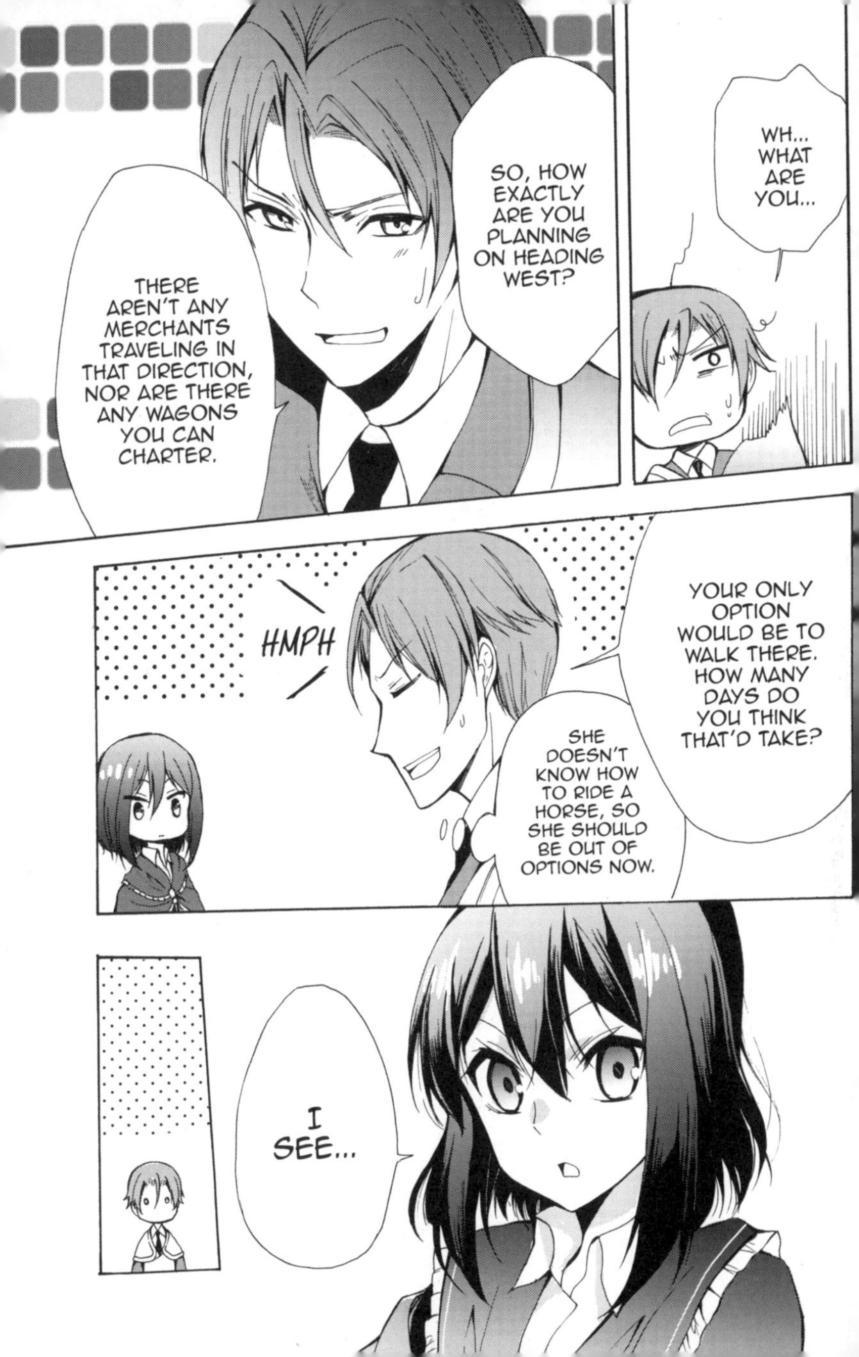
WH... WHAT ARE YOU...
SO, HOW EXACTLY ARE YOU PLANNING ON HEADING WEST?
THERE AREN'T ANY MERCHANTS TRAVELING IN THAT DIRECTION, NOR ARE THERE ANY WAGONS YOU CAN CHARTER.
YOUR ONLY OPTION WOULD BE TO WALK THERE. HOW MANY DAYS DO YOU THINK THAT'D TAKE?
HMPH
SHE DOESN'T KNOW HOW TO RIDE A HORSE, SO SHE SHOULD BE OUT OF OPTIONS NOW.
I SEE...

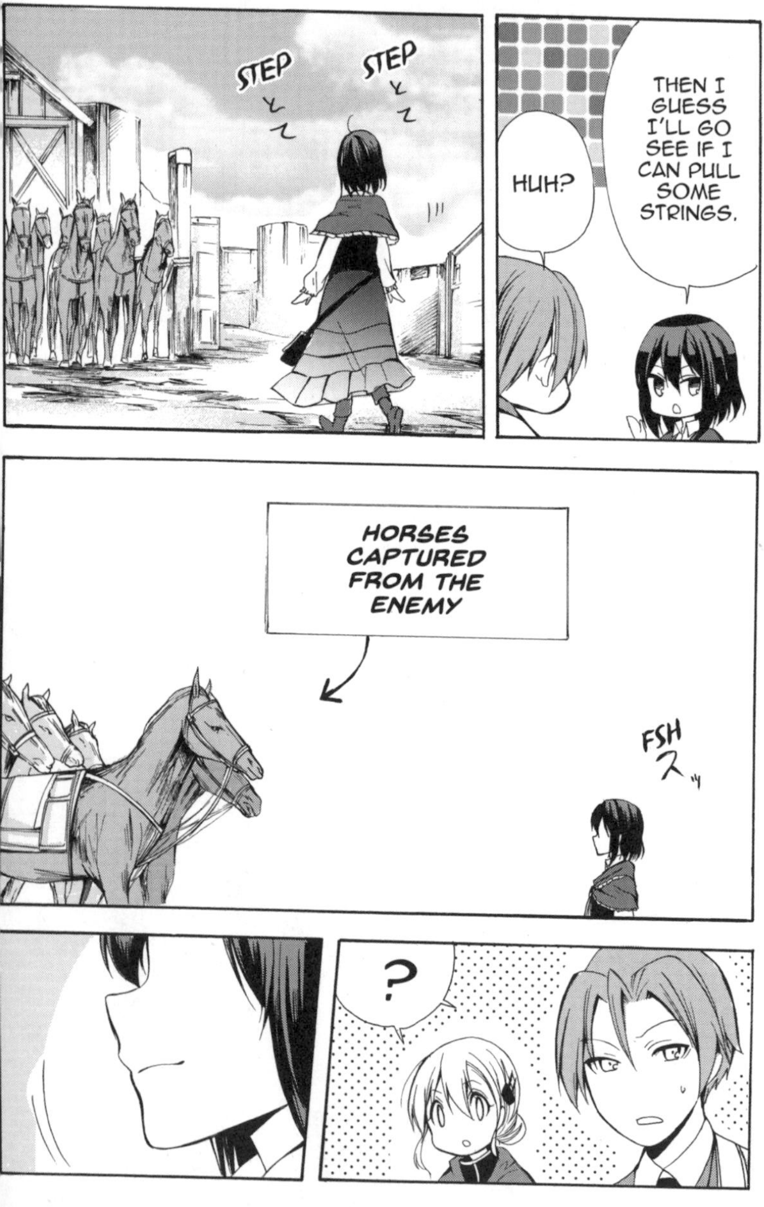
THEN I GUESS I'LL GO SEE IF I CAN PULL SOME STRINGS.
HUH?
STEP
STEP
HORSES CAPTURED FROM THE ENEMY
FSH
スッ
?

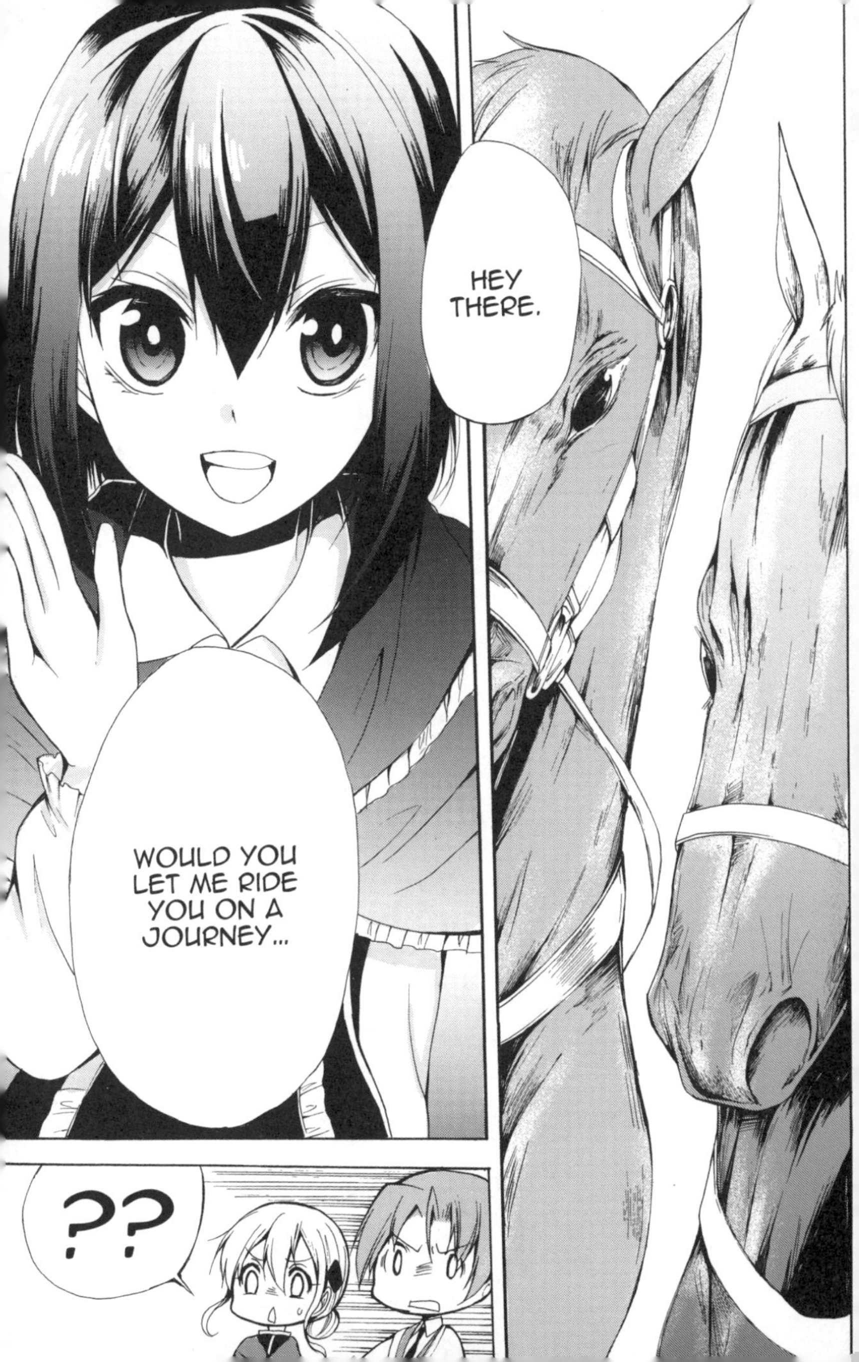
HEY THERE.
WOULD YOU LET ME RIDE YOU ON A JOURNEY...
??

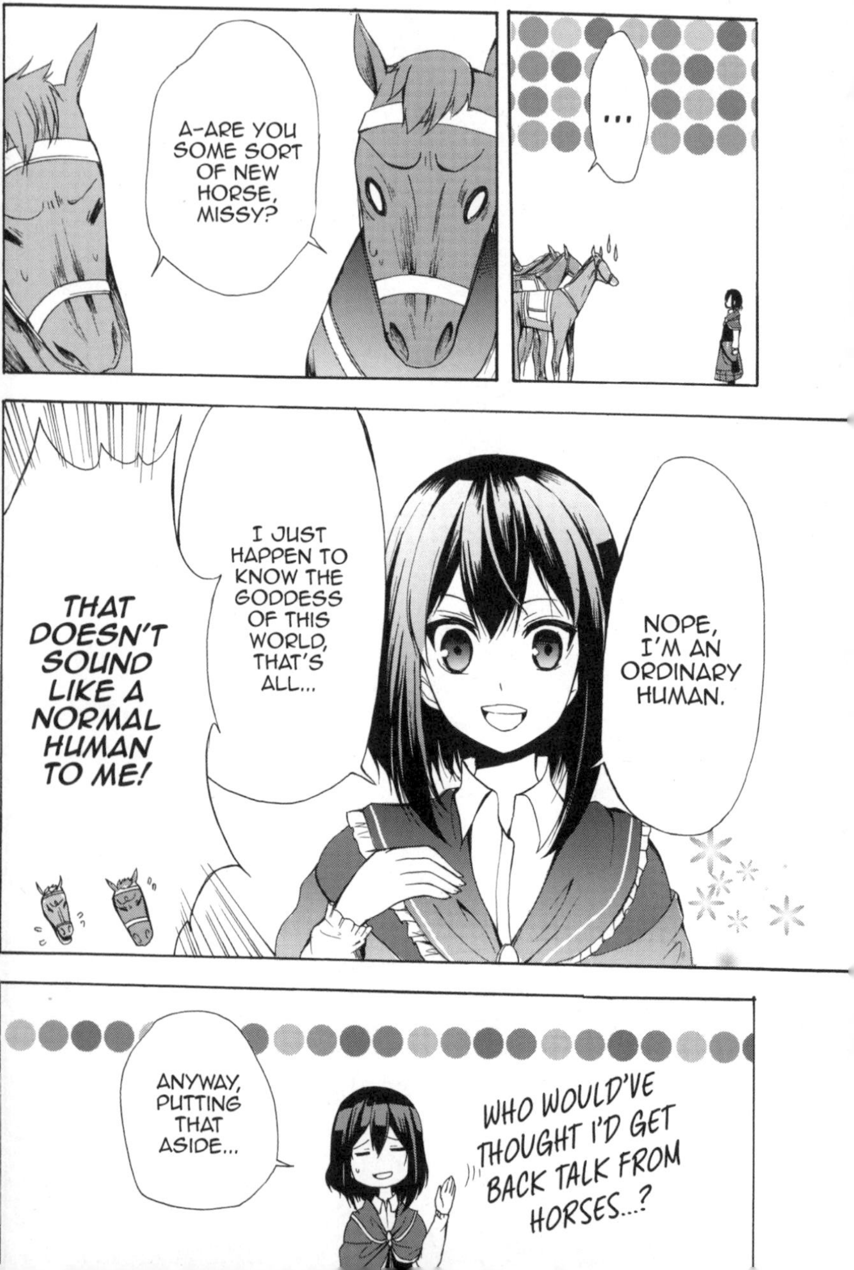
...
A-ARE YOU SOME SORT OF NEW HORSE, MISSY?
NOPE, I'M AN ORDINARY HUMAN.
I JUST HAPPEN TO KNOW THE GODDESS OF THIS WORLD, THAT'S ALL...
THAT DOESN'T SOUND LIKE A NORMAL HUMAN TO ME!
WHO WOULD'VE THOUGHT I'D GET BACK TALK FROM HORSES...?
ANYWAY, PUTTING THAT ASIDE...

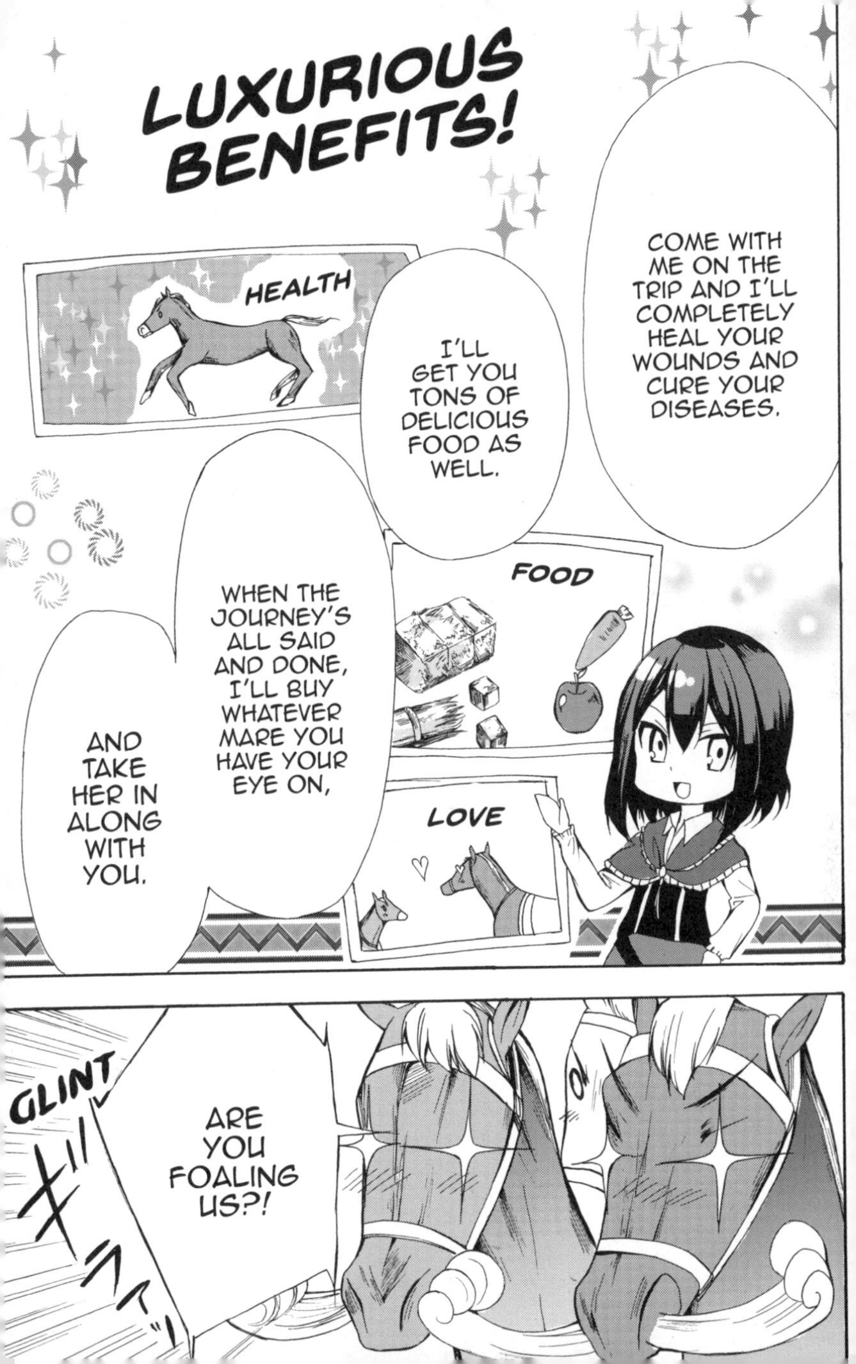
LUXURIOUS BENEFITS!
COME WITH ME ON THE TRIP AND I'LL COMPLETELY HEAL YOUR WOUNDS AND CURE YOUR DISEASES.
HEALTH
I'LL GET YOU TONS OF DELICIOUS FOOD AS WELL.
FOOD
WHEN THE JOURNEY'S ALL SAID AND DONE, I'LL BUY WHATEVER MARE YOU HAVE YOUR EYE ON,
LOVE
AND TAKE HER IN ALONG WITH YOU.
ARE YOU FOALING US?!
GLINT

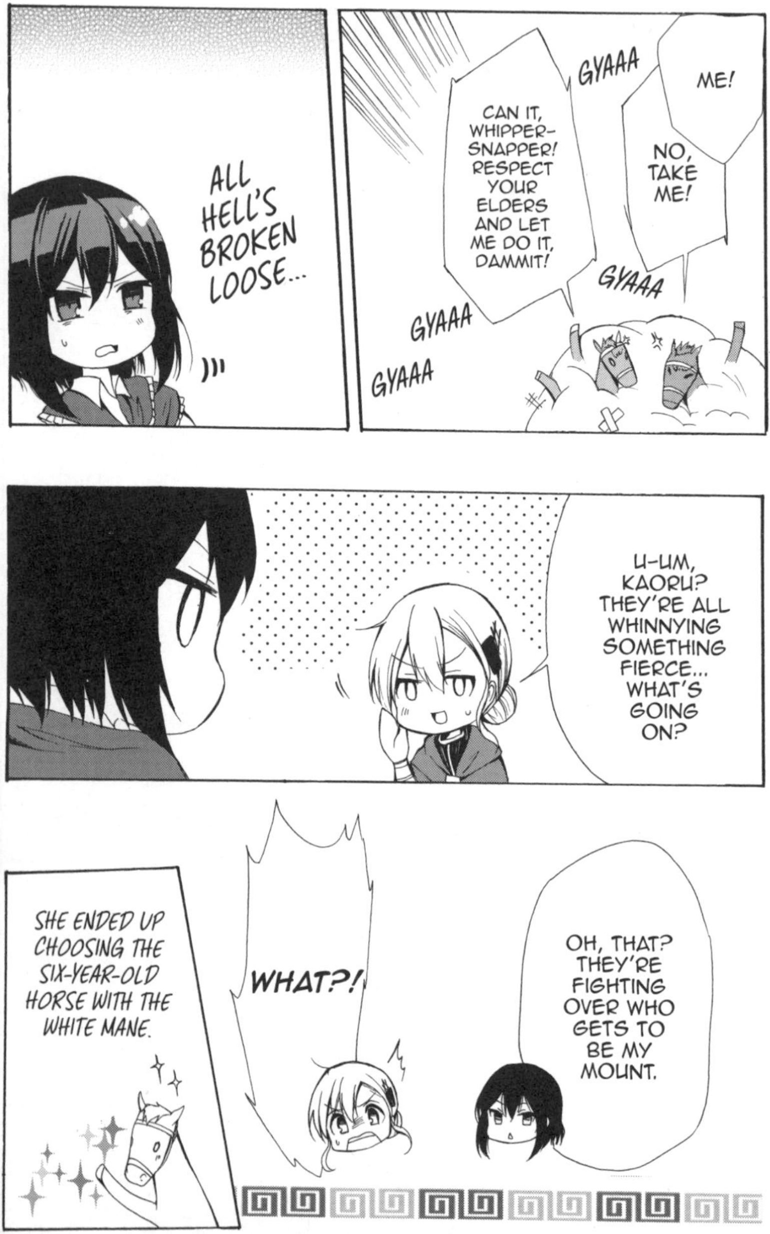
ME!
NO, TAKE ME!
GYAAA
CAN IT, WHIPPER-SNAPPER! RESPECT YOUR ELDERS AND LET ME DO IT, DAMMIT!
GYAAA
GYAAA
GYAAA
ALL HELL'S BROKEN LOOSE...
U-UM, KAORU? THEY'RE ALL WHINNYING SOMETHING FIERCE... WHAT'S GOING ON?
OH, THAT? THEY'RE FIGHTING OVER WHO GETS TO BE MY MOUNT.
WHAT?!
SHE ENDED UP CHOOSING THE SIX-YEAR-OLD HORSE WITH THE WHITE MANE.

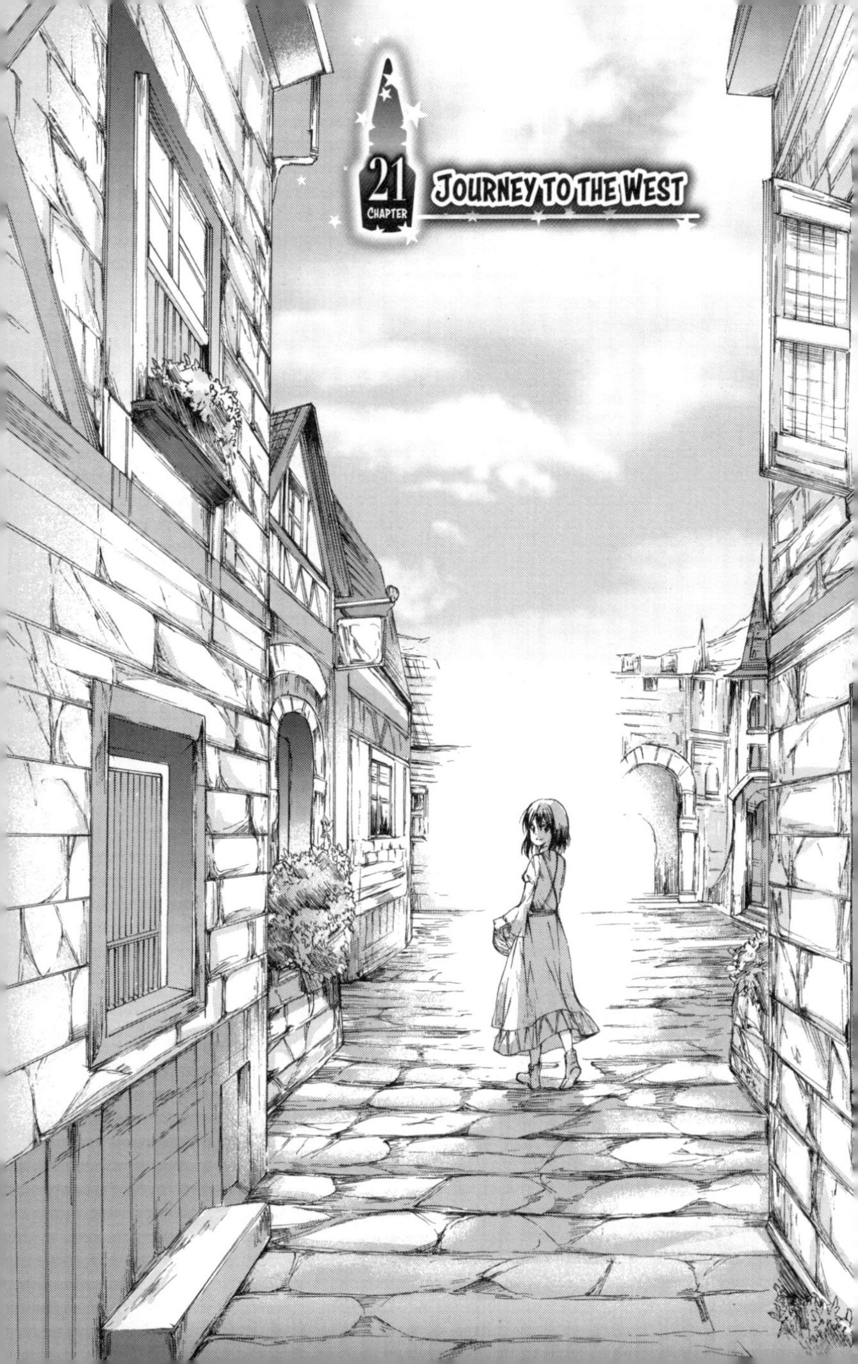
21
CHAPTER
JOURNEY TO THE WEST

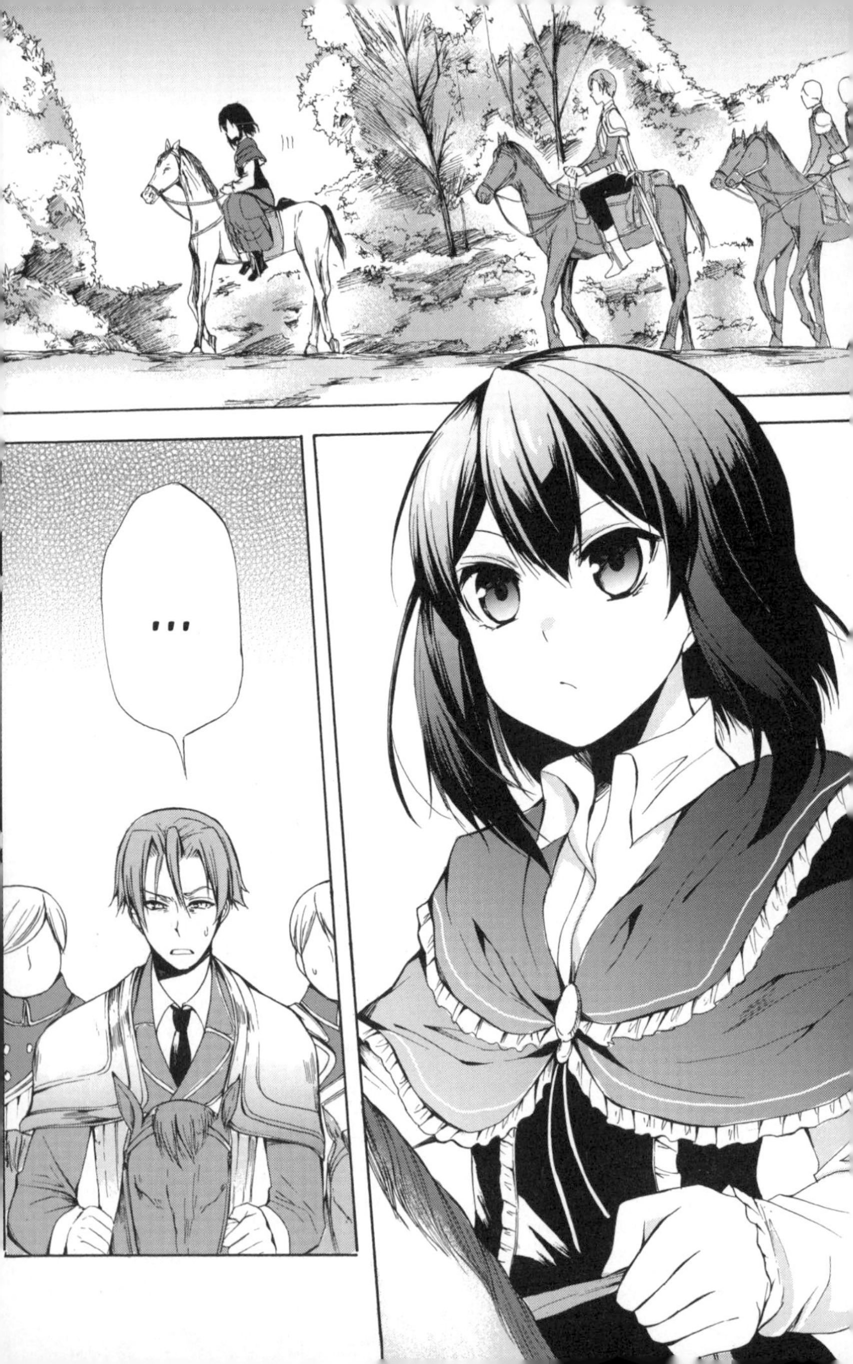
...

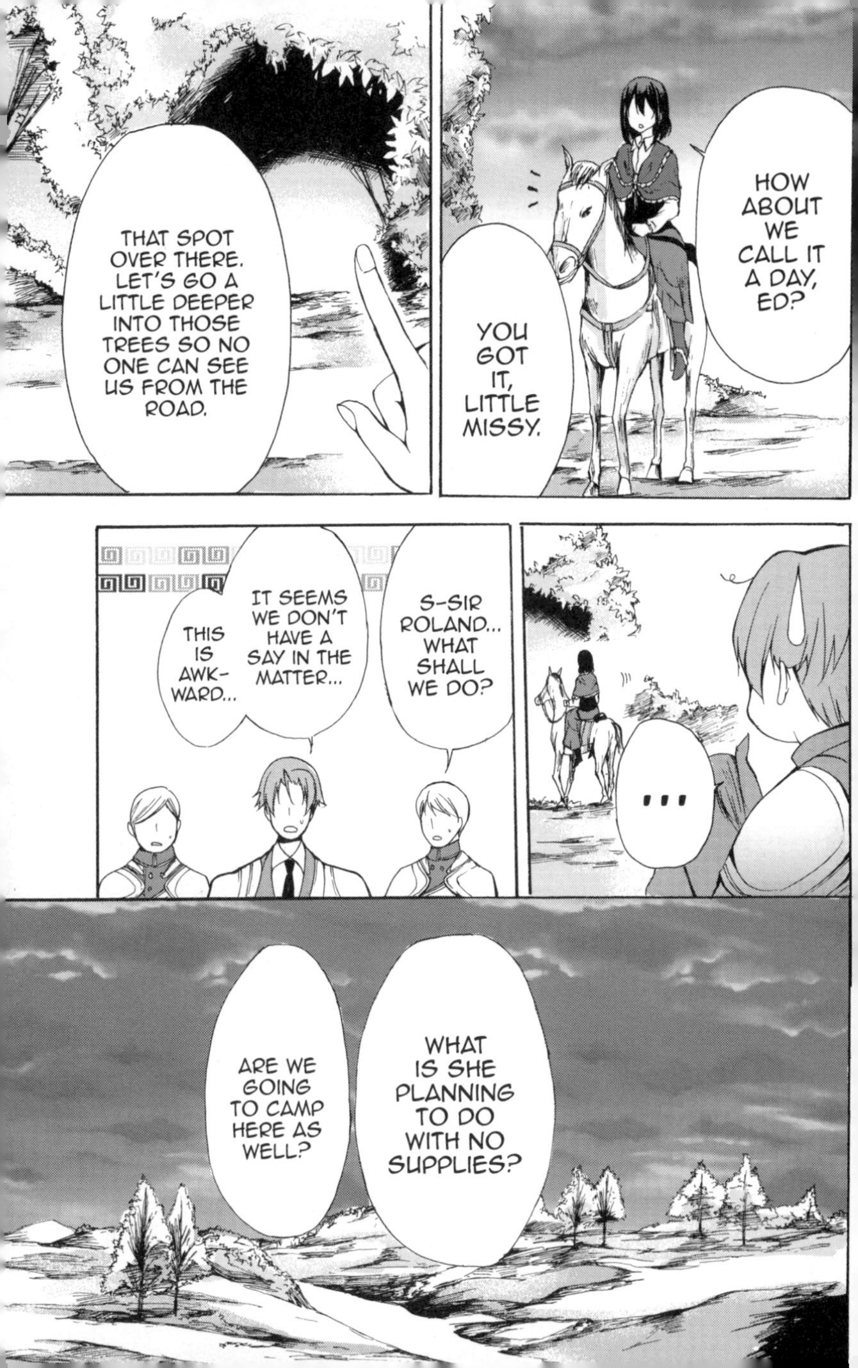
HOW ABOUT WE CALL IT A DAY, ED?
YOU GOT IT, LITTLE MISSY.
THAT SPOT OVER THERE. LET'S GO A LITTLE DEEPER INTO THOSE TREES SO NO ONE CAN SEE US FROM THE ROAD.
...
S-SIR ROLAND... WHAT SHALL WE DO?
IT SEEMS WE DON'T HAVE A SAY IN THE MATTER...
THIS IS AWK-WARD...
WHAT IS SHE PLANNING TO DO WITH NO SUPPLIES?
ARE WE GOING TO CAMP HERE AS WELL?

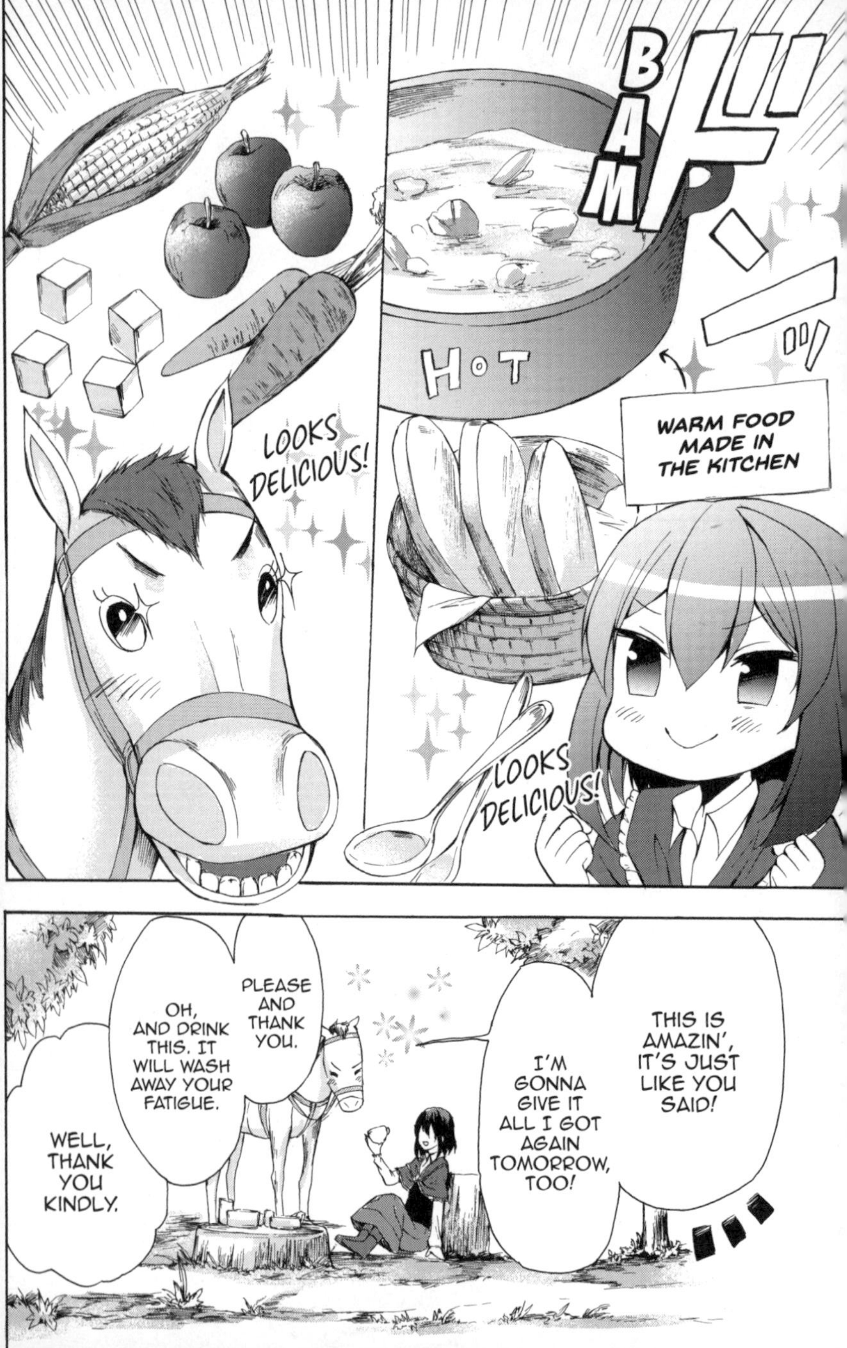
BAM
HOT
WARM FOOD MADE IN THE KITCHEN
LOOKS DELICIOUS!
LOOKS DELICIOUS!
THIS IS AMAZIN', IT'S JUST LIKE YOU SAID!
I'M GONNA GIVE IT ALL I GOT AGAIN TOMORROW, TOO!
PLEASE AND THANK YOU.
OH, AND DRINK THIS. IT WILL WASH AWAY YOUR FATIGUE.
WELL, THANK YOU KINDLY.

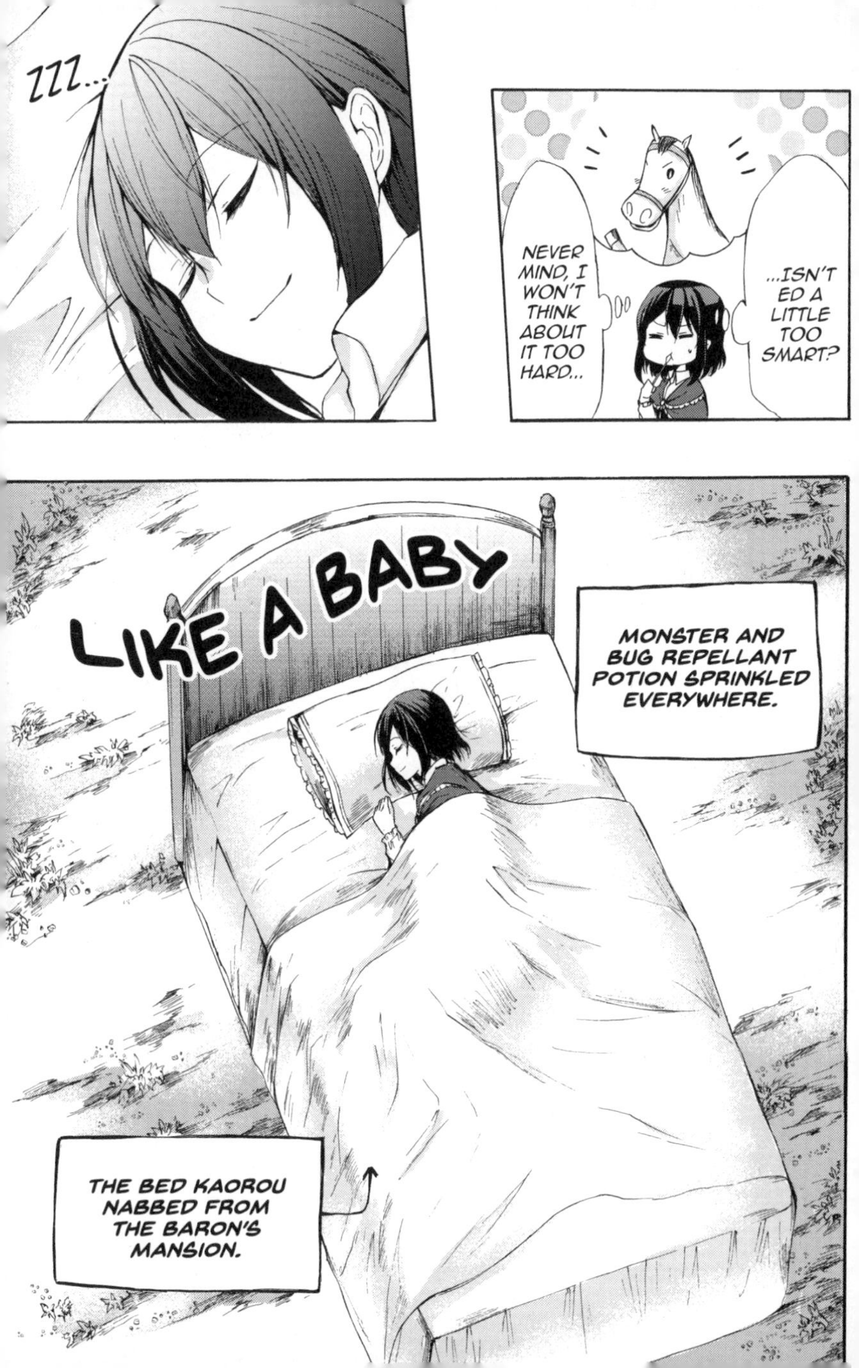
...ISN'T ED A LITTLE TOO SMART?
NEVER MIND, I WON'T THINK ABOUT IT TOO HARD...
ZZZ...
MONSTER AND BUG REPELLANT POTION SPRINKLED EVERYWHERE.
LIKE A BABY
THE BED KAOROU NABBED FROM THE BARON'S MANSION.

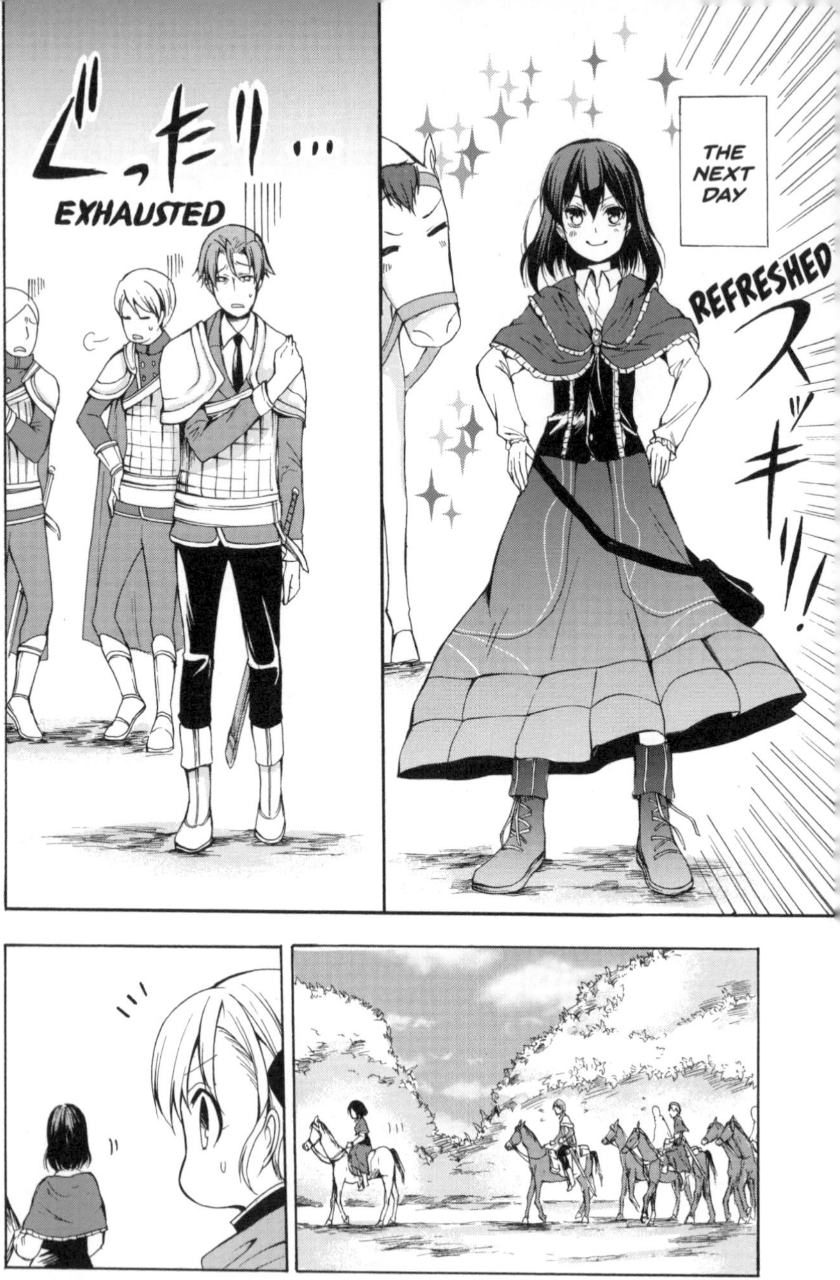
THE NEXT DAY
REFRESHED
スッキリ!!
ぐったり…
EXHAUSTED

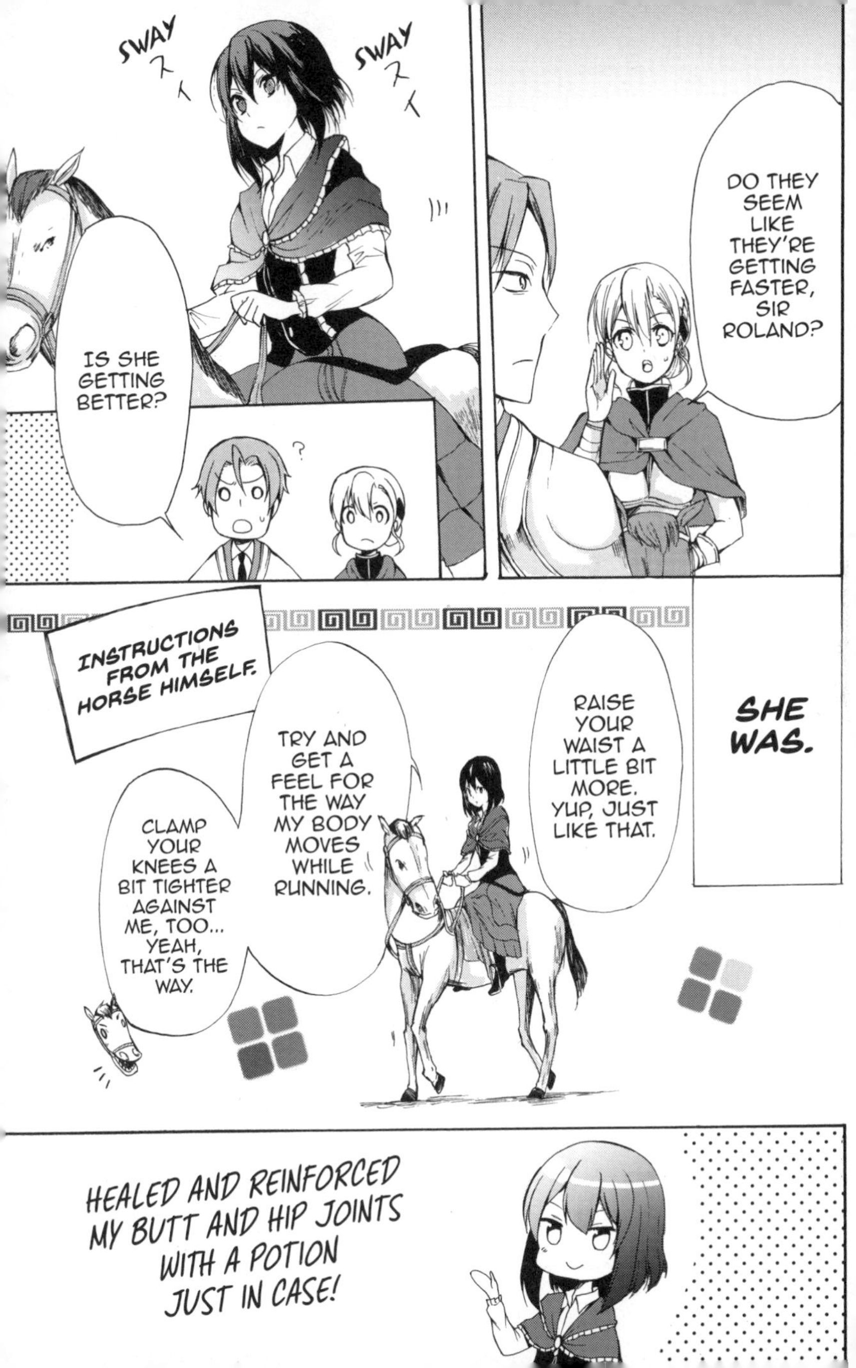
DO THEY SEEM LIKE THEY'RE GETTING FASTER, SIR ROLAND?
SWAY スイ
SWAY スイ
IS SHE GETTING BETTER?
SHE WAS.
RAISE YOUR WAIST A LITTLE BIT MORE. YUP, JUST LIKE THAT.
TRY AND GET A FEEL FOR THE WAY MY BODY MOVES WHILE RUNNING.
CLAMP YOUR KNEES A BIT TIGHTER AGAINST ME, TOO... YEAH, THAT'S THE WAY.
INSTRUCTIONS FROM THE HORSE HIMSELF.
HEALED AND REINFORCED MY BUTT AND HIP JOINTS WITH A POTION JUST IN CASE!

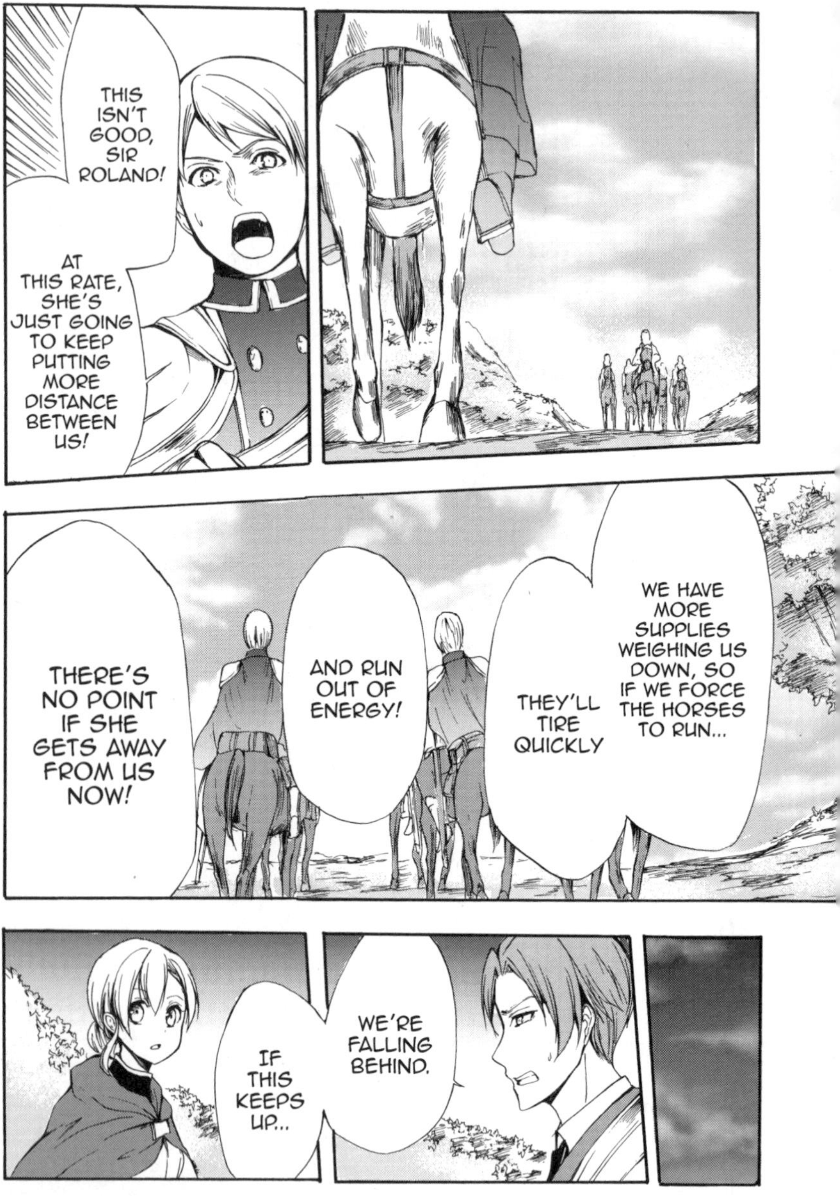
THIS ISN'T GOOD, SIR ROLAND!
AT THIS RATE, SHE'S JUST GOING TO KEEP PUTTING MORE DISTANCE BETWEEN US!
WE HAVE MORE SUPPLIES WEIGHING US DOWN, SO IF WE FORCE THE HORSES TO RUN...
THEY'LL TIRE QUICKLY
AND RUN OUT OF ENERGY!
THERE'S NO POINT IF SHE GETS AWAY FROM US NOW!
WE'RE FALLING BEHIND.
IF THIS KEEPS UP...

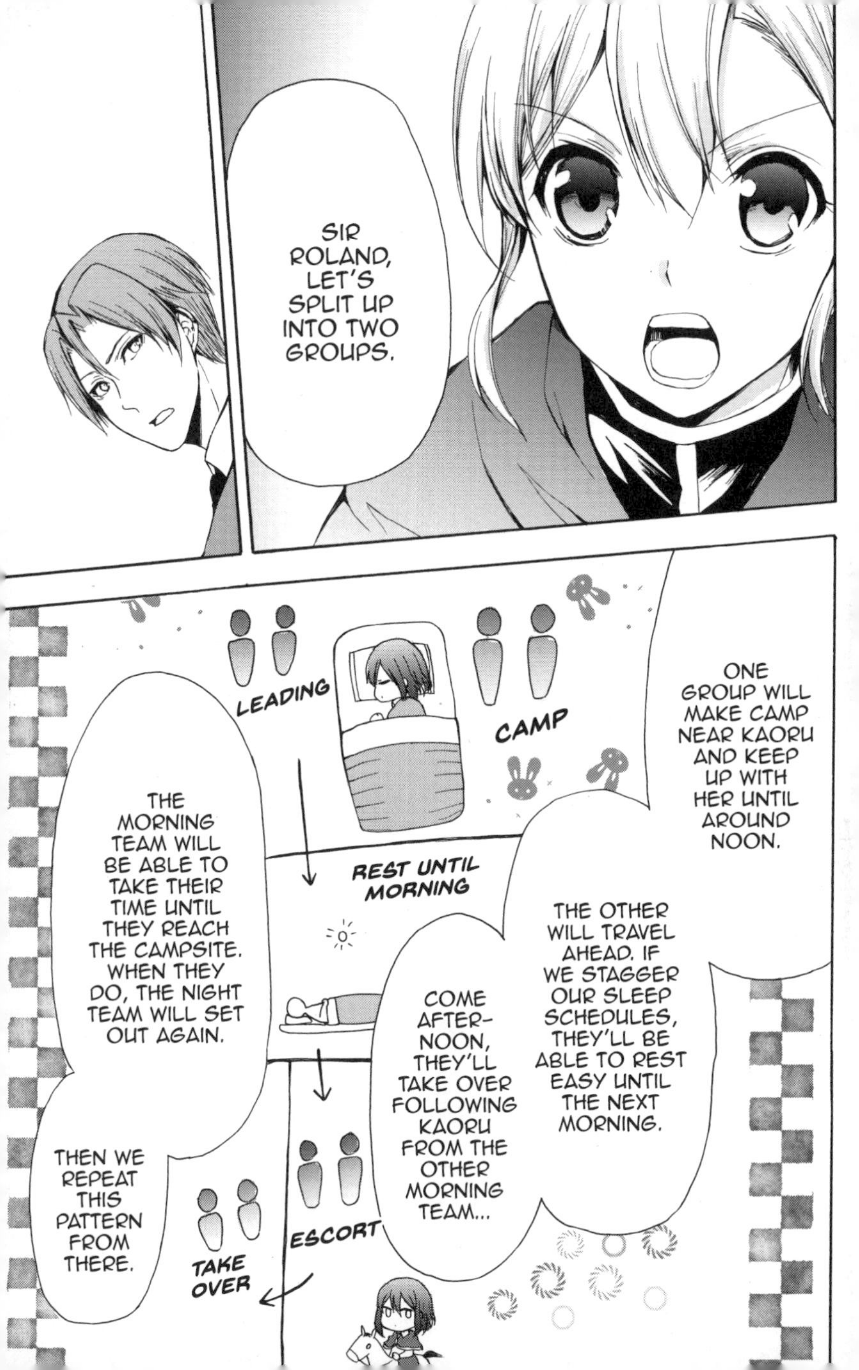
SIR ROLAND, LET'S SPLIT UP INTO TWO GROUPS.
ONE GROUP WILL MAKE CAMP NEAR KAORU AND KEEP UP WITH HER UNTIL AROUND NOON.
CAMP
LEADING
THE OTHER WILL TRAVEL AHEAD. IF WE STAGGER OUR SLEEP SCHEDULES, THEY'LL BE ABLE TO REST EASY UNTIL THE NEXT MORNING.
REST UNTIL MORNING
COME AFTER-NOON, THEY'LL TAKE OVER FOLLOWING KAORU FROM THE OTHER MORNING TEAM...
THE MORNING TEAM WILL BE ABLE TO TAKE THEIR TIME UNTIL THEY REACH THE CAMPSITE. WHEN THEY DO, THE NIGHT TEAM WILL SET OUT AGAIN.
ESCORT
TAKE OVER
THEN WE REPEAT THIS PATTERN FROM THERE.

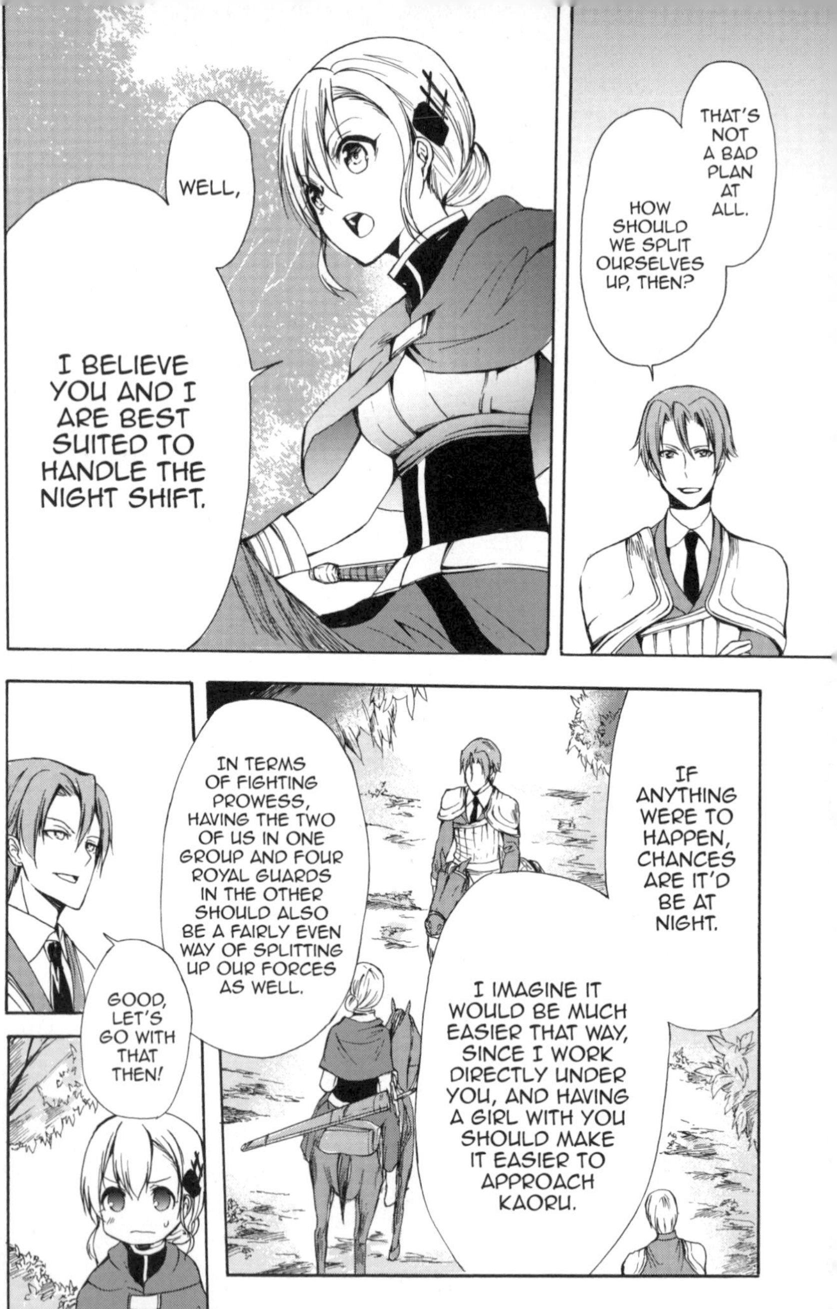
THAT'S NOT A BAD PLAN AT ALL.
HOW SHOULD WE SPLIT OURSELVES UP, THEN?
WELL,
I BELIEVE YOU AND I ARE BEST SUITED TO HANDLE THE NIGHT SHIFT.
IF ANYTHING WERE TO HAPPEN, CHANCES ARE IT'D BE AT NIGHT.
I IMAGINE IT WOULD BE MUCH EASIER THAT WAY, SINCE I WORK DIRECTLY UNDER YOU, AND HAVING A GIRL WITH YOU SHOULD MAKE IT EASIER TO APPROACH KAORU.
IN TERMS OF FIGHTING PROWESS, HAVING THE TWO OF US IN ONE GROUP AND FOUR ROYAL GUARDS IN THE OTHER SHOULD ALSO BE A FAIRLY EVEN WAY OF SPLITTING UP OUR FORCES AS WELL.
GOOD, LET'S GO WITH THAT THEN!

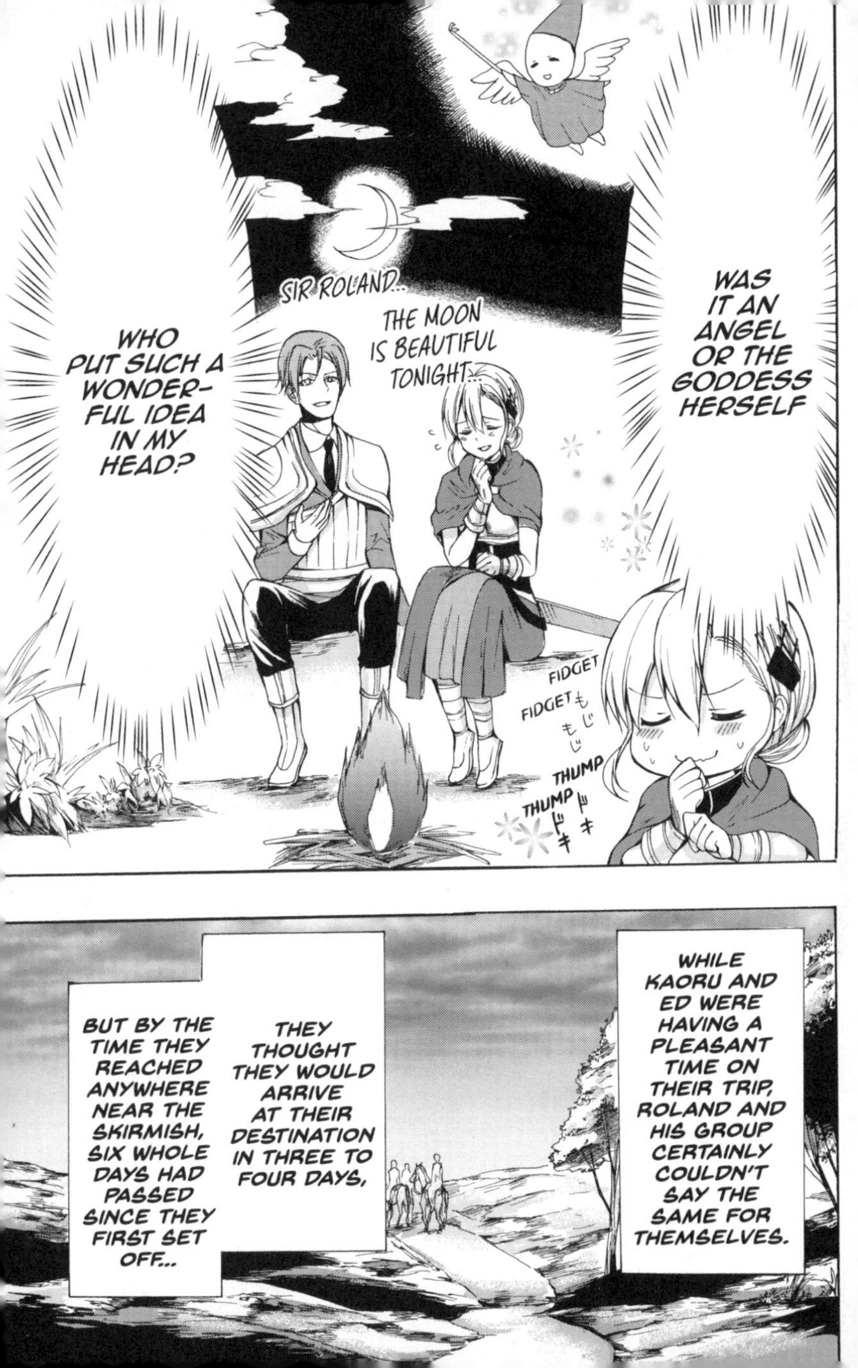
WAS IT AN ANGEL OR THE GODDESS HERSELF
WHO PUT SUCH A WONDER-FUL IDEA IN MY HEAD?
SIR ROLAND...
THE MOON IS BEAUTIFUL TONIGHT...
FIDGET FIDGET
もじもじ
THUMP THUMP
ドキドキ
WHILE KAORU AND ED WERE HAVING A PLEASANT TIME ON THEIR TRIP, ROLAND AND HIS GROUP CERTAINLY COULDN'T SAY THE SAME FOR THEMSELVES.
THEY THOUGHT THEY WOULD ARRIVE AT THEIR DESTINATION IN THREE TO FOUR DAYS,
BUT BY THE TIME THEY REACHED ANYWHERE NEAR THE SKIRMISH, SIX WHOLE DAYS HAD PASSED SINCE THEY FIRST SET OFF...

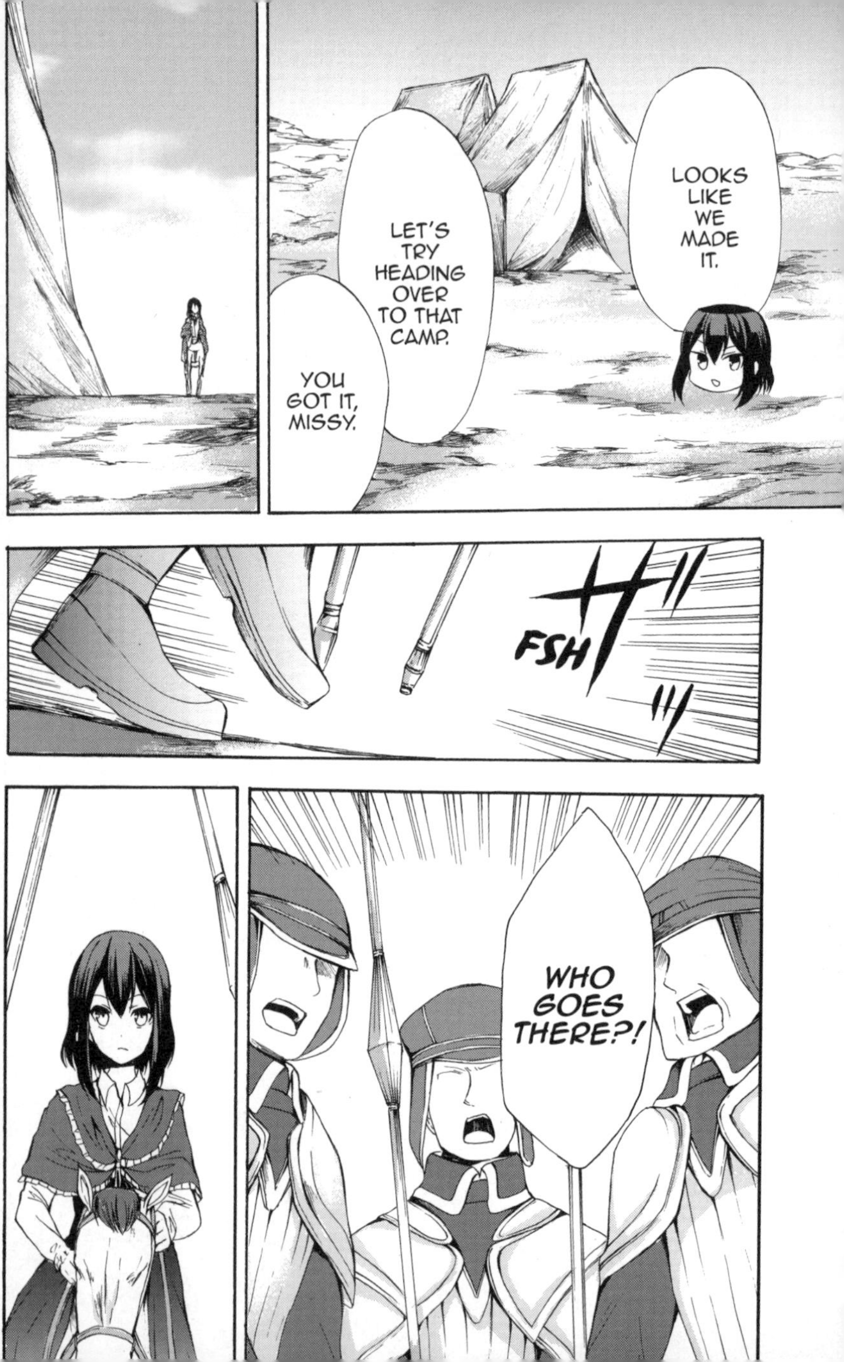
LOOKS LIKE WE MADE IT.
LET'S TRY HEADING OVER TO THAT CAMP.
YOU GOT IT, MISSY.
FSH
WHO GOES THERE?!

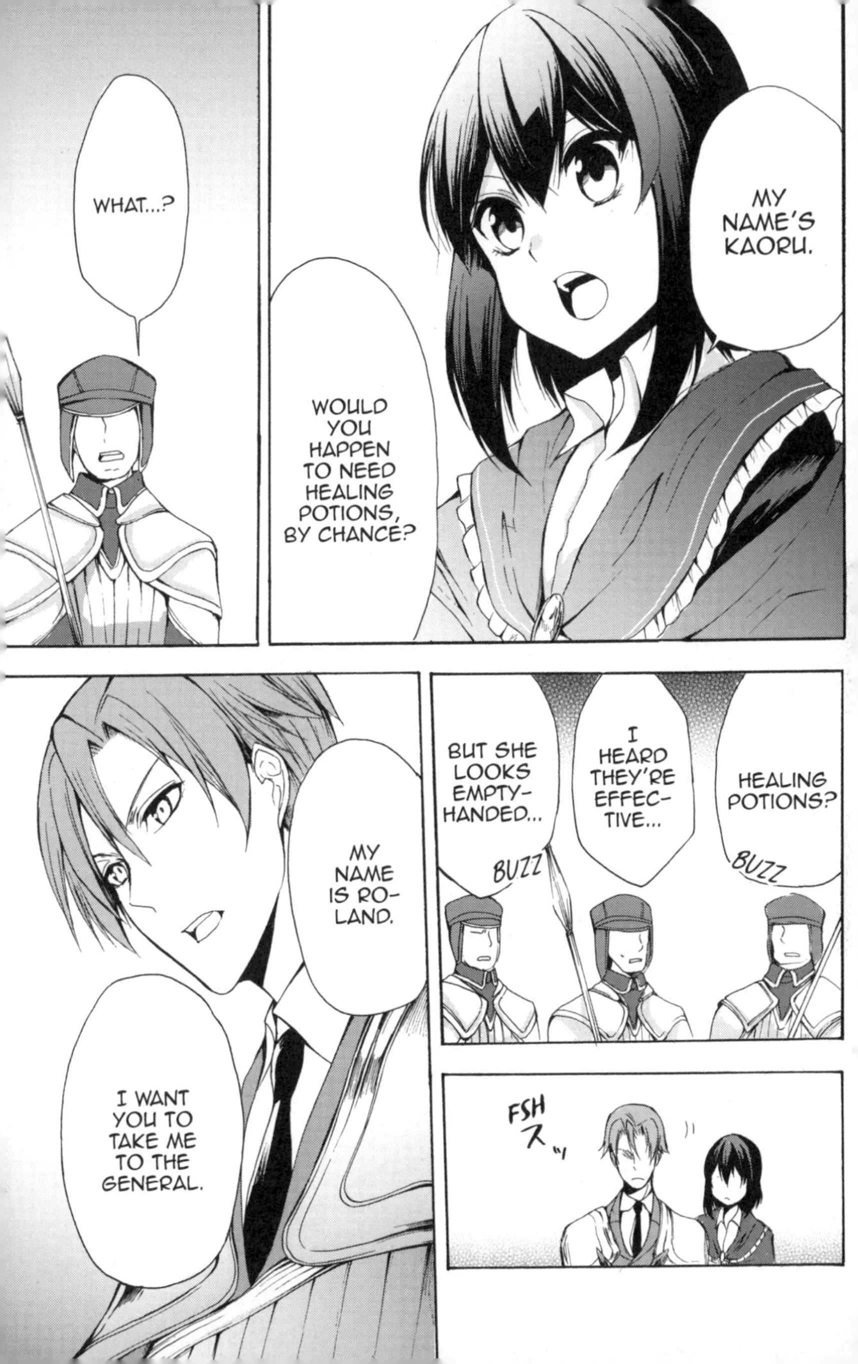
MY NAME'S KAORU.
WOULD YOU HAPPEN TO NEED HEALING POTIONS, BY CHANCE?
WHAT...?
HEALING POTIONS?
BUZZ
I HEARD THEY'RE EFFEC-TIVE...
BUT SHE LOOKS EMPTY-HANDED...
BUZZ
FSH
スッ
MY NAME IS RO-LAND.
I WANT YOU TO TAKE ME TO THE GENERAL.

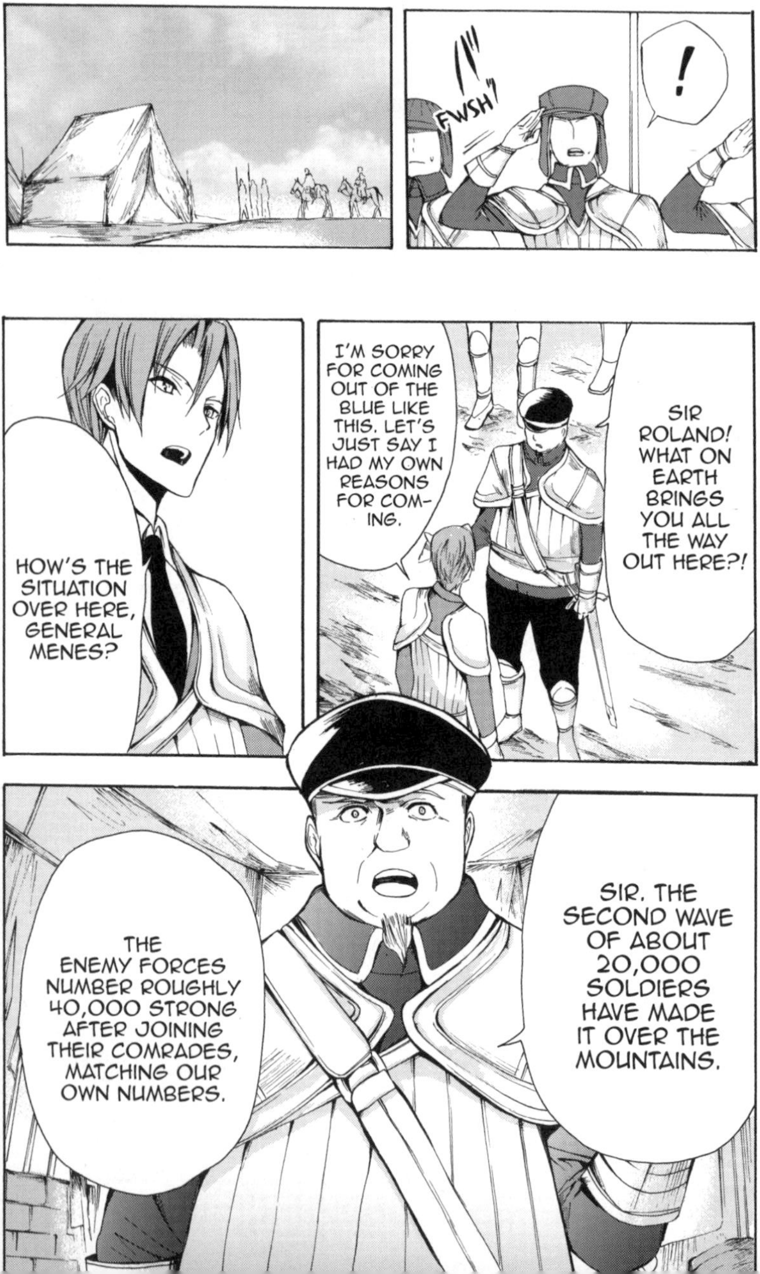
FWSH
!
SIR ROLAND! WHAT ON EARTH BRINGS YOU ALL THE WAY OUT HERE?!
I'M SORRY FOR COMING OUT OF THE BLUE LIKE THIS. LET'S JUST SAY I HAD MY OWN REASONS FOR COM-ING.
HOW'S THE SITUATION OVER HERE, GENERAL MENES?
SIR. THE SECOND WAVE OF ABOUT 20,000 SOLDIERS HAVE MADE IT OVER THE MOUNTAINS.
THE ENEMY FORCES NUMBER ROUGHLY 40,000 STRONG AFTER JOINING THEIR COMRADES, MATCHING OUR OWN NUMBERS.

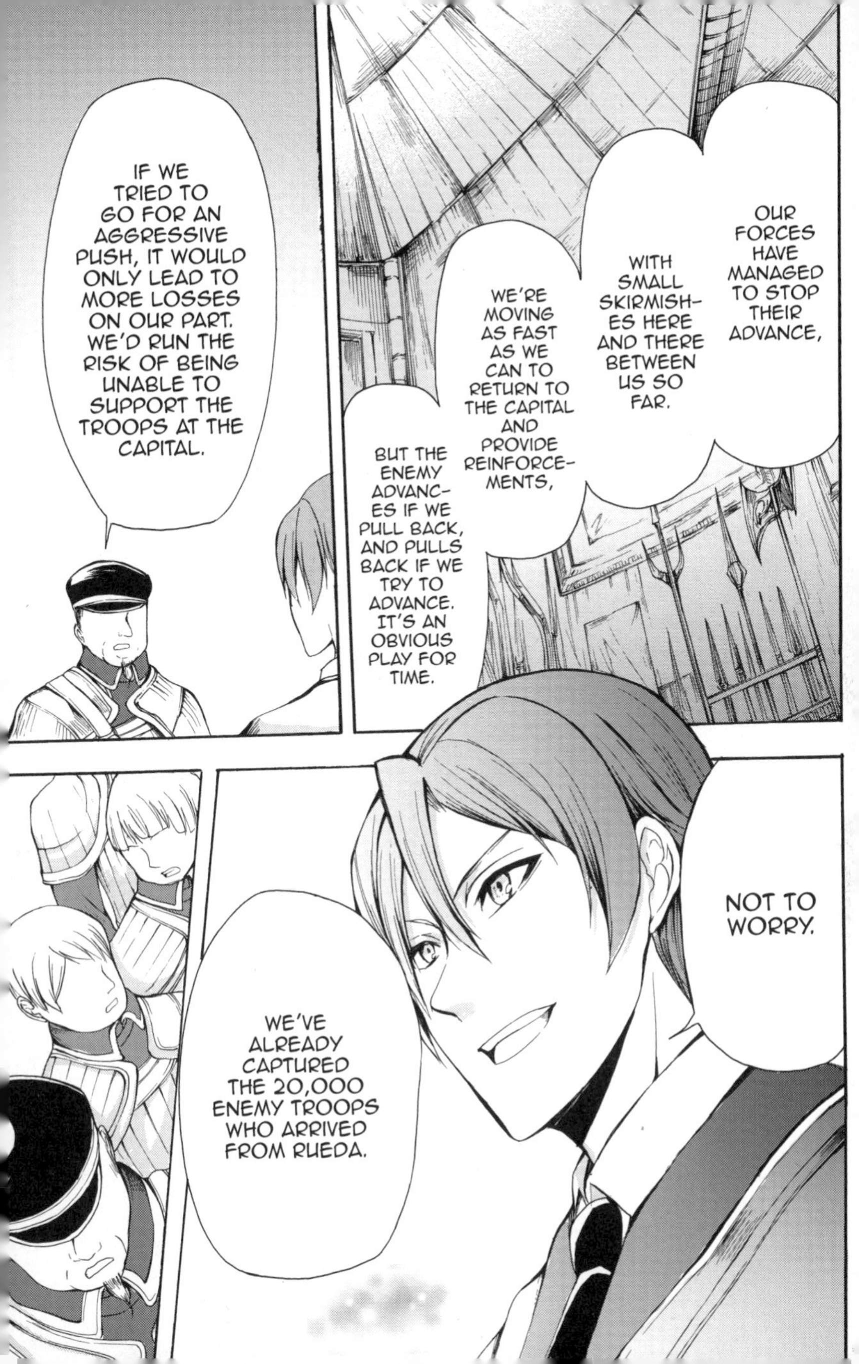
OUR FORCES HAVE MANAGED TO STOP THEIR ADVANCE,
WITH SMALL SKIRMISH-ES HERE AND THERE BETWEEN US SO FAR.
WE'RE MOVING AS FAST AS WE CAN TO RETURN TO THE CAPITAL AND PROVIDE REINFORCE-MENTS,
BUT THE ENEMY ADVANC-ES IF WE PULL BACK, AND PULLS BACK IF WE TRY TO ADVANCE. IT'S AN OBVIOUS PLAY FOR TIME.
IF WE TRIED TO GO FOR AN AGGRESSIVE PUSH, IT WOULD ONLY LEAD TO MORE LOSSES ON OUR PART. WE'D RUN THE RISK OF BEING UNABLE TO SUPPORT THE TROOPS AT THE CAPITAL.
NOT TO WORRY.
WE'VE ALREADY CAPTURED THE 20,000 ENEMY TROOPS WHO ARRIVED FROM RUEDA.

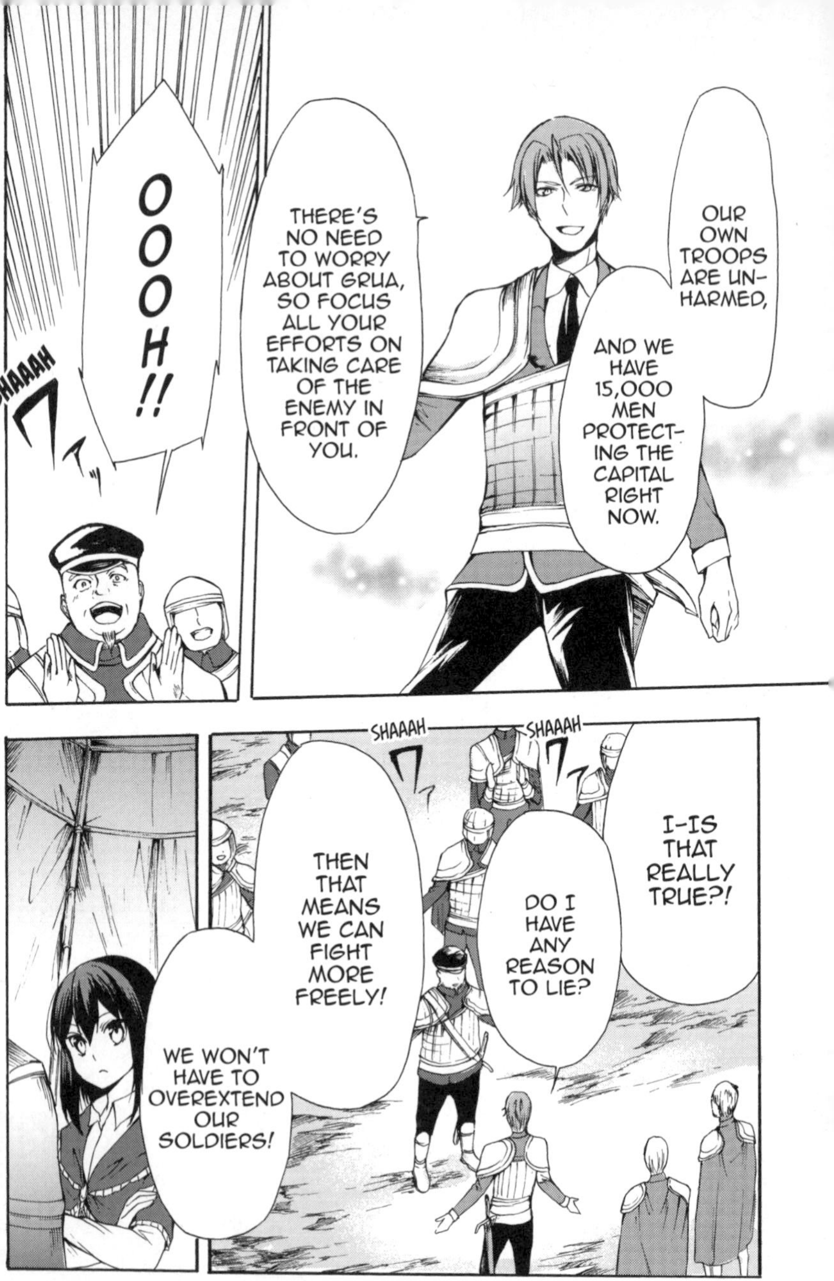
OUR OWN TROOPS ARE UN-HARMED,
AND WE HAVE 15,000 MEN PROTECTING THE CAPITAL RIGHT NOW.
THERE'S NO NEED TO WORRY ABOUT GRUA, SO FOCUS ALL YOUR EFFORTS ON TAKING CARE OF THE ENEMY IN FRONT OF YOU.
OOOH!!
SHAAAH
SHAAAH
SHAAAH
I-IS THAT REALLY TRUE?!
DO I HAVE ANY REASON TO LIE?
THEN THAT MEANS WE CAN FIGHT MORE FREELY!
WE WON'T HAVE TO OVEREXTEND OUR SOLDIERS!

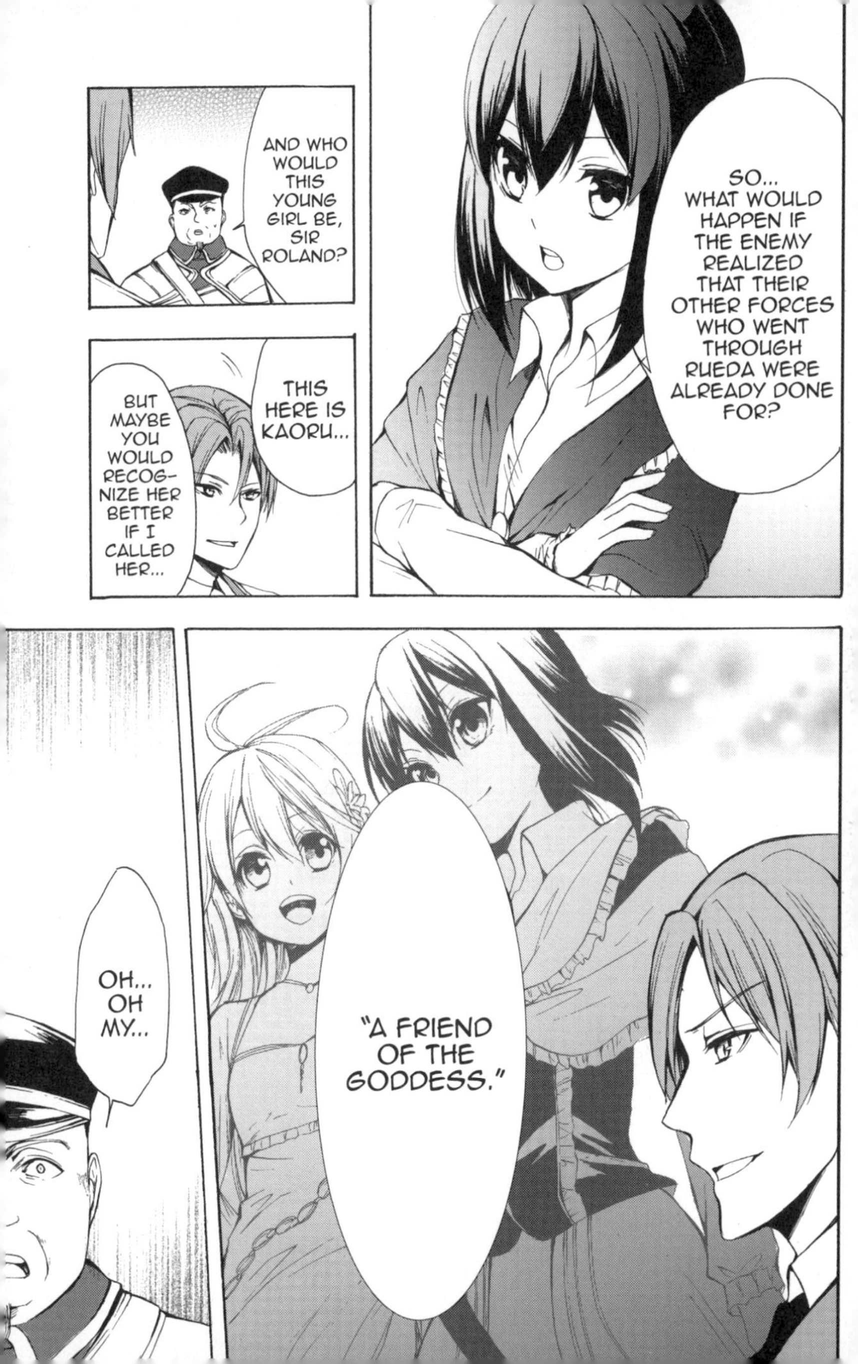
SO... WHAT WOULD HAPPEN IF THE ENEMY REALIZED THAT THEIR OTHER FORCES WHO WENT THROUGH RUEDA WERE ALREADY DONE FOR?
AND WHO WOULD THIS YOUNG GIRL BE, SIR ROLAND?
THIS HERE IS KAORU...
BUT MAYBE YOU WOULD RECOG-NIZE HER BETTER IF I CALLED HER...
"A FRIEND OF THE GODDESS."
OH... OH MY...

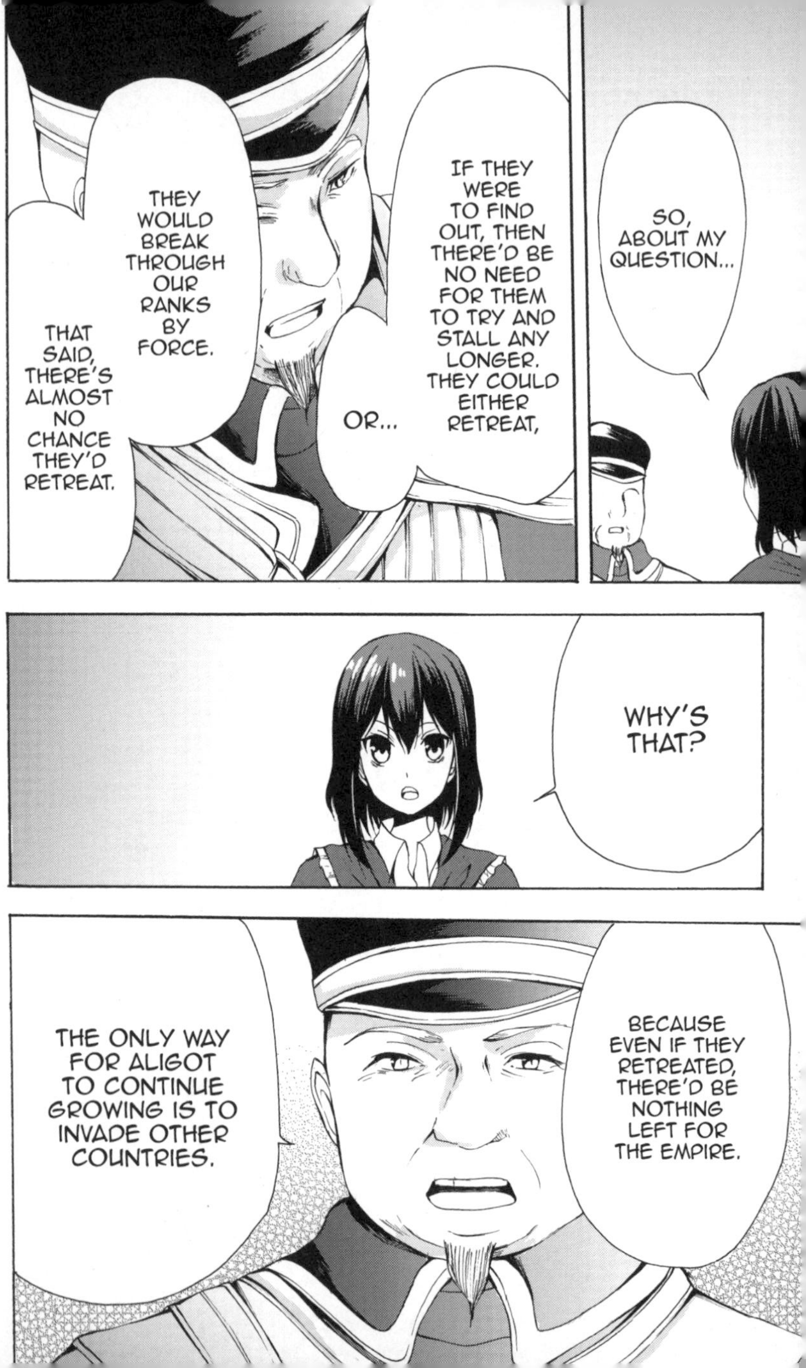
SO, ABOUT MY QUESTION...
IF THEY WERE TO FIND OUT, THEN THERE'D BE NO NEED FOR THEM TO TRY AND STALL ANY LONGER. THEY COULD EITHER RETREAT,
OR...
THEY WOULD BREAK THROUGH OUR RANKS BY FORCE.
THAT SAID, THERE'S ALMOST NO CHANCE THEY'D RETREAT.
WHY'S THAT?
BECAUSE EVEN IF THEY RETREATED, THERE'D BE NOTHING LEFT FOR THE EMPIRE.
THE ONLY WAY FOR ALIGOT TO CONTINUE GROWING IS TO INVADE OTHER COUNTRIES.

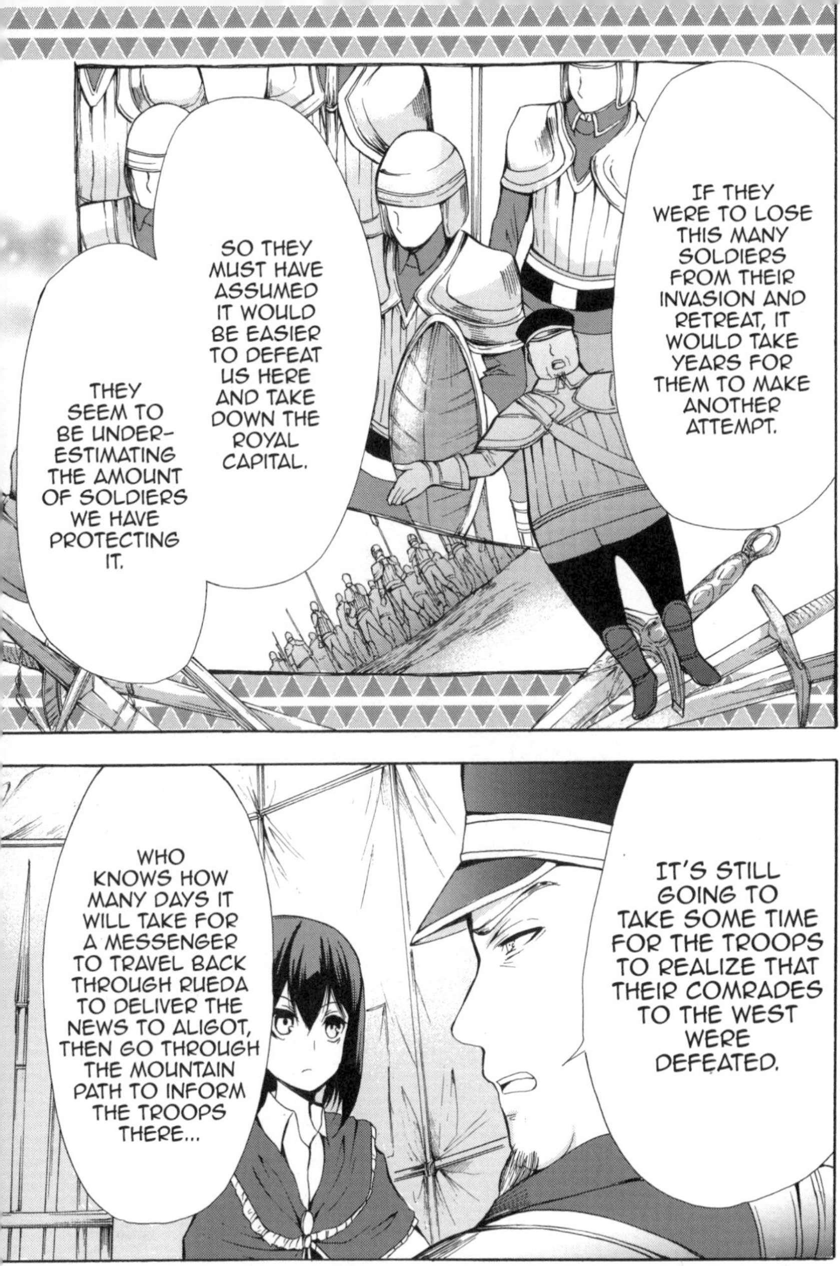
IF THEY WERE TO LOSE THIS MANY SOLDIERS FROM THEIR INVASION AND RETREAT, IT WOULD TAKE YEARS FOR THEM TO MAKE ANOTHER ATTEMPT.
SO THEY MUST HAVE ASSUMED IT WOULD BE EASIER TO DEFEAT US HERE AND TAKE DOWN THE ROYAL CAPITAL.
THEY SEEM TO BE UNDER-ESTIMATING THE AMOUNT OF SOLDIERS WE HAVE PROTECTING IT.
IT'S STILL GOING TO TAKE SOME TIME FOR THE TROOPS TO REALIZE THAT THEIR COMRADES TO THE WEST WERE DEFEATED.
WHO KNOWS HOW MANY DAYS IT WILL TAKE FOR A MESSENGER TO TRAVEL BACK THROUGH RUEDA TO DELIVER THE NEWS TO ALIGOT, THEN GO THROUGH THE MOUNTAIN PATH TO INFORM THE TROOPS THERE...

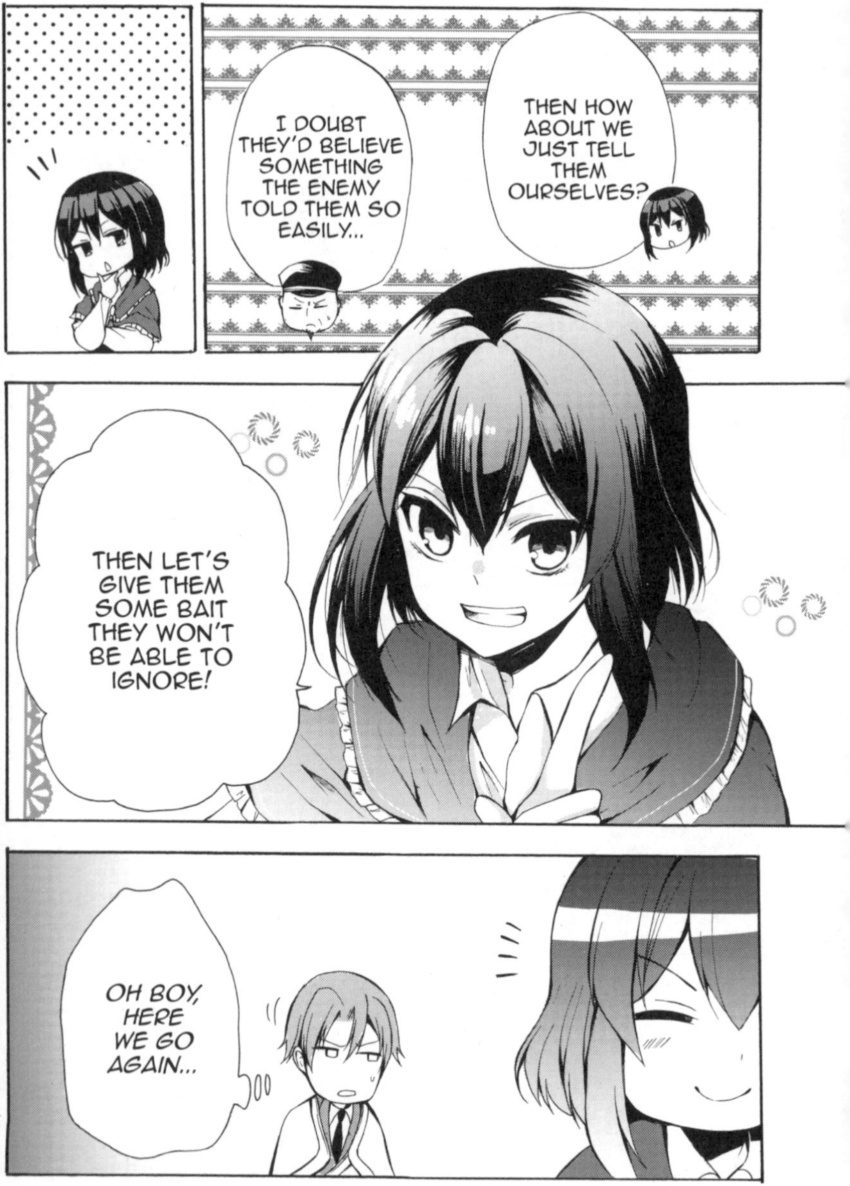
THEN HOW ABOUT WE JUST TELL THEM OURSELVES?
I DOUBT THEY'D BELIEVE SOMETHING THE ENEMY TOLD THEM SO EASILY...
THEN LET'S GIVE THEM SOME BAIT THEY WON'T BE ABLE TO IGNORE!
OH BOY, HERE WE GO AGAIN...

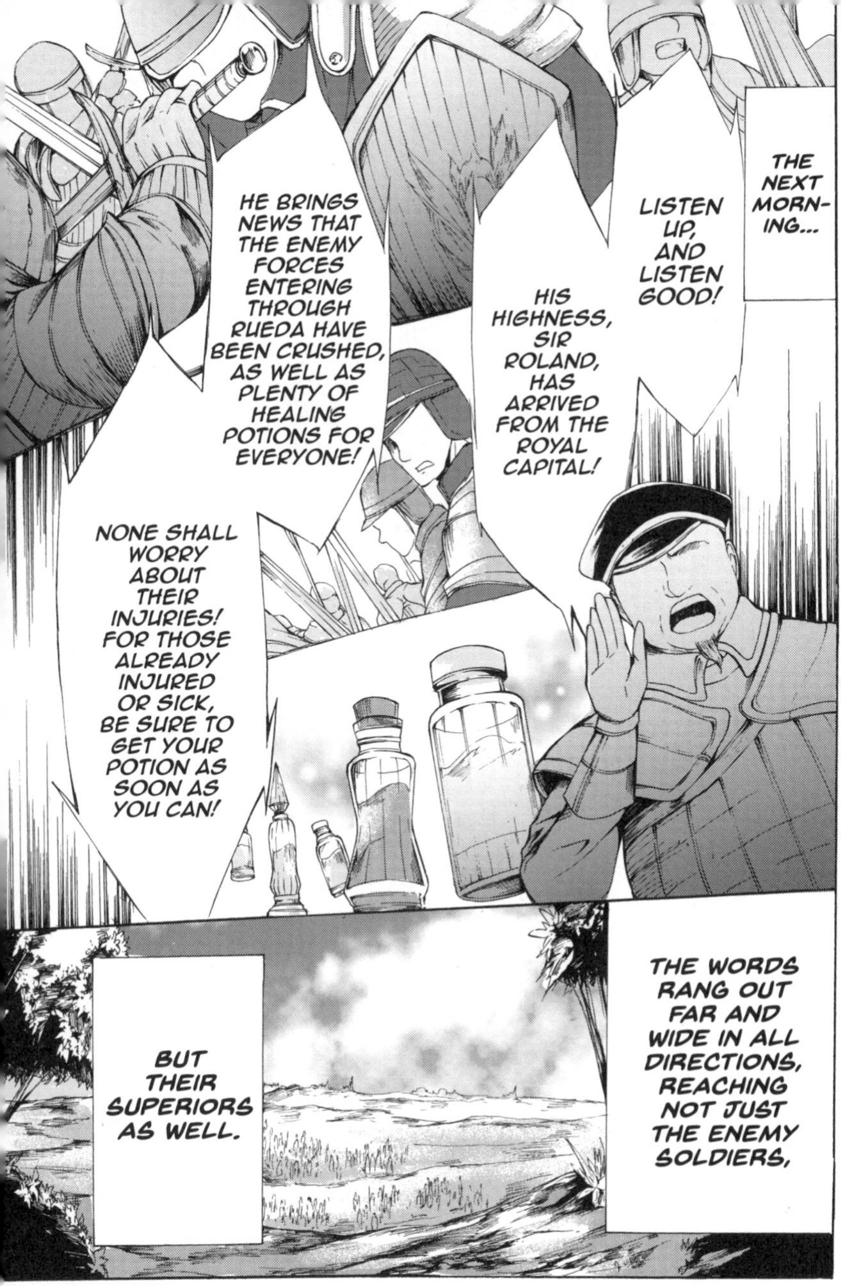
THE NEXT MORNING...
LISTEN UP, AND LISTEN GOOD!
HIS HIGHNESS, SIR ROLAND, HAS ARRIVED FROM THE ROYAL CAPITAL!
HE BRINGS NEWS THAT THE ENEMY FORCES ENTERING THROUGH RUEDA HAVE BEEN CRUSHED, AS WELL AS PLENTY OF HEALING POTIONS FOR EVERYONE!
NONE SHALL WORRY ABOUT THEIR INJURIES! FOR THOSE ALREADY INJURED OR SICK, BE SURE TO GET YOUR POTION AS SOON AS YOU CAN!
THE WORDS RANG OUT FAR AND WIDE IN ALL DIRECTIONS, REACHING NOT JUST THE ENEMY SOLDIERS,
BUT THEIR SUPERIORS AS WELL.

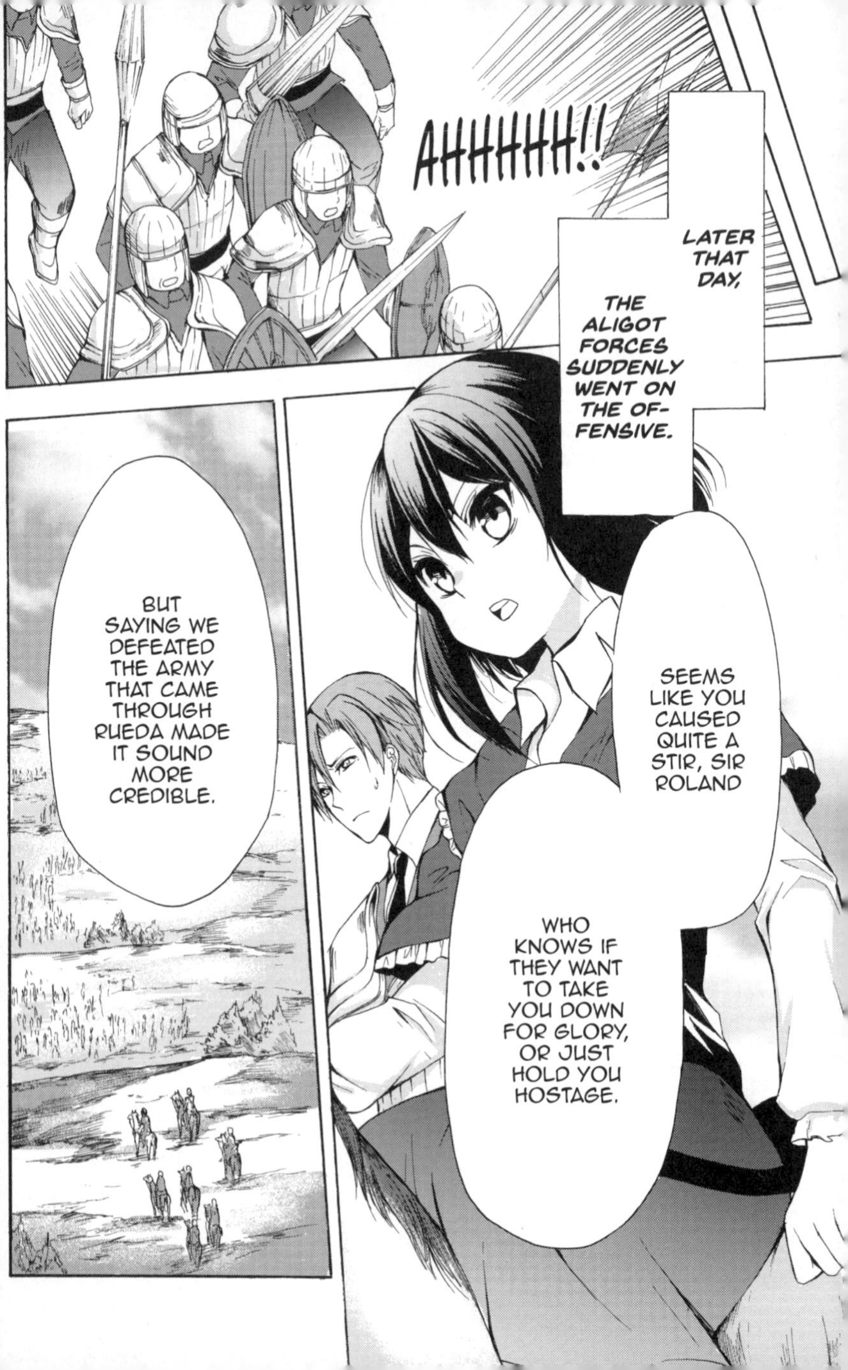
AHHHHH!!
LATER THAT DAY,
THE ALIGOT FORCES SUDDENLY WENT ON THE OFFENSIVE.
SEEMS LIKE YOU CAUSED QUITE A STIR, SIR ROLAND
WHO KNOWS IF THEY WANT TO TAKE YOU DOWN FOR GLORY, OR JUST HOLD YOU HOSTAGE.
BUT SAYING WE DEFEATED THE ARMY THAT CAME THROUGH RUEDA MADE IT SOUND MORE CREDIBLE.

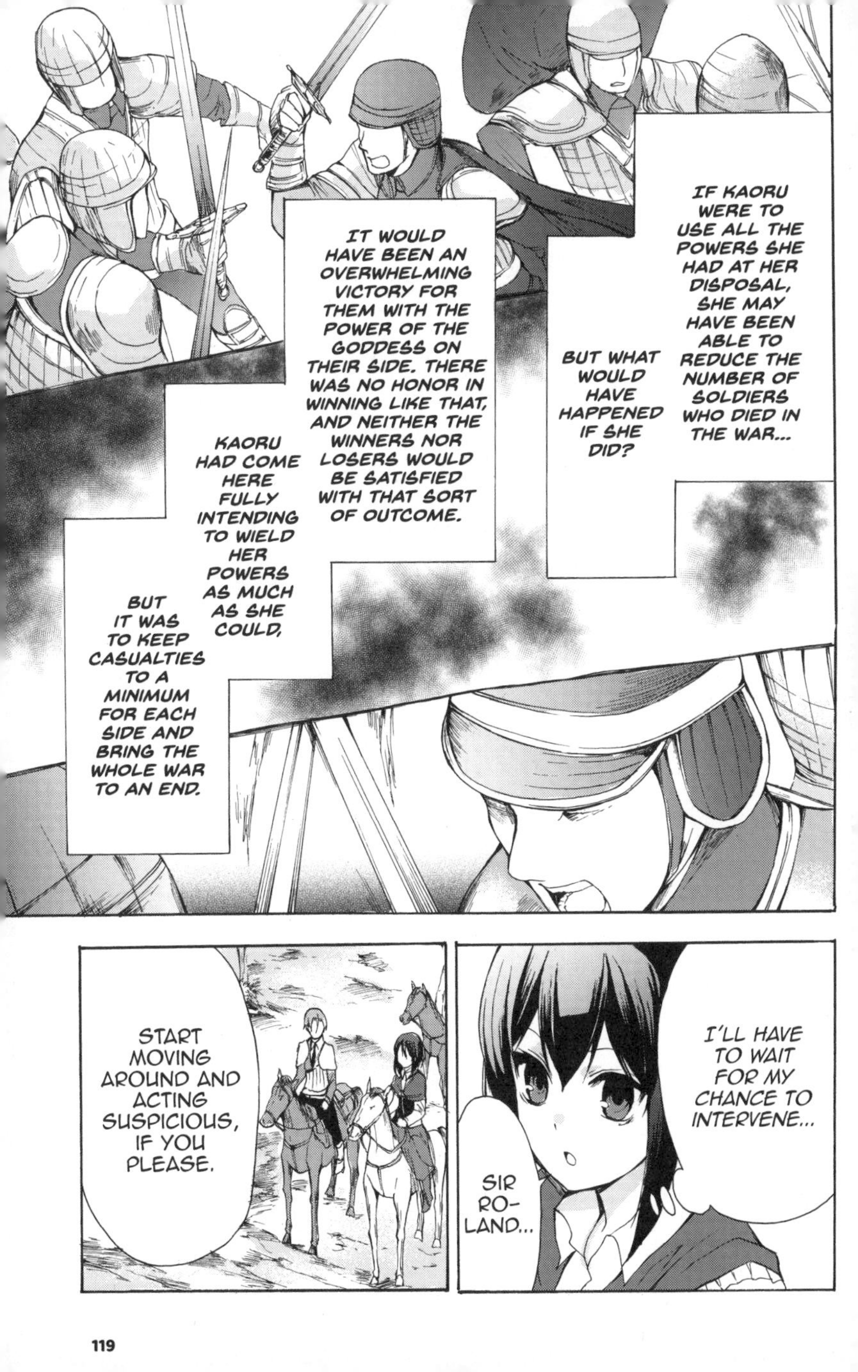
IF KAORU WERE TO USE ALL THE POWERS SHE HAD AT HER DISPOSAL, SHE MAY HAVE BEEN ABLE TO REDUCE THE NUMBER OF SOLDIERS WHO DIED IN THE WAR...
BUT WHAT WOULD HAVE HAPPENED IF SHE DID?
IT WOULD HAVE BEEN AN OVERWHELMING VICTORY FOR THEM WITH THE POWER OF THE GODDESS ON THEIR SIDE. THERE WAS NO HONOR IN WINNING LIKE THAT, AND NEITHER THE WINNERS NOR LOSERS WOULD BE SATISFIED WITH THAT SORT OF OUTCOME.
KAORU HAD COME HERE FULLY INTENDING TO WIELD HER POWERS AS MUCH AS SHE COULD,
BUT IT WAS TO KEEP CASUALTIES TO A MINIMUM FOR EACH SIDE AND BRING THE WHOLE WAR TO AN END.
I'LL HAVE TO WAIT FOR MY CHANCE TO INTERVENE...
SIR RO-LAND...
START MOVING AROUND AND ACTING SUSPICIOUS, IF YOU PLEASE.

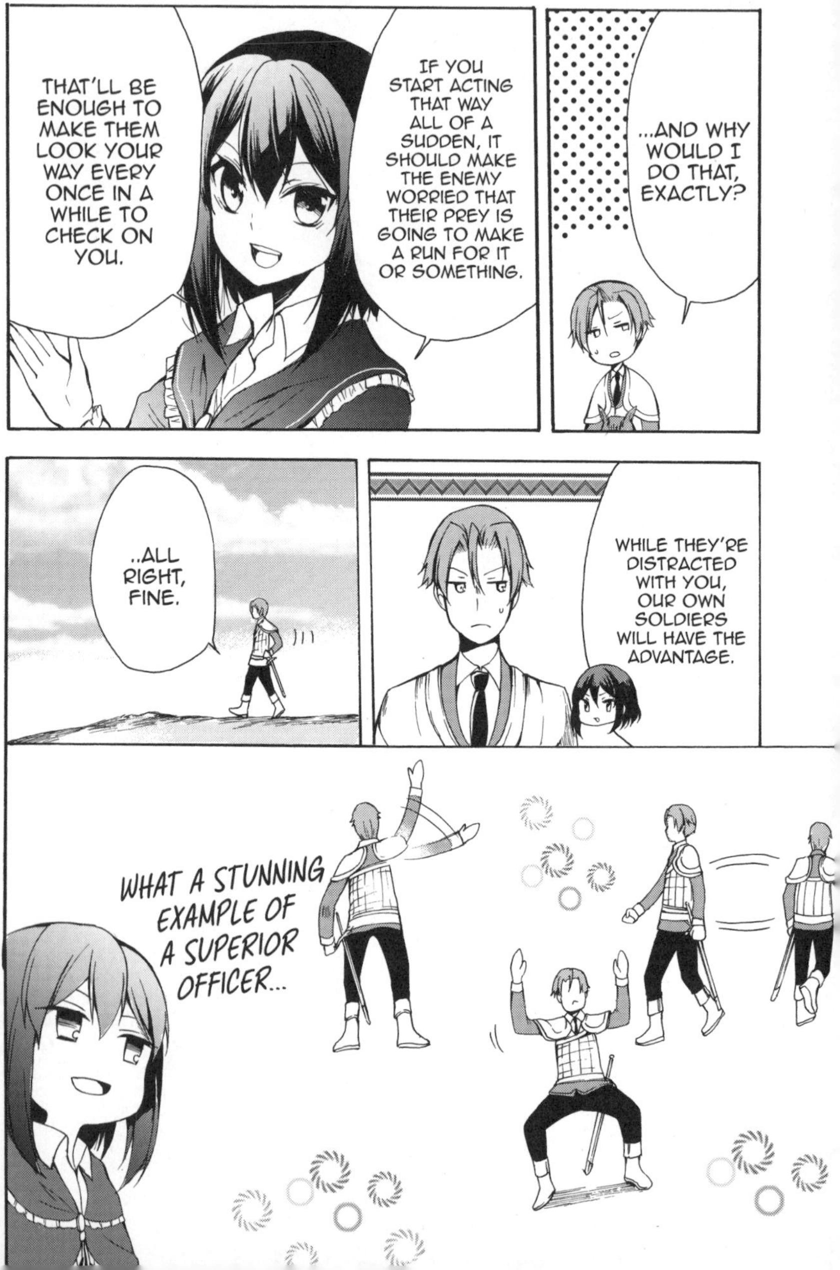
...AND WHY WOULD I DO THAT, EXACTLY?
IF YOU START ACTING THAT WAY ALL OF A SUDDEN, IT SHOULD MAKE THE ENEMY WORRIED THAT THEIR PREY IS GOING TO MAKE A RUN FOR IT OR SOMETHING.
THAT'LL BE ENOUGH TO MAKE THEM LOOK YOUR WAY EVERY ONCE IN A WHILE TO CHECK ON YOU.
WHILE THEY'RE DISTRACTED WITH YOU, OUR OWN SOLDIERS WILL HAVE THE ADVANTAGE.
..ALL RIGHT, FINE.
WHAT A STUNNING EXAMPLE OF A SUPERIOR OFFICER...

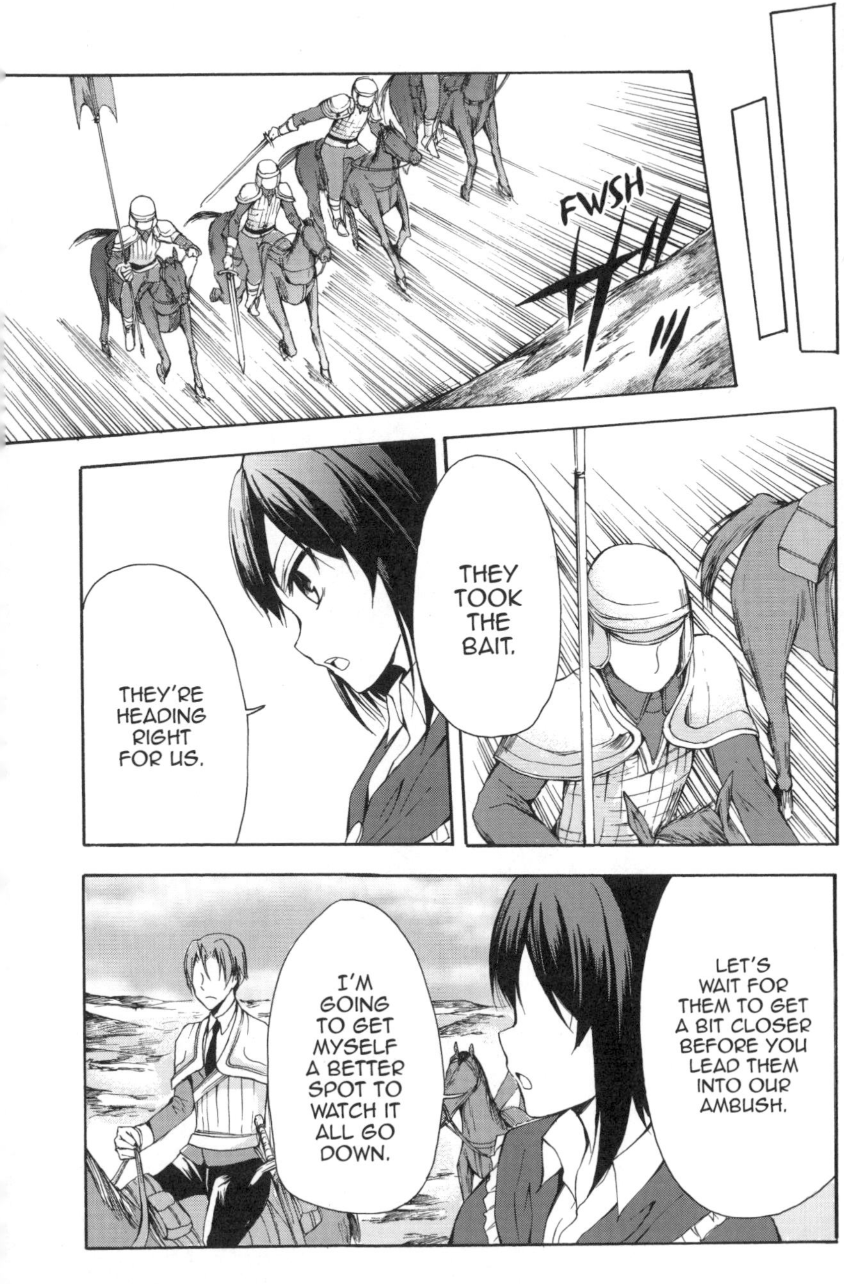
FWSH
THEY TOOK THE BAIT.
THEY'RE HEADING RIGHT FOR US.
LET'S WAIT FOR THEM TO GET A BIT CLOSER BEFORE YOU LEAD THEM INTO OUR AMBUSH.
I'M GOING TO GET MYSELF A BETTER SPOT TO WATCH IT ALL GO DOWN.

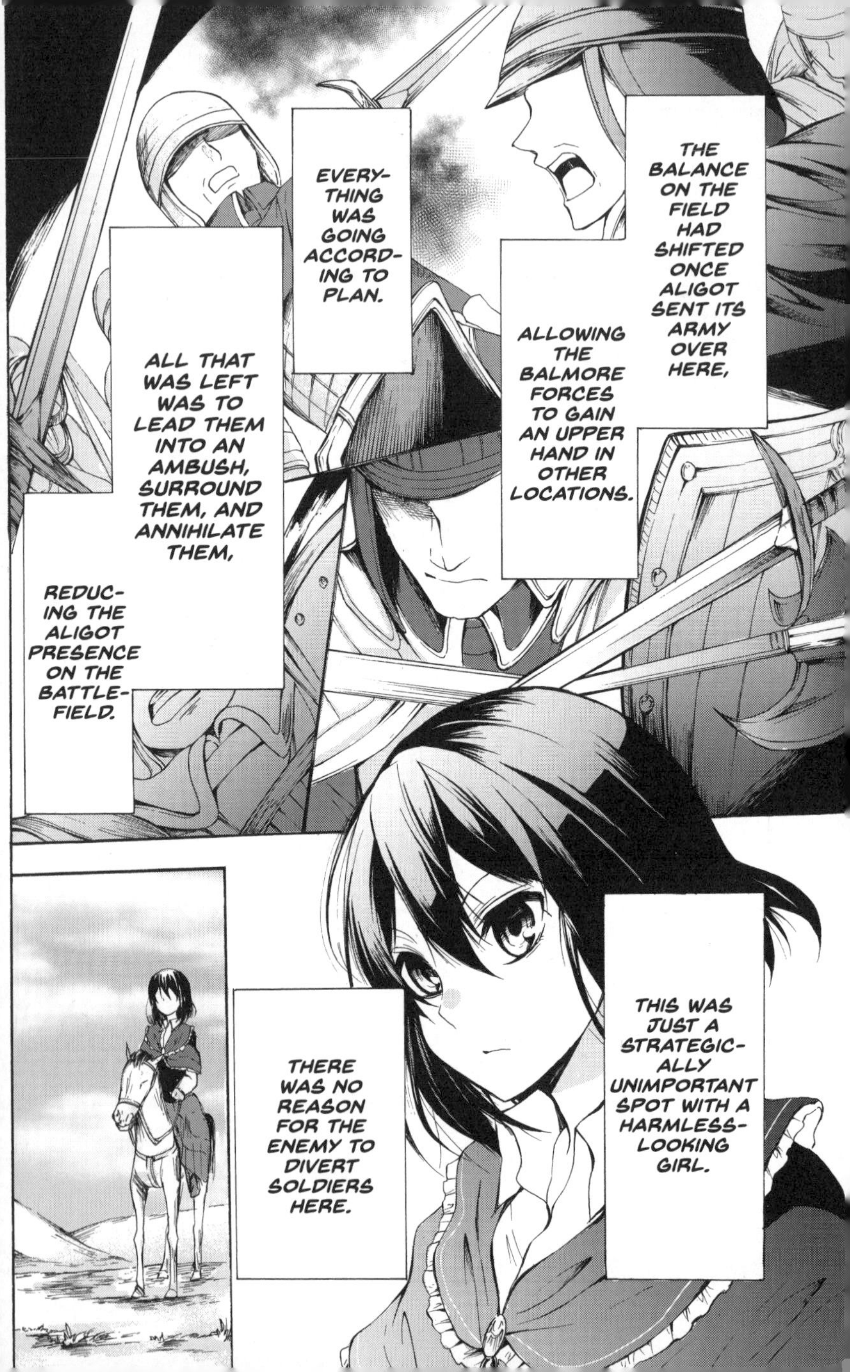
THE BALANCE ON THE FIELD HAD SHIFTED ONCE ALIGOT SENT ITS ARMY OVER HERE,
ALLOWING THE BALMORE FORCES TO GAIN AN UPPER HAND IN OTHER LOCATIONS.
EVERY-THING WAS GOING ACCORD-ING TO PLAN.
ALL THAT WAS LEFT WAS TO LEAD THEM INTO AN AMBUSH, SURROUND THEM, AND ANNIHILATE THEM,
REDUC-ING THE ALIGOT PRESENCE ON THE BATTLE-FIELD.
THIS WAS JUST A STRATEGIC-ALLY UNIMPORTANT SPOT WITH A HARMLESS-LOOKING GIRL.
THERE WAS NO REASON FOR THE ENEMY TO DIVERT SOLDIERS HERE.

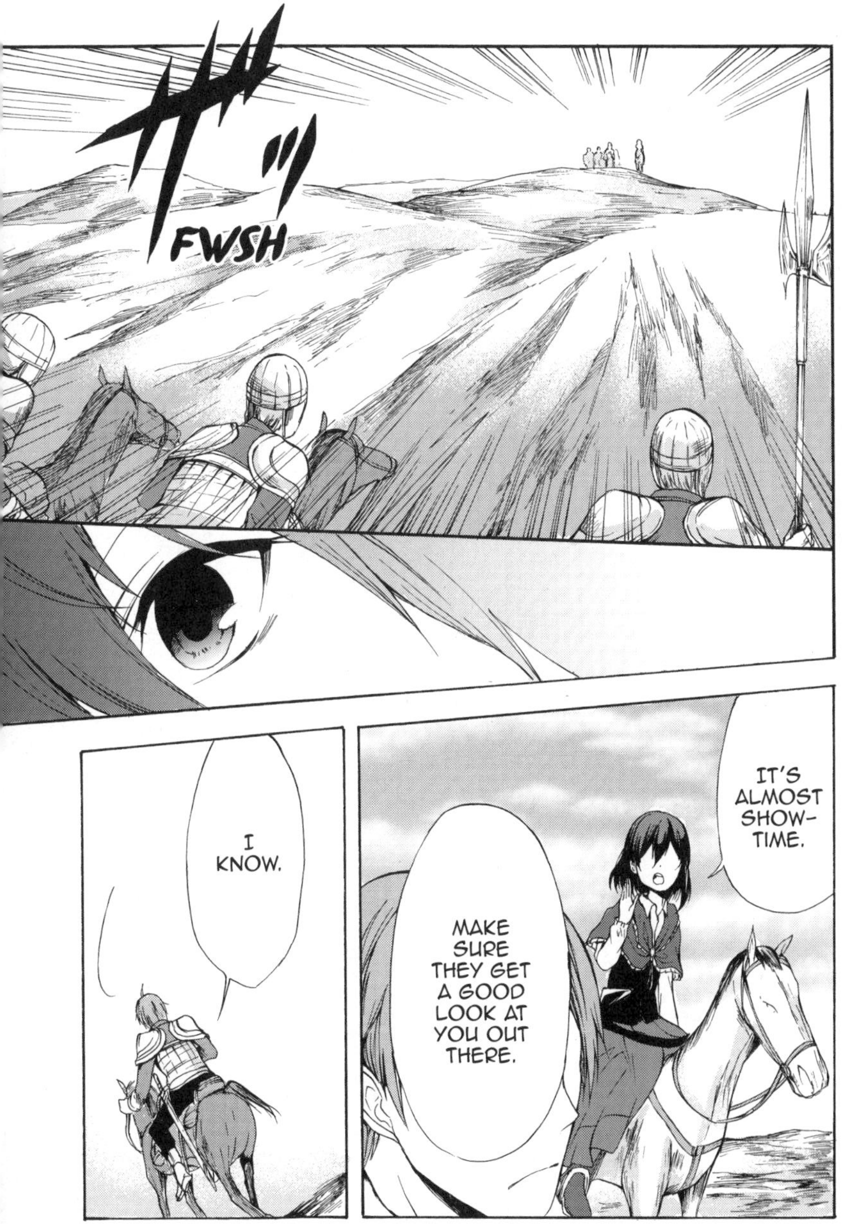
FWSH
IT'S ALMOST SHOW-TIME.
MAKE SURE THEY GET A GOOD LOOK AT YOU OUT THERE.
I KNOW.

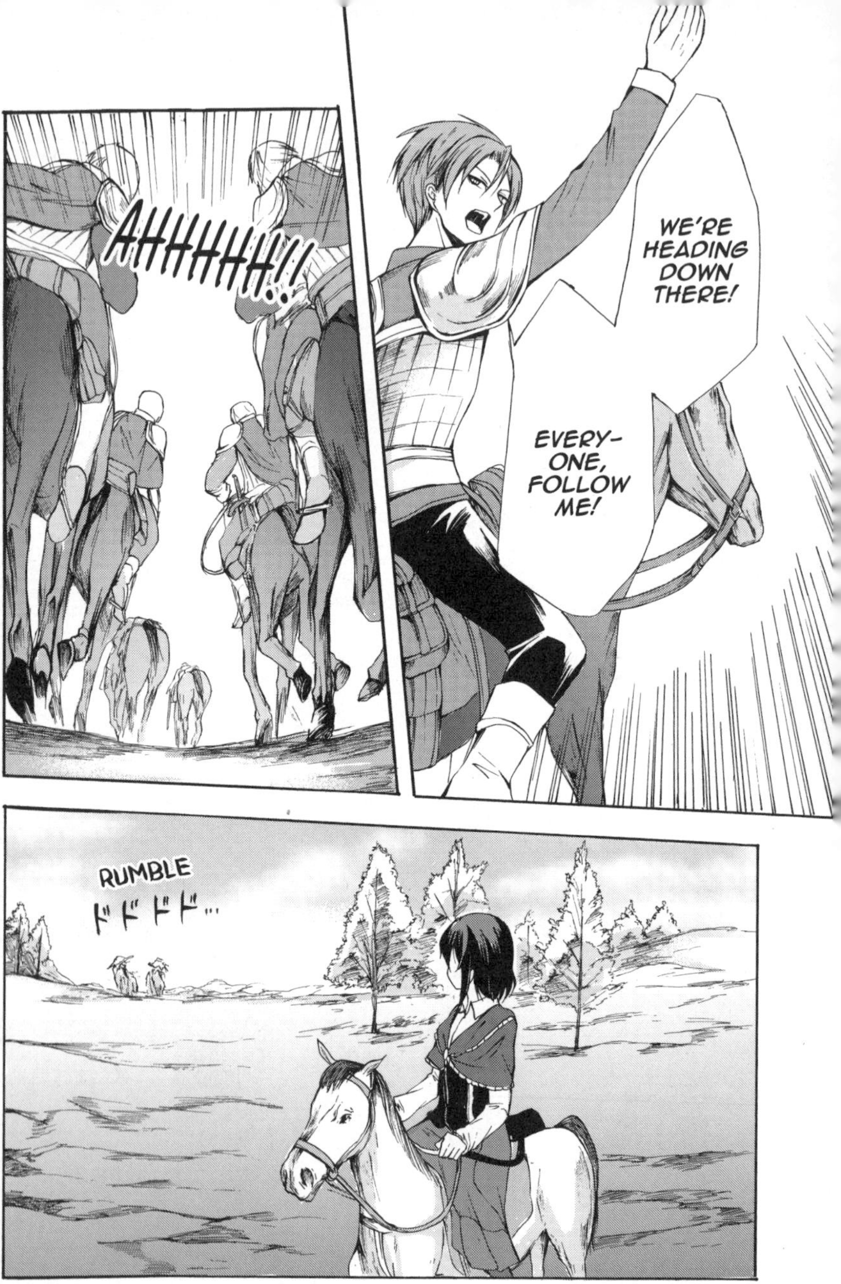
WE'RE HEADING DOWN THERE!
EVERY-ONE, FOLLOW ME!
AHHHHHH!!
RUMBLE
ドドドド…

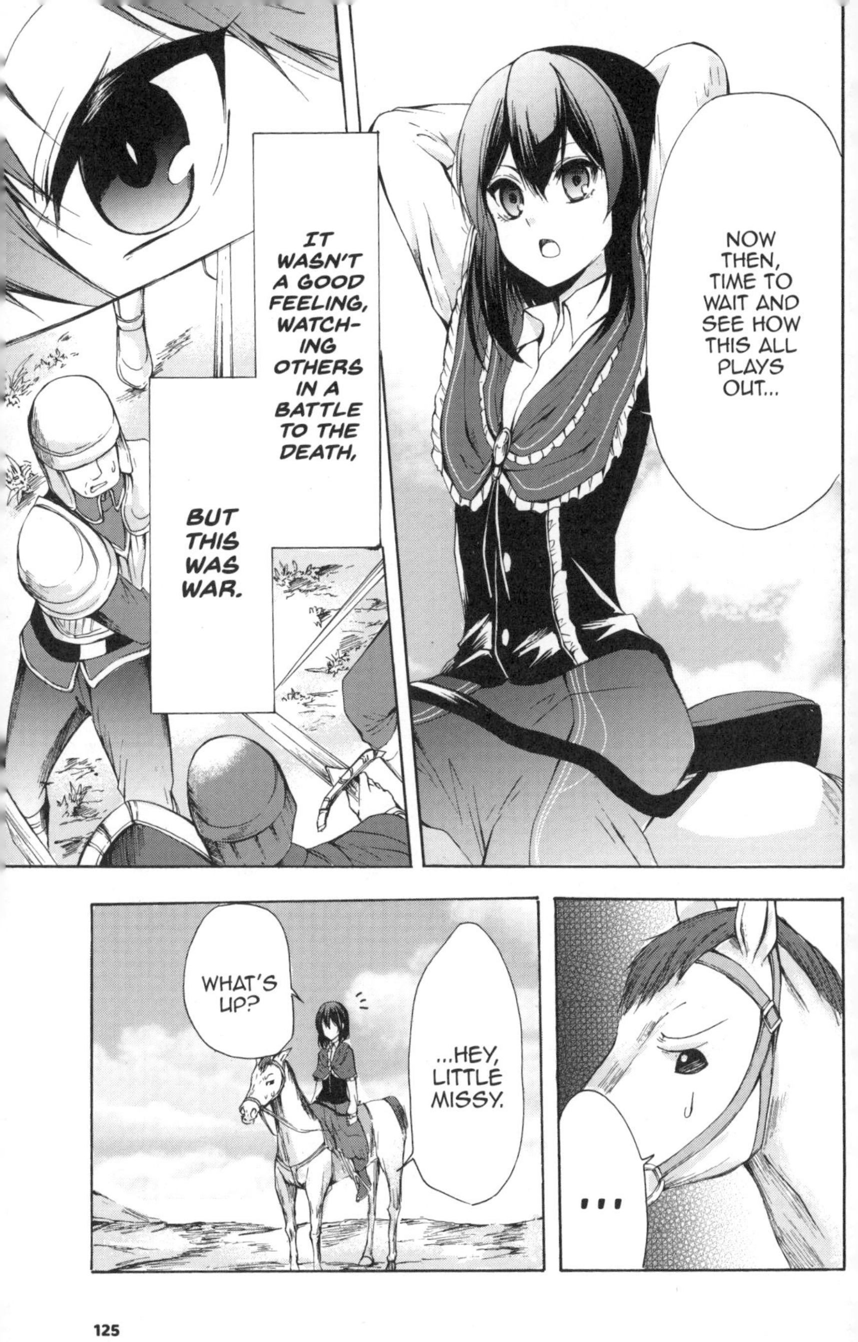
NOW THEN, TIME TO WAIT AND SEE HOW THIS ALL PLAYS OUT...
IT WASN'T A GOOD FEELING, WATCHING OTHERS IN A BATTLE TO THE DEATH,
BUT THIS WAS WAR.
...
...HEY, LITTLE MISSY.
WHAT'S UP?

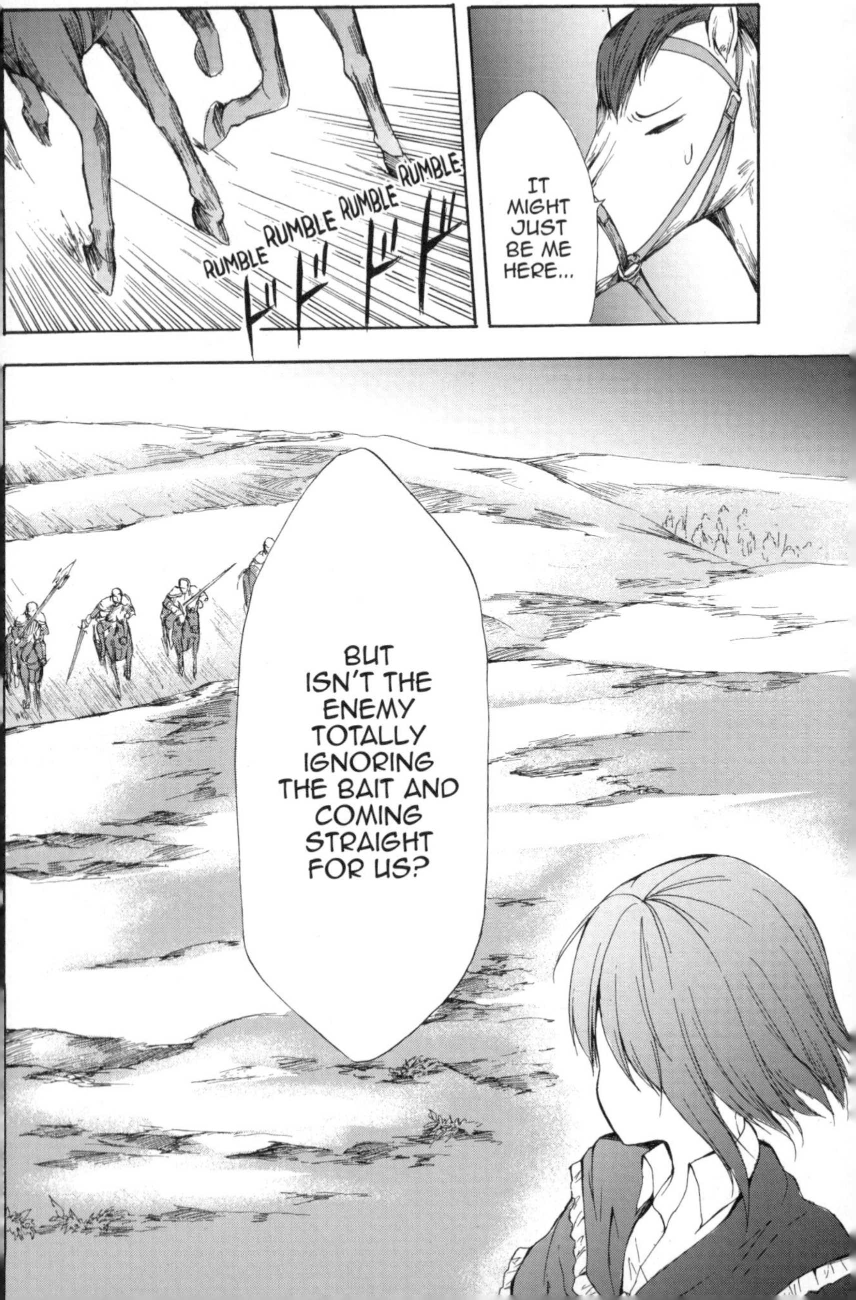
IT MIGHT JUST BE ME HERE...
RUMBLE RUMBLE RUMBLE RUMBLE
ドドドド
BUT ISN'T THE ENEMY TOTALLY IGNORING THE BAIT AND COMING STRAIGHT FOR US?

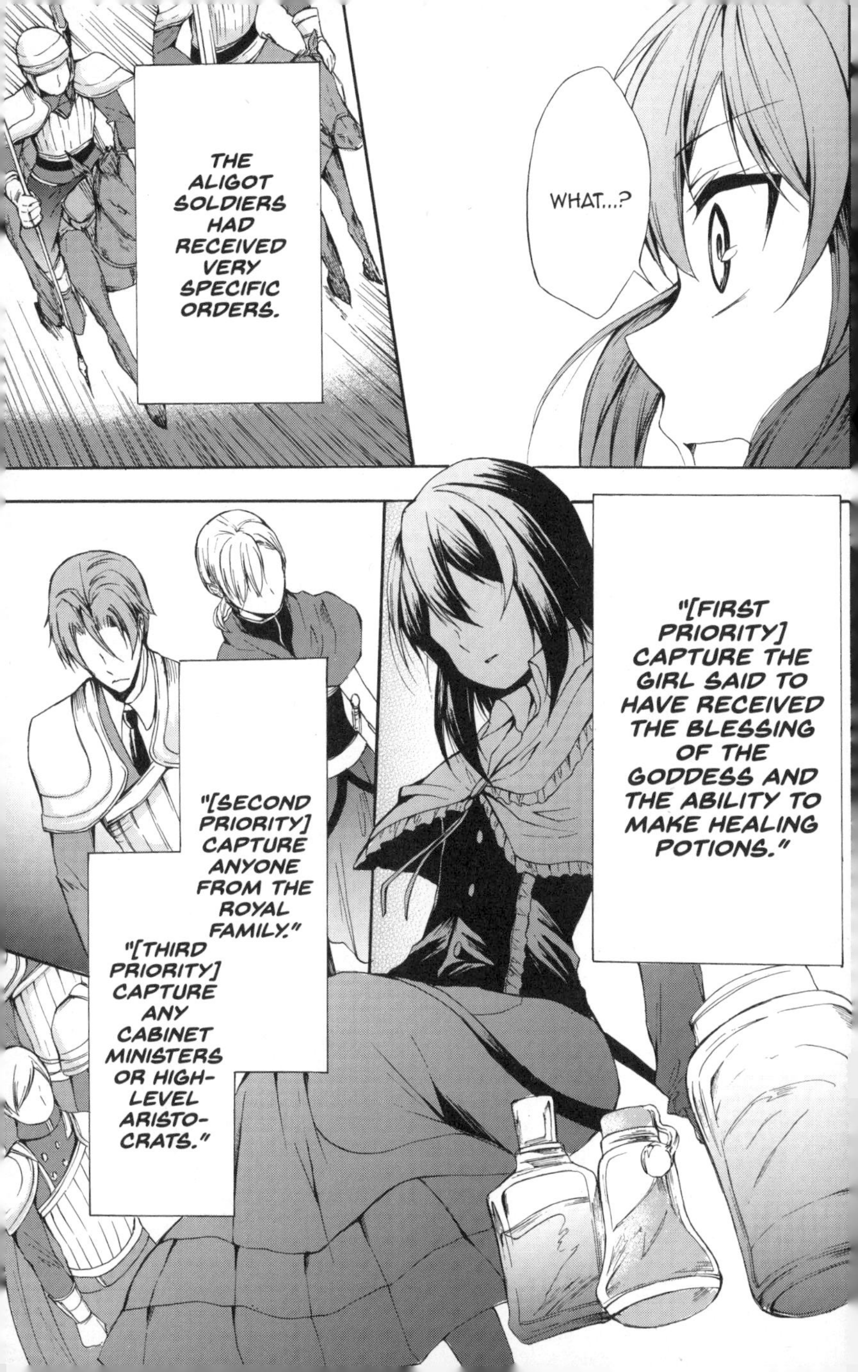
WHAT...?
THE ALIGOT SOLDIERS HAD RECEIVED VERY SPECIFIC ORDERS.
"[FIRST PRIORITY] CAPTURE THE GIRL SAID TO HAVE RECEIVED THE BLESSING OF THE GODDESS AND THE ABILITY TO MAKE HEALING POTIONS."
"[SECOND PRIORITY] CAPTURE ANYONE FROM THE ROYAL FAMILY."
"[THIRD PRIORITY] CAPTURE ANY CABINET MINISTERS OR HIGH-LEVEL ARISTO-CRATS."

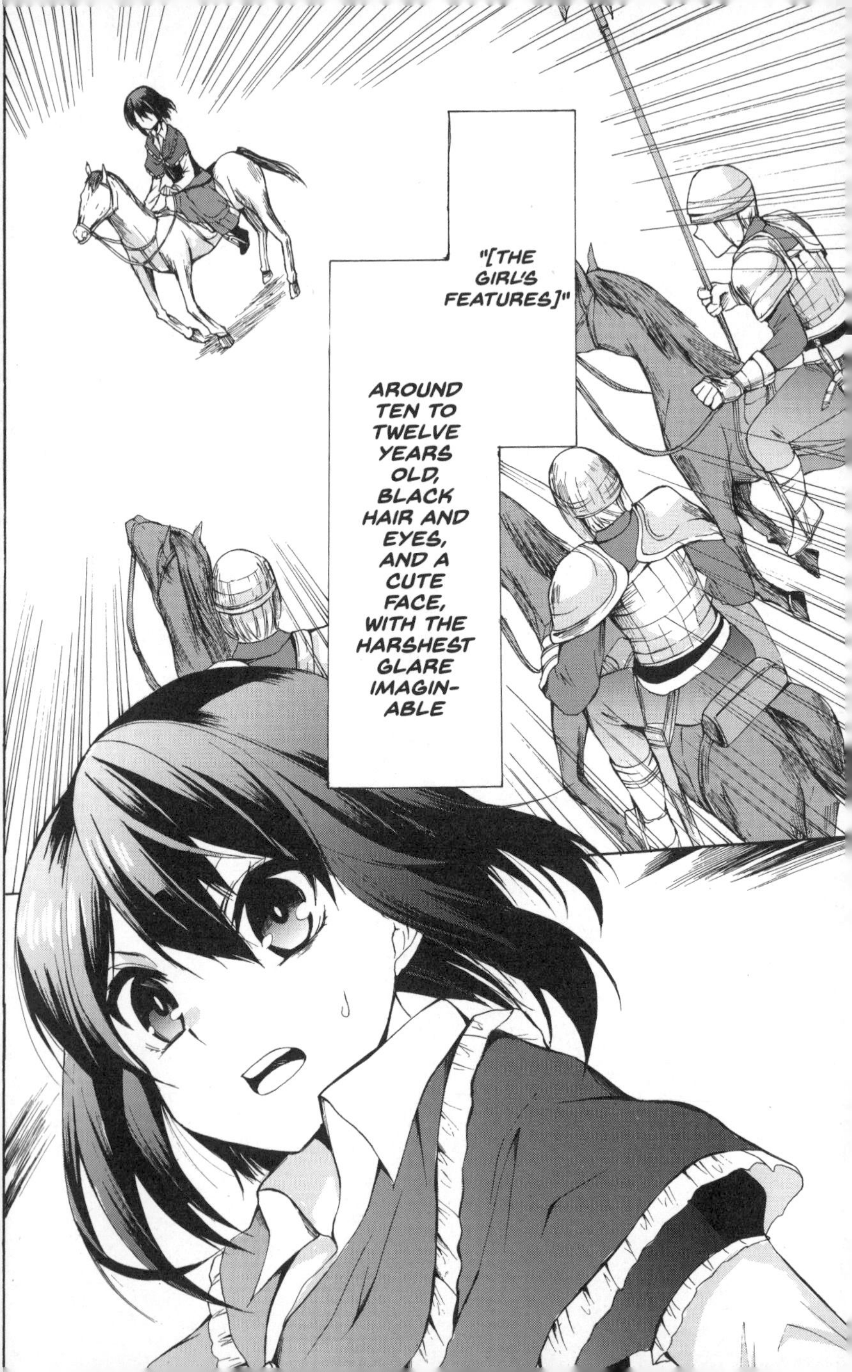
"[THE GIRL'S FEATURES]"
AROUND TEN TO TWELVE YEARS OLD, BLACK HAIR AND EYES, AND A CUTE FACE, WITH THE HARSHEST GLARE IMAGIN-ABLE

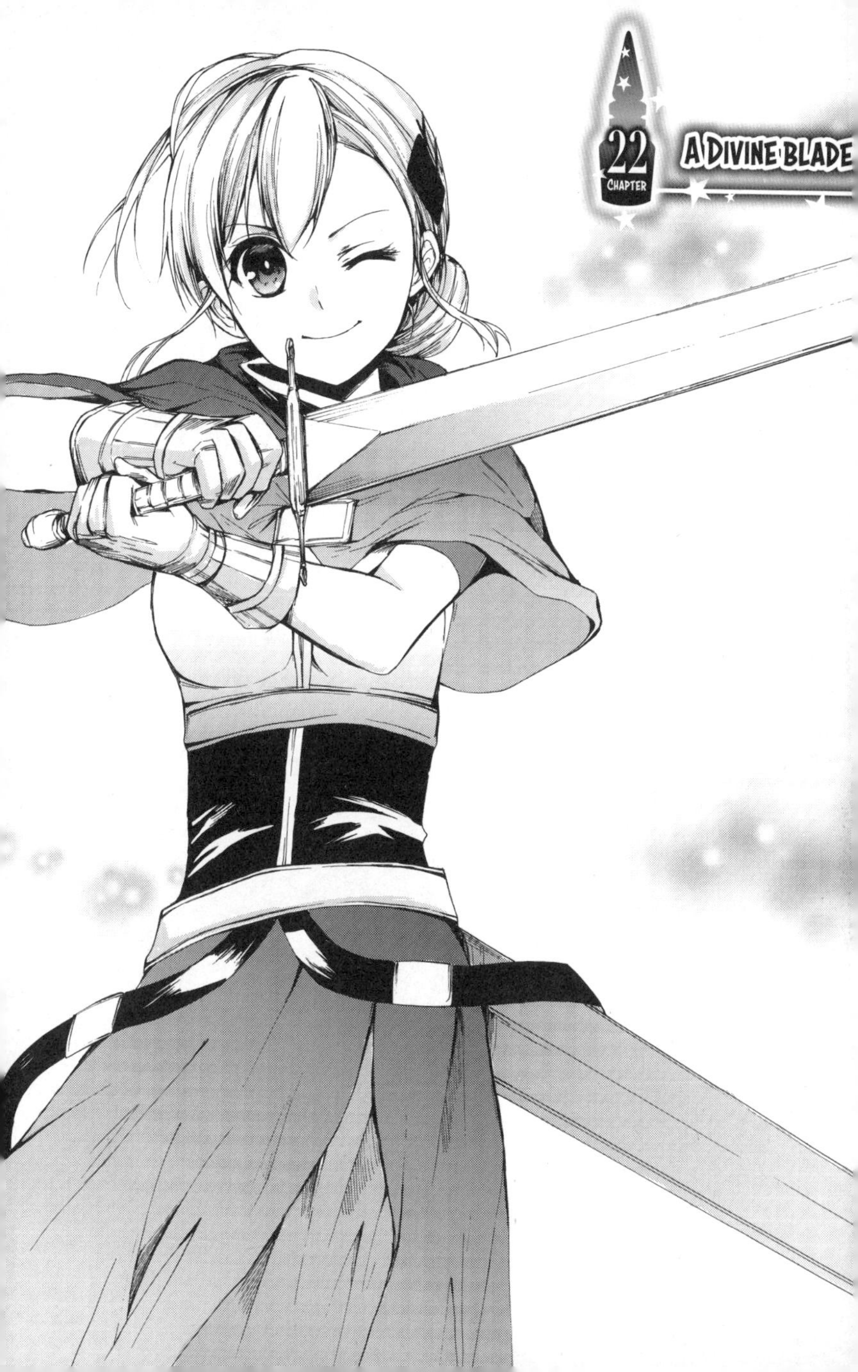
CHAPTER
22
A DIVINE BLADE

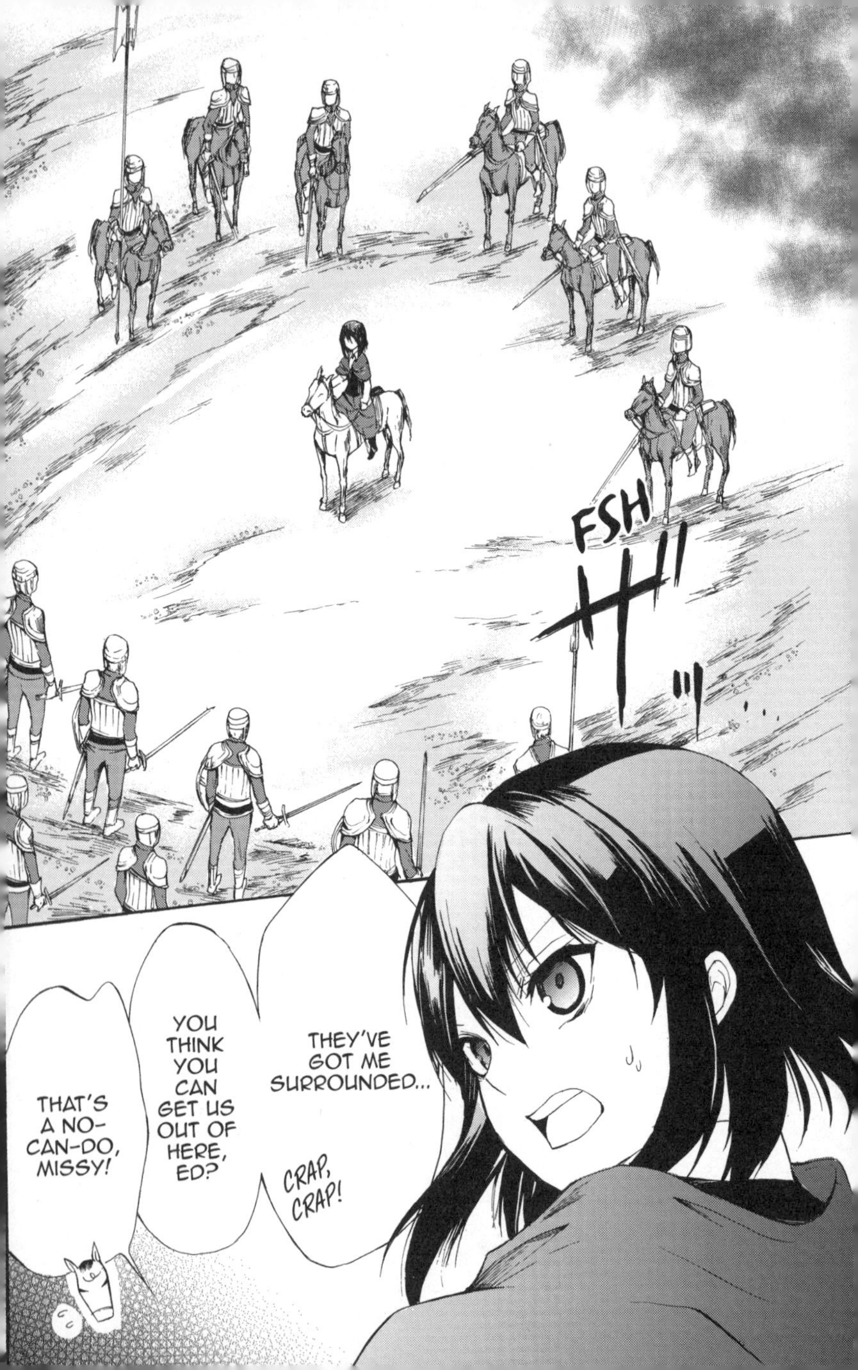
FSH
THEY'VE GOT ME SURROUNDED...
CRAP, CRAP!
YOU THINK YOU CAN GET US OUT OF HERE, ED?
THAT'S A NO-CAN-DO, MISSY!

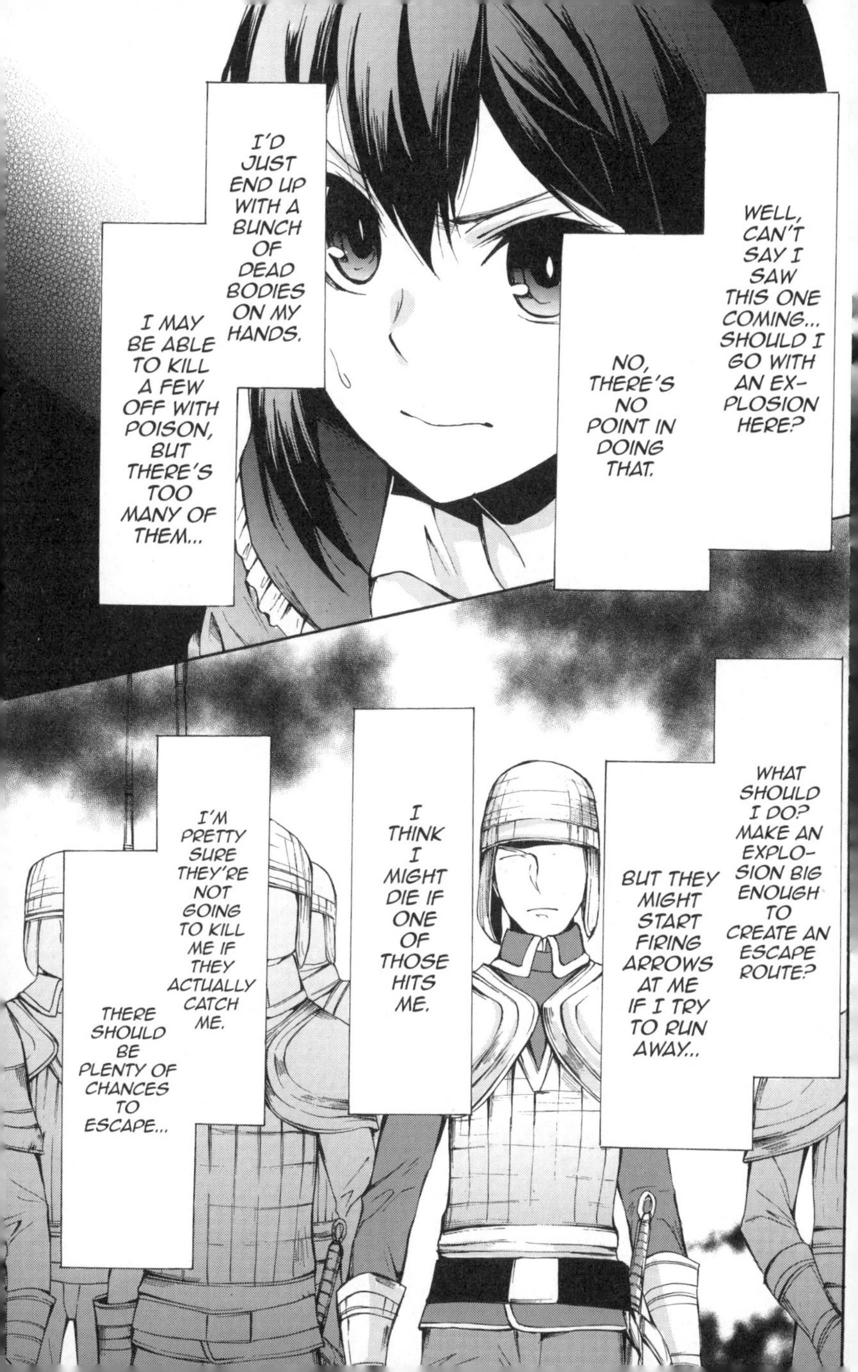
WELL, CAN'T SAY I SAW THIS ONE COMING... SHOULD I GO WITH AN EX-PLOSION HERE?
NO, THERE'S NO POINT IN DOING THAT.
I'D JUST END UP WITH A BUNCH OF DEAD BODIES ON MY HANDS.
I MAY BE ABLE TO KILL A FEW OFF WITH POISON, BUT THERE'S TOO MANY OF THEM...
WHAT SHOULD I DO? MAKE AN EXPLO-SION BIG ENOUGH TO CREATE AN ESCAPE ROUTE?
BUT THEY MIGHT START FIRING ARROWS AT ME IF I TRY TO RUN AWAY...
I THINK I MIGHT DIE IF ONE OF THOSE HITS ME.
I'M PRETTY SURE THEY'RE NOT GOING TO KILL ME IF THEY ACTUALLY CATCH ME.
THERE SHOULD BE PLENTY OF CHANCES TO ESCAPE...

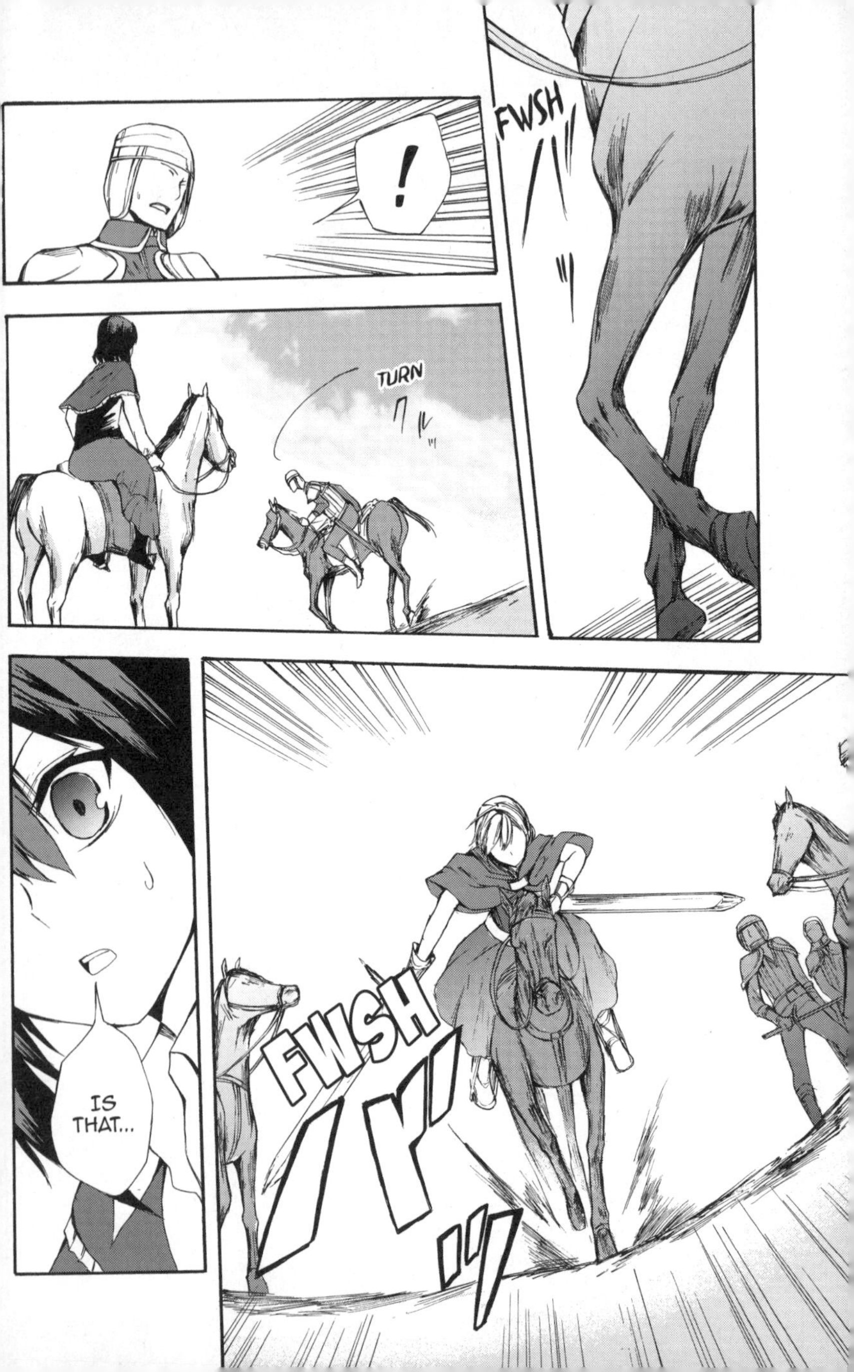
FWSH
!
TURN
FWSH
IS THAT...

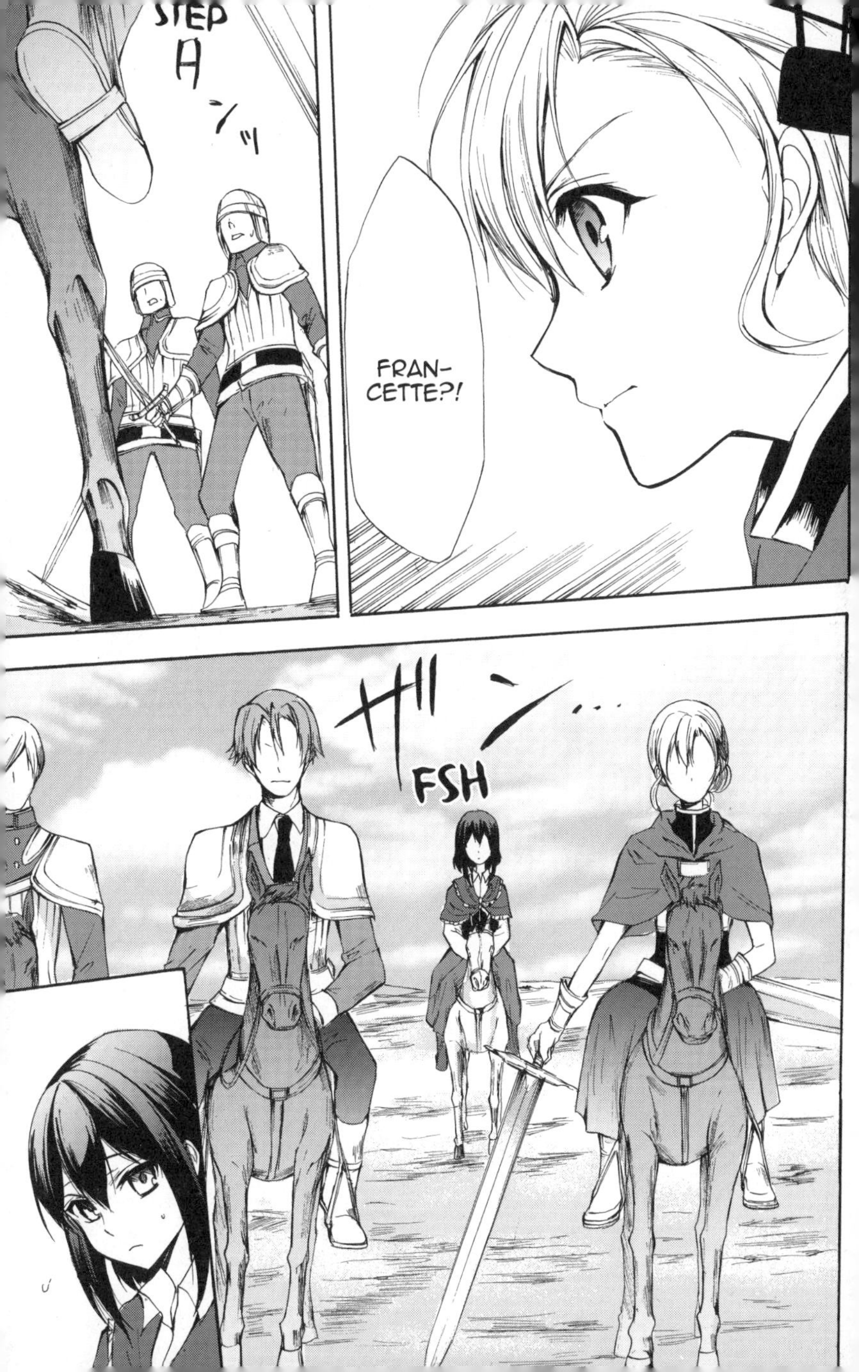
FRAN-
CETTE?!
STEP
FSH

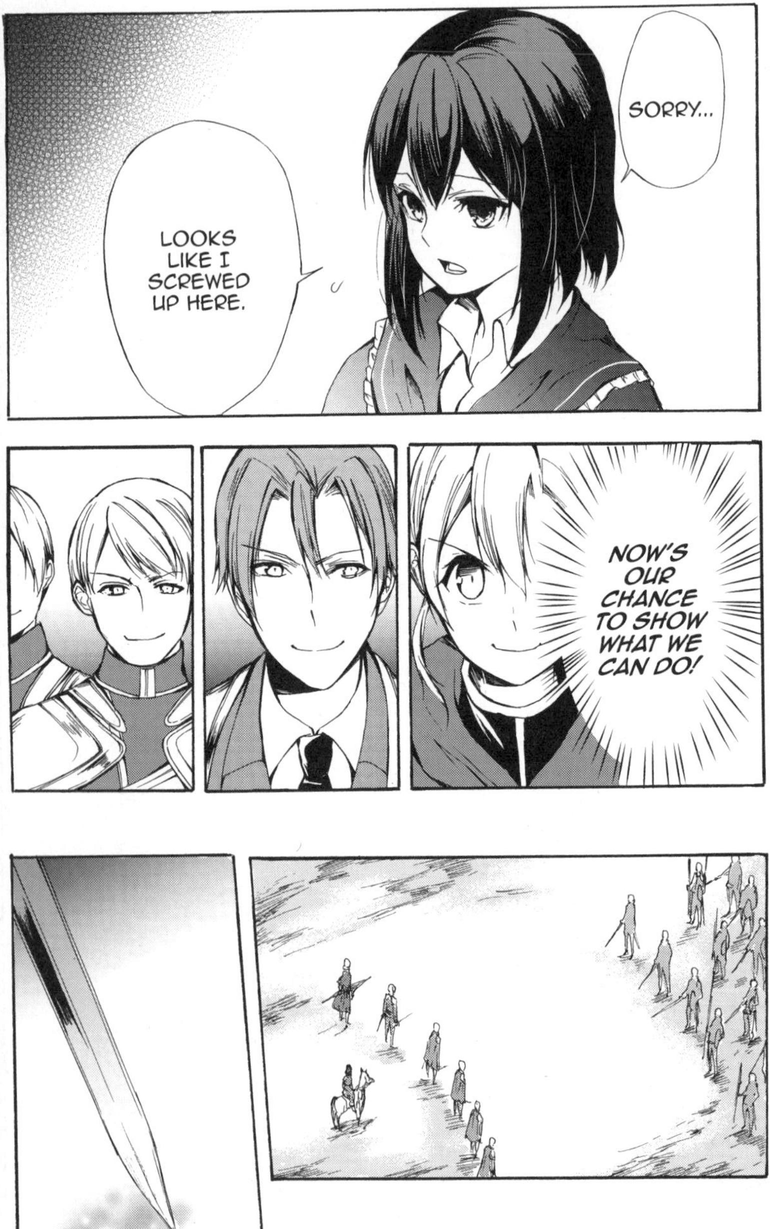
SORRY...
LOOKS LIKE I SCREWED UP HERE.
NOW'S OUR CHANCE TO SHOW WHAT WE CAN DO!

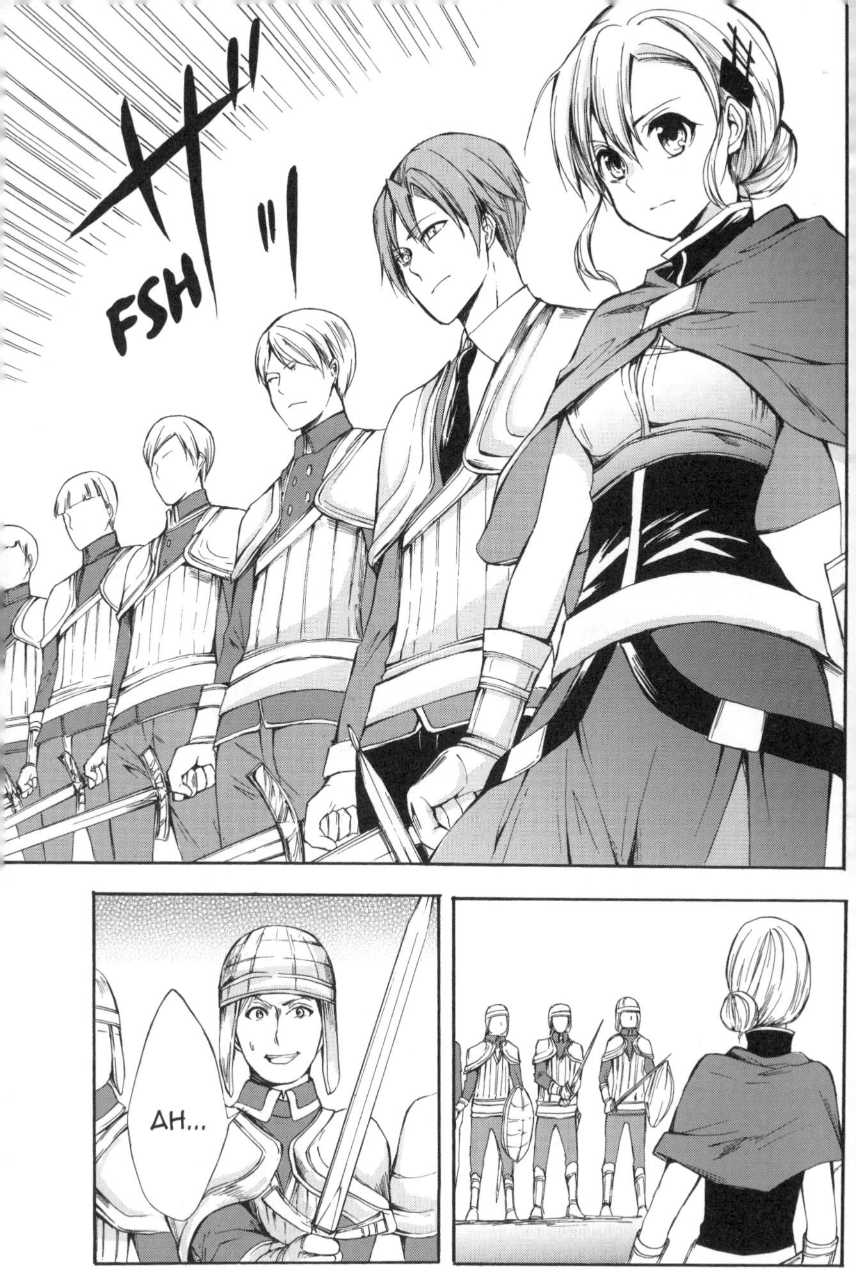
FSH
AH...

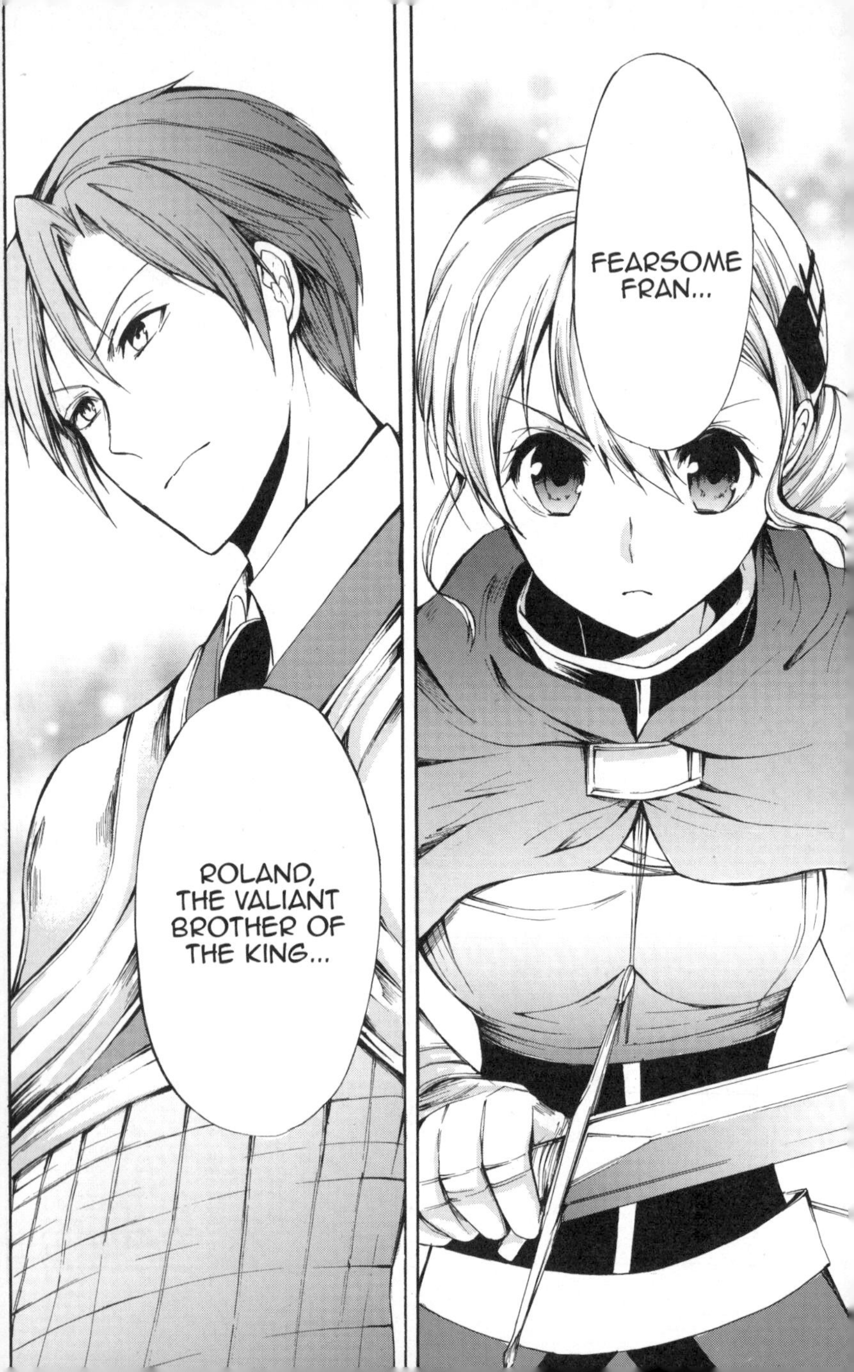
FEARSOME FRAN...
ROLAND, THE VALIANT BROTHER OF THE KING...

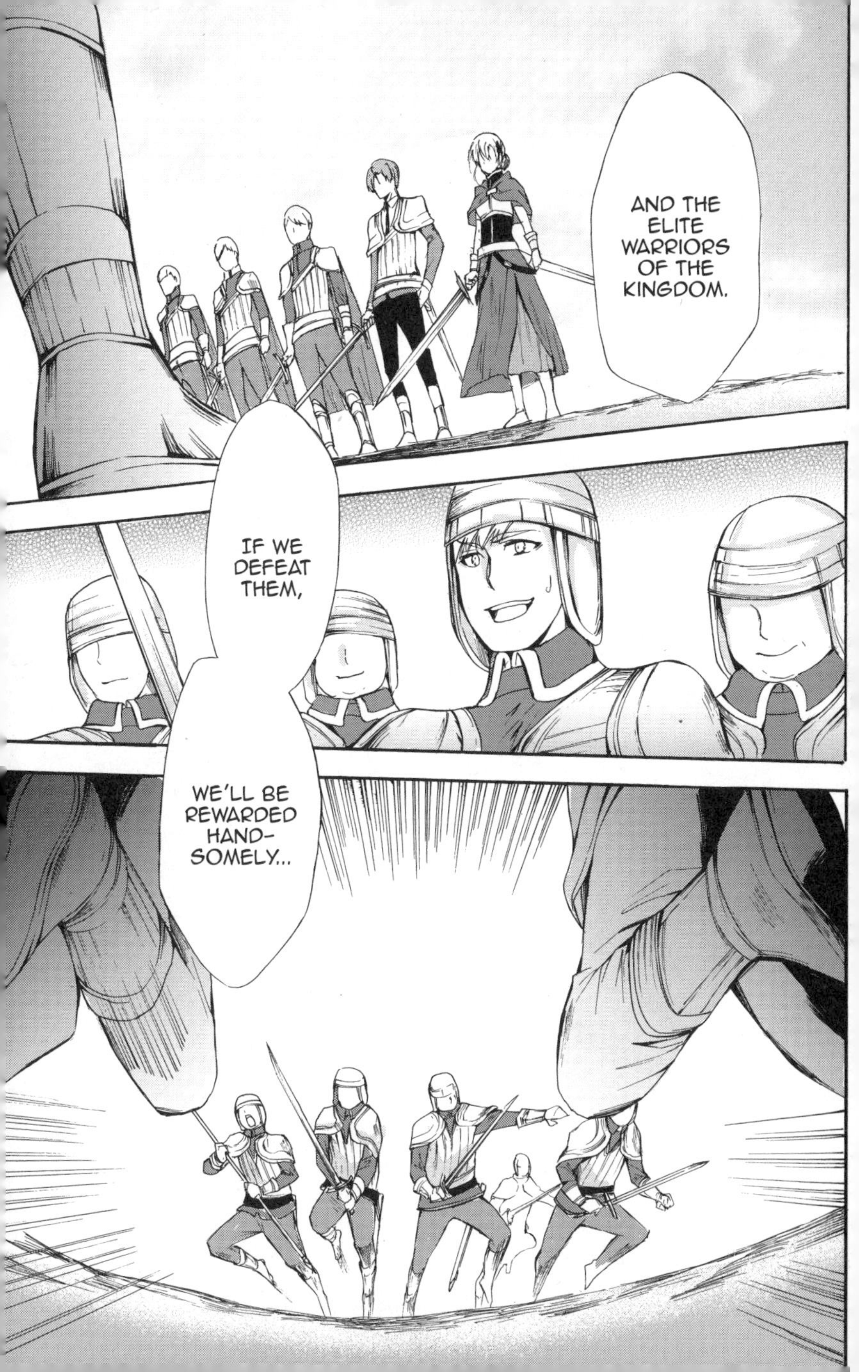
AND THE ELITE WARRIORS OF THE KINGDOM.
IF WE DEFEAT THEM,
WE'LL BE REWARDED HAND-SOMELY...

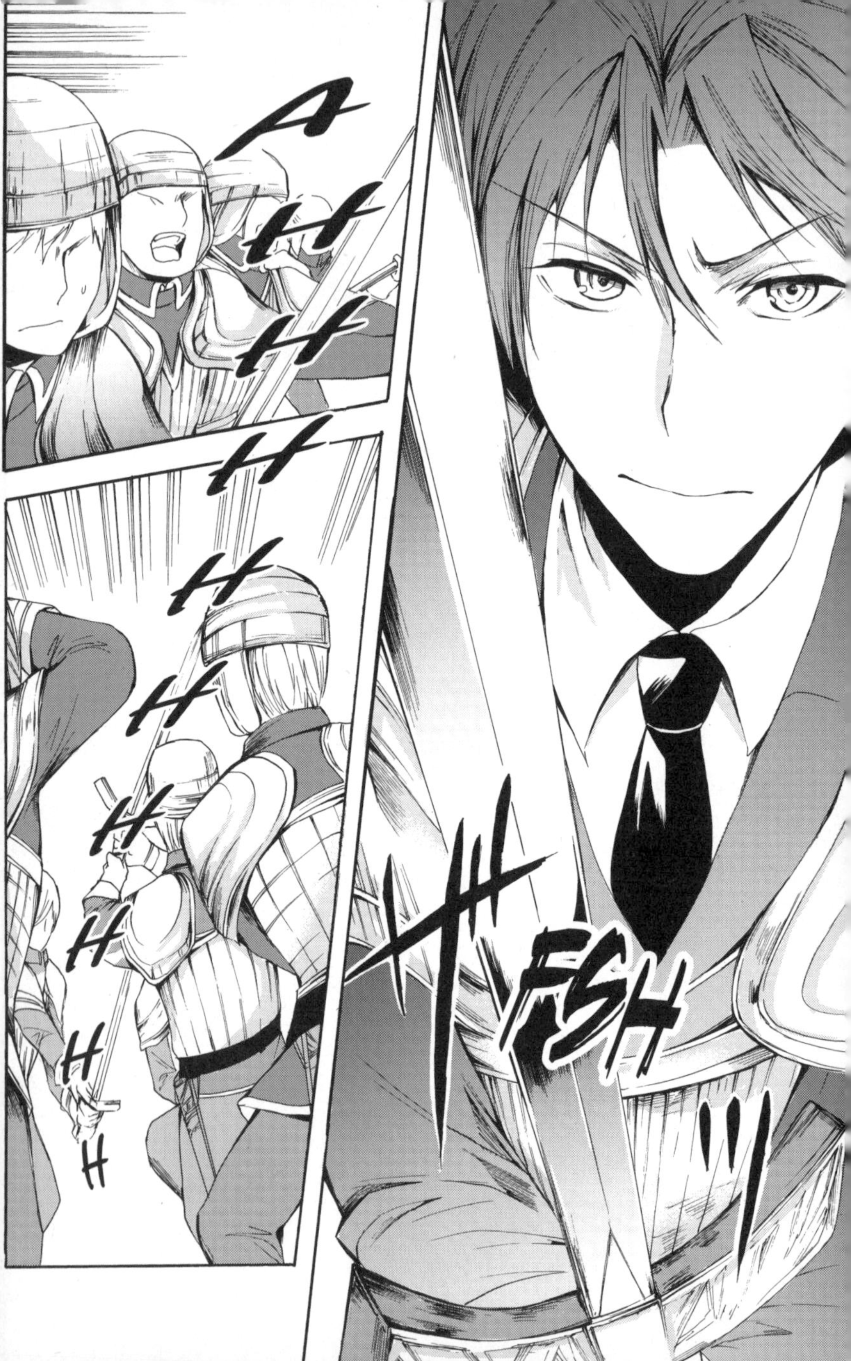
FSH
AHHHHHHHHH

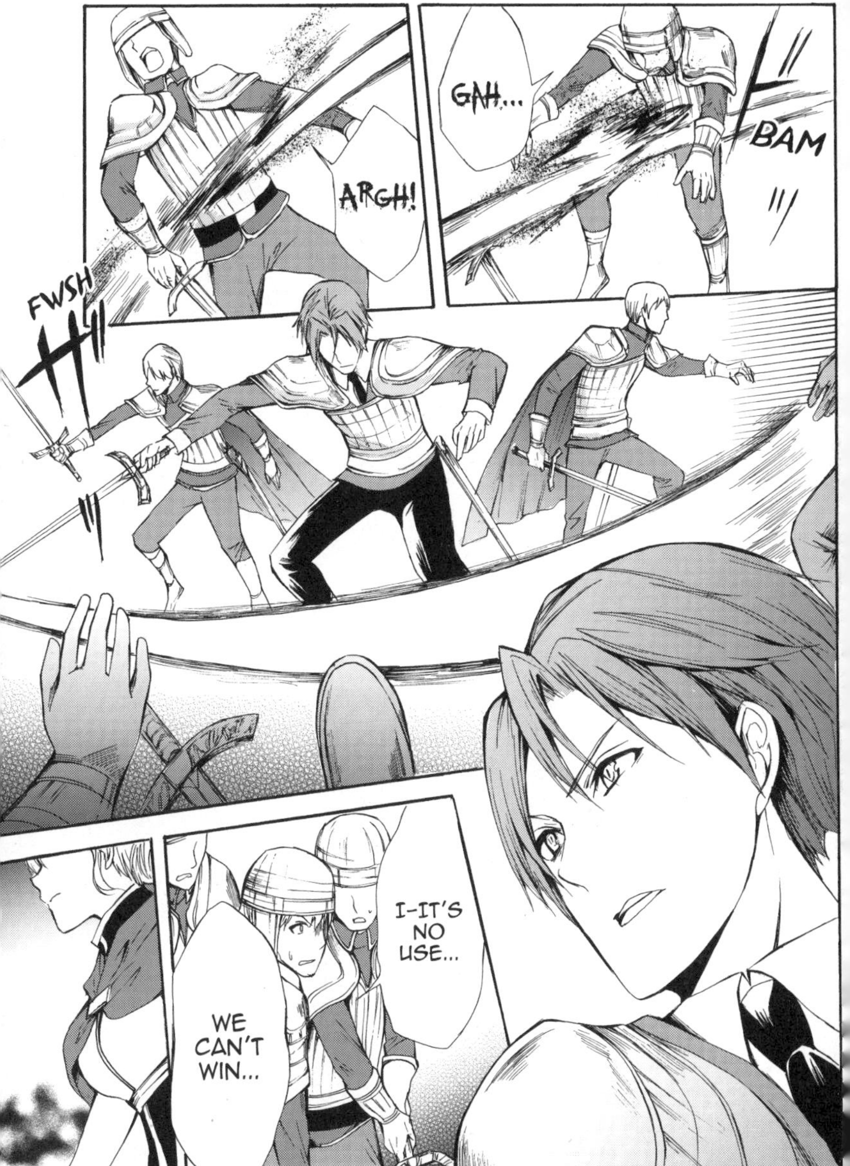

GAH...
BAM
ARGH!
FWSH
I-IT'S NO USE...
WE CAN'T WIN...

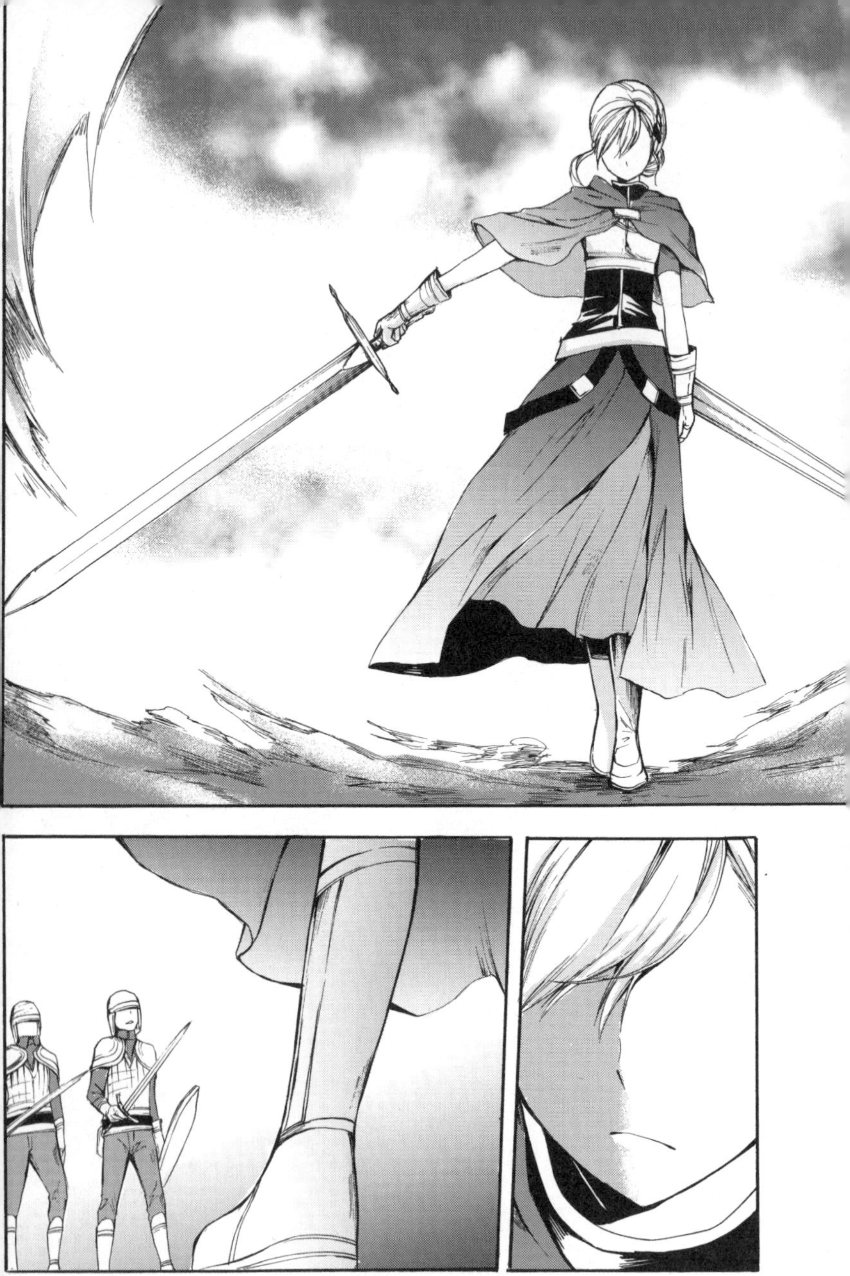

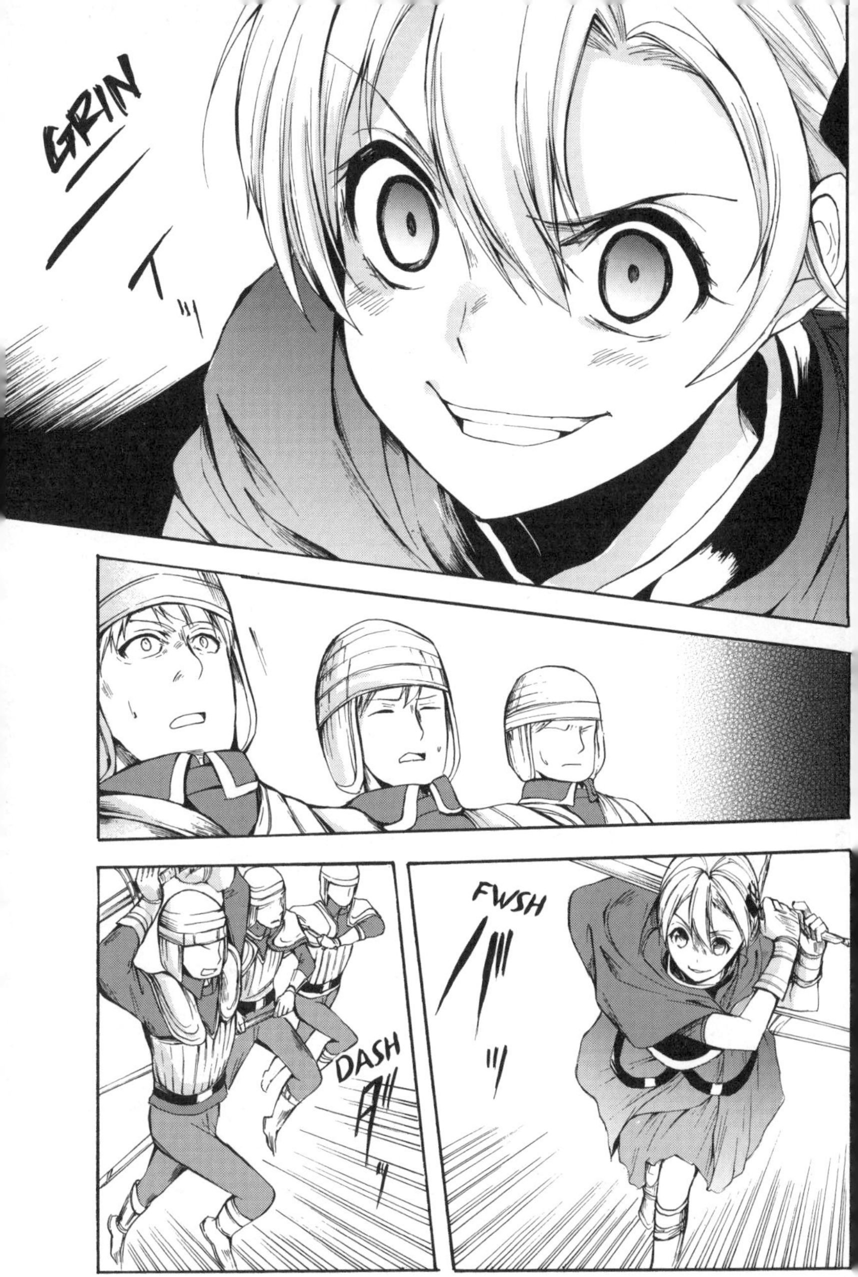
GRIN
FWSH
DASH

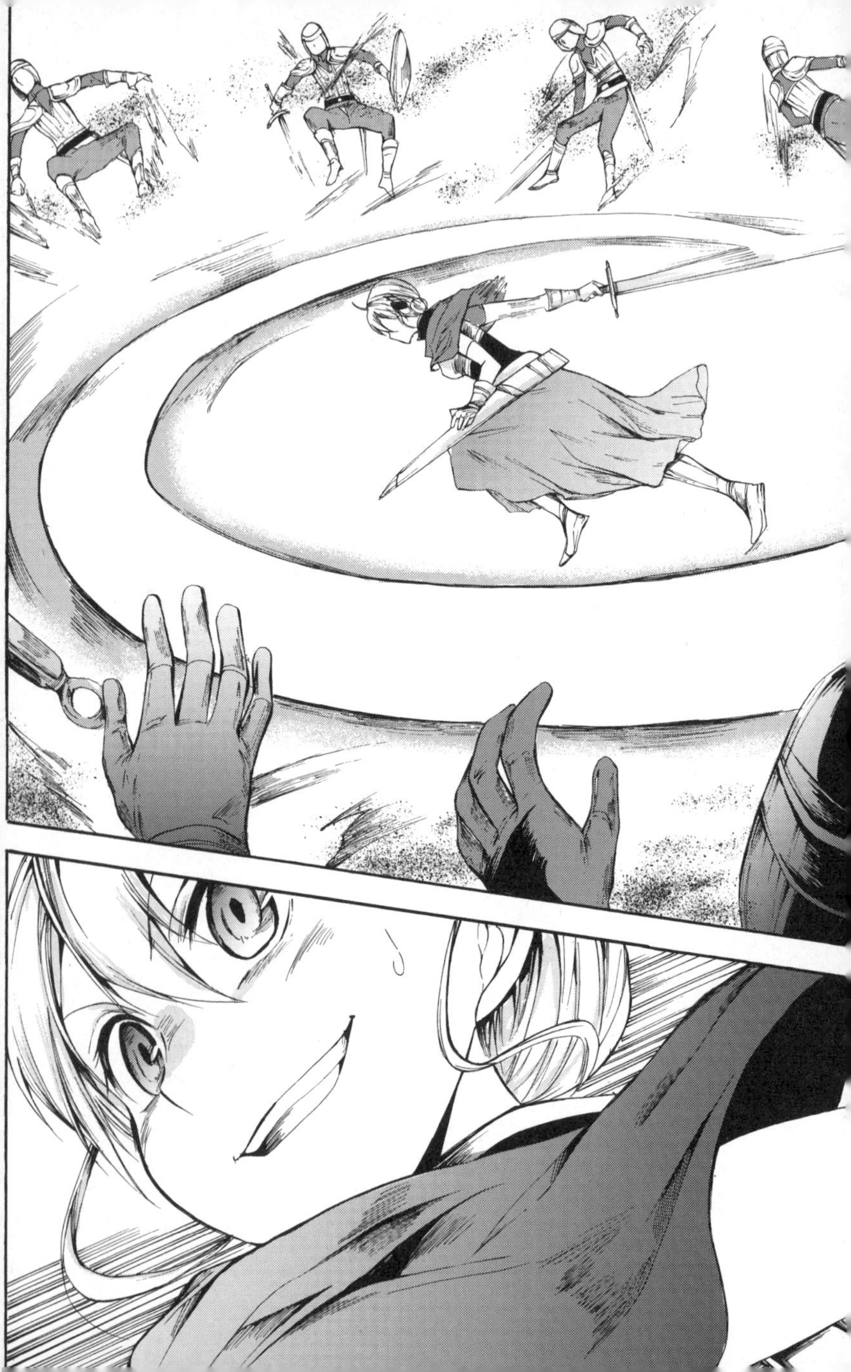

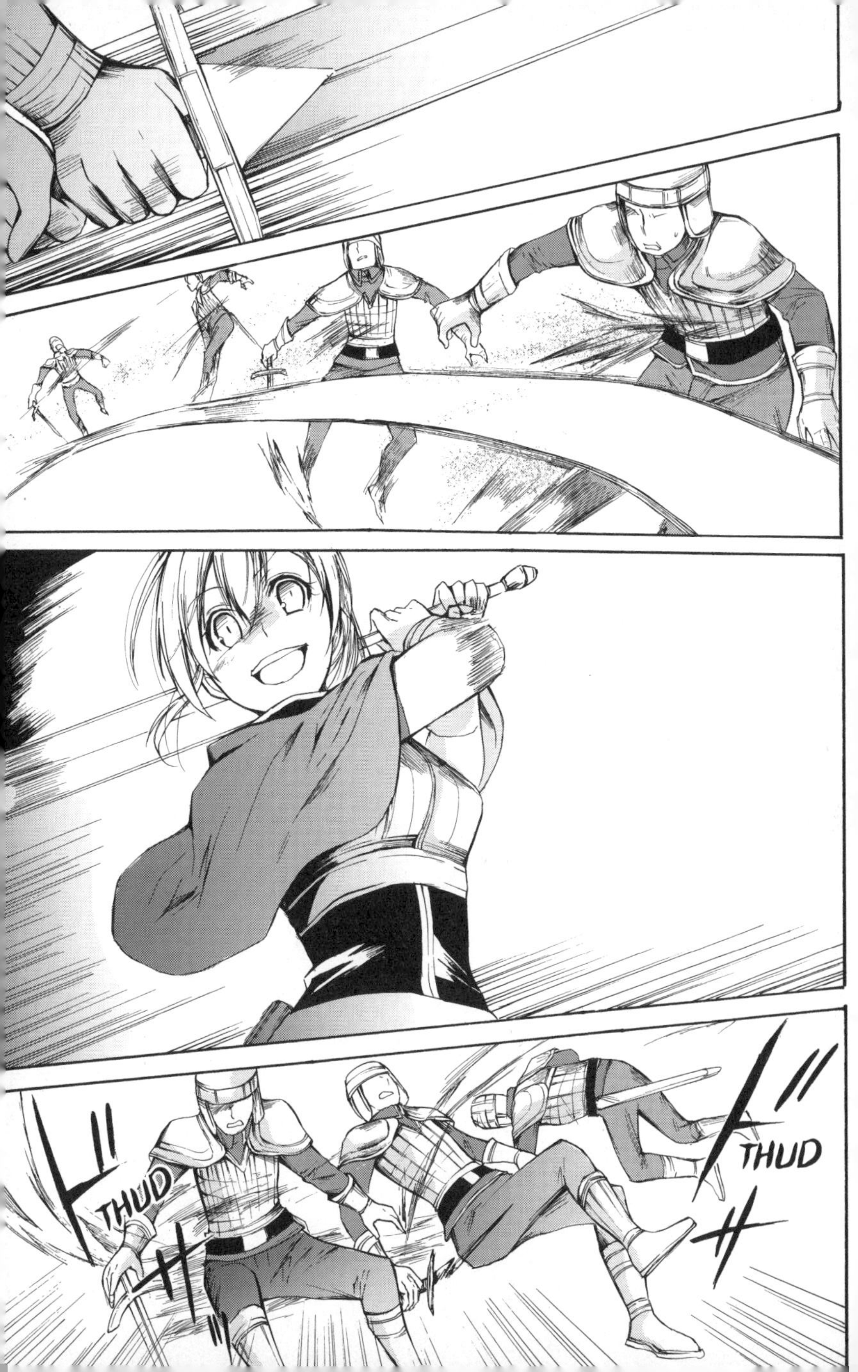
THUD
THUD

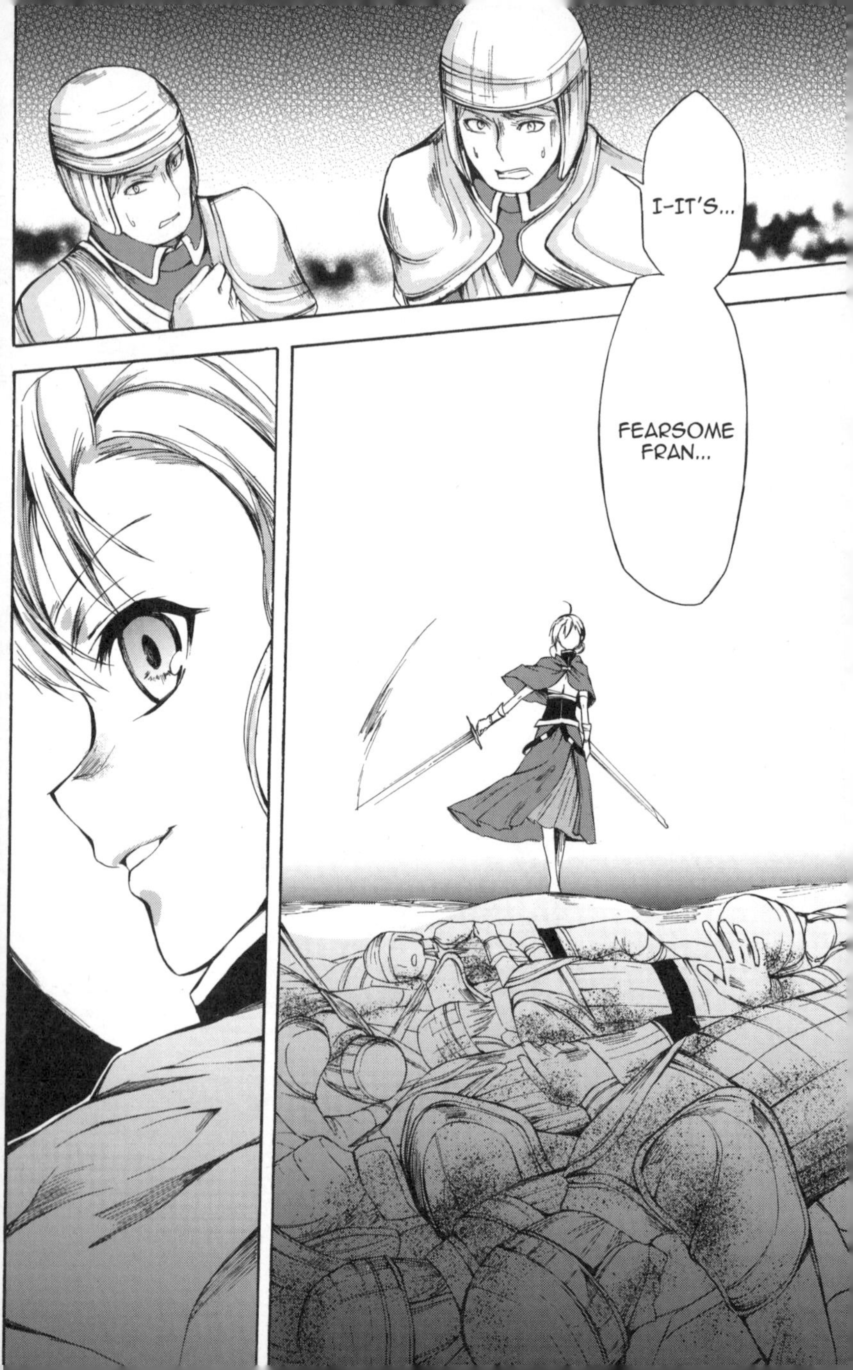
I-IT'S...
FEARSOME FRAN...

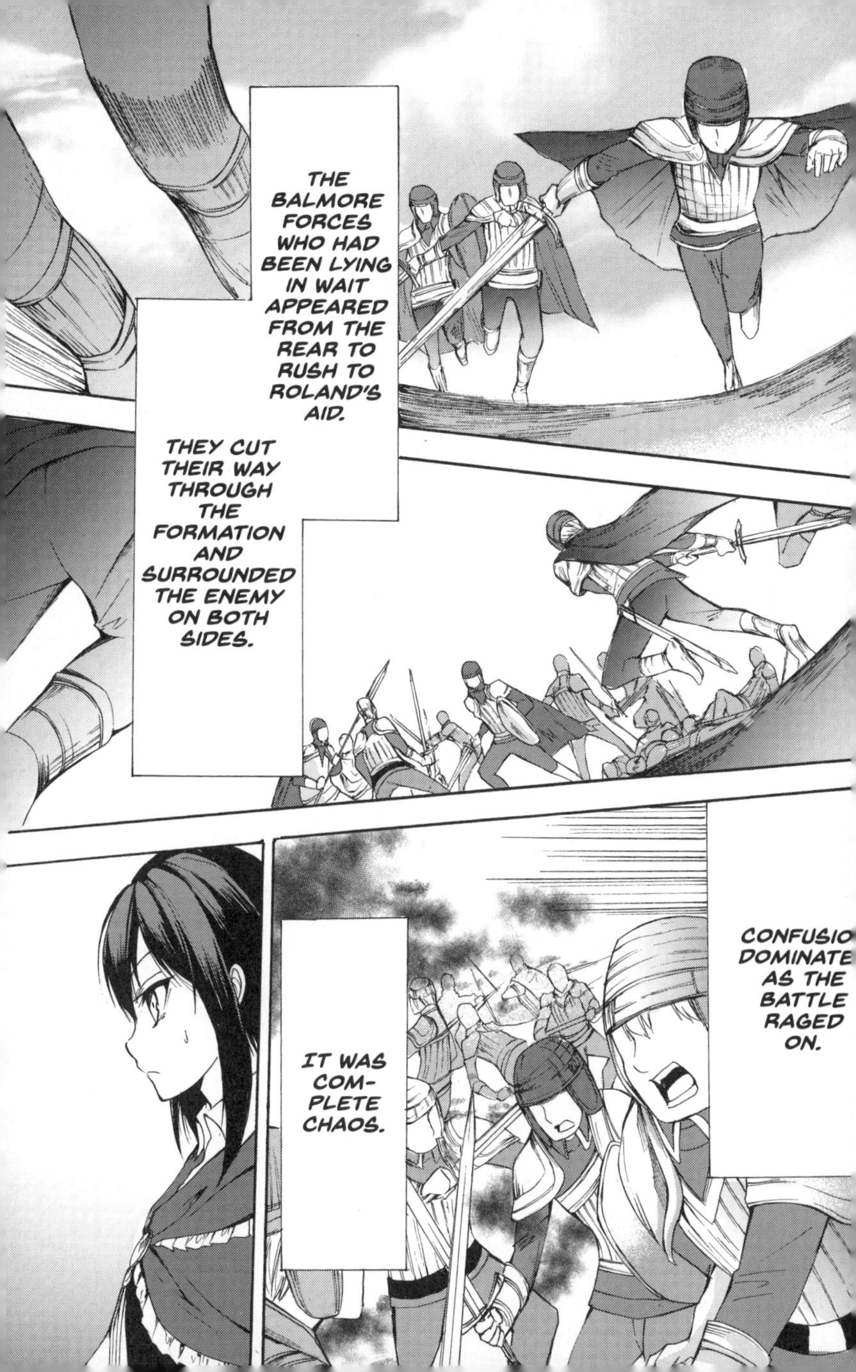
THE BALMORE FORCES WHO HAD BEEN LYING IN WAIT APPEARED FROM THE REAR TO RUSH TO ROLAND'S AID.
THEY CUT THEIR WAY THROUGH THE FORMATION AND SURROUNDED THE ENEMY ON BOTH SIDES.
CONFUSIO DOMINATE AS THE BATTLE RAGED ON.
IT WAS COM- PLETE CHAOS.

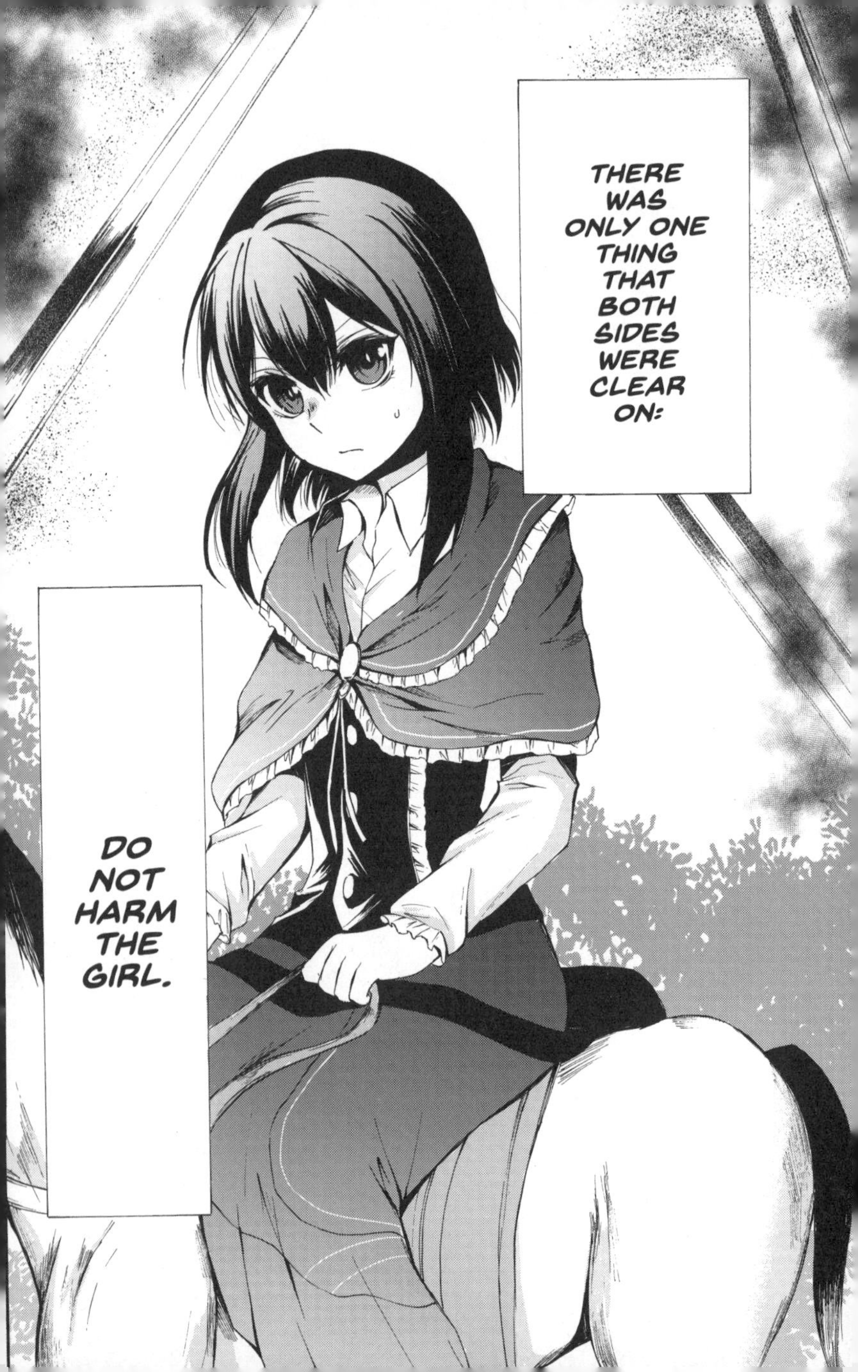
THERE WAS ONLY ONE THING THAT BOTH SIDES WERE CLEAR ON:
DO NOT HARM THE GIRL.

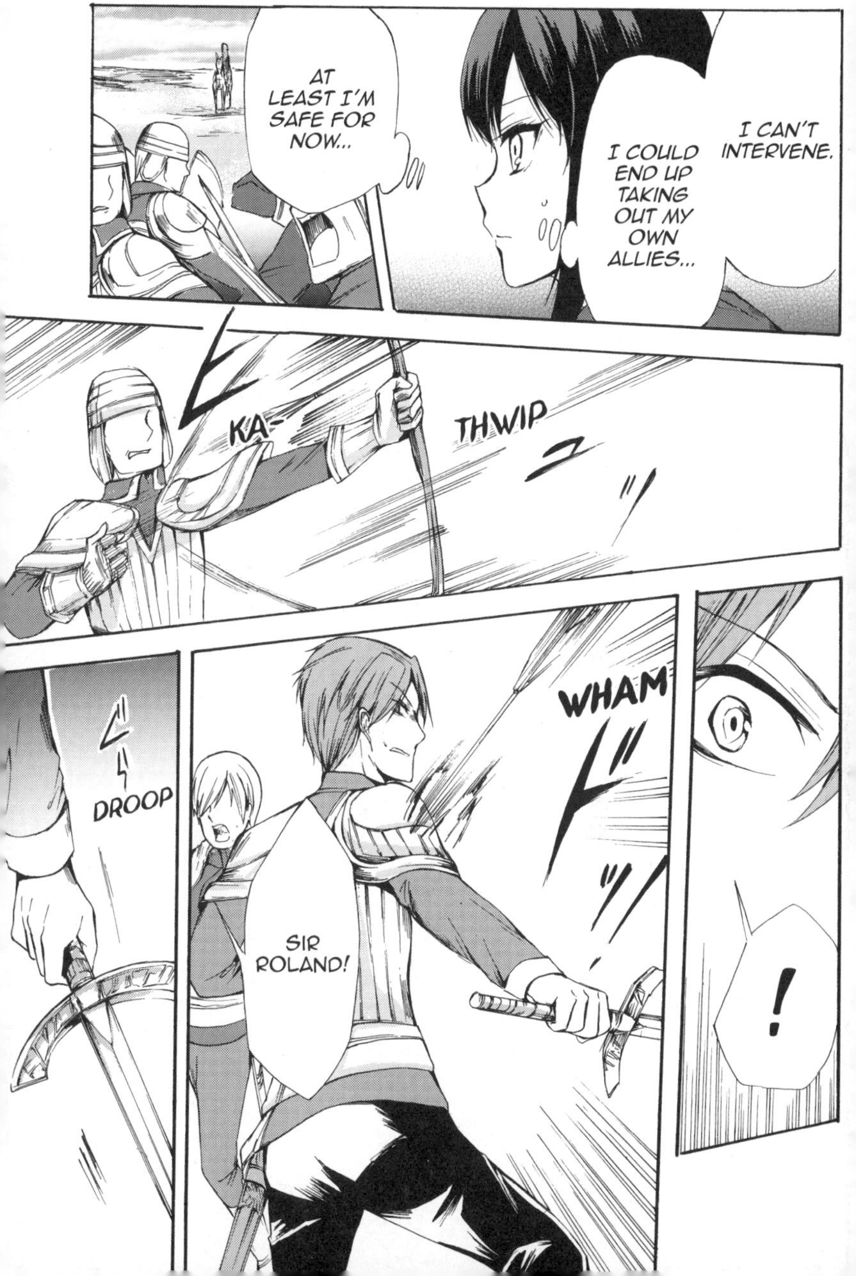
I CAN'T INTERVENE.
I COULD END UP TAKING OUT MY OWN ALLIES...
AT LEAST I'M SAFE FOR NOW...
KA-
THWIP
!
WHAM
SIR ROLAND!
DROOP

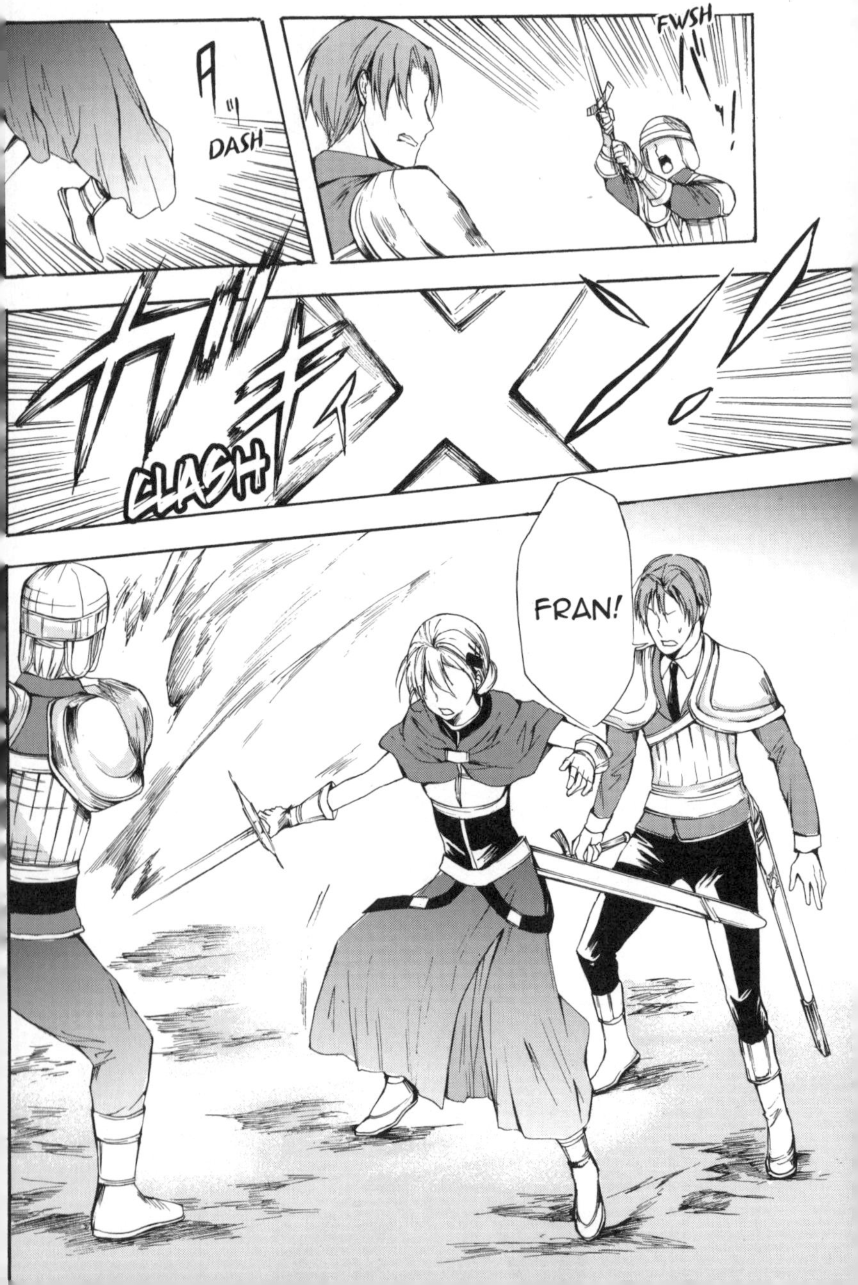
バッ!
FWSH
ダッ
DASH
ガギィン!!
CLASH
FRAN!

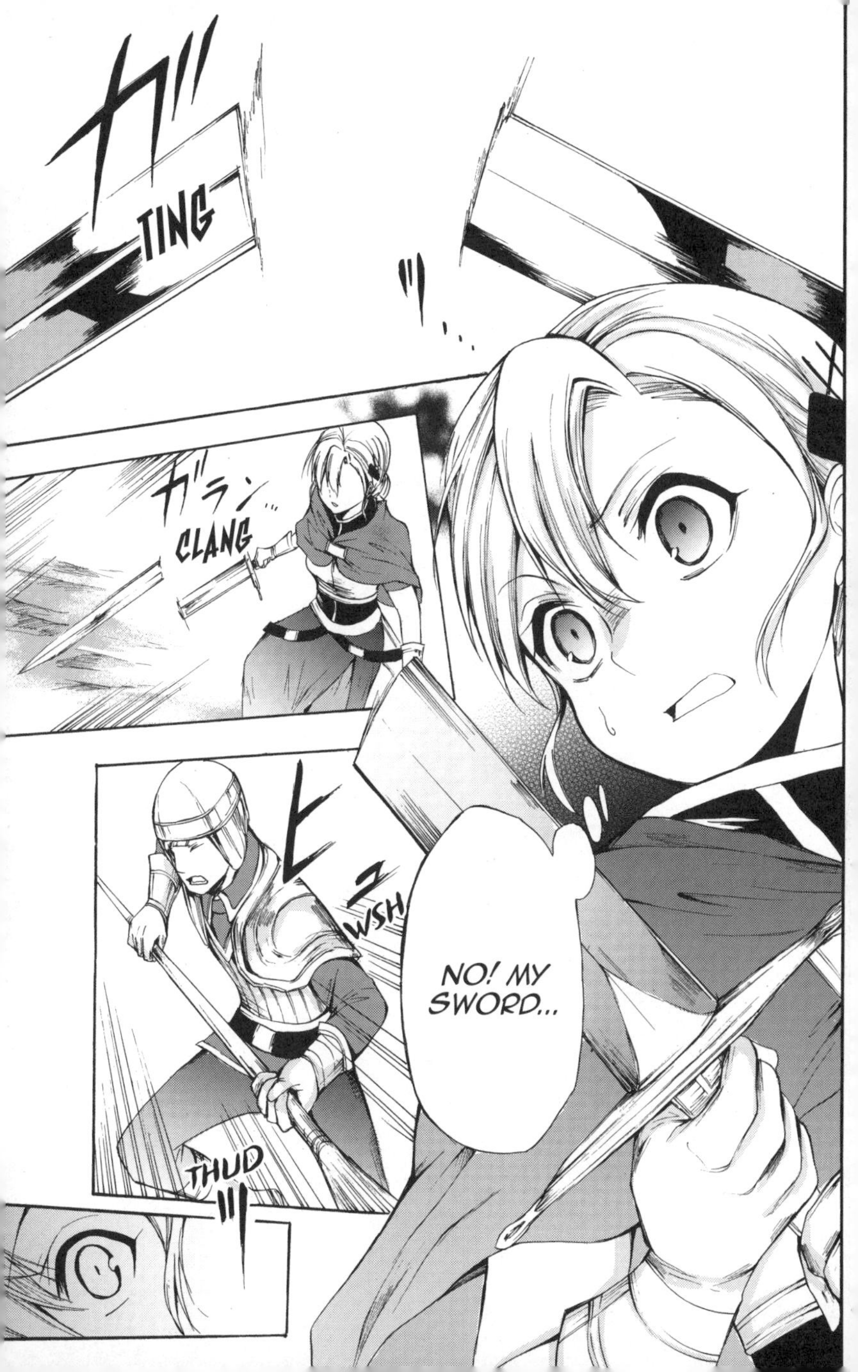
TING
NO! MY SWORD...
CLANG
WSH
THUD

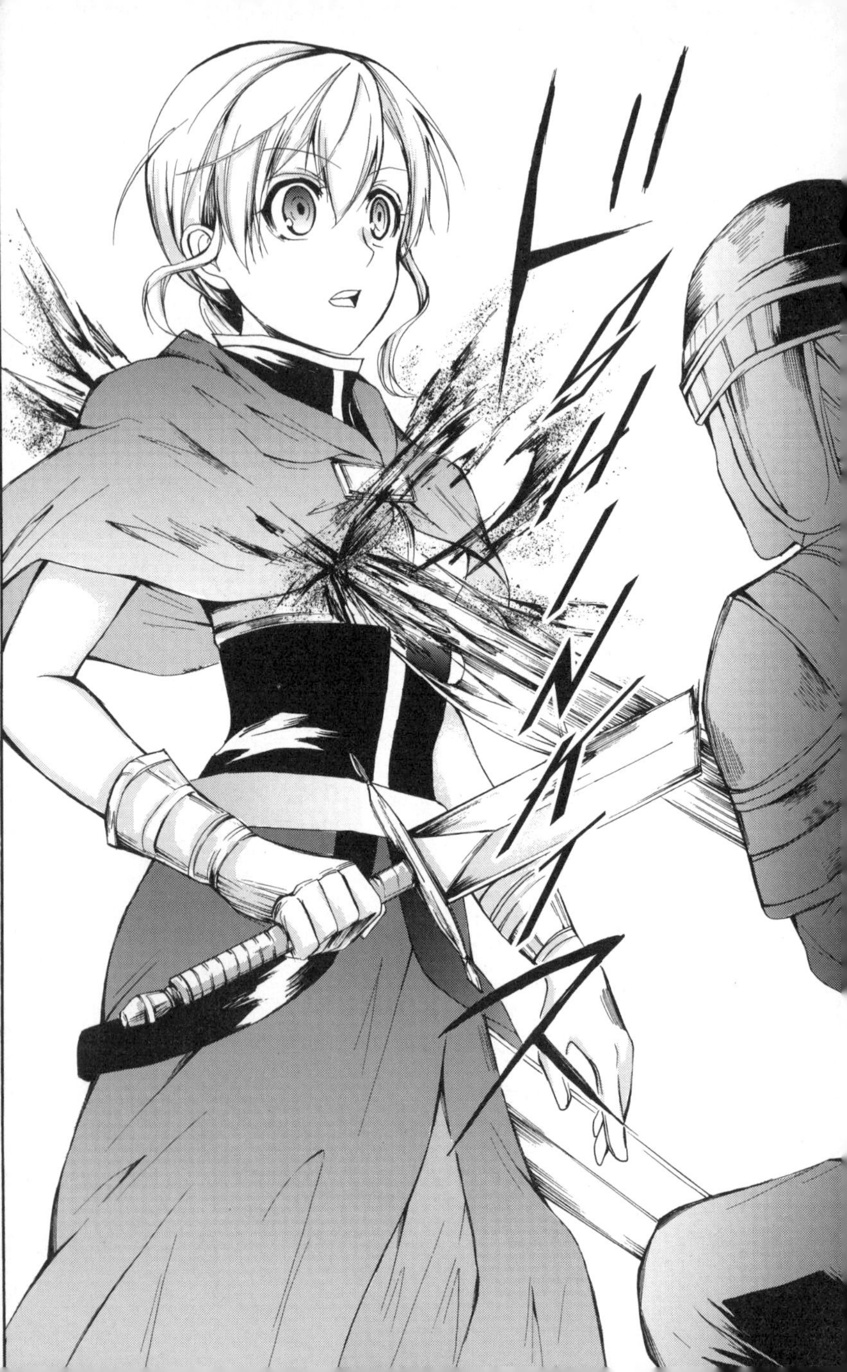

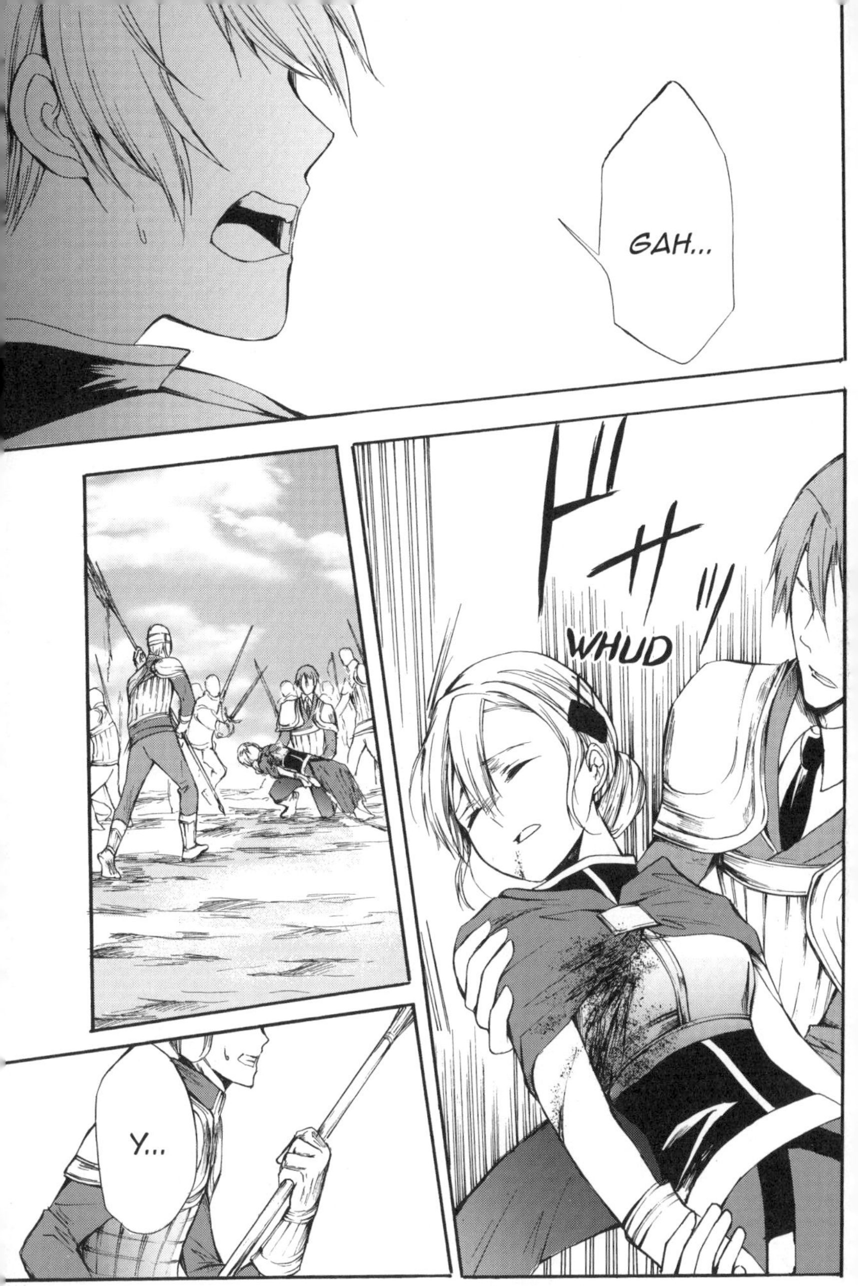
GAH...
WHUD
Y...

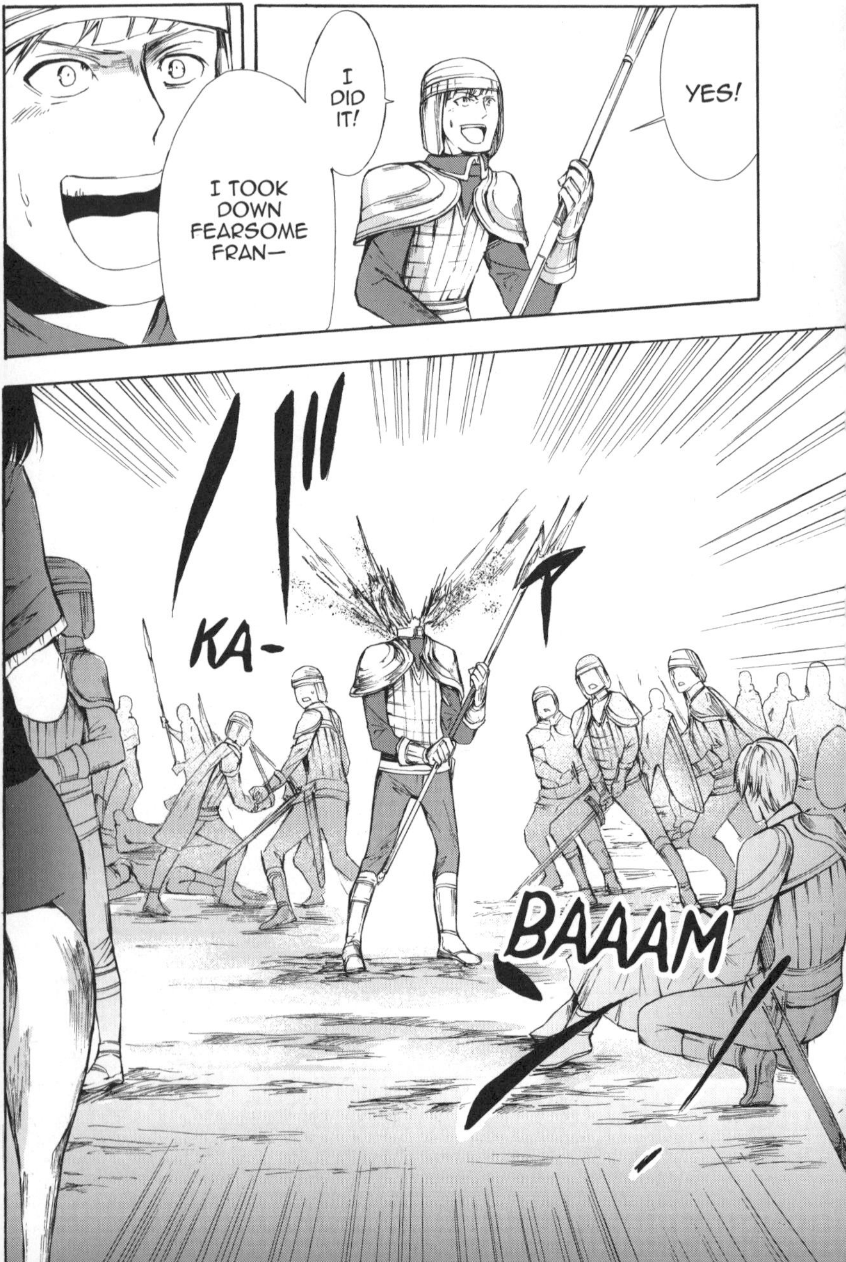
YES!
I DID IT!
I TOOK DOWN FEARSOME FRAN—
KA-
BAAAM

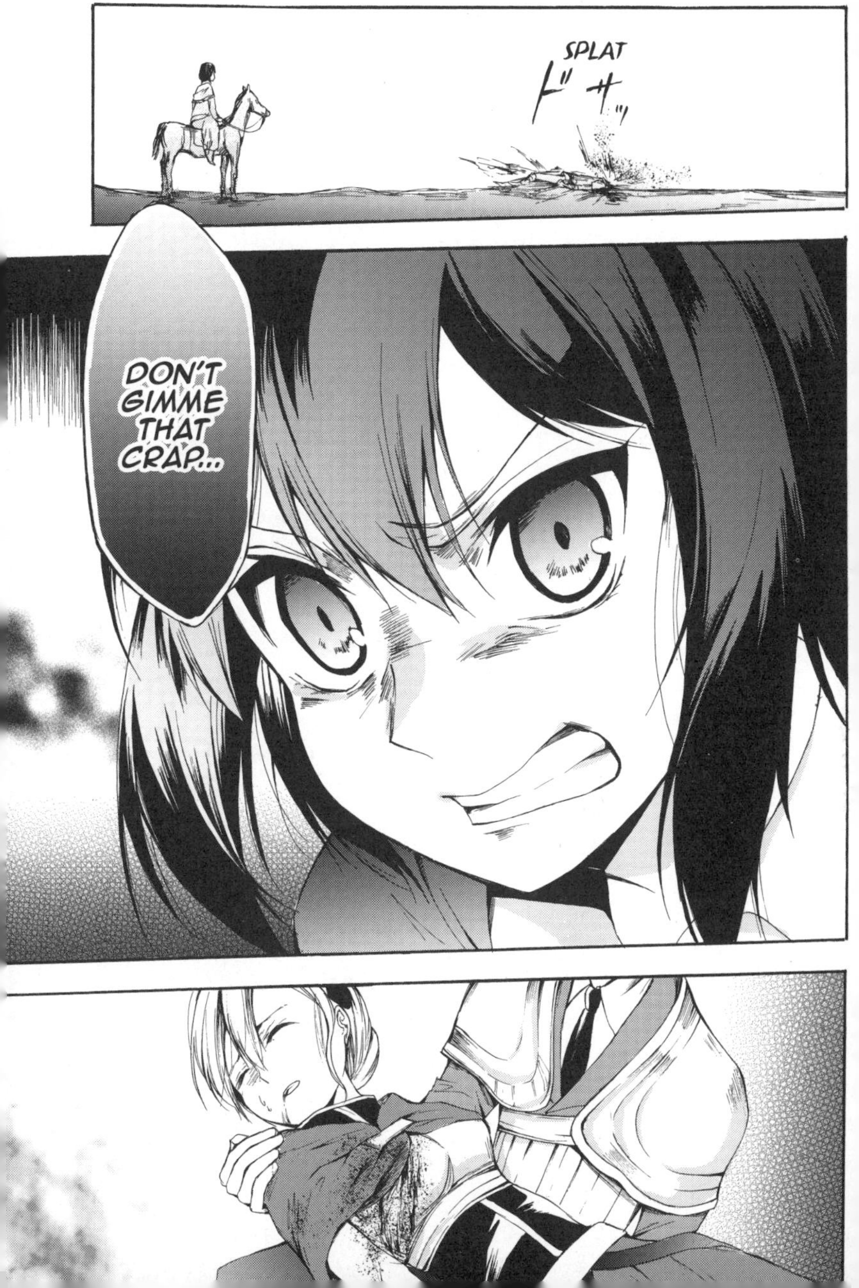
SPLAT
ドサッ
DON'T GIMME THAT CRAP...

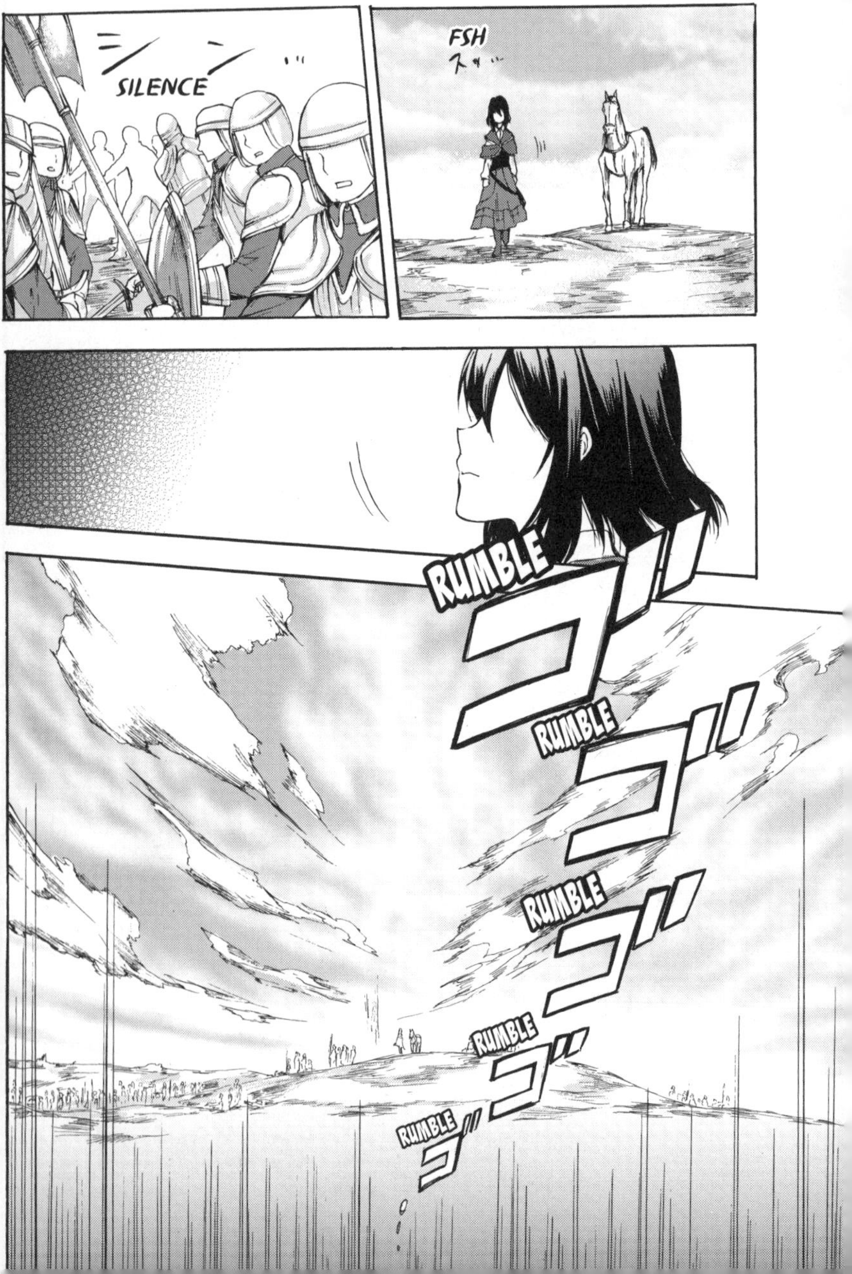
FSH
スッ…
SILENCE
RUMBLE
RUMBLE
RUMBLE
RUMBLE
RUMBLE

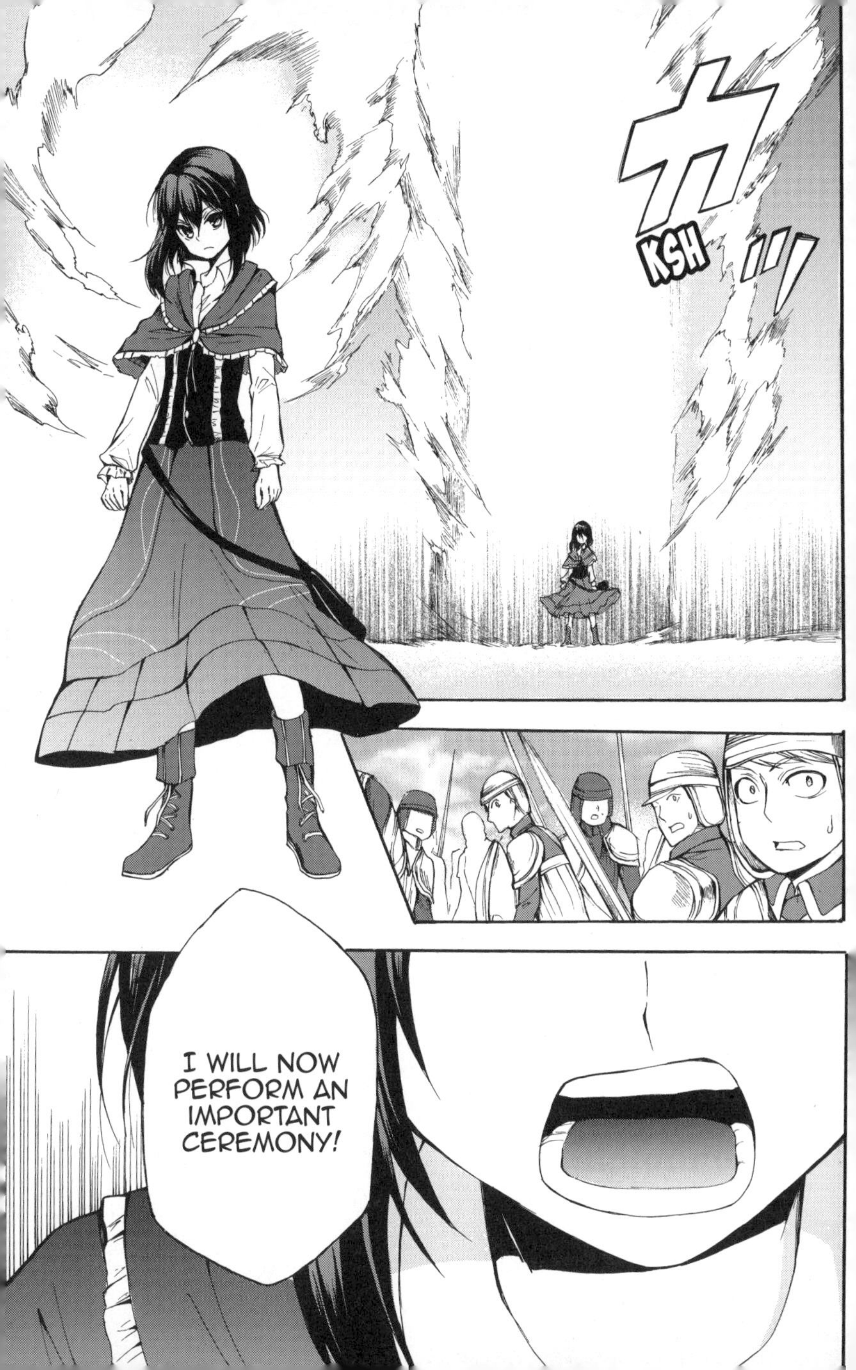
カッ
KSH
I WILL NOW PERFORM AN IMPORTANT CEREMONY!

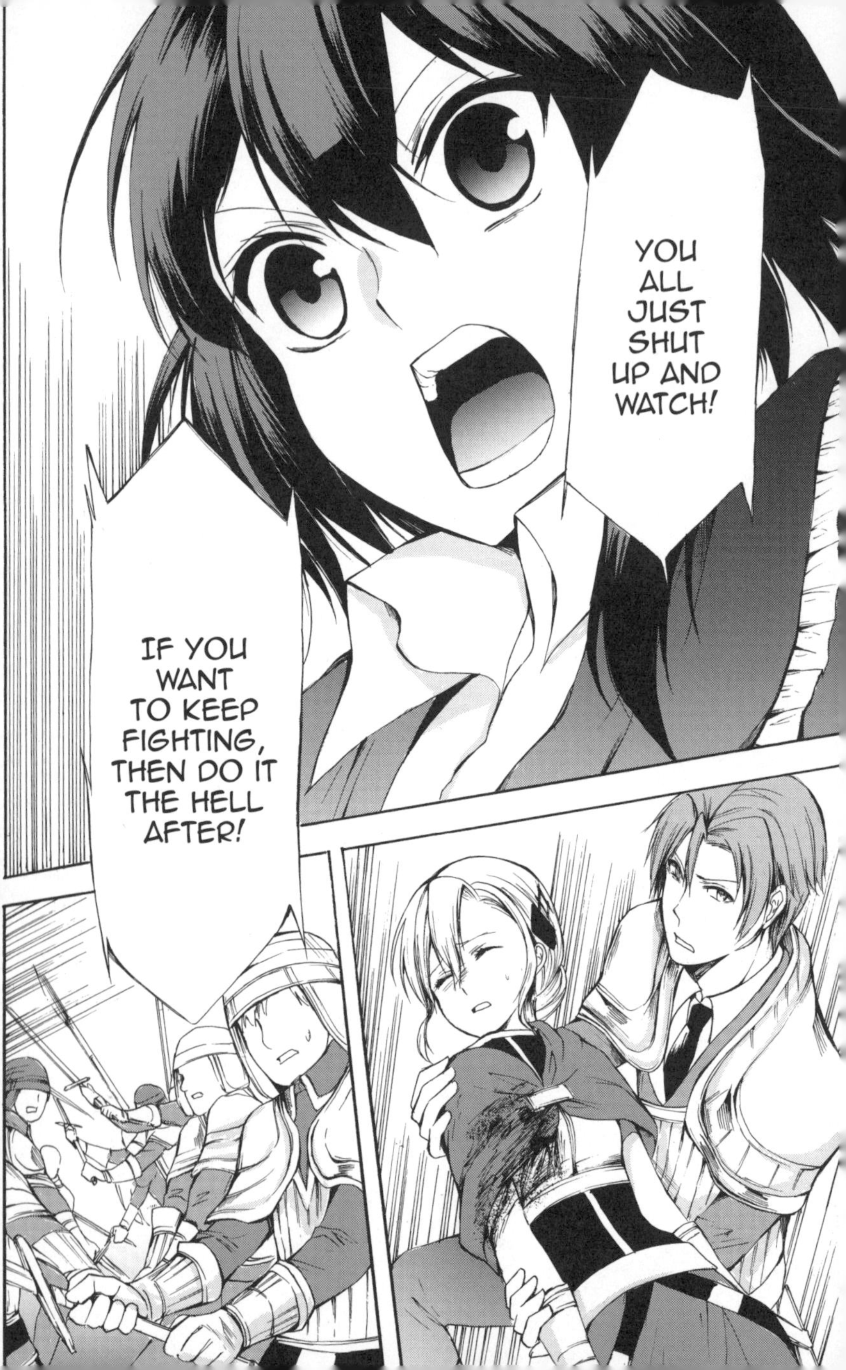
YOU ALL JUST SHUT UP AND WATCH!
IF YOU WANT TO KEEP FIGHTING, THEN DO IT THE HELL AFTER!

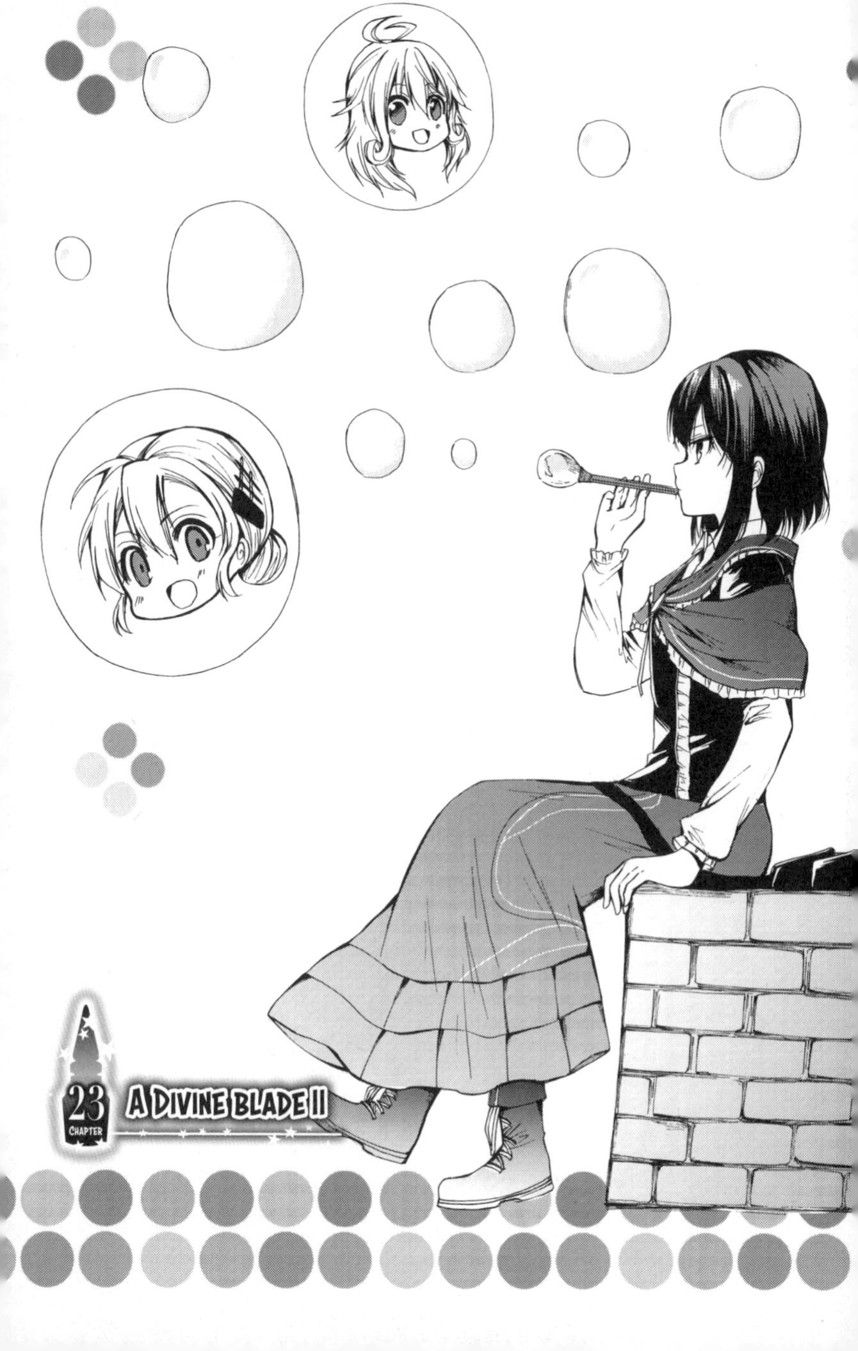
23
CHAPTER
A DIVINE BLADE II

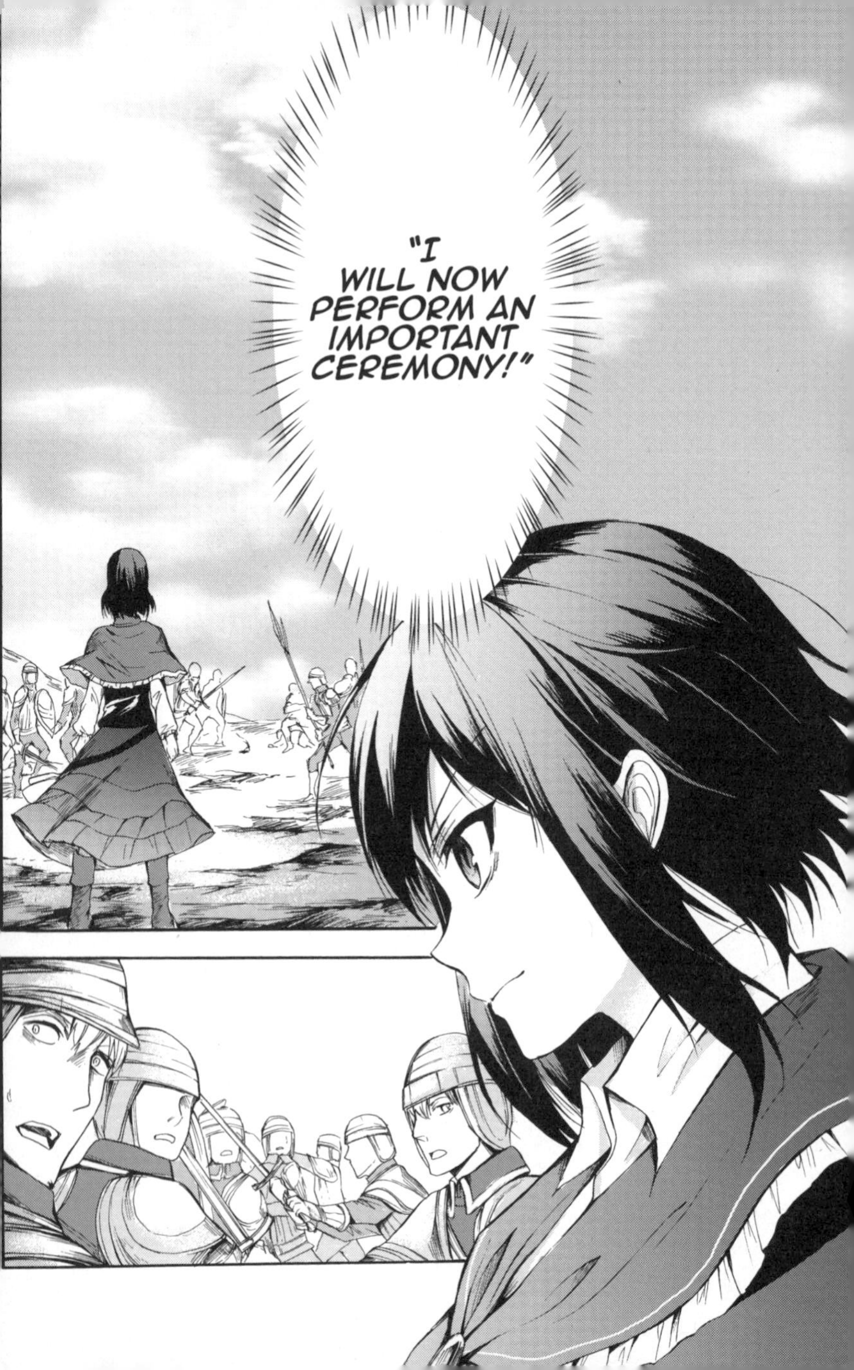
"I WILL NOW PERFORM AN IMPORTANT CEREMONY!"

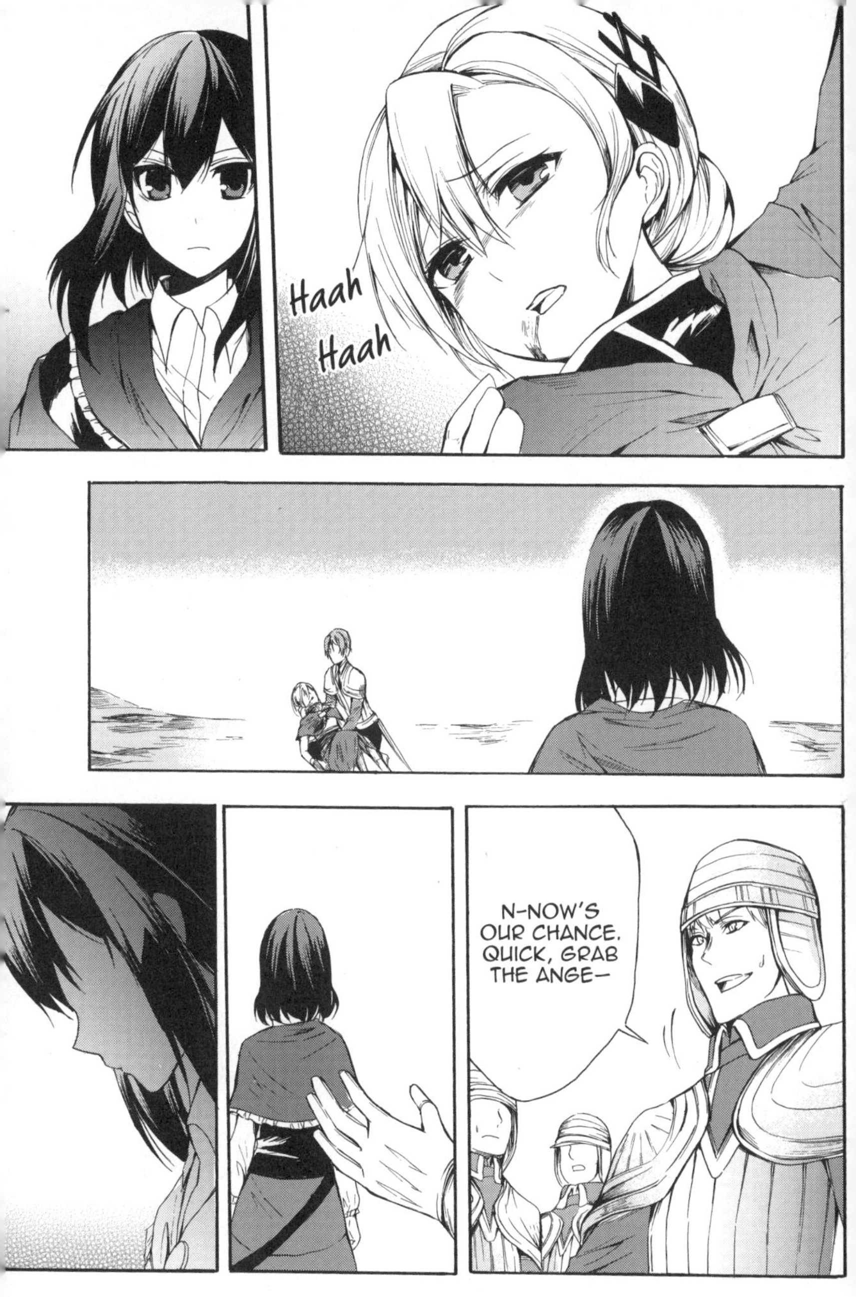
Haah
Haah
N-NOW'S OUR CHANCE. QUICK, GRAB THE ANGE—

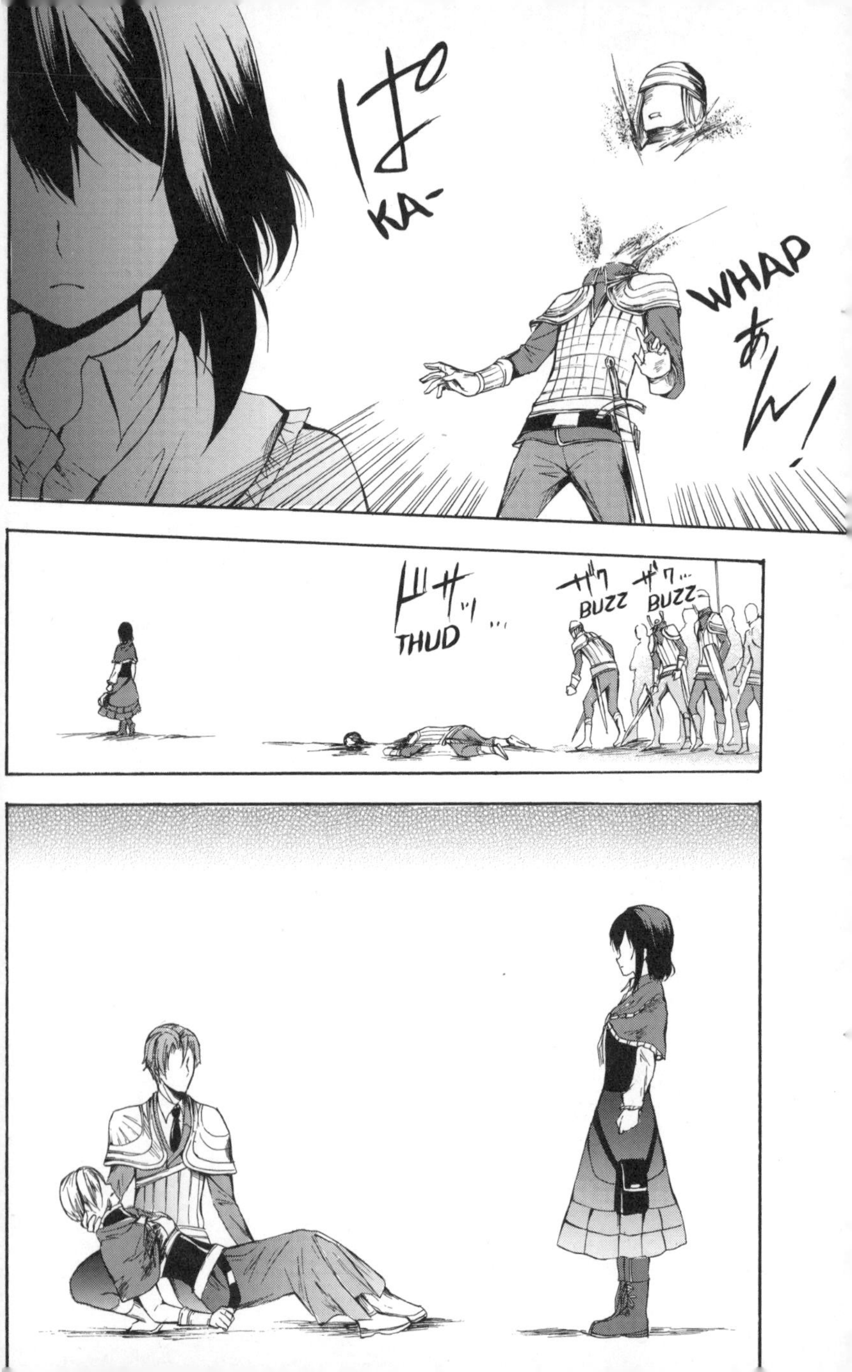

あん！
WHAP
ぱ
KA-
ザク ザク…
BUZZ BUZZ
ドサッ
THUD
…

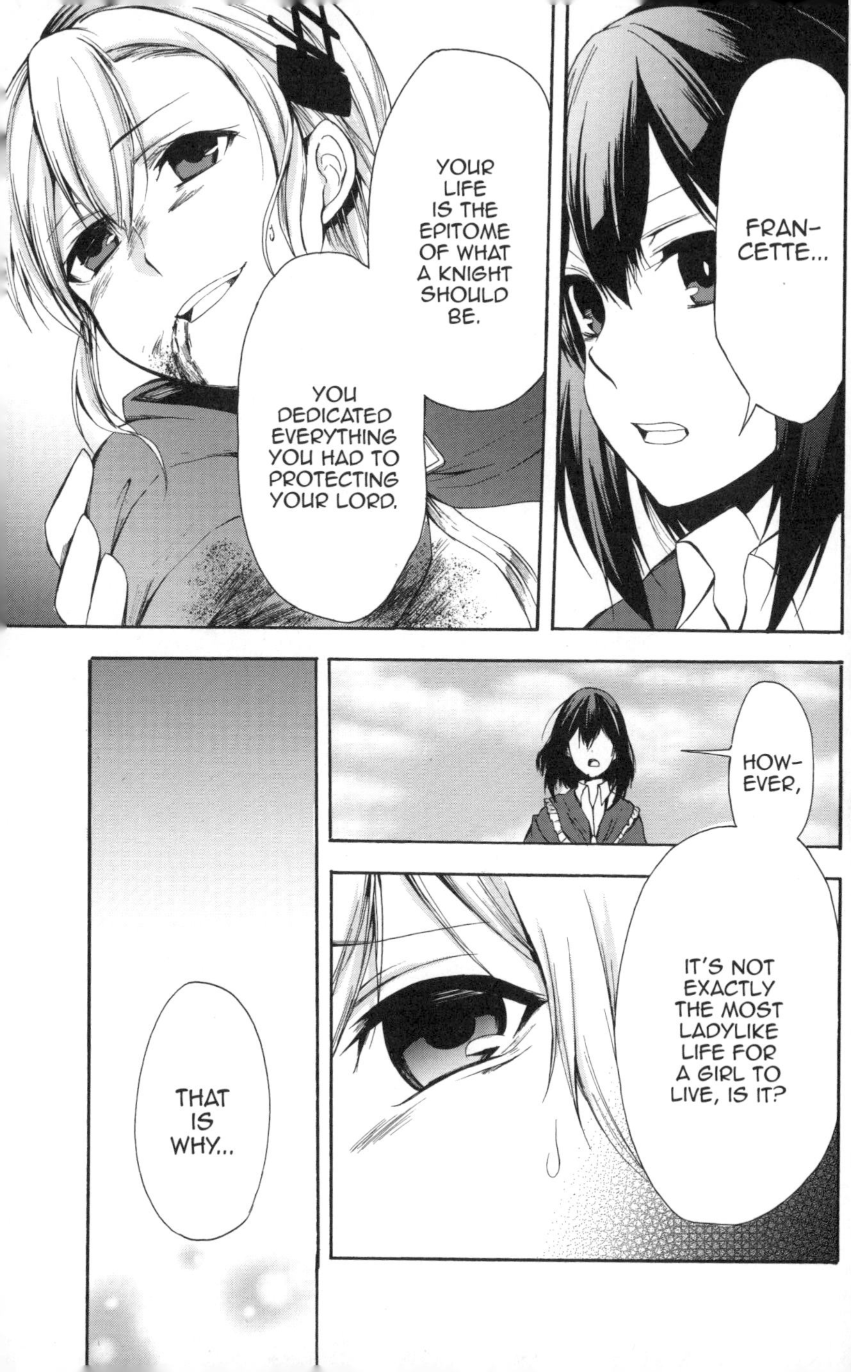
FRAN-CETTE...
YOUR LIFE IS THE EPITOME OF WHAT A KNIGHT SHOULD BE.
YOU DEDICATED EVERYTHING YOU HAD TO PROTECTING YOUR LORD.
HOW-EVER,
IT'S NOT EXACTLY THE MOST LADYLIKE LIFE FOR A GIRL TO LIVE, IS IT?
THAT IS WHY...

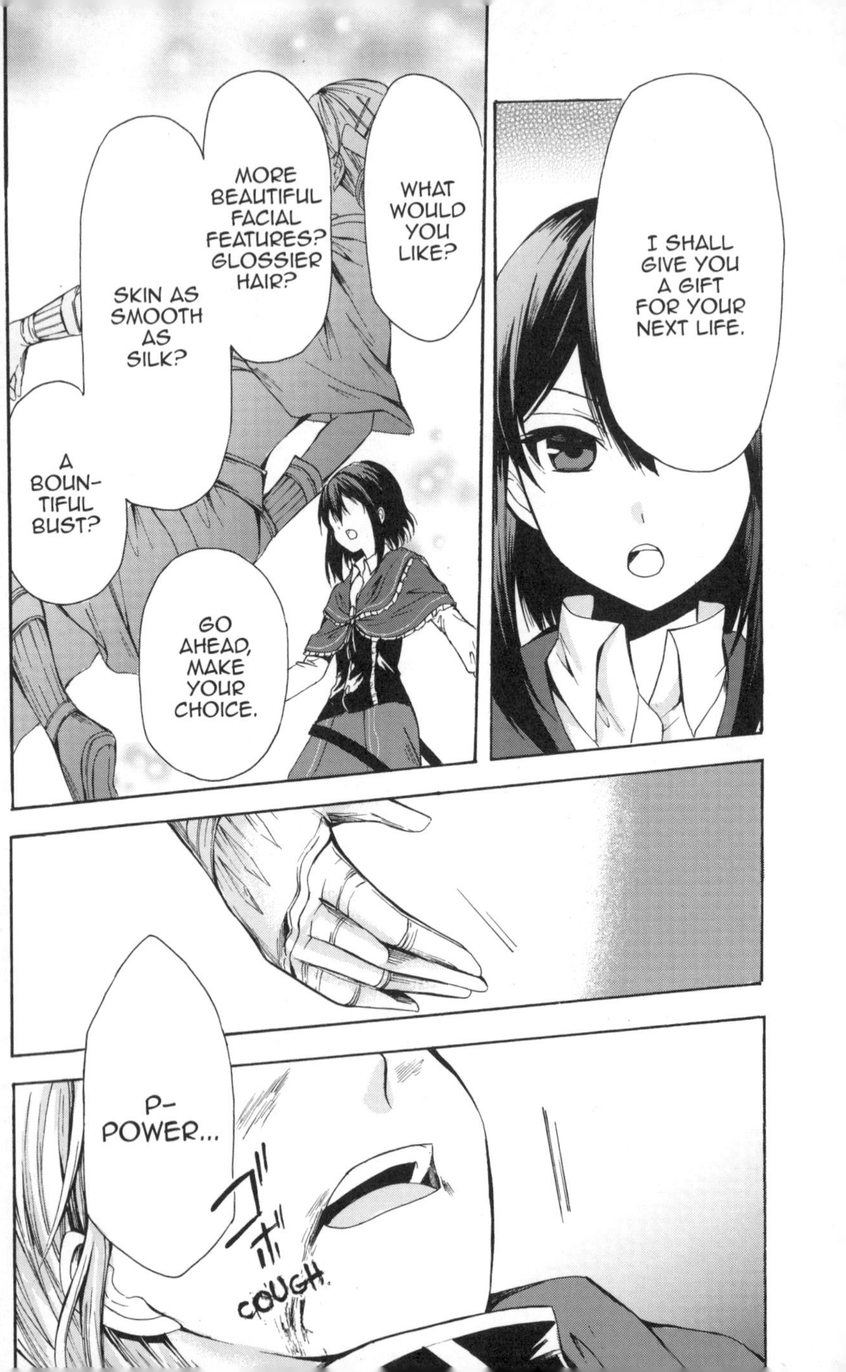
I SHALL GIVE YOU A GIFT FOR YOUR NEXT LIFE.
WHAT WOULD YOU LIKE?
MORE BEAUTIFUL FACIAL FEATURES? GLOSSIER HAIR?
SKIN AS SMOOTH AS SILK?
A BOUN-TIFUL BUST?
GO AHEAD, MAKE YOUR CHOICE.
P-POWER...
COUGH

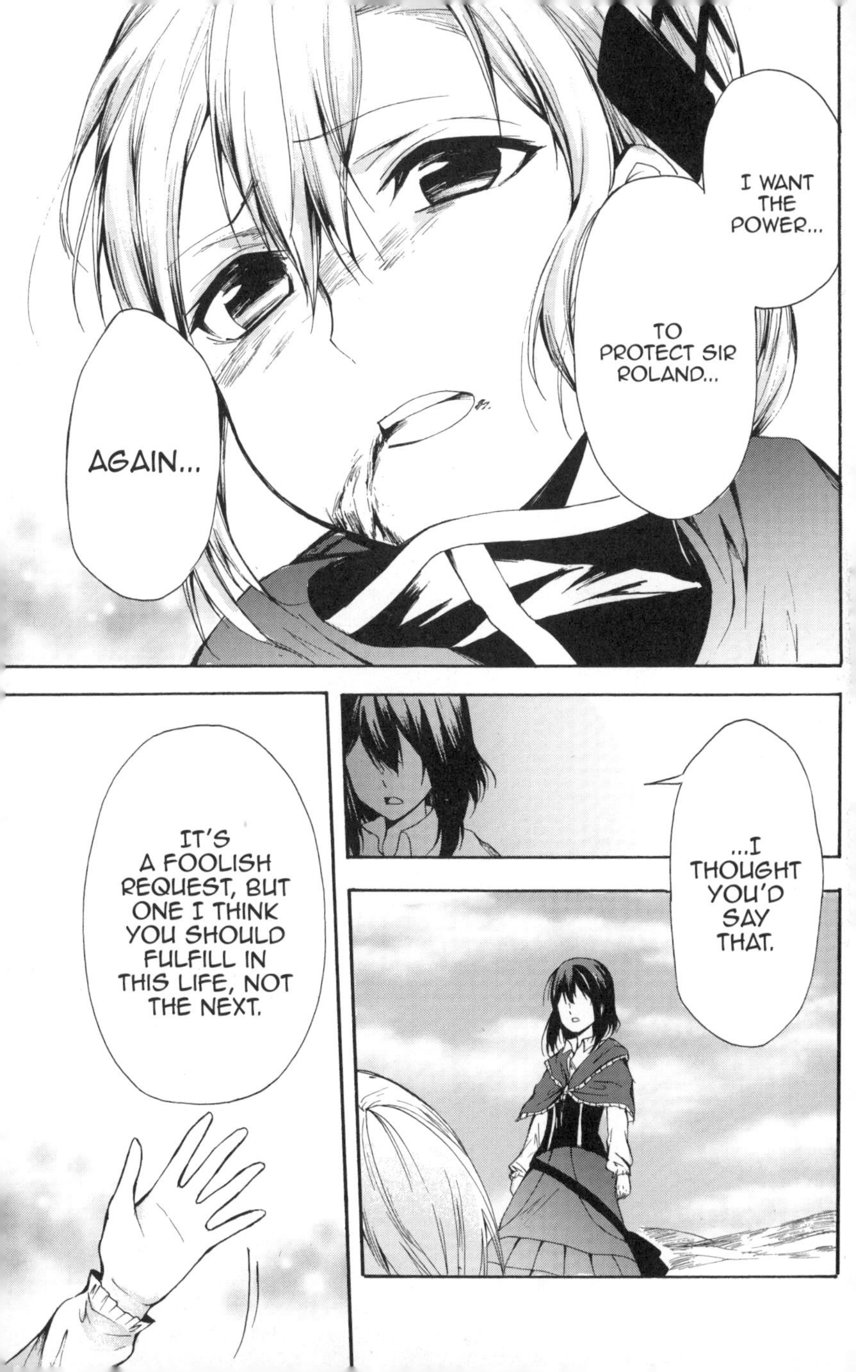
I WANT THE POWER...
TO PROTECT SIR ROLAND...
AGAIN...
...I THOUGHT YOU'D SAY THAT.
IT'S A FOOLISH REQUEST, BUT ONE I THINK YOU SHOULD FULFILL IN THIS LIFE, NOT THE NEXT.

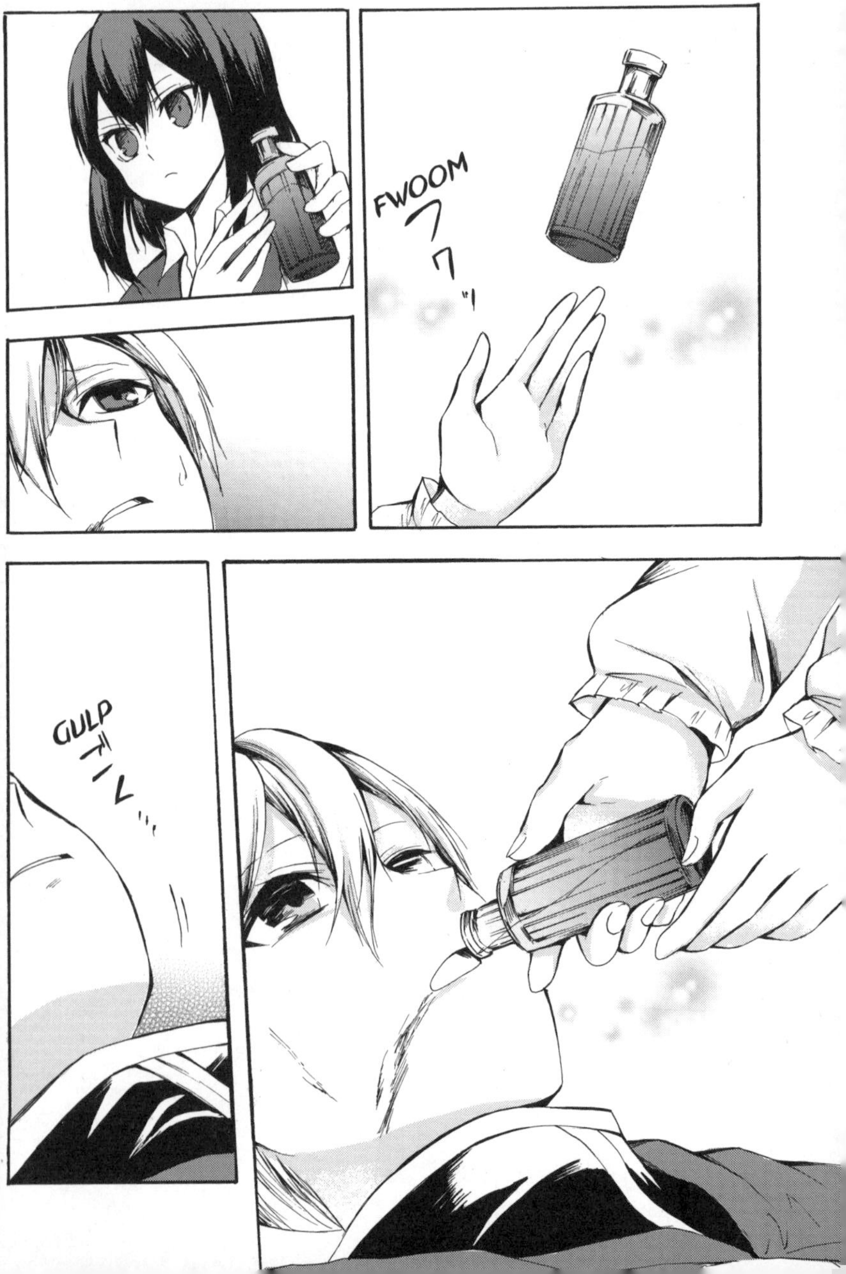
FWOOM
GULP

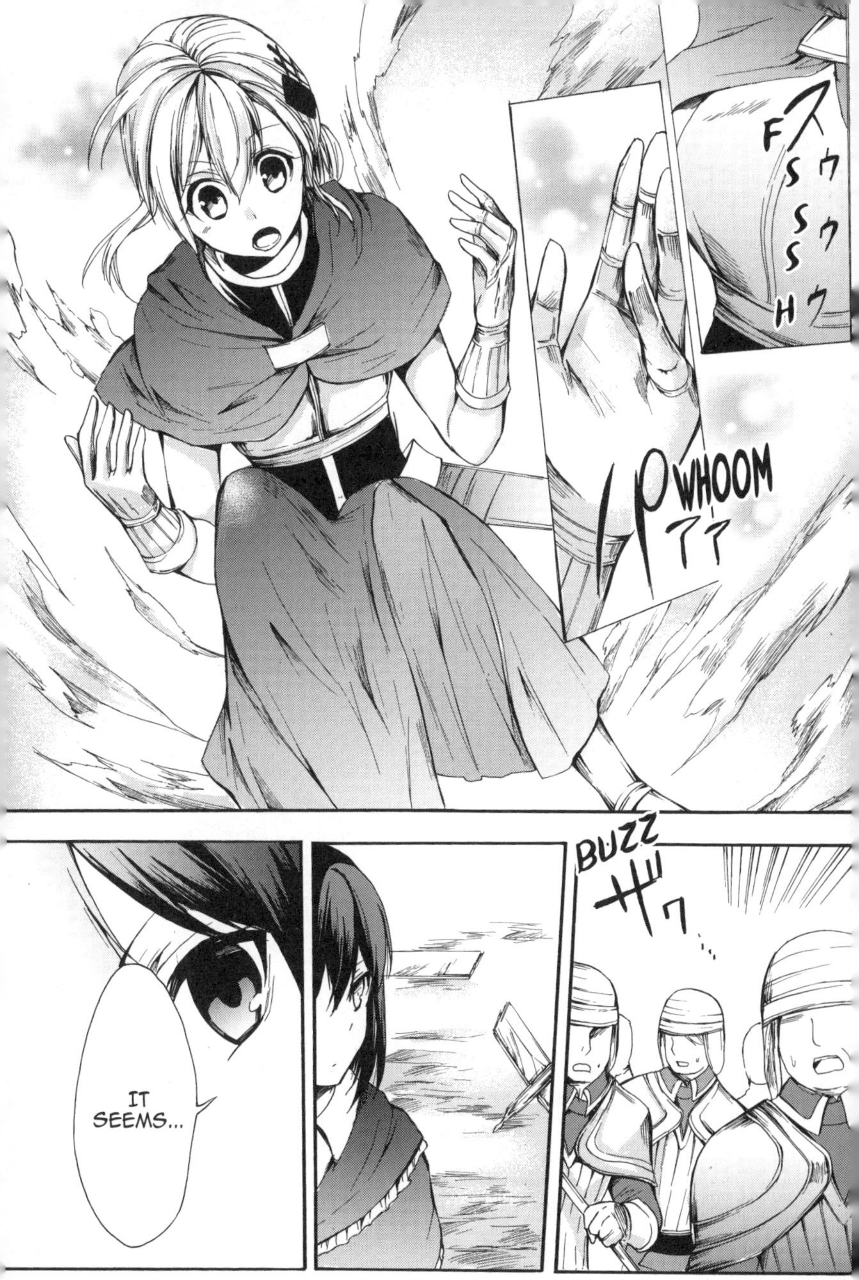
FSSSH
スウウウ
WHOOM
アア
BUZZ
ザワ…
IT SEEMS...

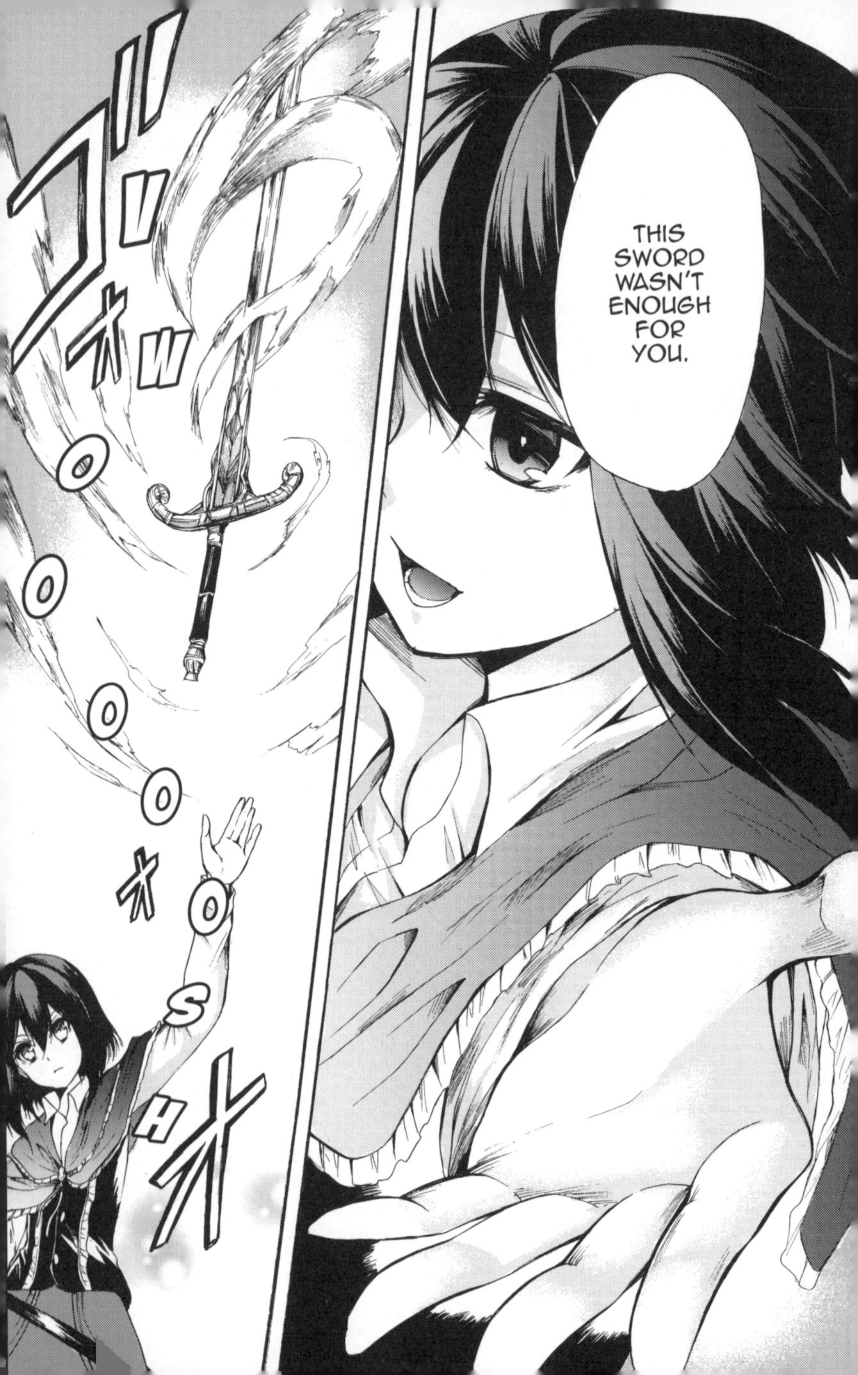
THIS SWORD WASN'T ENOUGH FOR YOU.
WOOOOOSH

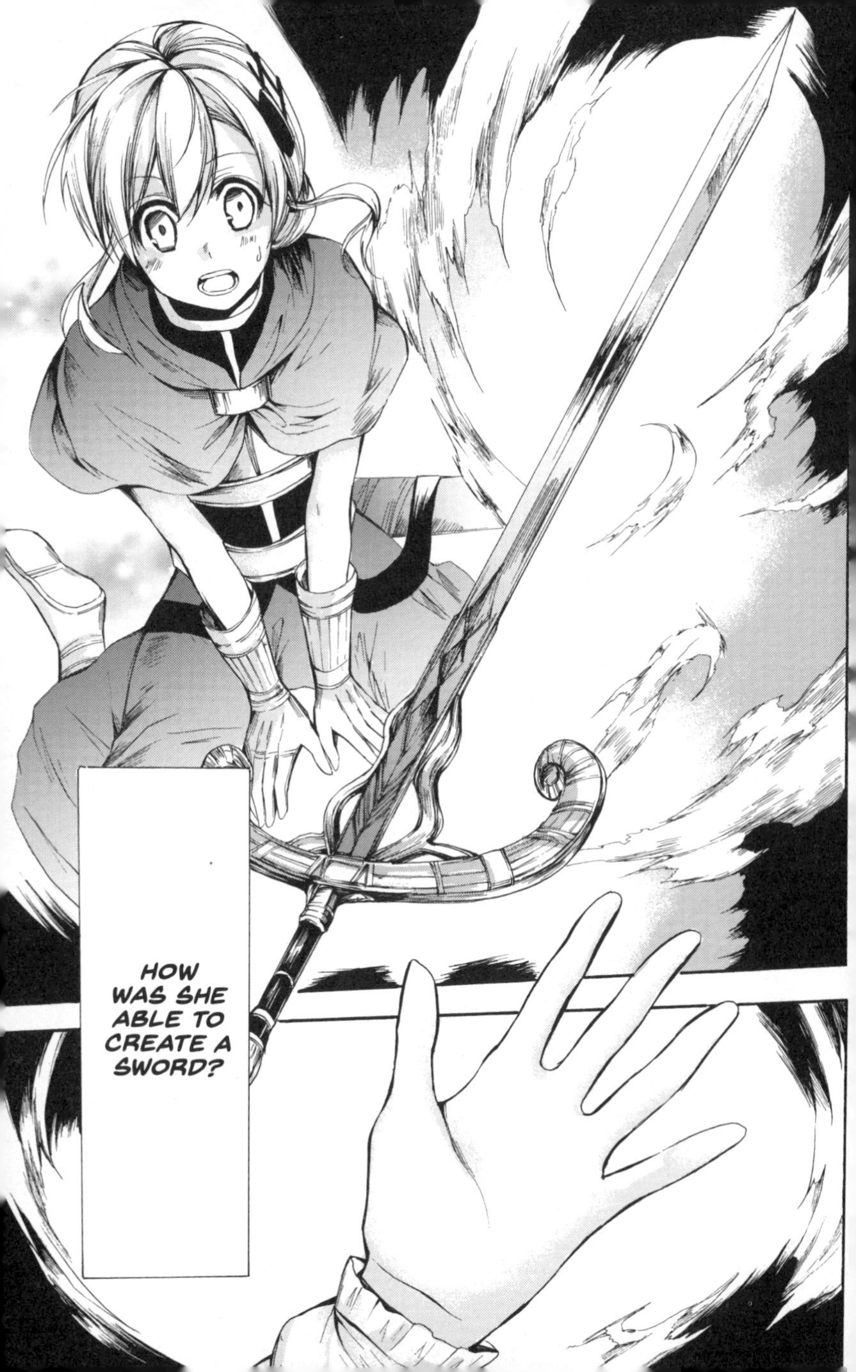
HOW WAS SHE ABLE TO CREATE A SWORD?

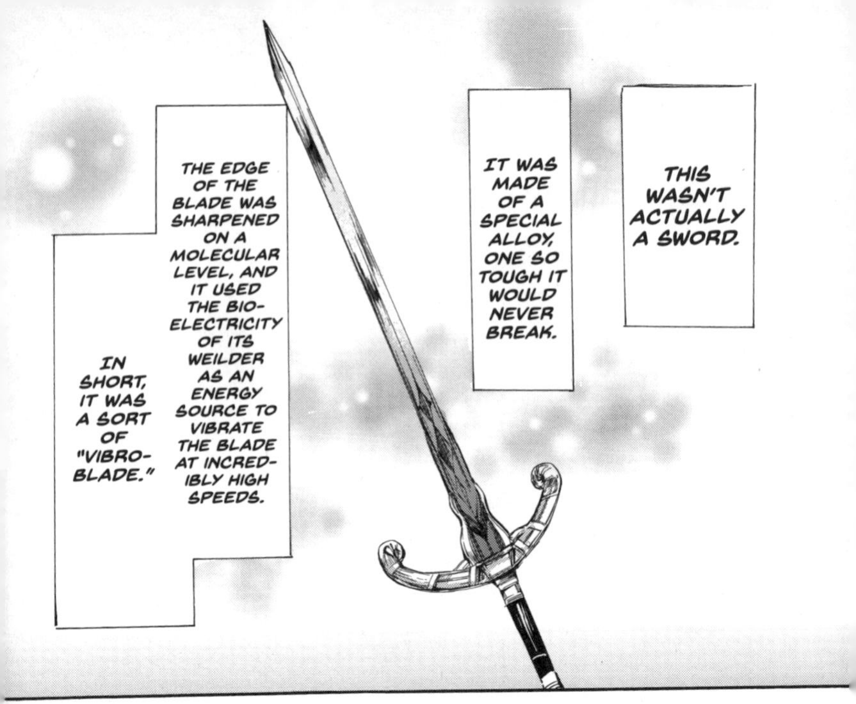
THIS WASN'T ACTUALLY A SWORD.
IT WAS MADE OF A SPECIAL ALLOY, ONE SO TOUGH IT WOULD NEVER BREAK.
THE EDGE OF THE BLADE WAS SHARPENED ON A MOLECULAR LEVEL, AND IT USED THE BIO-ELECTRICITY OF ITS WEILDER AS AN ENERGY SOURCE TO VIBRATE THE BLADE AT INCREDIBLY HIGH SPEEDS.
IN SHORT, IT WAS A SORT OF "VIBRO-BLADE."

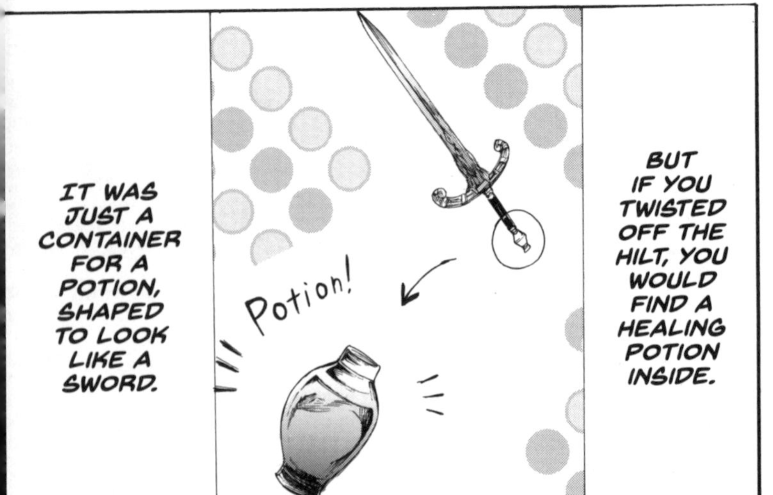
BUT IF YOU TWISTED OFF THE HILT, YOU WOULD FIND A HEALING POTION INSIDE.
Potion!
IT WAS JUST A CONTAINER FOR A POTION, SHAPED TO LOOK LIKE A SWORD.

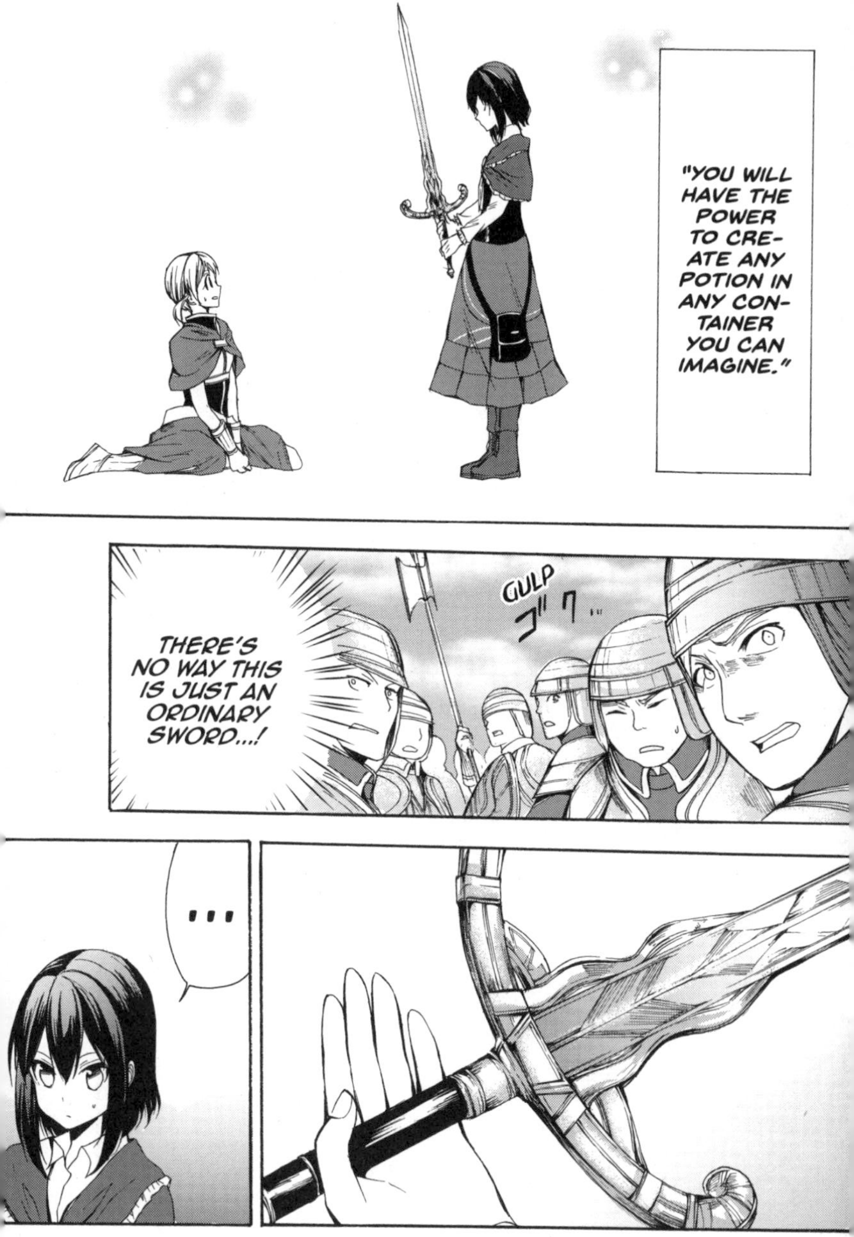
"YOU WILL HAVE THE POWER TO CRE-ATE ANY POTION IN ANY CON-TAINER YOU CAN IMAGINE."
GULP
ゴク
THERE'S NO WAY THIS IS JUST AN ORDINARY SWORD...!
...

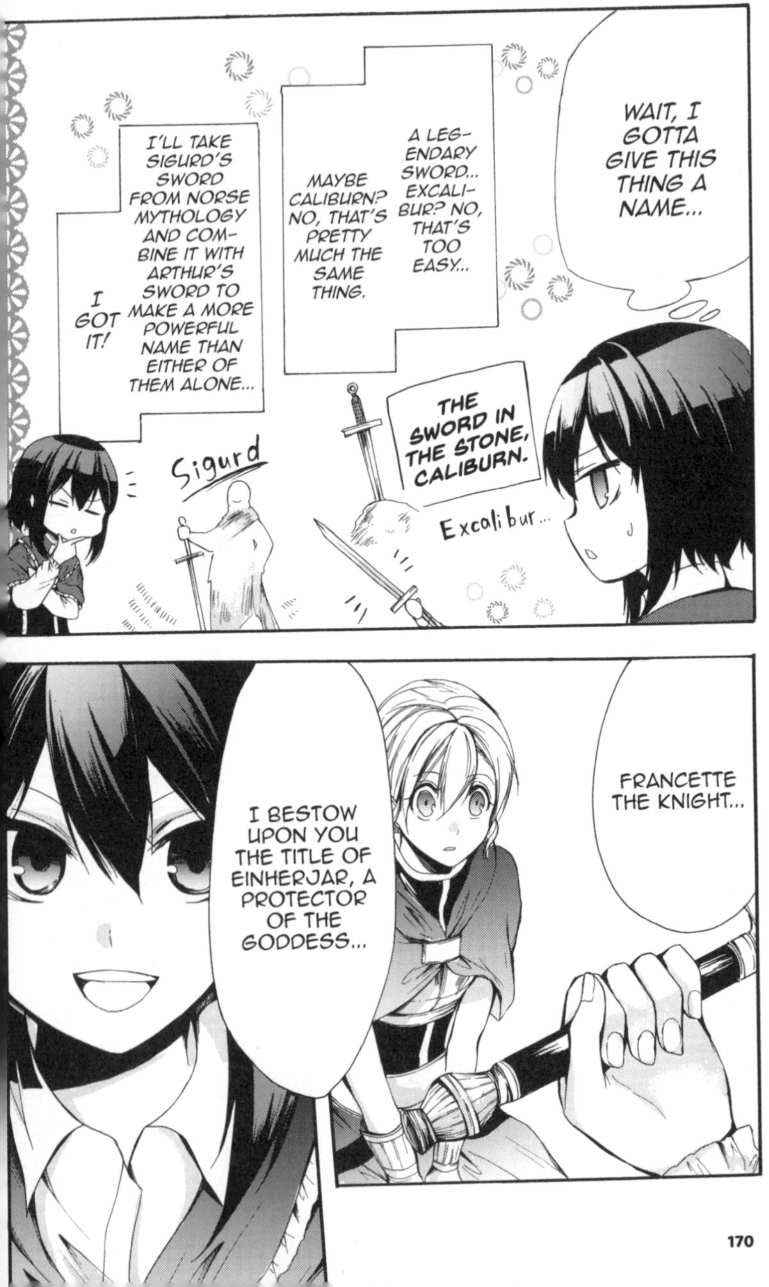
WAIT, I GOTTA GIVE THIS THING A NAME...
A LEG-ENDARY SWORD... EXCALI-BUR? NO, THAT'S TOO EASY...
THE SWORD IN THE STONE, CALIBURN.
Excalibur...
MAYBE CALIBURN? NO, THAT'S PRETTY MUCH THE SAME THING.
I'LL TAKE SIGURD'S SWORD FROM NORSE MYTHOLOGY AND COM-BINE IT WITH ARTHUR'S SWORD TO MAKE A MORE POWERFUL NAME THAN EITHER OF THEM ALONE...
Sigurd
I GOT IT!
FRANCETTE THE KNIGHT...
I BESTOW UPON YOU THE TITLE OF EINHERJAR, A PROTECTOR OF THE GODDESS...

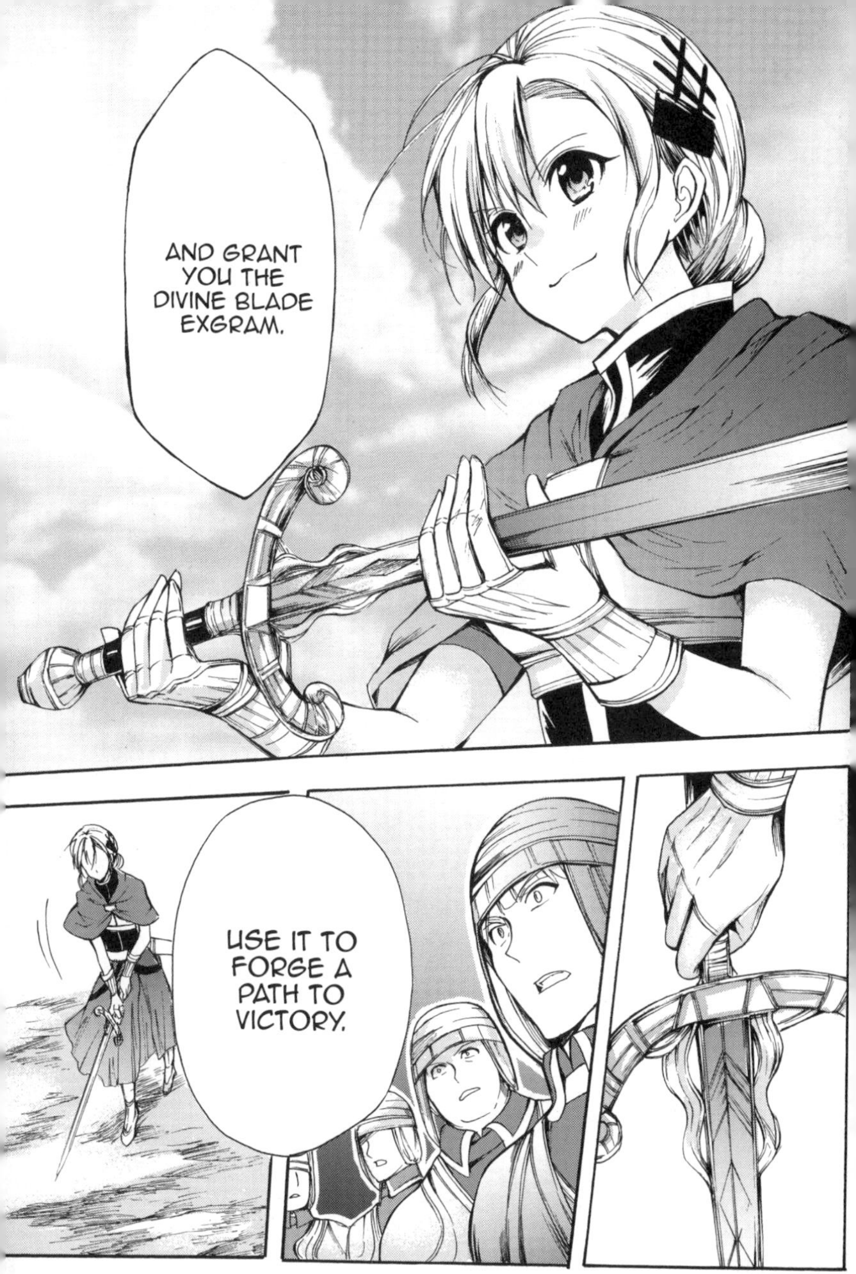
AND GRANT YOU THE DIVINE BLADE EXGRAM.
USE IT TO FORGE A PATH TO VICTORY.

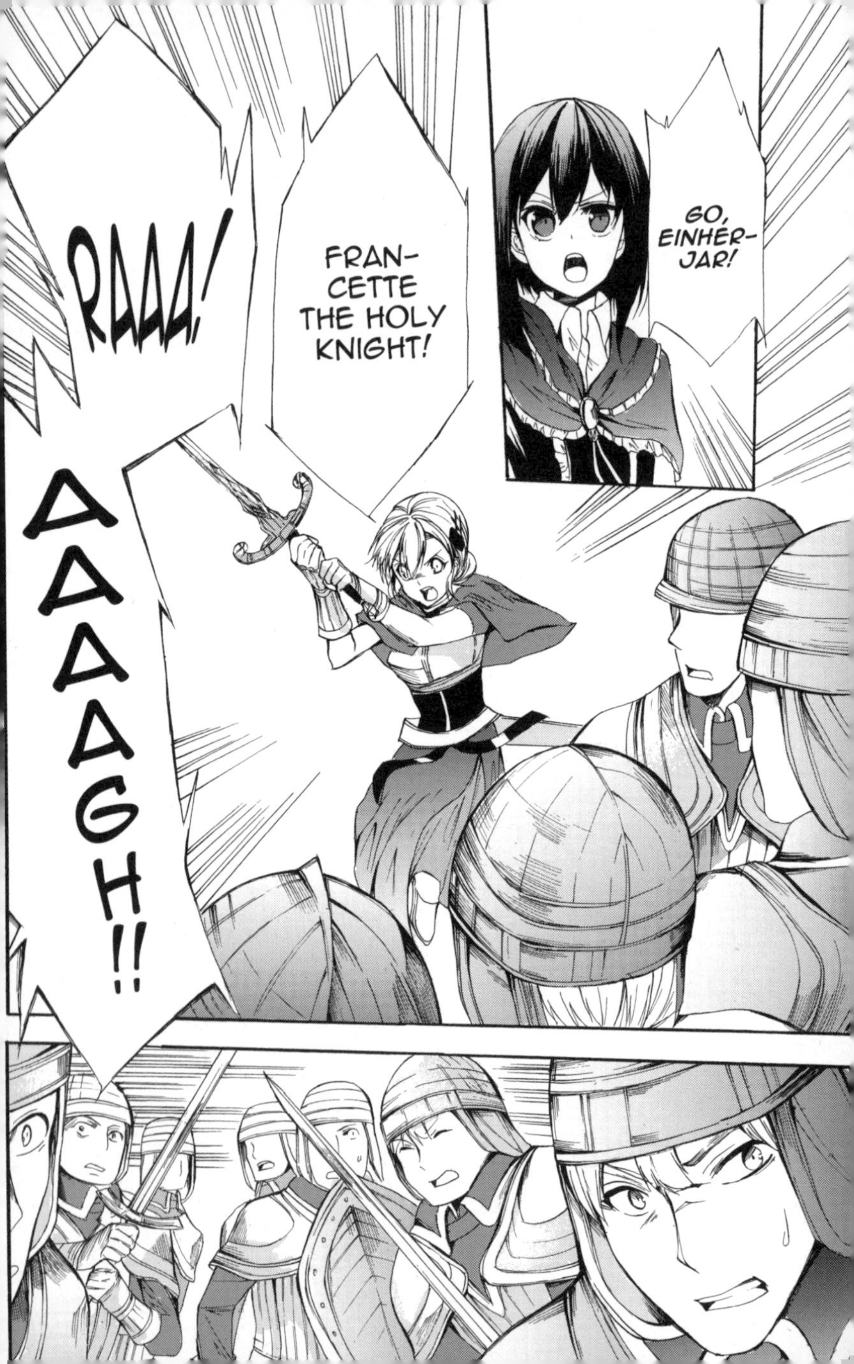
GO, EINHER-JAR!
FRAN-CETTE THE HOLY KNIGHT!
RAAA!
AAAAAGH!!

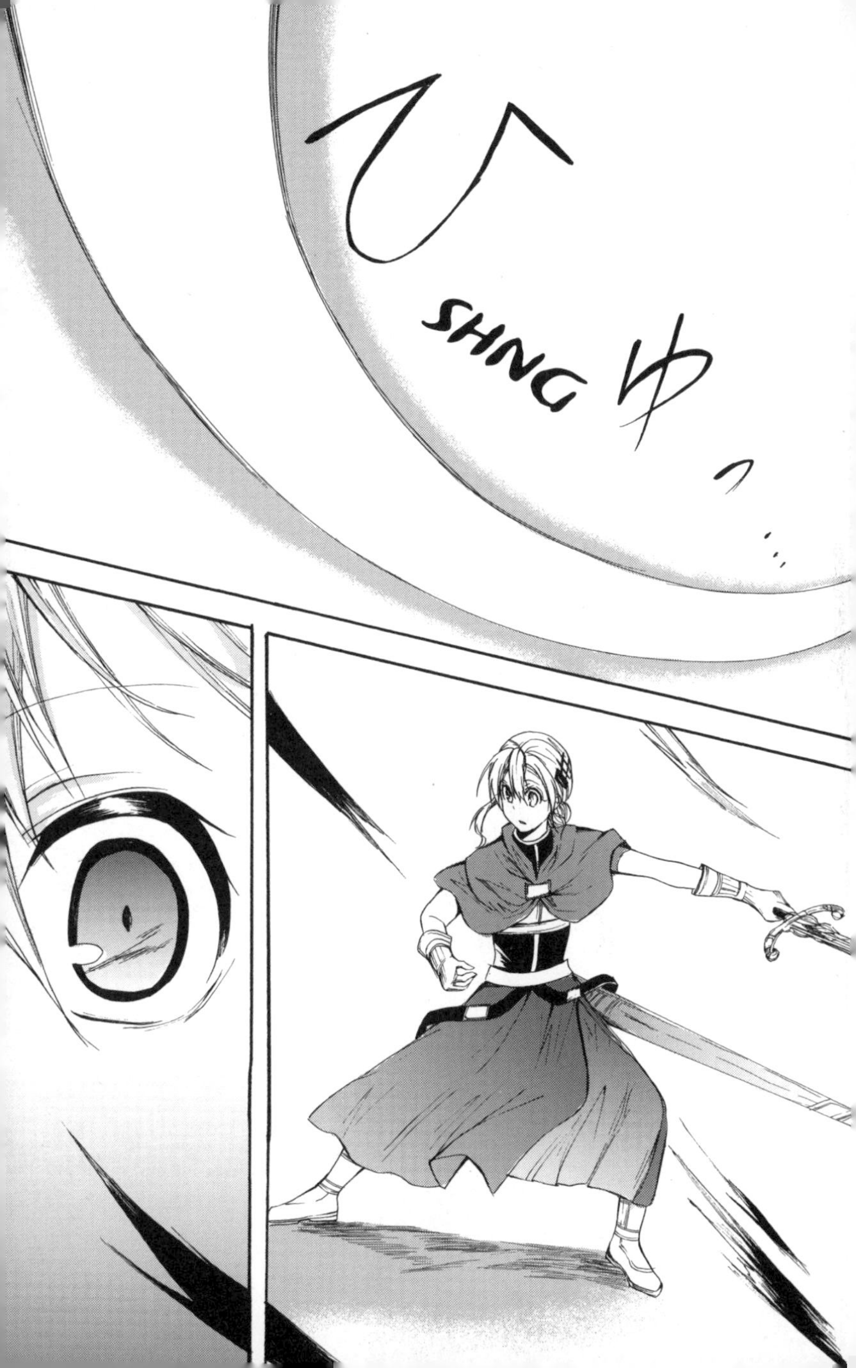
ひゅっ…
SHNG

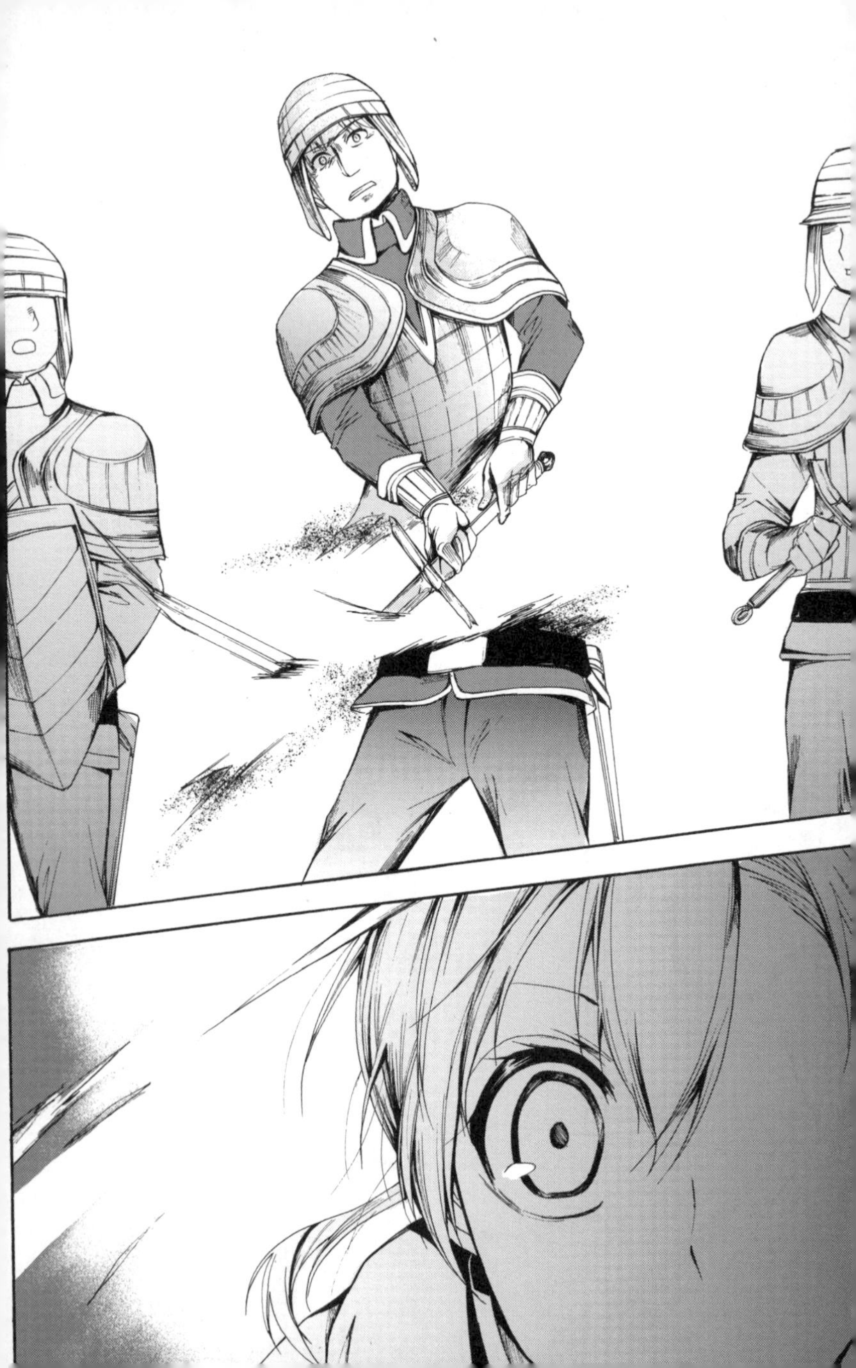

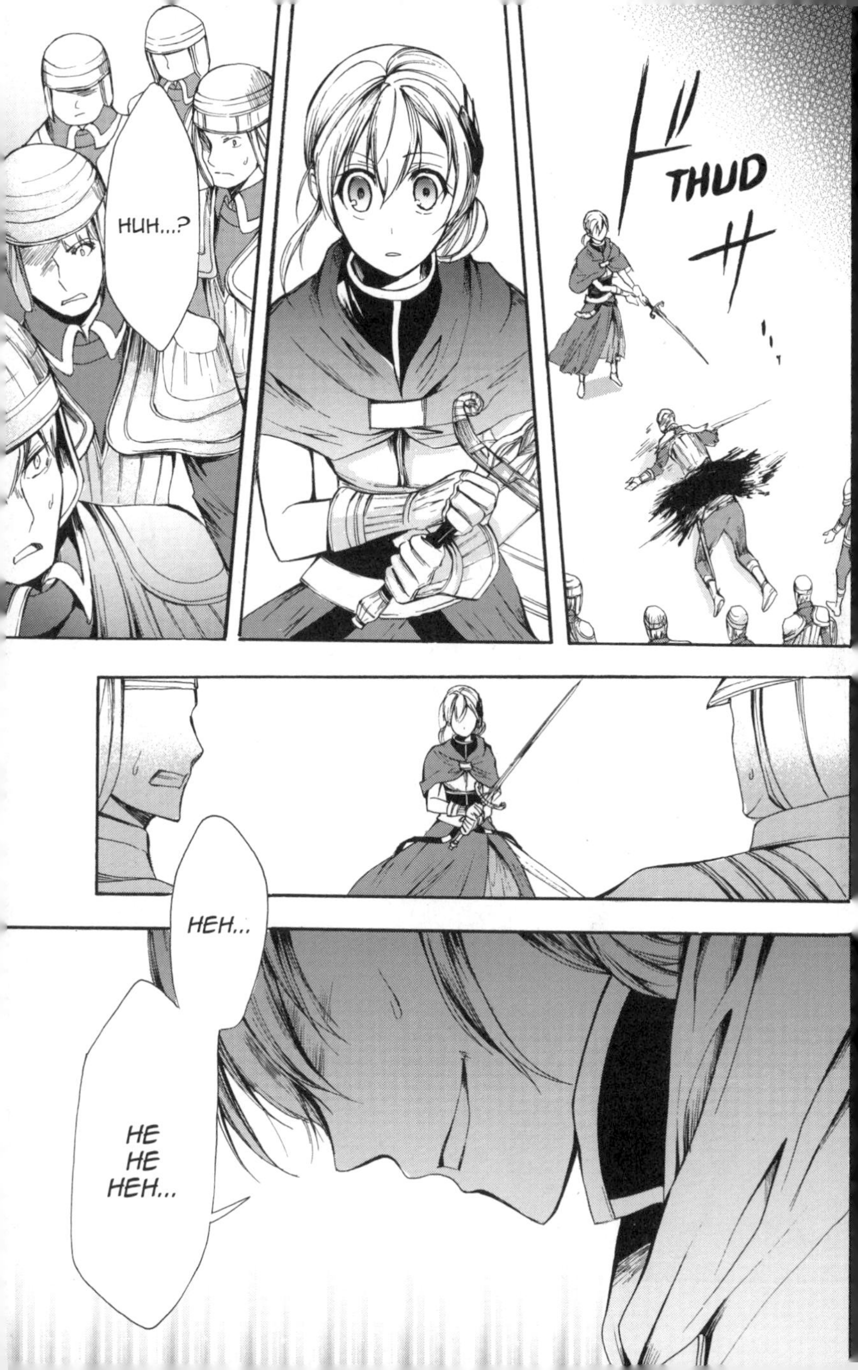
THUD
HUH...?
HEH...
HE HE HEH...

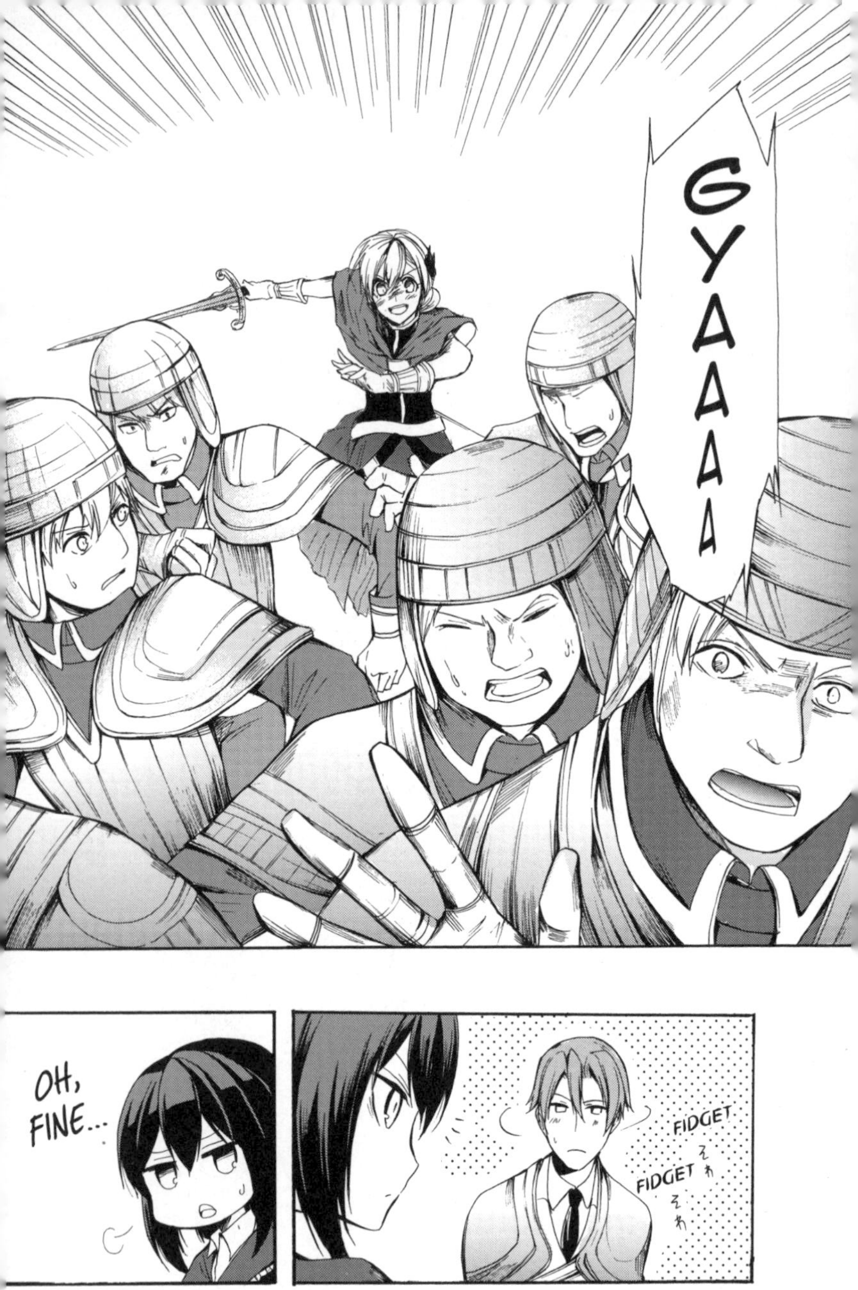
GYAAAA
FIDGET
FIDGET
そわ
そわ
OH, FINE...

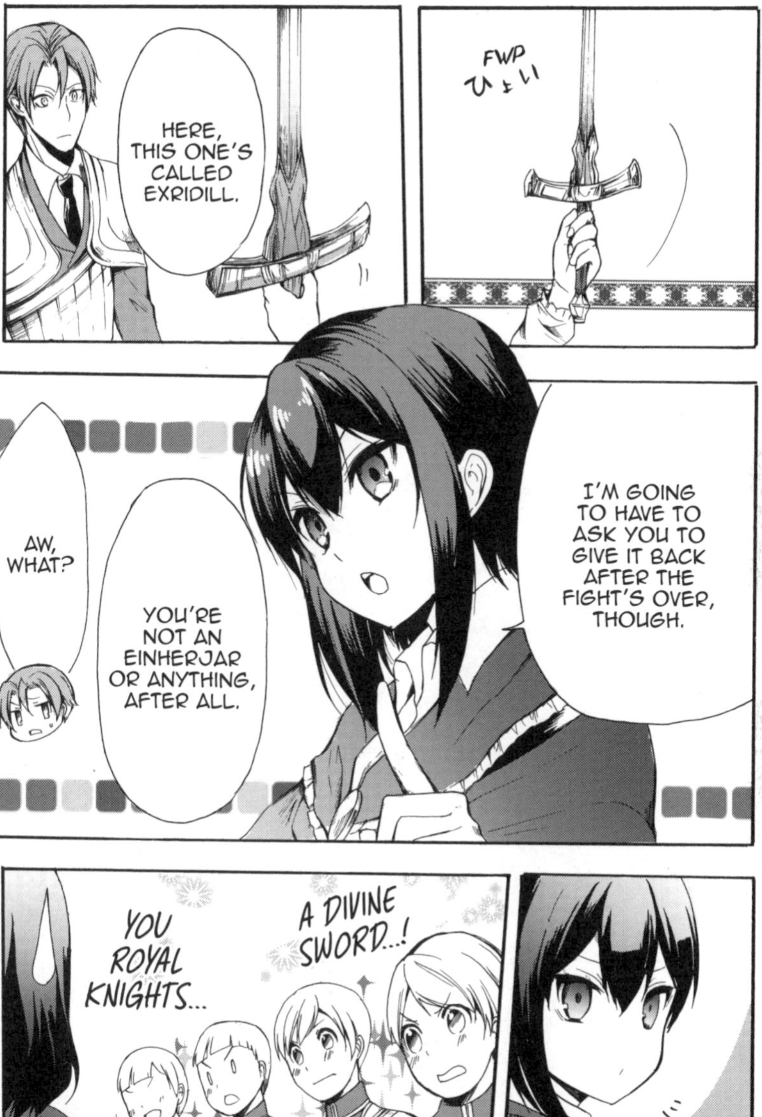
FWP
ひょい
HERE, THIS ONE'S CALLED EXRIDILL.
I'M GOING TO HAVE TO ASK YOU TO GIVE IT BACK AFTER THE FIGHT'S OVER, THOUGH.
YOU'RE NOT AN EINHERJAR OR ANYTHING, AFTER ALL.
AW, WHAT?
...
A DIVINE SWORD...!
YOU ROYAL KNIGHTS...

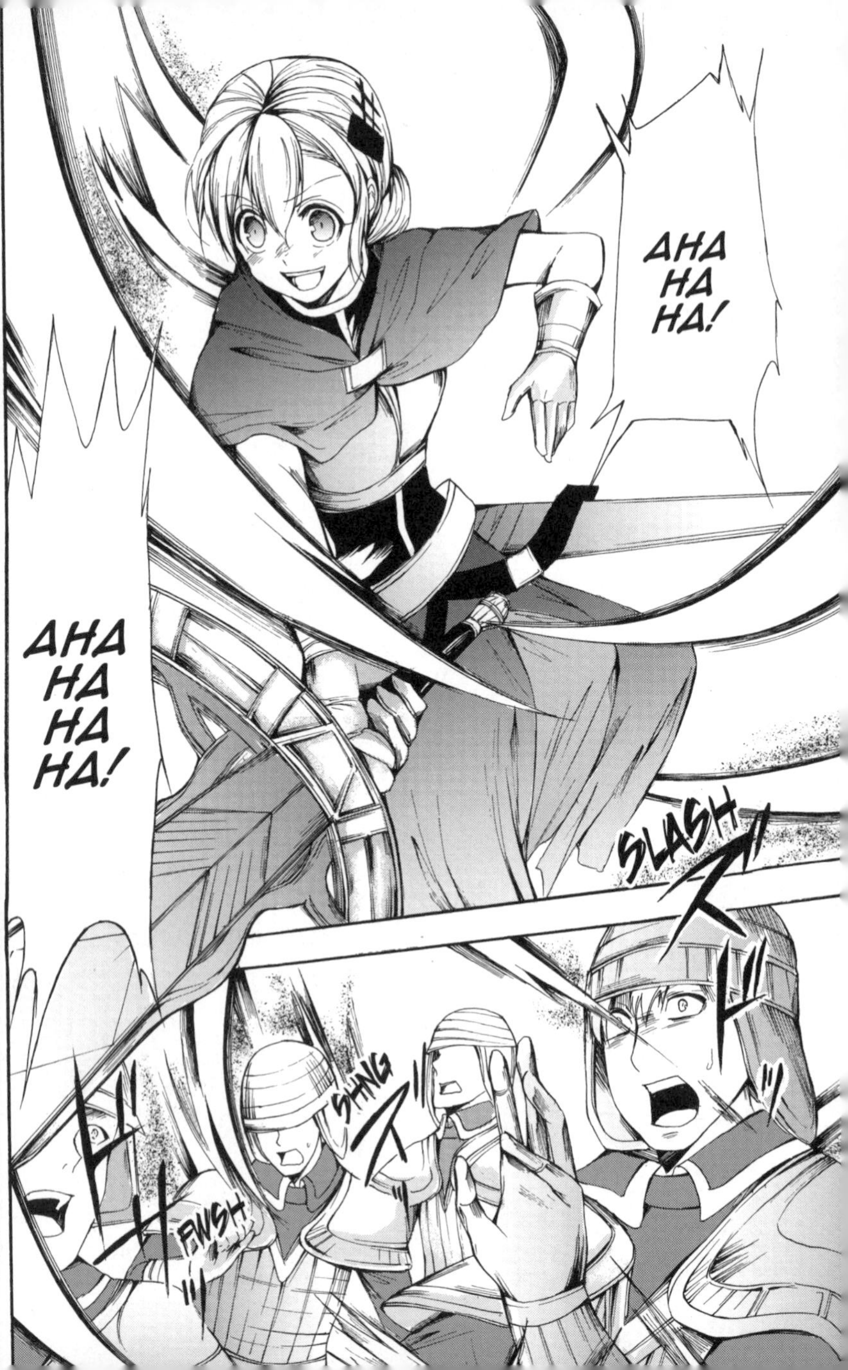
AHA HA HA!
AHA HA HA HA!
SLASH
SHNG
FWSH

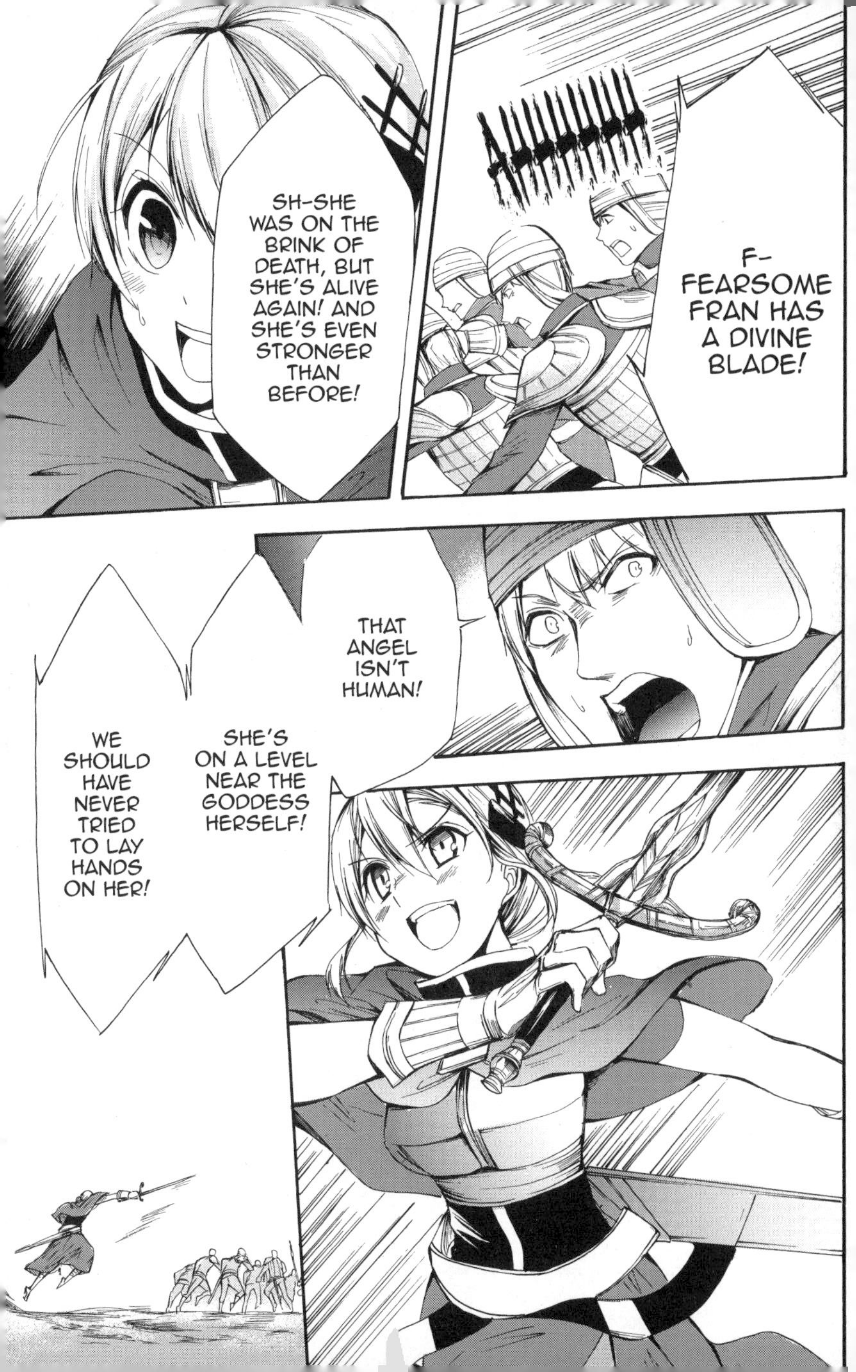
AHHHHHHHH
F-FEARSOME FRAN HAS A DIVINE BLADE!
SH-SHE WAS ON THE BRINK OF DEATH, BUT SHE'S ALIVE AGAIN! AND SHE'S EVEN STRONGER THAN BEFORE!
THAT ANGEL ISN'T HUMAN!
SHE'S ON A LEVEL NEAR THE GODDESS HERSELF!
WE SHOULD HAVE NEVER TRIED TO LAY HANDS ON HER!

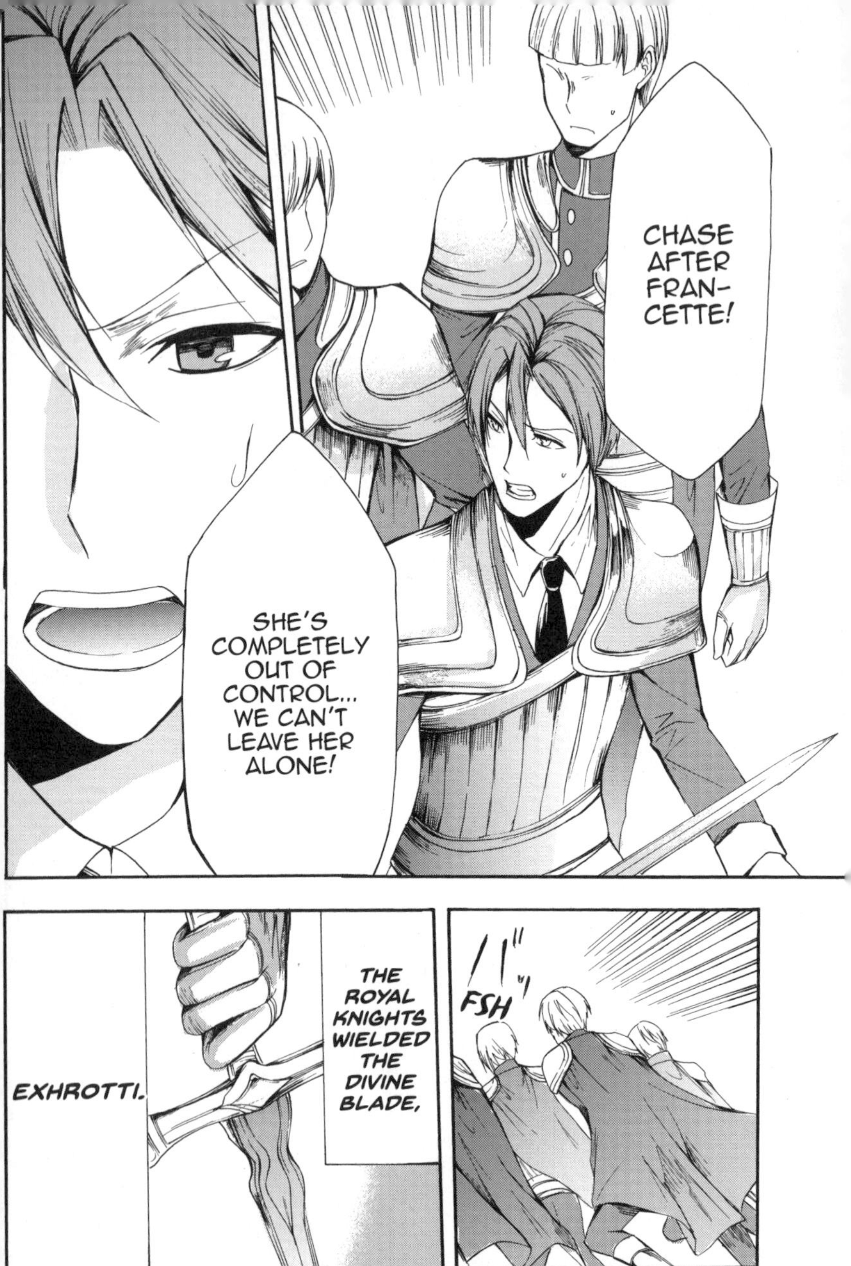
CHASE AFTER FRAN-CETTE!
SHE'S COMPLETELY OUT OF CONTROL... WE CAN'T LEAVE HER ALONE!
FSH
THE ROYAL KNIGHTS WIELDED THE DIVINE BLADE,
EXHROTTI.

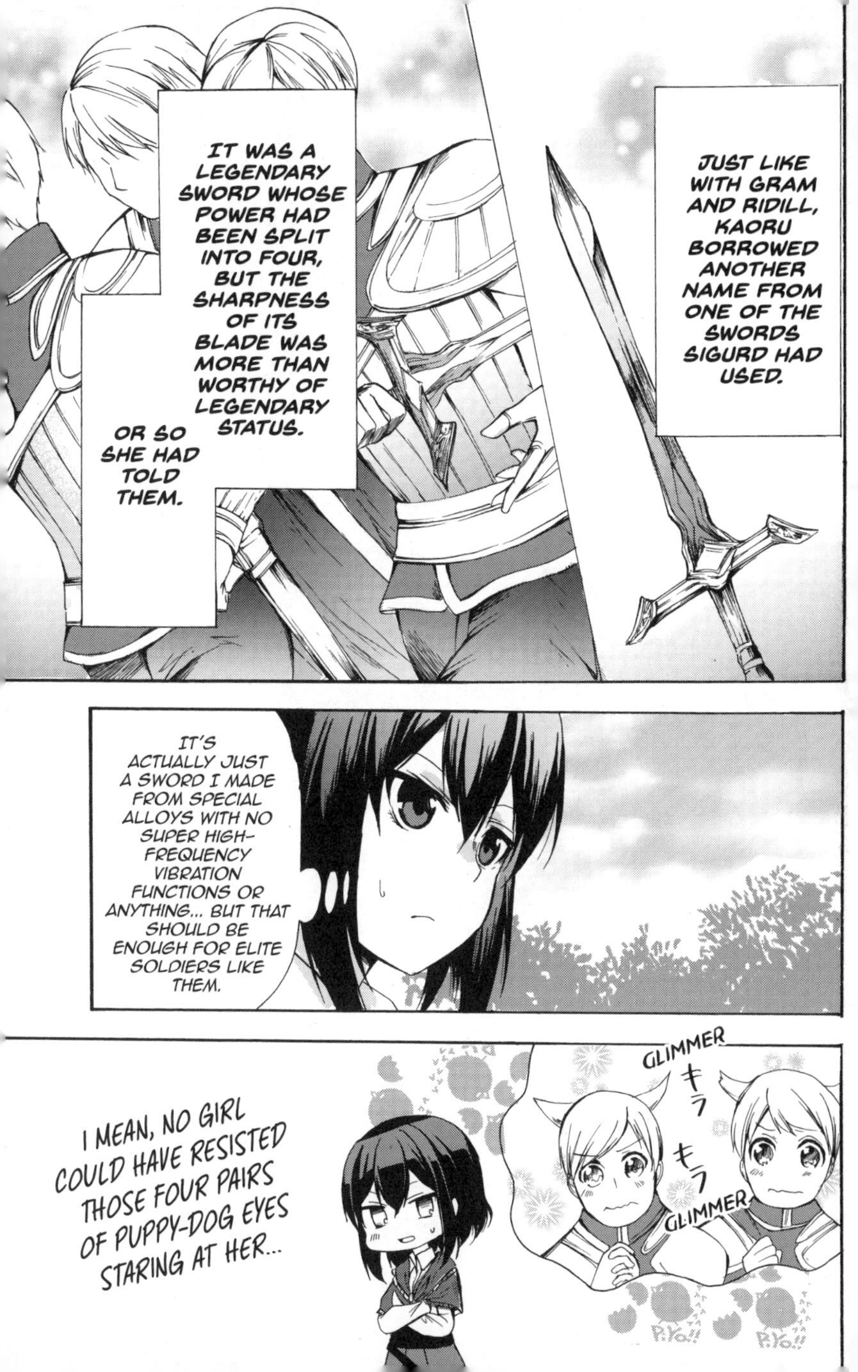
JUST LIKE WITH GRAM AND RIDILL, KAORU BORROWED ANOTHER NAME FROM ONE OF THE SWORDS SIGURD HAD USED.
IT WAS A LEGENDARY SWORD WHOSE POWER HAD BEEN SPLIT INTO FOUR, BUT THE SHARPNESS OF ITS BLADE WAS MORE THAN WORTHY OF LEGENDARY STATUS.
OR SO SHE HAD TOLD THEM.
IT'S ACTUALLY JUST A SWORD I MADE FROM SPECIAL ALLOYS WITH NO SUPER HIGH-FREQUENCY VIBRATION FUNCTIONS OR ANYTHING... BUT THAT SHOULD BE ENOUGH FOR ELITE SOLDIERS LIKE THEM.
GLIMMER
キラ
キラ
GLIMMER
P.Yo!!
P.Yo!!
I MEAN, NO GIRL COULD HAVE RESISTED THOSE FOUR PAIRS OF PUPPY-DOG EYES STARING AT HER...

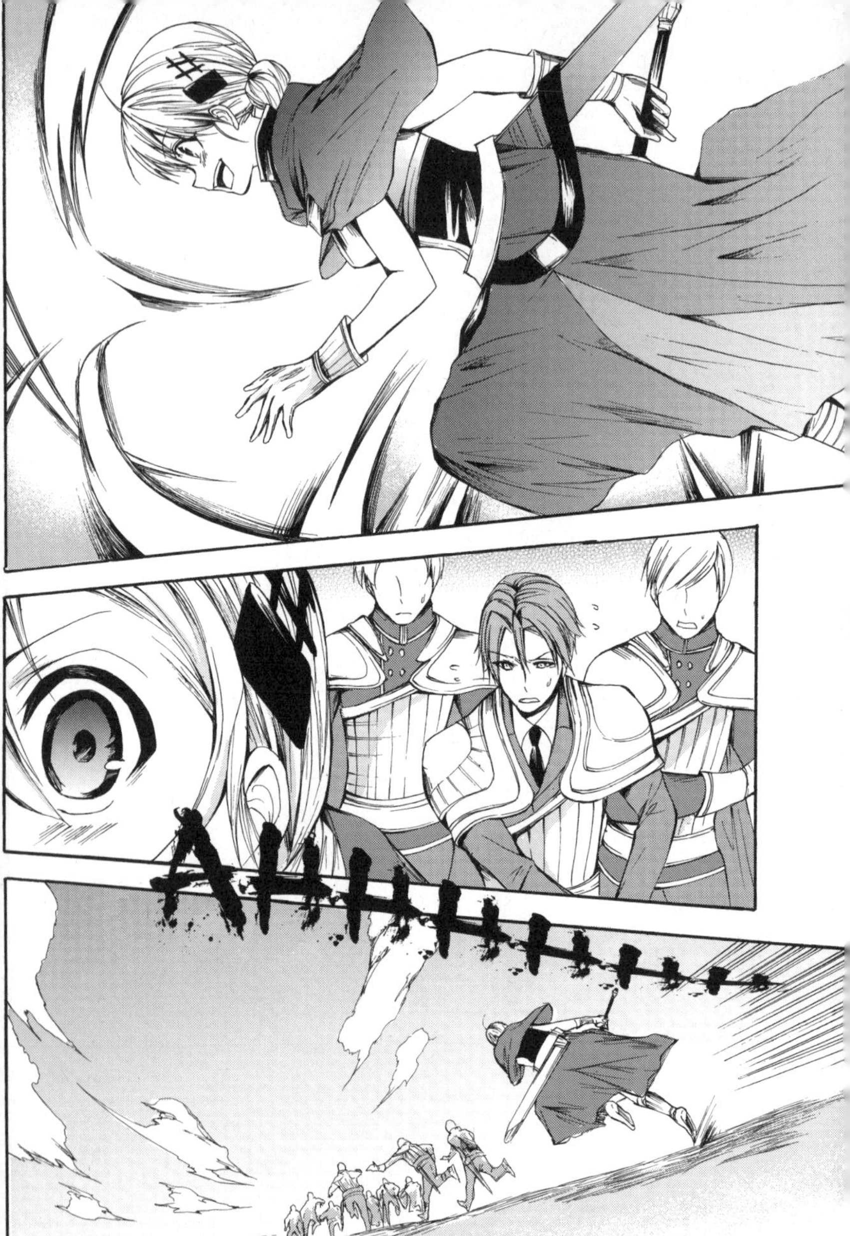
AHHHHHH...

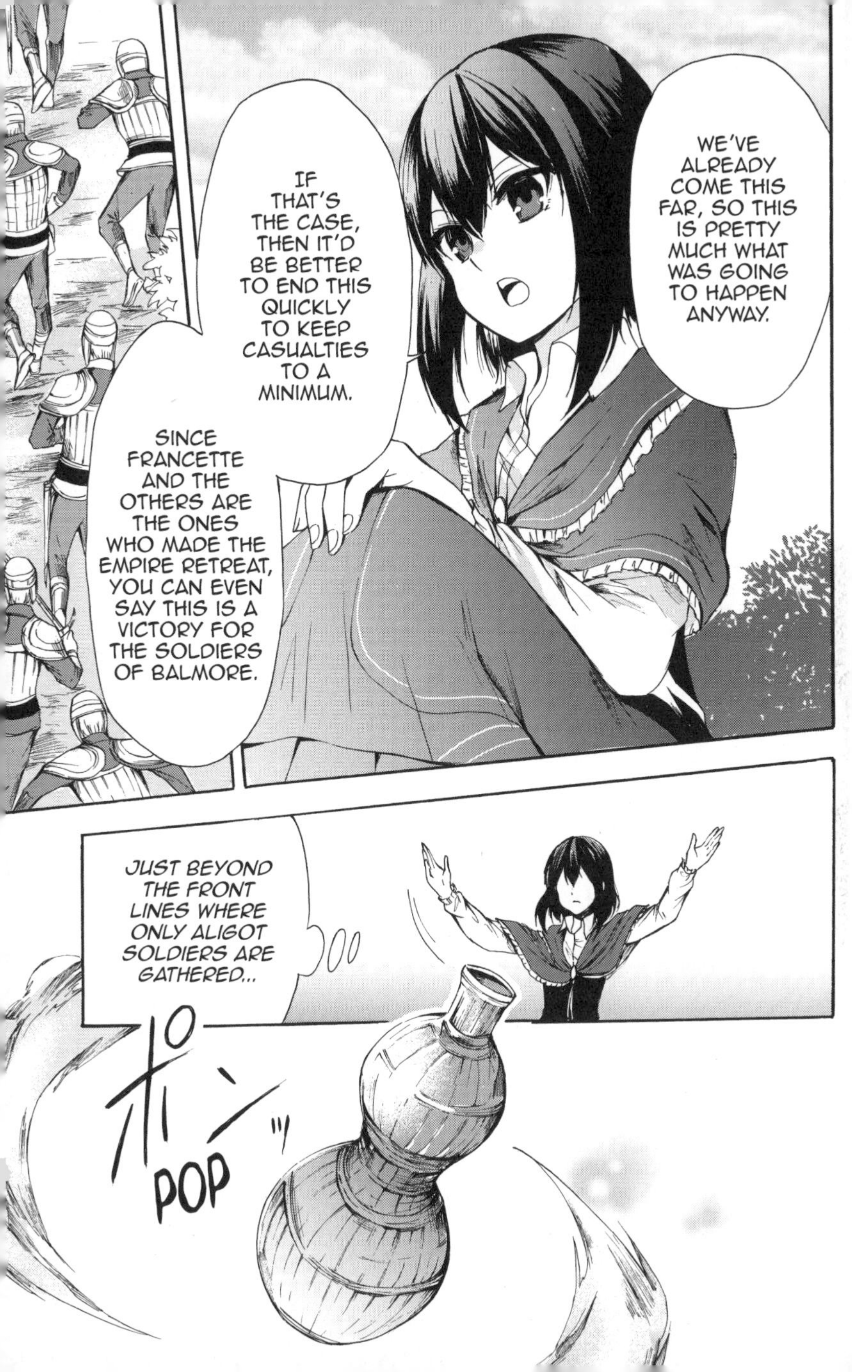
WE'VE ALREADY COME THIS FAR, SO THIS IS PRETTY MUCH WHAT WAS GOING TO HAPPEN ANYWAY.
IF THAT'S THE CASE, THEN IT'D BE BETTER TO END THIS QUICKLY TO KEEP CASUALTIES TO A MINIMUM.
SINCE FRANCETTE AND THE OTHERS ARE THE ONES WHO MADE THE EMPIRE RETREAT, YOU CAN EVEN SAY THIS IS A VICTORY FOR THE SOLDIERS OF BALMORE.
JUST BEYOND THE FRONT LINES WHERE ONLY ALIGOT SOLDIERS ARE GATHERED...
ポン
POP

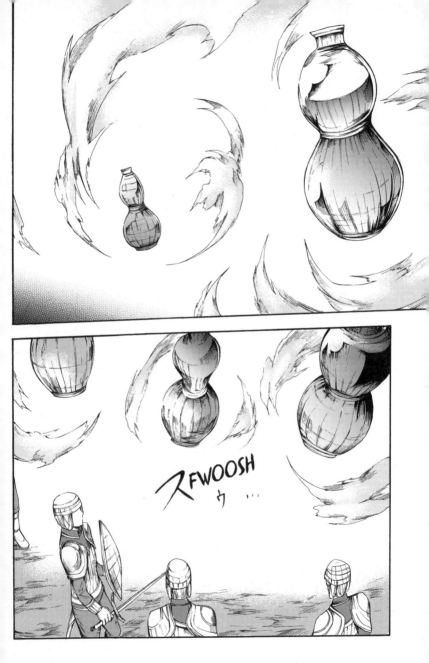

スFWOOSH
ウ ・・

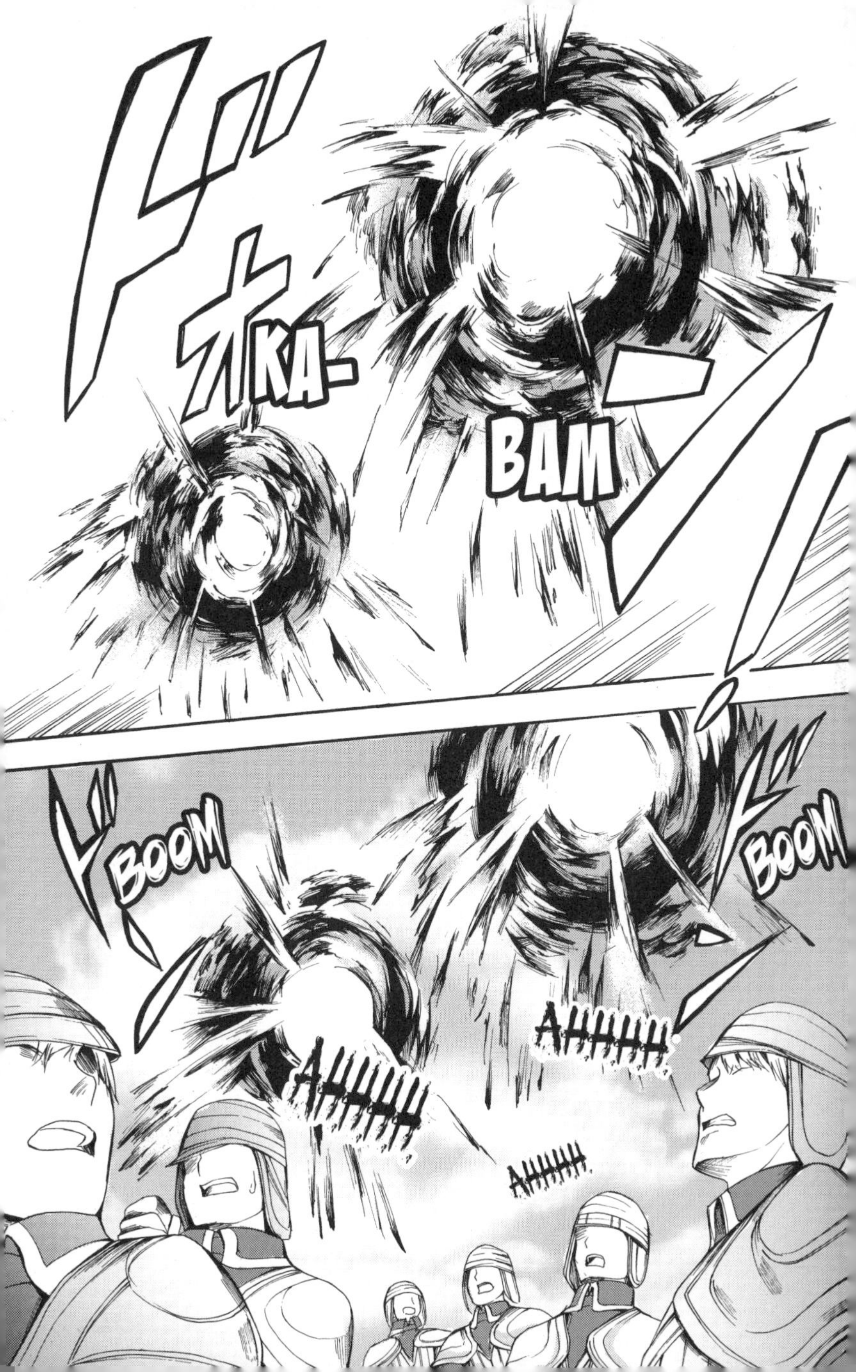
KA-
BAM
BOOM
AHHHHH
BOOM
AHHHHH
AHHHH

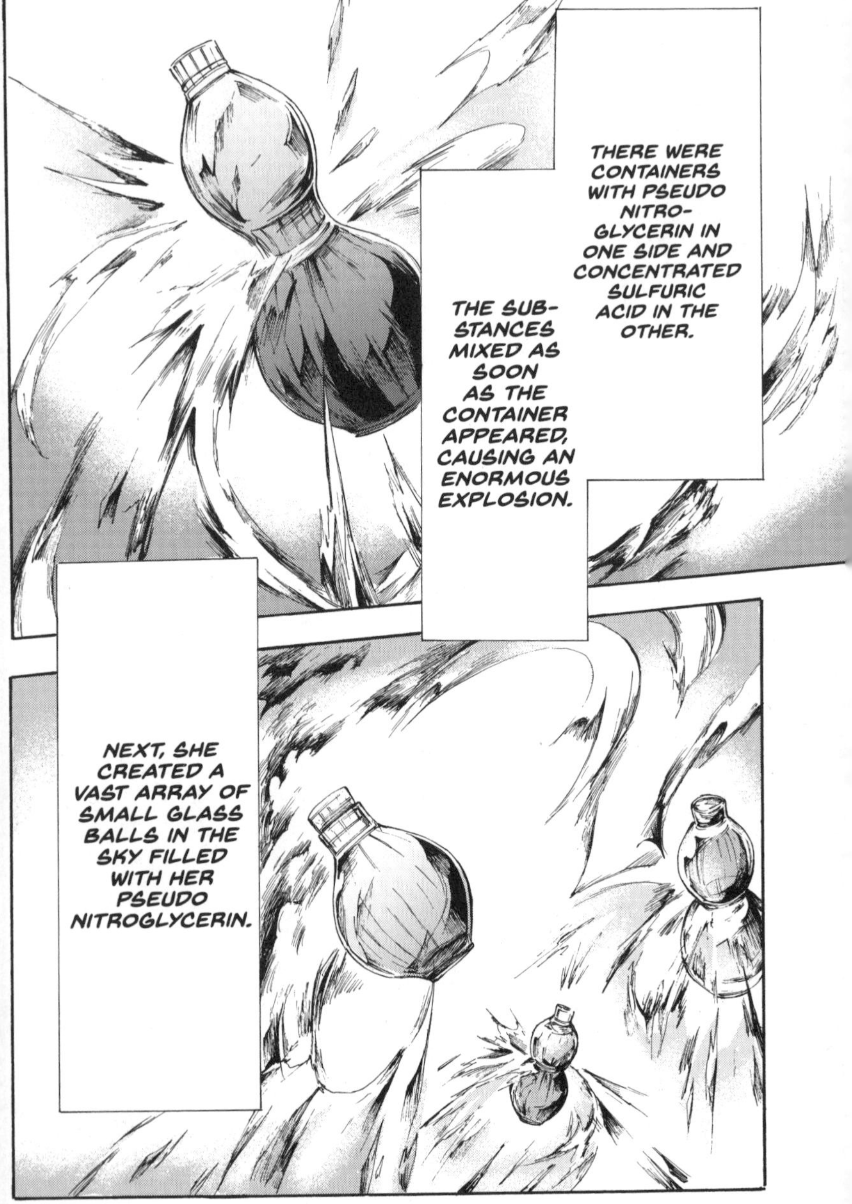
THERE WERE CONTAINERS WITH PSEUDO NITRO-GLYCERIN IN ONE SIDE AND CONCENTRATED SULFURIC ACID IN THE OTHER.
THE SUB-STANCES MIXED AS SOON AS THE CONTAINER APPEARED, CAUSING AN ENORMOUS EXPLOSION.
NEXT, SHE CREATED A VAST ARRAY OF SMALL GLASS BALLS IN THE SKY FILLED WITH HER PSEUDO NITROGLYCERIN.

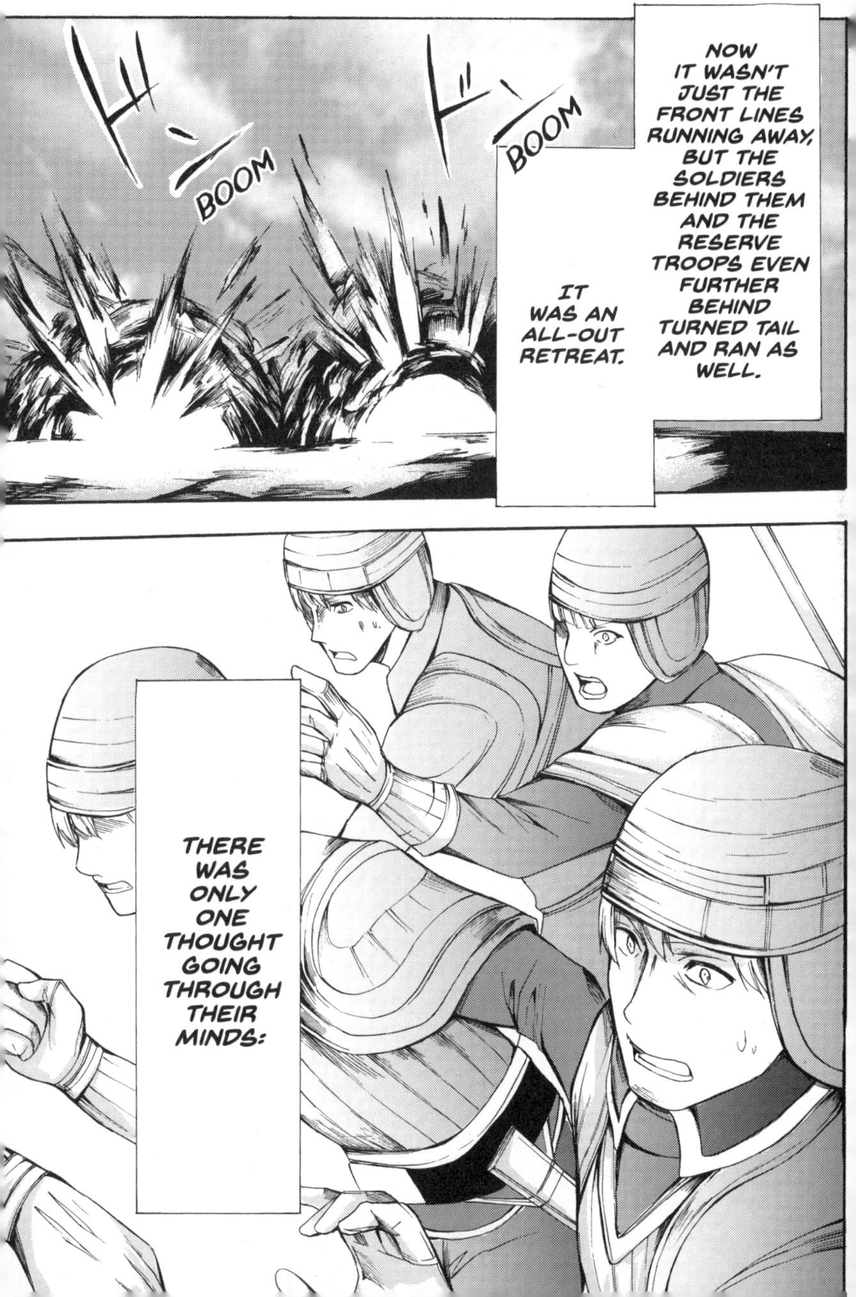
NOW IT WASN'T JUST THE FRONT LINES RUNNING AWAY, BUT THE SOLDIERS BEHIND THEM AND THE RESERVE TROOPS EVEN FURTHER BEHIND TURNED TAIL AND RAN AS WELL.
IT WAS AN ALL-OUT RETREAT.
BOOM
BOOM
THERE WAS ONLY ONE THOUGHT GOING THROUGH THEIR MINDS:

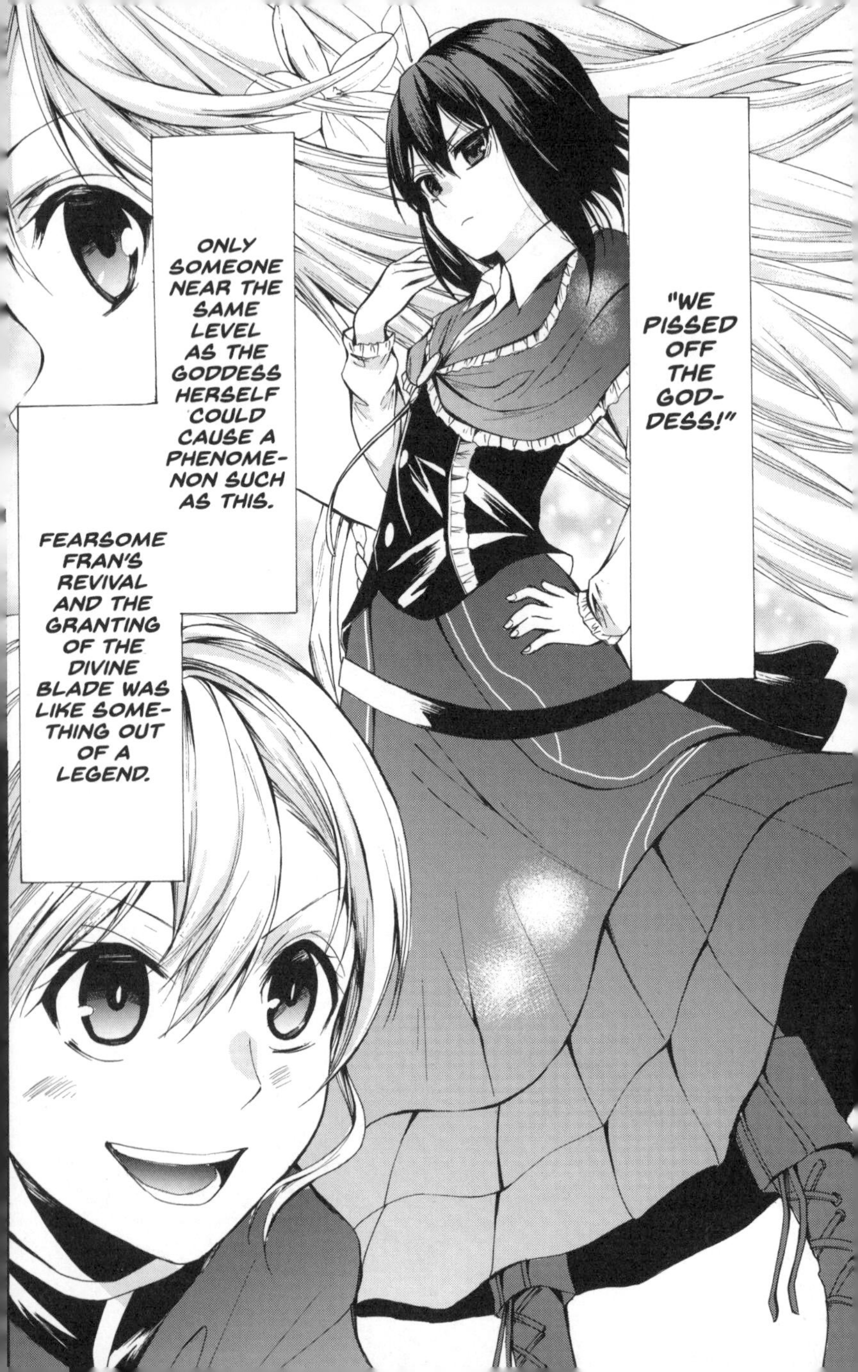
"WE PISSED OFF THE GOD-DESS!"
ONLY SOMEONE NEAR THE SAME LEVEL AS THE GODDESS HERSELF COULD CAUSE A PHENOME-NON SUCH AS THIS.
FEARSOME FRAN'S REVIVAL AND THE GRANTING OF THE DIVINE BLADE WAS LIKE SOME-THING OUT OF A LEGEND.

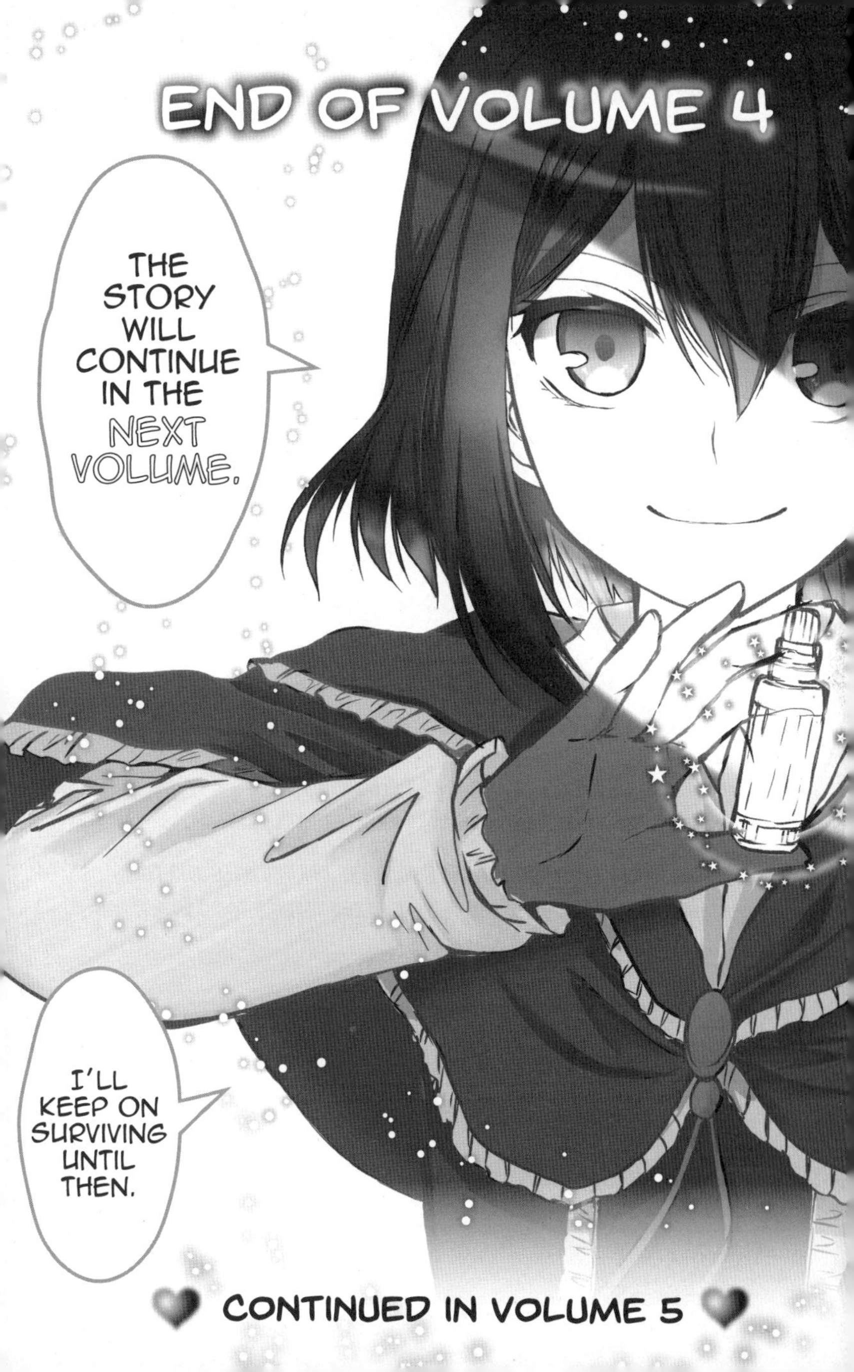
END OF VOLUME 4
THE STORY WILL CONTINUE IN THE NEXT VOLUME.
I'LL KEEP ON SURVIVING UNTIL THEN.
CONTINUED IN VOLUME 5

AFTERWORD

MANGA HIBIKI KOKONOE -SENSEI

AT DID YOU THINK OF VOLUME 4?
OULD BE THRILLED IF YOU FOUND
ENJOYABLE. I WANT TO IMPROVE MY
'T! SEE YOU NEXT TIME...

FUNA-SAN, SUKIMA-SAN, MY COORDINATOR,
D MY READERS, THANK YOU SO MUCH.

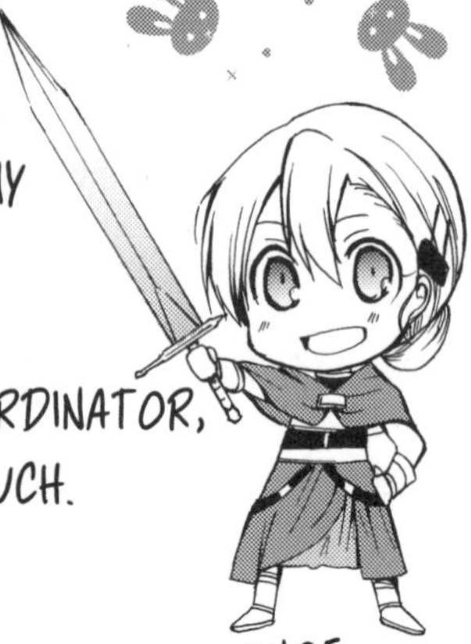

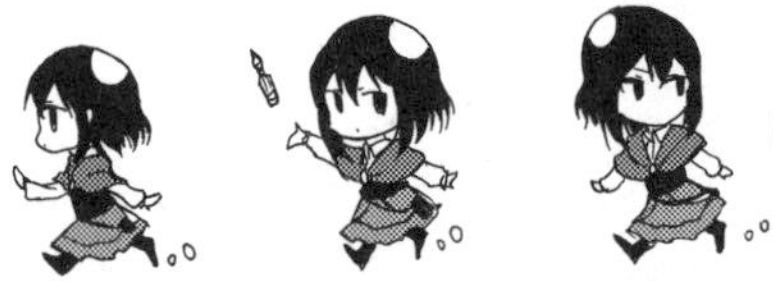

HIBIKI KOKONOE

AUTHOR FUNA -SENSEI

CONGRATULATIONS ON
RELEASING VOLUME 4 OF THE MANGA! KAORU
DEFEATS THE IMPERIAL ARMY AND PROTECTS THE KINGDOM.

KAORU: FRAN AND THE KINGDOM'S SOLDIERS ARE THE ONES WHO TOOK THEM DOWN, SO THE GODDESS AND HER ANGEL HAD NOTHING TO DO WITH IT...

FRANCETTE: IS THAT SO?

KAORU: I JUST WANT TO LIVE A NORMAL LIFE WITHOUT BEING IN THE SPOTLIGHT...

FRANCETTE: IT'S A BIT LATE FOR THAT...

WILL KAORU EVER FIND STABILITY AND HAPPINESS?

CELES: I'M SURE THEY'LL FIND OUT IF THEY BUY THE NEXT VOLUME!

KAORU/FRANCETTE: THERE IT IS!

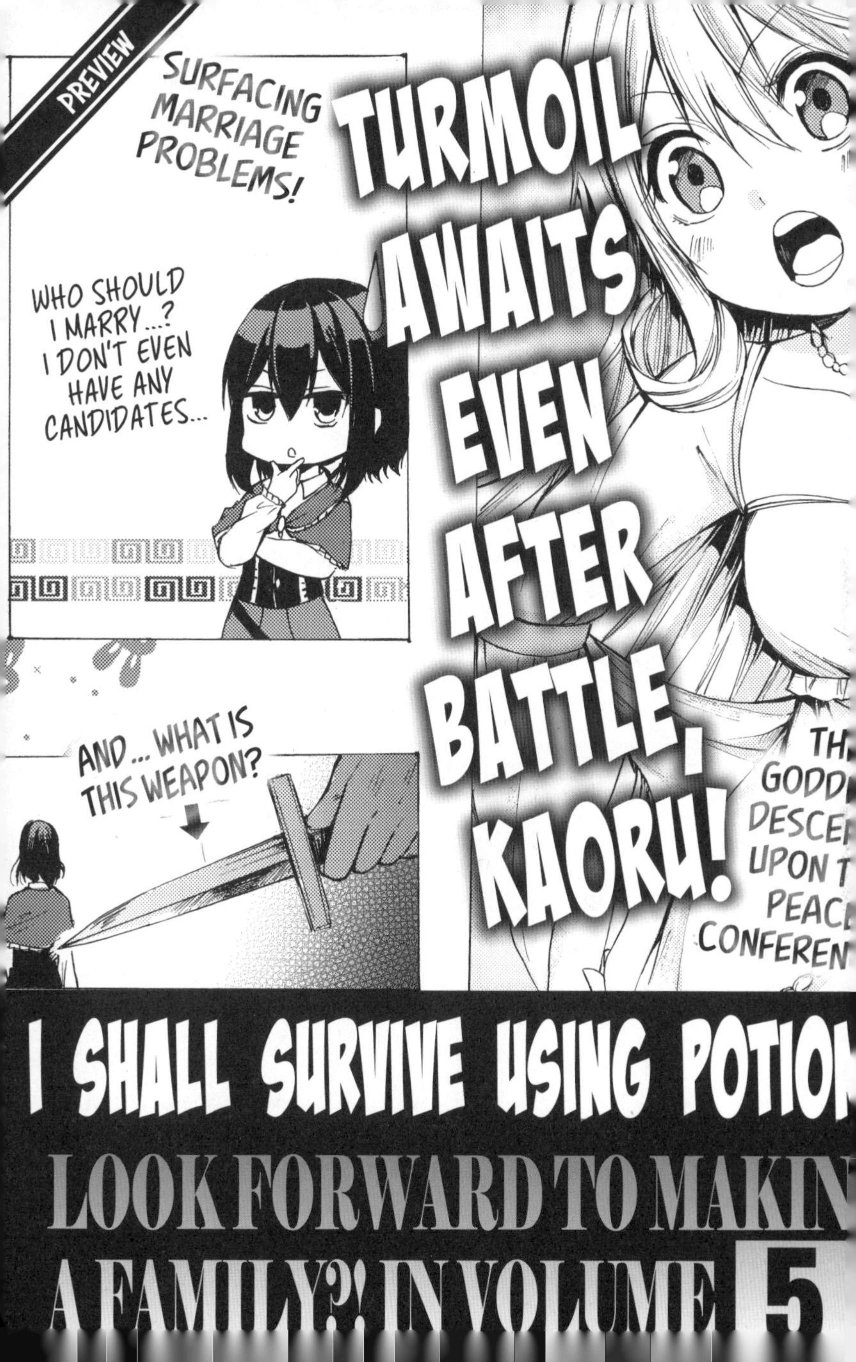
PREVIEW
TURMOIL AWAITS EVEN AFTER BATTLE, KAORU!
TH GODD DESCE UPON T PEAC CONFEREN
SURFACING MARRIAGE PROBLEMS!
WHO SHOULD I MARRY...? I DON'T EVEN HAVE ANY CANDIDATES...
AND... WHAT IS THIS WEAPON?
I SHALL SURVIVE USING POTIO
LOOK FORWARD TO MAKIN
A FAMILY?! IN VOLUME 5

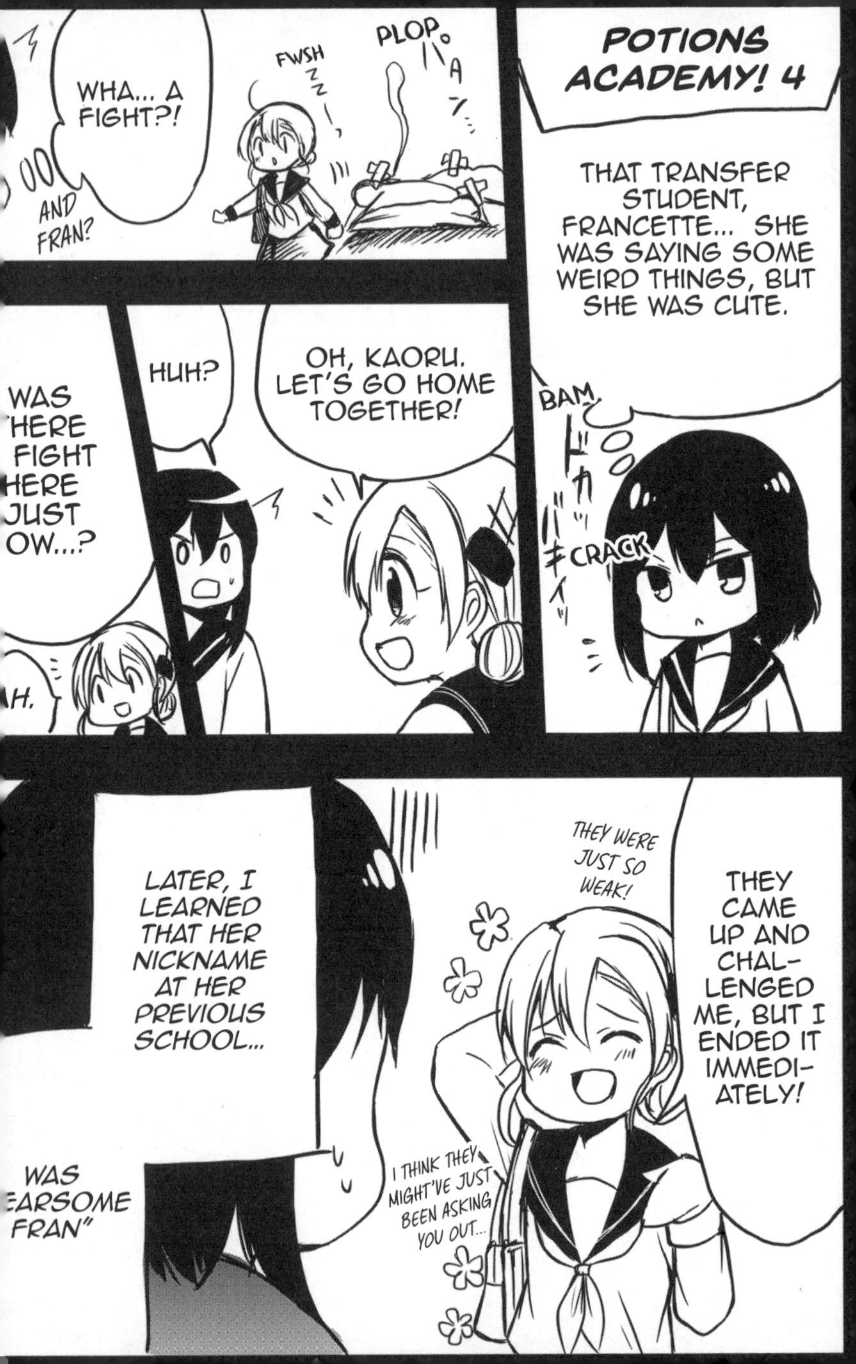
POTIONS ACADEMY! 4
THAT TRANSFER STUDENT, FRANCETTE... SHE WAS SAYING SOME WEIRD THINGS, BUT SHE WAS CUTE.
BAM
CRACK
PLOP
FWSH
WHA... A FIGHT?!
AND FRAN?
OH, KAORU. LET'S GO HOME TOGETHER!
HUH?
WAS HERE FIGHT HERE JUST OW...?
H.
THEY CAME UP AND CHAL-LENGED ME, BUT I ENDED IT IMMEDI-ATELY!
THEY WERE JUST SO WEAK!
I THINK THEY MIGHT'VE JUST BEEN ASKING YOU OUT...
LATER, I LEARNED THAT HER NICKNAME AT HER PREVIOUS SCHOOL...
WAS EARSOME FRAN"

I SHALL SURVIVE USING POTIONS! (MANGA) VOLUME 4
by FUNA (story) and Hibiki Kokonoe (artwork)
Original character designs by Sukima

Translated by Hiro Watanabe
Edited by William Haggard
Lettered by Richard Brown
English Print Cover by Kelsey Denton

This book is a work of fiction. Names, characters, places, and incidents are the product of the author's imagination or are used fictitiously. Any resemblance to actual events, locales, or persons, living or dead, is coincidental.

First published in Japan in 2019 by Kodansha Ltd., Tokyo.
Publication rights for this English edition arranged through Kodansha Ltd., Tokyo.

President and Publisher: Samuel Pinansky
Managing Editor (Manga): J. Collis
Managing Translator: Kristi Fernandez
QA Manager: Hannah N. Carter
Marketing Manager: Stephanie Hii

ISBN: 978-1-7183-7233-7
Printed in Korea
First Printing: July 2021
10 9 8 7 6 5 4 3 2 1

Original Work: **FUNA**

Manga: **Hibiki Kokonoe**

Character Design: **Sukima**

5

MANGA VOLUME 5
ON SALE
NOVEMBER 2021!

NOVEL VOLUME 6
ON SALE
OCTOBER 2021!

I SHALL SURVIVE USING POTIONS!

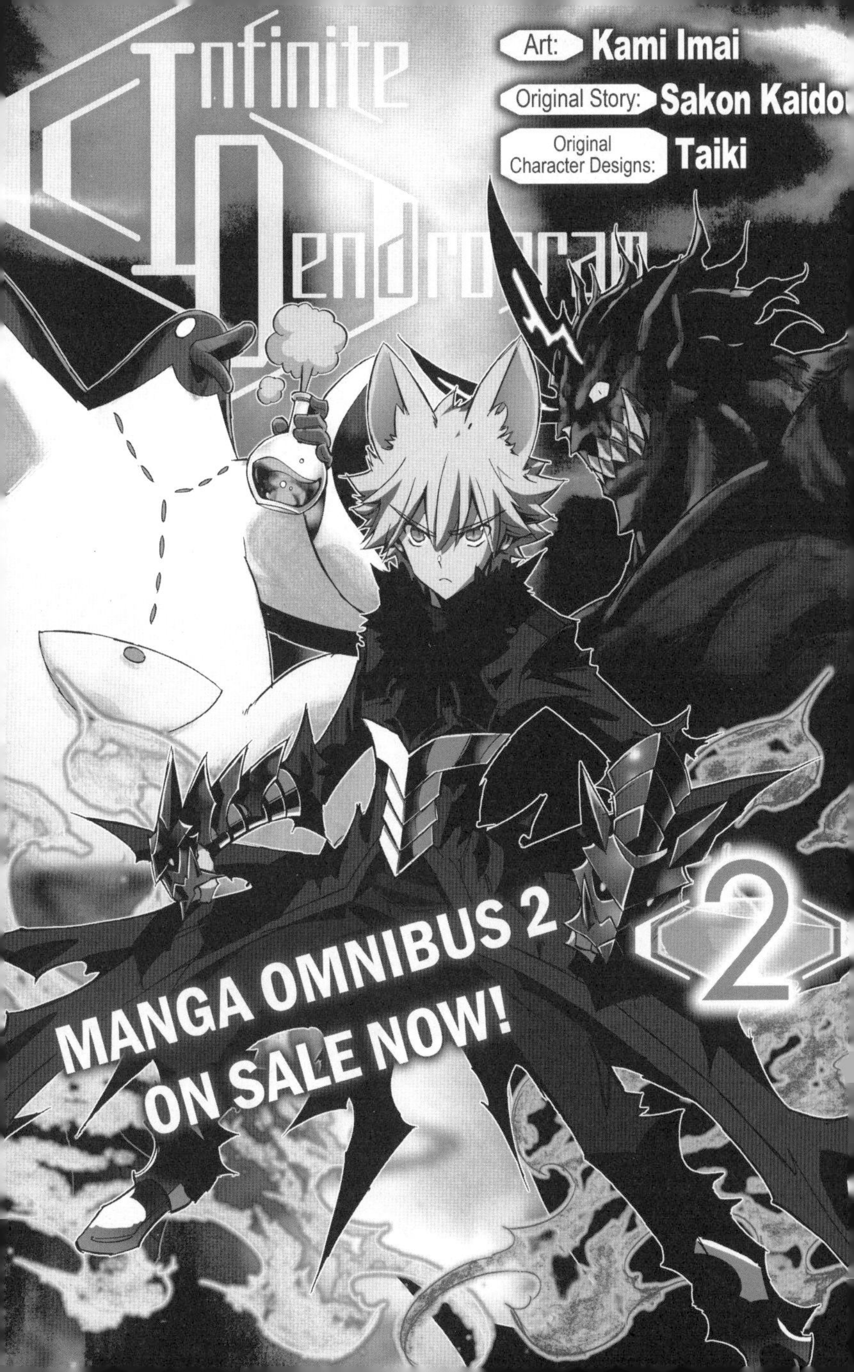

Infinite Dendrogram
Art: Kami Imai
Original Story: Sakon Kaido
Original Character Designs: Taiki
2
MANGA OMNIBUS 2
ON SALE NOW!

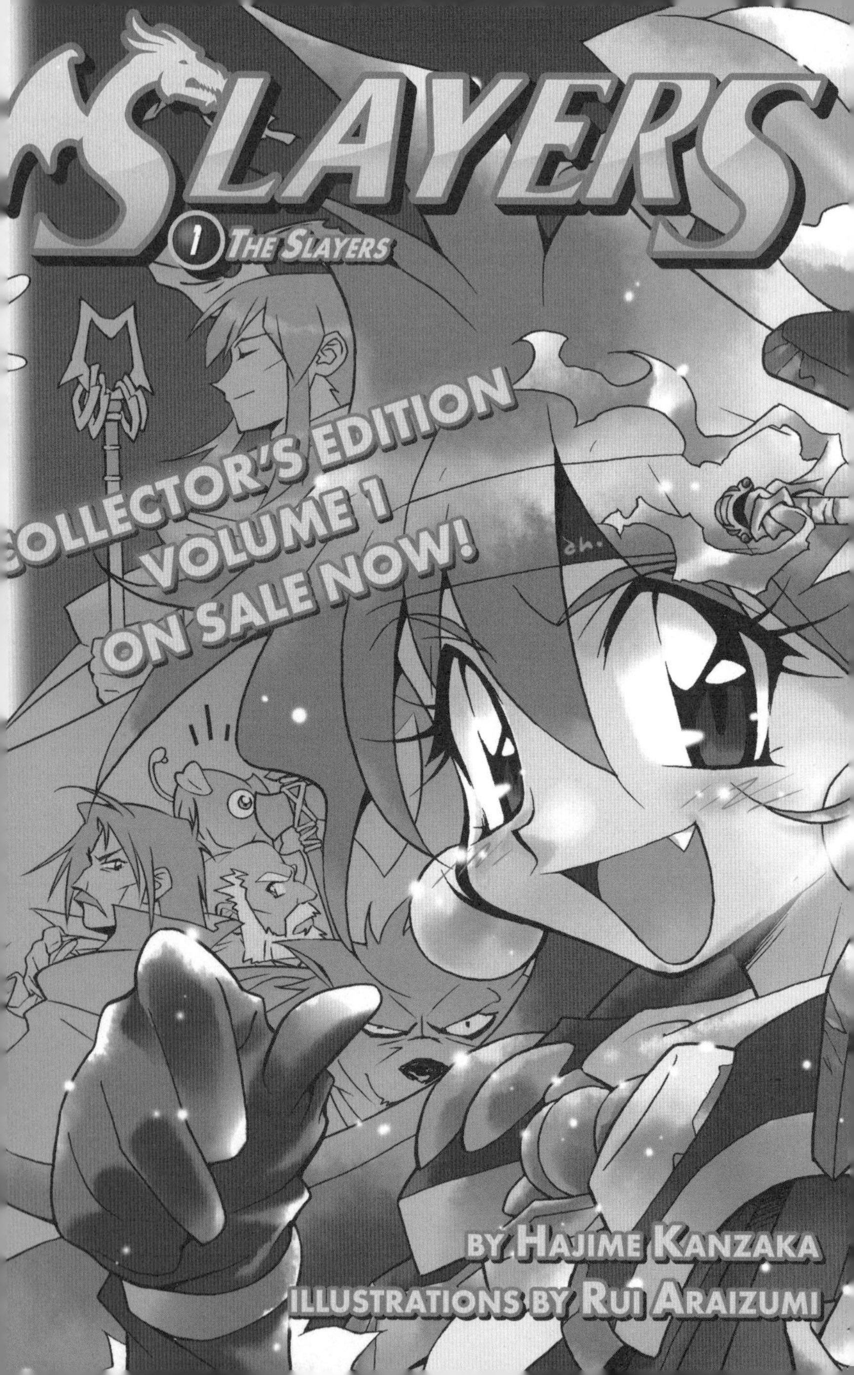
SLAYERS
1 THE SLAYERS
COLLECTOR'S EDITION
VOLUME 1
ON SALE NOW!
BY HAJIME KANZAKA
ILLUSTRATIONS BY RUI ARAIZUMI

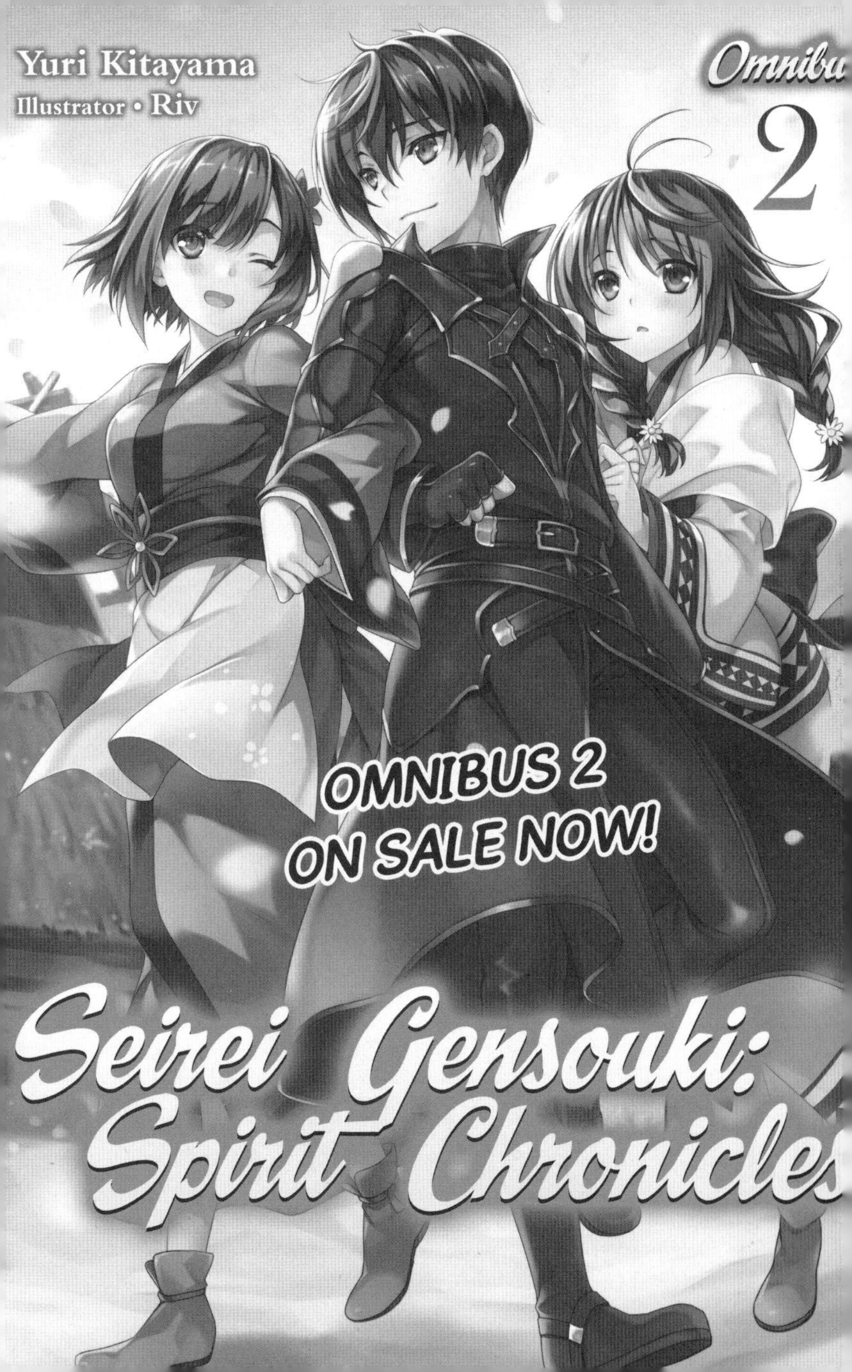
Yuri Kitayama
Illustrator • Riv
Omnibus
2
OMNIBUS 2
ON SALE NOW!
Seirei Gensouki:
Spirit Chronicles

How a Realist Hero

Rebuilt the Kingdom

OMNIBUS II

On Sale Now!

Manga ✚ Satoshi Ueda
Original Work ✚ Dojyomaru
Original Character Design ✚ Fuyuyuki

J-Novel Club Lineup

Ebook Releases Series List

A Lily Blooms in Another World
A Very Fairy Apartment**
A Wild Last Boss Appeared!
Altina the Sword Princess
Amagi Brilliant Park
An Archdemon's Dilemma: How to Love Your Elf Bride*
Animeta!**
The Apothecary Diaries
Are You Okay With a Slightly Older Girlfriend?
Arifureta: From Commonplace to World's Strongest
Arifureta Zero
Ascendance of a Bookworm*
Banner of the Stars
Beatless
Bibliophile Princess*
Black Summoner*
The Bloodline
By the Grace of the Gods
Campfire Cooking in Another World with My Absurd Skill*
Can Someone Please Explain What's Going On?!
The Combat Baker and Automaton Waitress
Cooking with Wild Game*
Deathbound Duke's Daughter
Demon King Daimaou
Demon Lord, Retry!*
Der Werwolf: The Annals of Veight*
Discommunication**
Dungeon Busters
The Economics of Prophecy
The Epic Tale of the Reincarnated Prince Herscherik
The Extraordinary, the Ordinary, and SOAP!
The Faraway Paladin*
From Truant to Anime Screenwriter: My Path to "Anohana" and "The Anthem of the Heart"
Full Metal Panic!
Fushi no Kami: Rebuilding Civilization Starts With a Village
The Great Cleric
The Greatest Magicmaster's Retirement Plan
Girls Kingdom
Grimgar of Fantasy and Ash
Her Majesty's Swarm
Holmes of Kyoto
The Holy Knight's Dark Road
How a Realist Hero Rebuilt the Kingdom*
How NOT to Summon a Demon Lord
I Love Yuri and I Got Bodyswapped with a Fujoshi!**
I Refuse to Be Your Enemy!
I Saved Too Many Girls and Caused the Apocalypse
I Shall Survive Using Potions!*
I'll Never Set Foot in That House Again!
The Ideal Sponger Life
If It's for My Daughter, I'd Even Defeat a Demon Lord
In Another World With My Smartphone
Infinite Dendrogram*
Infinite Stratos
Invaders of the Rokujouma!?
Isekai Rebuilding Project
JK Haru is a Sex Worker in Another World
Kobold King
Kokoro Connect
Last and First Idol
Lazy Dungeon Master
The Magic in this Other World is Too Far Behind!*
The Magician Who Rose From Failure
Mapping: The Trash-Tier Skill That Got Me Into a Top-Tier Party*
Marginal Operation**
The Master of Ragnarok & Blesser of Einherjar*
Middle-Aged Businessman, Arise in Another World!
Mixed Bathing in Another Dimension
Monster Tamer
My Big Sister Lives in a Fantasy World
My Friend's Little Sister Has It In For Me!
My Instant Death Ability is So Overpowered, No One in This Other World Stands a Chance Against Me!
My Next Life as a Villainess: All Routes Lead to Doom!
Our Crappy Social Game Club Is Gonna Make the Most Epic Game
Otherside Picnic
Outbreak Company
Outer Ragna
Record of Wortenia War*
Seirei Gensouki: Spirit Chronicles*
Sexiled: My Sexist Party Leader Kicked Me Out, So I Teamed Up With a Mythical Sorceress!
She's the Cutest... But We're Just Friends!
Slayers
The Sorcerer's Receptionist
Sorcerous Stabber Orphen*
Sweet Reincarnation**
The Tales of Marielle Clarac*
Tearmoon Empire
Teogonia
The Underdog of the Eight Greater Tribes
The Unwanted Undead Adventurer*
WATARU!!! The Hot-Blooded Fighting Teen & His Epic Adventures After Stopping a Truck with His Bare Hands!!
Welcome to Japan, Ms. Elf!*
When the Clock Strikes Z
The White Cat's Revenge as Plotted from the Dragon King's Lap
Wild Times with a Fake Fake Princess
The World's Least Interesting Master Swordsman
Yume Nikki: I Am Not in Your Dream

* Novel and Manga Editions
** Manga Only

Keep an eye out at j-novel.club for further new title announcements!